Books 1–4

EMILY RODDA

Scholastic Inc.

New York   Toronto   London   Auckland   Sydney
Mexico City   New Delhi   Hong Kong   Buenos Aires

ISBN 0-439-48265-8

First published in 2000.
Text and graphics copyright © 2000 Emily Rodda.
Graphics by Kate Rowe.
Cover illustrations copyright © 2000 Scholastic Australia.
Cover illustration by Marc McBride.

All rights reserved. Published by Scholastic, Inc., 557 Broadway, New York, NY 10012, by arrangement with Scholastic Press, an imprint of Scholastic Australia.

12 11 10 9 8 7 6 5 4 3 2 1   2 3 4 5 6 7/0

23

Printed in the U.S.A.
First bind-up edition, November 2002

Contents

The Forests of Silence 1

The Lake of Tears 139

City of the Rats 277

The Shifting Sands 417

DELTORA QUEST

The Forests of
Silence

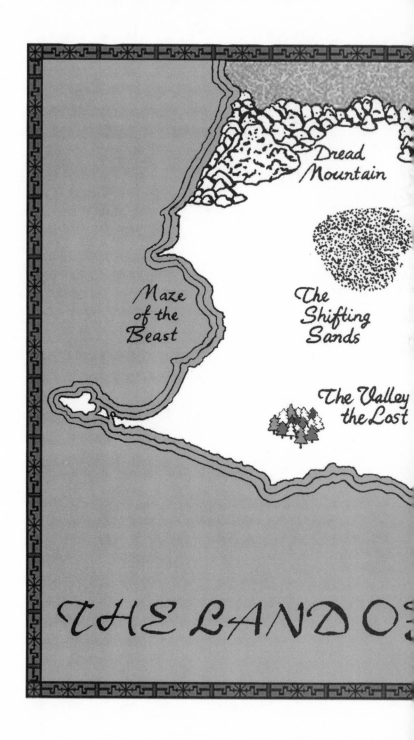

Dread
Mountain

Maze
of the
Beast

The
Shifting
Sands

The Valley
the Lost

THE LAND OF

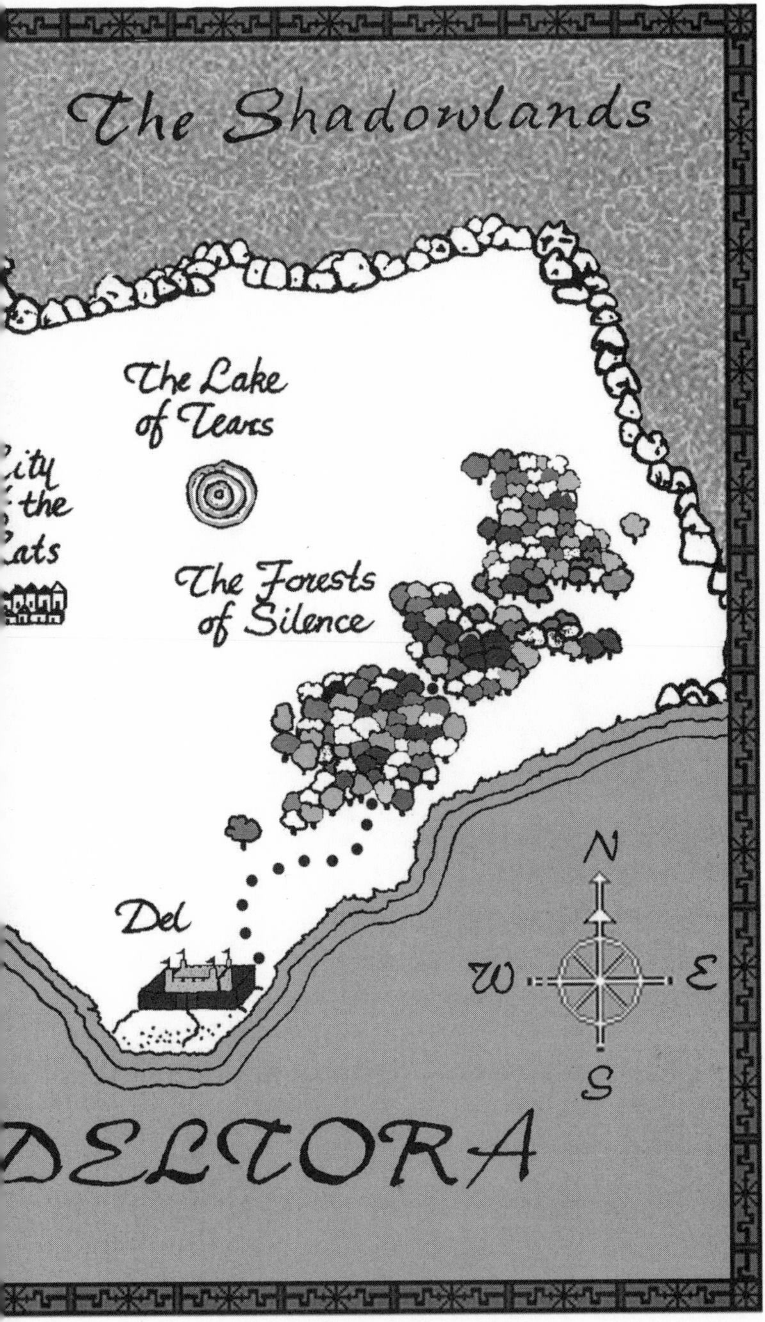
The Shadowlands
The Lake of Tears
The Forests of Silence
Del
N
W
E
S
DELTORA

Contents

Part I: THE BELT OF DELTORA

1 The King 7
2 The Belt of Deltora 16
3 Escape 23
4 The Forge 30
5 The Enemy Strikes 38
6 Friends to the Death 46
7 Treachery 53

Part II: UNDER THE SHADOW

8 Lief 62
9 The Secret 73
10 Decisions 83
11 Beware! 90
12 The Wennbar 98
13 The Nest 107
14 The Dark 115
15 The Lilies of Life 123
16 The Topaz 130

1 ~ The King

Jarred stood unnoticed in the crowd thronging the great hall of the palace. He leaned against a marble pillar, blinking with tiredness and confusion.

It was midnight. He had been roused from his bed by shouts and bells. He had pulled on his clothes and joined the crowd of noble folk surging towards the hall.

"The king is dead," the people were whispering. "The young prince is to be crowned at once."

Jarred could hardly take it in. The king of Deltora, with his long, plaited beard and his golden robes, had died of the mysterious fever that had kept him to his bed for the last few weeks. Never again would his deep, booming voice be heard in the hallways of the palace. Never again would he sit laughing in the feasting hall.

King Alton was dead, like his wife, the queen,

before him. The fever had taken them both. And now . . .

Now Endon will be king, Jarred thought. He shook his head, trying to make himself believe it. He and Endon had been friends since they were young children. But what a difference there was between them!

For Endon was the son of the king and queen, the prince of Deltora. And Jarred was the son of a trusted servant who had died in the king's service when Jarred was only four years old.

Jarred had been given to Endon as a companion, so that the young prince would not be lonely. They had grown up together, like brothers. Together they did their lessons in the schoolroom, teased the guards, and persuaded the cooks in the kitchens to give them treats. Together they played in the vast green gardens.

The other children who lived in the palace — the sons and daughters of nobles and servants — kept to their own rooms and their own parts of the grounds. As was the palace custom, Jarred and Endon never even saw them, except in the great hall on feast days. But the two boys did what they could to entertain themselves.

They had a secret hiding place — a huge, hollow tree near the palace gates. There they hid from fussy old Min, their nursemaid, and Prandine, the king's chief advisor, a tall, thin, sour man they both disliked.

They practiced archery together, playing a game called "Aim High," where the first to shoot an arrow into the topmost fork of the hollow tree would win.

They invented a secret code and used it to pass messages, jokes, and warnings to each other under the noses of their teachers, Min or Prandine.

Jarred would be hiding in the hollow tree, for example, because Min wanted him to take a dose of the fish-oil medicine he detested. Endon would walk by, and drop a note where he could reach it.

```
DEL ONEL O TELGEL O TELO TEL
HELE KEL ITEL CEL HELE NEL SEL
MEL I NELI SEL TELHEL E RELE
```

The message looked like nonsense, and no one in the palace could guess the meaning if they picked up a note by accident. But the code was simple.

All you had to do to decode a message was write down all the letters in a line, leaving out "EL" wherever it appeared.

DONOTGOTOTHEKITCHENSMINISTHERE

Then you divided the letters into words that made sense.

DO NOT GO TO THE KITCHENS. MIN IS THERE.

✳

As Endon and Jarred grew older there was less time for games. Their days were filled with tasks and duties.

Much of their time was spent learning the Rule — the thousands of laws and customs by which the royal family lived. The Rule governed their lives.

They sat — Endon patiently and Jarred not so patiently — while their long hair was plaited and twined with golden cord, according to the Rule. They spent hours learning to hammer red-hot metal into swords and shields. The first king of Deltora had been a blacksmith and it was part of the Rule that his art should be continued.

Each late afternoon they had a precious hour of free time. The only thing they were not allowed to do was to climb the high wall that surrounded the palace gardens, or go through the gates to the city beyond. For the prince of Deltora, like the king and queen, never mingled with the ordinary people. This was an important part of the Rule.

It was a part that Jarred was sometimes tempted to break. But Endon, quiet, dutiful, and obedient, anxiously begged him not even to think of climbing the wall.

"It is forbidden," he would say. "And Prandine already fears that you are a bad influence on me, Jarred. He has told my father so. If you break the Rule you will be sent away. And I do not want that."

Jarred did not want it, either. He knew he would miss Endon sorely. And where would he go if he had to leave the palace? It was the only home he had ever known. So he tamed his curiosity, and the city beyond the wall remained as much a mystery to him as it was to the prince.

The sound of the crystal trumpets broke into Jarred's thoughts. He turned, like everyone else, towards the back of the hall.

Endon was entering between two rows of royal guards in pale blue uniforms trimmed with gold.

Poor Endon, Jarred thought. He is grieving.

He wished that he could be beside his friend, to comfort him. But he had not been summoned. Instead, Chief Advisor Prandine stalked at Endon's right hand.

Jarred looked at Prandine with dislike. The advisor looked even taller and thinner than usual. He wore a long purple robe and carried what looked like a box covered by a gold cloth. As he walked, his head poked forward so that he looked like a great bird of prey.

Endon's eyes were shadowed with sadness and he looked very small and pale in his stiff silver jacket with its high, jewelled collar. But he held up his head bravely, as he had been taught to do.

All his life he had been trained for this moment. "When I die, you will be king, my son," his father had told him so many times. "Do not fail in your duty."

"I will not fail, Father," Endon would answer

him obediently. "I will do what is right, when the time comes."

But neither Jarred nor Endon had thought the time would come so soon. The king was so strong and healthy that it had seemed that he would live forever.

Endon had reached the front of the hall now, and was mounting the steps to the platform. When he had reached the top, he turned and faced the sea of faces.

"He is so young," a woman near Jarred breathed to her neighbor.

"Ssh," the neighbor warned. "He is the rightful heir." As she spoke, she glanced nervously in Jarred's direction. Jarred did not recognize her face, but he realized that she knew him and feared he might tell Endon that her friend had been disloyal. He looked away quickly.

But now the crystal trumpets were sounding again and a low, excited murmuring had begun in the crowd.

Prandine had put his burden down on a small table beside the throne. He was sweeping the gold cloth aside to reveal a glass box. He was opening the box and taking out something that shone and glittered.

The magic Belt of Deltora. The crowd gave a hissing sigh, and Jarred, too, caught his breath. He had heard about the Belt since his earliest childhood, but he had never seen it before.

And here it was, in all its beauty and mystery —

the ancient object that for thousands of years had kept Deltora safe from invasion by the evil Shadow Lord who ruled beyond the Mountains.

Hanging between Prandine's bony fingers, the Belt seemed as delicate as lace, and the seven huge gems set along its length looked like beautiful decorations. But Jarred knew that the Belt was made of the strongest steel, and that each of the gems played its own special part in the magic that protected Deltora.

There was the topaz, symbol of faithfulness, gold as the setting sun. There was the amethyst, symbol of truth, purple as the violets that grew by the banks of the river Del. For purity and strength there was the diamond, clear and sparkling as ice. For honor there was the emerald, green as lush grass. There was the lapis lazuli, the heavenly stone, midnight blue with pinpoints of silver like the night sky. There was the ruby for happiness, red as blood. And the opal, symbol of hope, sparkling with all the colors of the rainbow.

The crowd seemed to hold its breath as Prandine bent to loop the Belt around Endon's waist. The advisor's fingers fumbled with the fastening, and he was standing well back. He almost seems afraid, Jarred thought curiously. I wonder why?

Then, suddenly, the fastening snapped closed, and his question was answered. Prandine sprang backwards, there was a crackling sound, and, at the same moment, the Belt seemed to explode with light.

The gems blazed like fire, lighting the hall with their rainbow brilliance. The people cried out and turned away, hiding their eyes.

Endon stood with his arms upraised, almost hidden by the flashing, darting light. No longer was he just a young boy with sad eyes. The magic Belt had recognized him as the true heir to the throne of Deltora. He, and he alone, could now use its mystery, magic, and power.

But *will* Endon use them? Jarred thought suddenly. Did his father use them? Did his father ever do anything but follow rules laid down ages ago?

He watched as the fires of the gems slowly died to a winking glow. He watched as the young king took off the Belt and handed it to Prandine. He watched as Prandine, smiling now, put it back into its glass case.

Jarred knew what would happen to the Belt now. As the Rule stated, it would be carried back to the topmost room of the palace tower. The door of the room would be locked with three gold locks. Three guards in gold uniforms would be put outside the door.

And then . . . life would go on as before. Prandine and the other government officials would make all the real decisions affecting the kingdom.

The king would attend ceremonies and feasts, laugh at the clowns and acrobats in the great hall, practice archery and the blacksmith's art. He would sit for hours while his hair, and, one day, his beard were plaited. He would sign endless documents and stamp them with the ring that bore the royal seal. He would follow the Rule.

In a few years he would marry a young woman chosen for him by Prandine. A daughter of one of the noble families, who had also spent her life inside the palace walls. They would have a child, to take Endon's place when he died. And that child would also wear the Belt only once, before it was again locked away.

Now, for the first time in his life, Jarred wondered if this was a good idea. For the first time he wondered how and why the Belt was made. For the first time he began to doubt the wisdom of letting such a power for good remain idle in a tower room while the realm it was supposed to protect lay, unseen, outside high walls.

He slipped unnoticed out of the great hall and ran up the stairs to the palace library. This was another first for him. He had never loved study.

But there were things he needed to know. And the library was the only place he was likely to find them out.

2 - The Belt of Deltora

After hours of searching, Jarred finally found a book that he thought might help him. It was covered in faded pale blue cloth and the gold lettering on the outside had been worn away.

But the title inside was still very clear.

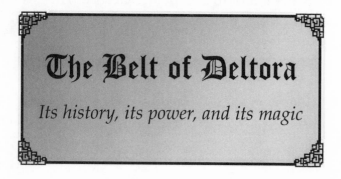

The Belt of Deltora

Its history, its power, and its magic

This book was nothing like the splendid hand-painted volumes that he and Endon read in the schoolroom. And nothing like the many other weighty books on the library shelves.

It was small, thin, and very dusty. It had been tucked away in the library's darkest corner among piles of papers, as though someone had wanted it forgotten.

Jarred carried the old book carefully to a table. He planned to read it from beginning to end. His task might take him all night, but he did not expect to be disturbed. No one would be looking for him. Endon would go straight from the great hall to the chapel, where his father's body lay surrounded by candles. He would keep watch there alone till dawn, following the Rule.

Poor Endon, thought Jarred. It has only been a few days since he did the same for his mother. Now he is alone in the world, as I am. But at least we have each other. We are friends to the death. And I will protect him as best I can.

Protect him from what?

The question pierced his mind like a sharp knife. Why had he suddenly begun to fear for Endon? Who or what could threaten the all-powerful king of Deltora?

I am tired, thought Jarred. I am imagining things.

He shook his head impatiently and lit a fresh candle to brighten the darkness. But the memory of Prandine's thin smile as he locked the magic Belt away kept drifting into his mind like the shadow of a remembered nightmare. He frowned, lowered his head to the book, turned to the first page, and began to read.

✝ In ancient days, Deltora was divided into seven tribes. The tribes fought on their borders but otherwise stayed in their own place. Each had a gem from deep within the earth, a talisman with special powers.

✝ There came a time when the Enemy from the Shadowlands cast greedy eyes on Deltora. The tribes were divided, and singly none of them could repel the invader, who began to triumph.

✝ A hero called Adin rose from the ranks of the people. He was an ordinary man, a blacksmith who made swords and armor and shoes for horses. But he had been blessed with strength, courage, and cleverness.

✝ One night, Adin dreamed of a special and splendid belt — seven steel medallions beaten to the thinness of silk and connected together with fine chain. To each medallion was fixed one of the tribal gems.

✝ Realizing that the dream had been sent to him for a purpose, Adin worked in secret over many months to create a likeness of the belt he had been shown. Then he traveled around the kingdom to persuade each tribe to allow its talisman to be added to it.

✝ The tribes were at first suspicious and wary, but, one by one, desperate to save their land, they agreed. As each gem became part of the belt, its tribe grew stronger. But the people kept their strength secret, and bided their time.

✝ And when at last the belt was complete, Adin fastened it around his waist, and it flashed like the sun. Then all the tribes united behind him to form a great army, and together they drove the Enemy from their land.

✝ And so Adin became the first king of the united tribes of Deltora, and he ruled the land long and wisely. But he never forgot that he was a man of the people, and that their trust in him was the source of his power. Neither did he forget that the Enemy, though defeated, was not destroyed. He knew that the Enemy is clever and sly, and that to its anger and envy a thousand years is like the blink of an eye. So he wore the belt always, and never let it out of his sight . . .

Jarred read on and on, and the more he read, the more troubled he became. He had a pencil and some paper in his pocket, but he did not need to take notes. The words of the book seemed to be burning themselves into his brain. He was learning more than he expected. Not just about the Belt of Deltora, but about the Rule.

✝   **The first to leave the belt aside was Adin's grandson, King Elstred, who in his middle years grew fat with good living and found the steel cut sadly into his belly. Elstred's chief advisor soothed his fears, saying that the belt need only be worn on great occasions. Elstred's daughter, Queen Adina, followed her father's ways, wearing the belt only five times in her reign. Her son, King Brandon, wore it only three times. And at last it became the custom for the belt to be worn only on the day the heir took the throne . . .**

✝   **At the urging of his chief advisor, King Brandon caused the Ralad builders to raise a great palace on the hill at the center of the city of Del. The royal family moved from the old blacksmith's forge to the palace, and over time it became the custom for them to remain within its walls, where no harm could come to them . . .**

When Jarred closed the book at last, his heart was heavy. His candle had burned low and the first dawn light was showing at the window. He sat for a moment, thinking. Then he slipped the book into his shirt and ran to seek Endon.

✳

The chapel was below ground level, in a quiet corner of the palace. It was still and cold. The old king's body was lying on a raised marble platform in the center, surrounded by candles. Endon was kneeling beside it, with his head bowed.

He looked up as Jarred burst in. His eyes were red from weeping. "You should not be here, Jarred," he whispered. "It is against the Rule."

"It is dawn," Jarred panted. "And I had to see you."

Endon stood up stiffly and came over to him. "What is it?" he asked in a low voice.

Jarred's head was full of everything he had read. The words came tumbling out of him. "Endon, you should wear the Belt of Deltora always, as the ancient kings and queens did."

Endon stared at him in puzzlement.

"Come!" Jarred urged, taking his arm. "Let us go and get it now."

But Endon held back, shaking his head. "You know I cannot do that, Jarred. The Rule — "

Jarred stamped his foot with impatience. "Forget the Rule! It is just a collection of traditions that have grown up over the years and been made law by the chief advisors. It is dangerous, Endon! Because of it, every new ruler of Deltora has been more powerless than the one before. This must stop — with you! You must get the Belt and put it on. Then you must come with me outside the palace gates."

He was speaking too fast and too wildly. By now Endon was frowning, backing away from him. "You

21

are ill, my friend," he was whispering nervously. "Or you have been dreaming."

"No!" Jarred insisted, following him. "It is you who are living in a dream. You must see how things are outside the palace — in the city and beyond."

"I see the city, Jarred," argued Endon. "I look out at it from my window every day. It is beautiful."

"But you do not talk to the people. You do not walk among them!"

"Of course I do not! That is forbidden by the Rule!" Endon gasped. "But I know that all is well."

"You know nothing, except what you are told by Prandine!" shouted Jarred.

"And is that not enough?" The cold voice cut through the air like sharp steel.

3 - Escape

Startled, Endon and Jarred spun around. Prandine was standing in the doorway. His eyes, fixed on Jarred, glittered with hatred.

"How dare you tempt the king to turn from his duty and the Rule, servant boy?" he hissed, striding into the chapel. "You have always been jealous of him. And now you seek to destroy him. Traitor!"

"No!" exclaimed Jarred. He turned again to Endon. "Believe me!" he begged. "I have only your good at heart." But Endon shrank away from him, horrified.

Jarred plunged his hand into his shirt to get the book — to show it to Endon, prove to him that he had good reason for what he said.

"Beware, your majesty! He has a knife!" shouted Prandine, leaping forward and sweeping Endon under his cloak as if to protect him. He raised his voice to a shriek. "Murderer! Traitor! Guards! Guards!"

For a single moment Jarred stood frozen. Then he heard bells of warning ringing. He heard shouts of alarm and heavy feet thudding towards the chapel. He saw Prandine's mocking, triumphant smile. He realized that Prandine had been given the chance he had been waiting for — the chance to rid himself of Jarred for good.

Jarred knew that if he valued his life he would have to flee. Pushing Prandine aside, he ran like the wind from the chapel, up the stairs and to the back of the palace. He plunged into the huge, dim kitchens, where the cooks were just beginning to light the fires in the great stoves. Behind him he could hear the shouts of the guards: "Traitor! Stop him! Stop him!"

But the cooks did not try to stop Jarred. How could they think that he was the one the guards were pursuing? He was the young king's friend, and they had known him all his life. So they only watched as Jarred tore open the kitchen door and ran outside.

The grounds were deserted, except for a ragged old man tipping food scraps into a horse-drawn cart. He took no notice as Jarred plunged under the cover of the thick bushes that grew against the palace walls.

Keeping low, Jarred crawled through the bushes to the front of the palace. Then he ran, dodging and weaving, till he reached the tree near the gates, where so often he and Endon had hidden from Min in the old days.

He crept into the tree's hollow and huddled

there, panting. He knew that the guards would surely find him in the end. Perhaps Endon would even tell them where to look. And when they found him they would kill him. Of that he had no doubt.

He cursed himself for being impatient. For scaring Endon with wild talk while he was still confused, tired, and grieving. For playing into Prandine's hands.

There was a squeaking, rattling sound not far away. Peering cautiously out of his hollow, Jarred saw the rubbish cart trundling around the side of the palace, heading for the gates. The old man sat at the front, urging his tired horse on with sad shakes of the reins.

Jarred's heart leapt. Perhaps there was a chance of escape from the palace after all! But how could he run away, leaving Endon alone and unprotected? He was sure now that Prandine was evil.

If you stay, you will die. And then you will never be able to help Endon. Never.

The thought brought him to his senses. He pulled out his pencil and paper and scrawled a note.

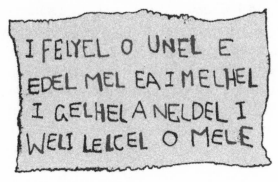

I FELYEL O UNEL E
EDEL MEL EA I MELHEL
I GELHEL A NELDEL I
WELI LELCEL O MELE

He tucked the note into a hole in the tree's trunk, wondering if his friend would ever see it. Perhaps Endon, believing what Prandine said of him, would never come to this place again.

But he had done what he could, and the cart was coming closer. Soon it would pass under the tree. That would be his chance.

As he had done so many times before, he climbed up through the hollow trunk of the tree and squeezed out of the hole that gaped just above its lowest branch.

From here he could see that there were guards everywhere. But he was used to hiding. He lay on his stomach, flattening himself against the branch, being careful not to make it sway.

The rubbish cart was underneath him now. He waited until just the right moment, then dropped lightly onto the back, burrowing quickly into the sticky mess of scraps until he was completely covered.

Bread crusts, apple peel, moldy cheese, gnawed bones, and half-eaten cakes pressed against his face. The smell nearly made him choke. He screwed his eyes shut and held his breath.

He could hear the sound of the horse's feet. He could hear the distant shouting of the guards searching for him. And at last he could hear the sound of the first pair of great wooden gates creaking open.

His heart thudded as the cart trundled on. Then he heard the gates closing behind him and the second pair of gates opening. Soon, soon . . .

The cart moved on, swaying and jolting. With a creak the second pair of gates slammed shut. And then Jarred knew that, for the first time in his life, he was outside the palace walls. The cart was trundling down the hill now. Soon he would actually be in the beautiful city he had seen so often from his window.

He had to look. His curiosity was too great. Slowly he wriggled until his eyes and nose were above the mound of scraps.

He was facing back towards the palace. He could see the wall, and the gates. He could see the top of the hollow. But — Jarred squinted in puzzlement — why could he not see the turrets of the palace, or the tops of the other trees in the gardens? Above the wall there was only shining mist.

He thought his eyes were at fault, and rubbed them. But the mist did not disappear.

Confused, he turned his head to look down towards the city. And his shock, dismay, and horror were so great that he almost cried out. For instead of beauty he saw ruin.

The fine buildings were crumbling. The roads were filled with holes. The grain fields were brown and choked with weeds. The trees were stunted and bent. Waiting at the bottom of the hill was a crowd of thin, ragged people carrying baskets and bags.

Jarred began struggling to free himself from the rubbish. In his confusion he no longer cared if the driver of the cart heard him or not, but the old man did not look around. Jarred realized that he was deaf. Unable to speak, too, no doubt, for he had not uttered a single word, even to the horse.

Jarred leapt from the back of the cart and rolled into a ditch at the side of the road. He lay, watching, as the cart moved on to the bottom of the hill and stopped. The old man sat staring ahead of him while the ragged people swarmed onto the pile of rubbish. Jarred saw them fighting one another for the scraps from the palace tables, stuffing old bones, crusts, and vegetable peelings into their baskets and into their mouths.

They were starving.

Sick at heart, Jarred looked back at the palace. From here he could just see the tips of the palace turrets, rising above the shimmering mist.

Endon might be looking from his window at this moment, staring down at the city. He would be seeing peace, beauty, and plenty. He would be seeing a lie. A lie created by pictures on a misty screen.

For how many years had this evil magic blinded the eyes of the kings and queens of Deltora? And who had created it?

Words from the book came to Jarred's mind. He shuddered with dread.

. . . the Enemy is clever and sly, and to its anger and envy a thousand years is like the blink of an eye.

The Shadow Lord was stirring.

4 ~ The Forge

fterwards, Jarred could barely remember
scrambling from the ditch. He could not
remember stumbling through the tangled
weeds and thorny bushes beyond the road. He did
not know what guided him to the blacksmith's forge,
where at last he fell, fainting, to the ground.

Perhaps he saw the glow of the fire. Perhaps he
heard the hammer beating on the red-hot metal, and
the sound reminded him of his lessons with Endon.
Or perhaps the spirit of Adin was looking after him.
For Crian the blacksmith, stubborn and fearless, was
perhaps the only man in Del who would have taken
him in.

Crian roused him and helped him into the small
house behind the forge. At Crian's call, a sweet-faced
girl came running. Her eyes were full of questions, but

she was silent as she helped Crian give Jarred water and bread and bathe his cuts and scratches. They took his filthy, torn clothes, gave him a long, plain night-shirt, and tucked him into a narrow bed.

Then Jarred slept.

When he woke, the great hammer was ringing on metal once more, the girl was singing in the kitchen, and the sun was setting. He had slept the day through.

At the end of his bed he found a set of clothes. He pulled them on, tidied the bed, and crept outside.

He found Crian at work in the forge. The old man turned and looked at him without speaking.

"I thank you for your kindness with all my heart," Jarred said awkwardly. "I will leave now, for I do not want to cause you trouble. But I beg you not to say I was here if the palace guards come searching. They will tell you I tried to kill the new king. But I did not do it."

"So much the worse," the old man answered grimly, returning to his work. "Many in Del would thank you if you had."

Jarred caught his breath. So this was how things were. The king was not loved, but hated. And no wonder. As far as his people knew, he lived in lux-ury behind his high walls while they suffered. They did not understand that he had no idea of their trouble.

"The guards will not come," the old man said, without turning around. "I threw your clothes over a cliff into the sea and watched as they found them. They think that you are drowned."

Jarred did not know what to say. He saw that Crian had finished the horseshoe he had been hammering. Without thinking, he picked up the heavy tongs beside the forge and stepped forward. Crian glanced at him in surprise, but let him pick up the shoe and dip it into the barrel of water standing ready. The water hissed and bubbled as the iron cooled.

"You have done this work before," the old man murmured.

Jarred nodded. "A little," he said. Carefully, he lifted the horseshoe from the water and laid it aside.

"I am old," Crian said, watching him. "My son, whose clothes you are wearing now, was killed three years ago. His dear wife died before him, when their child was born. I have only that child, Anna, now. We live simply, but there is always food on the table. And will be, while I keep my strength."

He glanced down at Jarred's hands — soft and white, with long, rounded nails. "You could stay here, boy," he said. "But you would have to work hard to earn your keep. Could you do it?"

"I could," said Jarred strongly.

Nothing would please him more than to stay. He liked the old blacksmith. He liked the calm, sweet-faced Anna. Here, too, he would be close to the palace. He could do nothing for Endon now except to keep watch. But he had vowed that this he would do.

Prandine thought he was dead. But he would be unlikely to tell Endon so. It would suit his purpose better to let the king think Jarred was still alive, and dangerous. If he feared for his life, Endon would be even more willing to do exactly as he was told.

But one day Endon may realize that after all I was right, thought Jarred. One day he may call me. And if ever that happens, I will be ready.

So, it was settled. Jarred took shears and cut off the long plaits of hair that marked him so plainly as coming from the palace. And after that, every day, he worked in the forge.

He already knew how to hammer hot iron and steel to make fine swords and shields. Now he had to learn to make simpler things, like horseshoes, axes, and blades for ploughs. But this he did quickly, and as his muscles hardened and his soft hands grew tough he took over more and more of the blacksmith's work.

The forge was busy, but still Crian and Anna were poor. Jarred soon discovered that this was because most of the people in Del were even poorer, and could pay little for the work the blacksmith did for them. Some, indeed, could give nothing. And these Crian would help all the same, saying, "Pay me when you can."

By the second day, Jarred had realized with a sinking heart that everything he and Endon had been taught about life outside the palace had been a lie. The city was a place of hunger, illness, and struggle. Beyond its walls, strange, terrible beasts and bands of robbers prowled. For many years no news had come from the towns and villages scattered through the countryside.

Many people were weak with hunger. Yet it was said that in the dead of night heavily guarded carts piled high with food and drink trundled into the city and up to the palace gates. No one knew where the carts came from.

"Somewhere far away, in any case," Crian muttered, as they sat by the fire on the second night. "Such luxuries could not be found here."

"It is said that Deltora was once a land of peace and plenty," Anna added. "But that was a long time ago."

"The new king knows nothing of this!" Jarred cried. "Neither did the old king. You should have told him — "

"*Told* him?" Crian growled angrily. "We told him time and again!" He swung around in his chair and pulled an old tin box from the shelf. He thrust the box at Jarred. "Open it!" he ordered.

Jarred lifted the lid of the box. Inside were many small rolls of parchment edged with gold. Confused, he picked out one of the rolls and straightened it.

The King thanks you for your
message. He will attend to your
request when time allows.
Alton

Frowning, Jarred thrust the parchment back into the box and picked out another. It was exactly the same. And so was the next he looked at, and the next. The only difference in the fourth was that it spoke of "The Queen" instead of "The King" and was signed "Lilia." Queen Lilia had been Alton's mother, Jarred remembered.

He scrabbled through the parchments. There were hundreds of them, all stamped with the royal seal. Some were much older than others, signed with royal names he remembered from his history lessons.

"They are all the same," Crian said, watching him reading one after the other. "The only difference between them is the name at the bottom. For centuries messages have been sent to the palace, begging for help. And these accursed parchments are all the people have ever received in return. Nothing has ever been done. Nothing!"

Jarred's throat tightened with pain and anger.

"King Alton, at least, never received your messages, Crian," he said, as calmly as he could. "I think they were kept from him by his chief advisor. A man called Prandine."

"The king signed these replies and fixed to them his royal seal," Crian pointed out coldly, flicking his finger at the box. "As did his mother and grandfather before him."

"It is the Rule — the custom — that the chief advisor prepares all replies for the king to sign," exclaimed Jarred. "The old king signed and sealed whatever Prandine put in front of him."

"Then he was a fool and a weakling!" Crian snapped back. "As no doubt his son is also! Endon will be as useless to us as his father." He shook his head. "I fear for Deltora," he muttered. "We are now so weak that should invasion come from the Shadowlands we could do nothing to protect ourselves."

"The Shadow Lord will not invade, Grandfather," Anna soothed. "Not while the Belt of Deltora protects us. And our king guards the Belt. That, at least, he does for us."

Jarred felt a chill of fear. But he could not bring himself to tell Anna that she was wrong. If she found out that the king did not wear the Belt but let it be shut away, under the care of others, she would lose the last of her hope.

Oh, Endon, he thought, as he went to bed that night. I cannot reach you unless you wish it. You are too well guarded. But you can reach me. Go to the hollow tree. Read my note. Send the signal.

From that time on, before he started work each morning, Jarred looked up at the tree rising against the misty cloud on the hill. He would look carefully, searching for the glint of the king's golden arrow at the top. The signal that Endon needed him.

But it was a long, long time before the signal came. And by then it was too late.

5 - The Enemy Strikes

Years passed and life went on. Jarred and Anna married. Then old Crian died and Jarred took his place as blacksmith.

Sometimes Jarred almost forgot that he had ever had another life. It was as if his time at the palace had been a dream. But still, every dawn, he looked up to the tree on the hill. And still he often read the small book he had found in the palace library. Then he feared for what the future might hold. He feared for his beloved Anna and the child they were expecting. He feared for himself, for Endon, and for the whole of Deltora.

One night, exactly seven years after the night Endon was crowned, Jarred tossed restlessly in his bed.

"It is nearly daybreak and you have not slept, Jarred," Anna said gently, at last. "What is troubling you?"

"I do not know, dear heart," Jarred murmured. "But I cannot rest."

"Perhaps the room is too warm," she said, climbing out of bed. "I will open the window a little more."

She had pulled the curtains aside and was reaching for the window fastening when suddenly she screamed and jumped back.

Jarred leapt up and ran to her.

"There!" Anna exclaimed, pointing, as he put his arm around her. "Oh, Jarred, what are they?"

Jarred stared through the window and caught his breath. In the sky above the palace on the hill, monstrous shapes were wheeling and circling.

It was still too dark to see them clearly. But there was no doubt that they were huge birds. There were seven. Their necks were long. Their great, hooked beaks were cruel. Their mighty wings flapped clumsily but strongly, beating at the air. As Jarred watched, they swooped, rose again, and then separated, flying off swiftly in different directions.

A name came to him. A name from the schoolroom of his past.

"Ak-Baba," he hissed. His arm tightened around Anna's shoulders.

She turned to him, her eyes wide and frightened.

"Ak-Baba," he repeated slowly, still staring at the palace. "Great birds that eat dead flesh and live for a thousand years. Seven of them serve the Shadow Lord."

"Why are they here?" Anna whispered.

"I do not know. But I fear — " Jarred broke off abruptly and leaned forward. He had seen something glinting brightly in the first feeble rays of the sun.

For a moment he stood motionless. Then he turned to Anna, his face grim and pale.

"Endon's arrow is in the tree," he said. "The call has come."

✳

In moments Jarred had dressed and run from the house behind the forge. He hurried up the hill to the palace, his mind racing.

How was he to reach Endon? If he climbed the wall, the guards inside would certainly see him. He would be hit by a dozen arrows before he reached the ground. The cart that collected the food scraps would be of no use to him. Prandine must have guessed that Jarred had used it to escape, because it was no longer permitted to enter the palace. These days it waited between the two sets of gates while guards loaded it with sacks.

Endon himself is the only one who can help me, Jarred thought as he ran. Perhaps he will be watching for me, waiting for me . . .

But as he slowed, panting, in sight of the palace gates, he could see that they were firmly closed and the road outside was deserted.

Jarred moved closer, his spine prickling. The long grass that ringed the palace walls whispered in the breeze of dawn. He could be walking into a trap. Perhaps at any moment guards would spring from their hiding places in the grass and lay hands on him. Perhaps Endon had at last decided to betray him to Prandine.

His feet brushed something lying in the dust of the road. He looked down and saw a child's wooden arrow. A small piece of paper had been rolled around the arrow's shaft and tied there.

His heart beating hard, Jarred picked up the arrow and pulled away the paper. But as he flattened it out and looked at it, his excitement died.

It was just a child's drawing. Some palace child had been playing a game, practicing shooting arrows over the wall as he and Endon once had done.

Jarred screwed up the paper in disgust and threw it to the ground. He looked around again at the closed gates, the empty road. Still there was no movement, no sign. There was nothing but the wooden arrow lying in the dust and the little ball of paper rolling slowly away from him, driven by the breeze. He stared at it, and the foolish little rhyme came back to him.

Strange, he thought idly. That rhyme sounds almost like a set of instructions. Instructions that a small child could chant and remember.

An idea seized him. He ran after the paper and snatched it up again. He smoothed out the creases and looked at it closely, this time seeing two things that he had overlooked before. The paper was yellowed with age. And the writing, though childish, was strangely familiar.

This is the way Endon used to print when he was small, he thought in wonder. And Endon drew the picture, too. I am sure of it!

Suddenly he realized what must have happened. Endon had had little time. Yet he had wanted to send Jarred a message. So he had snatched up one of his old childhood drawings and sent it over the wall. He had used a child's wooden arrow so that the guards

42

would take no notice if they saw it lying on the road.

And if Jarred was right, Endon had not chosen just any drawing. This one had a special meaning for him. Why else would he have kept it?

Wake the bear,

Do not fear . . .

Jarred waited no longer. With the paper clutched in his hand he left the road and moved left, following the wall.

The road was out of sight by the time he found what he was searching for. Even overgrown with long grass and shadowed by a clump of straggly bushes, the shape of the huge rock was clear. It really did look exactly like a sleeping animal.

Jarred forced his way through the undergrowth to the rock. He saw that at one end, where the bear's nose rested on its paws, the grass grew less strongly than it did anywhere else. Why would that be? Unless . . .

"Time to wake up, old bear," Jarred muttered aloud. He ran to the place, threw himself to his knees, and began pulling at the weak grass. It came away easily, and as he scrabbled in the earth beneath it Jarred realized with a wave of relief that he had been right. There was only a thin layer of soil here. Beneath it was a large, round metal plate.

It took only moments for his powerful hands to uncover the plate completely and pull it aside. A dark hole was revealed. Its walls were lined with stone. In wonder, Jarred realized that he had found the entrance to a tunnel.

Scurry, mouse,
Into your house . . .

He knew what he must do. He lay flat on his stomach and wriggled into the hole, pulling himself forward on his elbows until the space broadened and his way became easier.

So now the mouse is in the mouse hole, he thought grimly, as he crawled along in the darkness. Let us hope that no cat is waiting at the other end.

For a short time the tunnel sloped downwards, then it became more level and Jarred realized that he was moving through the center of the hill. The air was still, the walls around him were ancient stone, and the blackness was complete. He crawled on, losing all track of time.

At last the tunnel ended in a set of steep stone steps that led upwards. His heart thudding, Jarred began to climb blindly. He had to feel his way — up, up, one step at a time. Then, without warning, the top of his head hit hard stone. With a shock he realized that the way above was blocked. He could go no further.

Hot panic flared in him. Had this been a trap after all? Were guards even now creeping through the tunnel after him, knowing that they would find him cowering here, without hope of escape?

Then, through the confusion of his thoughts, he remembered.

Lift the lid,
Be glad you did.

The panic died. Jarred stretched up his arms, pushed firmly, and felt the stone above his head move. He pushed harder, then staggered and nearly fell as with a grating sound the stone moved smoothly aside.

He climbed the last few steps and crawled out of blackness into soft, flickering light.

"Who are you?" barked a deep, angry voice.

A tall, shimmering figure was looming over him. Jarred blinked up at it. After being so long in darkness, his eyes were watering, dazzled by the light. "My name is Jarred," he cried. "Stay back!"

He scrambled to his feet, blindly feeling for his sword.

Then, suddenly, with a rustle of rich silk and the clinking of golden ornaments, the figure was falling to its knees before him.

"Oh, Jarred, how could I not have known you?" the voice cried. "For the sake of our old friendship, I beg you to forgive the past. You are the only one I can trust. Please help us!"

And only then did Jarred realize that the man at his feet was Endon.

6 ~ Friends to the Death

With a shaky laugh, Jarred bent to raise the kneeling king. "Endon! I did not know you, either! Get up, for mercy's sake!"

As he stared, his eyes slowly adjusting to the light, he thought that it was no wonder he had not recognized his old friend.

The slim, solemn boy he had left behind him seven years ago had become a man. Endon had grown as tall and broad-shouldered as Jarred himself. His stiff robes and high collar were encrusted with tiny gems that glittered in the light. His eyes were outlined with black and his eyelids colored blue, in the palace fashion. His long hair and beard were plaited and twined with gold. He smelt of perfume and spices. To Jarred, who had been so long away from the palace and its ways, he made a strange, awesome picture.

Jarred realized that Endon was staring at him,

too, and suddenly he became aware of his workman's clothes, his thick boots, his rough beard, and untidy hair. He felt clumsy and awkward. To hide this he turned away.

As he did, he at last realized where he was. He was in the chapel. One of the marble tiles that surrounded the raised platform in the center had been pushed aside, and a dark hole gaped where it had lain.

"The tunnel through the hill is known only to the royal family, and is only to be used in times of great danger," he heard Endon say softly. "King Brandon caused it to be made when the palace was built. My father taught me of it when I was very young, as he had been taught in his time — in words that even a small child would remember. There is a rhyme for entering the palace, and a rhyme for leaving it. It is a dark secret. Even the chief advisors have never known of it."

Jarred did not reply. He had raised his eyes to the platform and seen what was lying there. It was the body of an old woman. Her work-worn hands were folded on her chest. Her wrinkled face was peaceful in the flickering light of the candles that surrounded her.

"Min!" he whispered. His eyes burned with sudden tears as he looked at the old nurse who had cared for him through his childhood. He had not seen her for many years, but he had thought of her often. It was hard to believe that she was dead.

"She had a grown-up son, you know," Endon murmured. "He lived in the palace, but I never met him. I asked for him, when I heard she had died. They told me he had run away — escaped through the gates during the feast. He was afraid, Jarred. Min must have told him what she heard. He knew she had been killed . . ."

"Killed?" gasped Jarred. "But — "

Endon's face was twisted with sorrow. "She came to me in my chamber. I was about to leave for the feast celebrating my seven years as king," he muttered. "She was troubled. She had been working in her sewing room, and had overheard whisperings outside that frightened her. She told me that there were enemies within the palace, and that some great evil was to strike this night."

He bowed his head. "I would not listen to her. I thought she had fallen asleep over her work, and dreamed. I smiled at her fears and sent her away. And within the hour, she was dead. She had fallen from the top of the stairs to the hall below. They said it was an accident. But . . ."

"But you do not think so," Jarred finished for him, looking sadly at Min's still, pale face. "You think she was killed because of what she knew."

"Yes," said Endon in a low voice. "And my wife thinks it, too."

Jarred glanced at him. "You are married, then," he said. "I, too."

48

Endon half smiled. "That is good," he murmured politely. "I hope that you are as happy in your marriage as I am in mine. My wife, the queen, is called Sharn. We had never spoken to each other before our wedding day, as is the Rule, but she grows more dear to me with every year that passes. Our first child will be born at summer's end."

"And ours in the early autumn," said Jarred.

There was a moment's silence as each of them thought of the changes that seven years had brought. Then Endon looked straight into Jarred's eyes. "It is good to see you again, my friend," he said softly. "I have been cruelly punished for believing that you could betray me. I have missed you sorely."

And suddenly all the strangeness between them melted away. Jarred thrust out his hand and clasped Endon's warmly. "Friends to the death we were as boys, and friends to the death we will always be," he said. "You must have always known this in your heart, Endon, because you sent for me when trouble came. I wish only that the summons had been sooner. I fear we have little time."

"Then Min was right," Endon whispered. "There is evil here."

"There has been evil here for a long time," said Jarred. "And now — "

Both of them swung around, their hands on their swords, as they heard the door behind them click open.

"Endon, it is past dawn," a voice called softly.

"Sharn!" exclaimed Endon. He ran to meet the pretty young woman who was slipping into the chapel. She was as richly robed as he, and her glossy hair was twisted high on her head. There were deep shadows under her eyes as if she had kept watch all night.

She gasped and shrank back as she saw Jarred.

"Do not be afraid, Sharn," Endon said gently. "It is only Jarred."

"Jarred! You came!" she exclaimed, her tired face breaking into a relieved smile.

"I did," nodded Jarred. "And I will do what I can to help you fight the trouble that has come to our land. But we must act quickly. We must go at once to the tower, so that Endon can reclaim the Belt of Deltora."

Endon stared at him, white-faced. "Jarred, I — I cannot," he stammered. "The Rule — "

"Forget the Rule, Endon!" Jarred hissed, striding towards the door. "I told you this once and you would not listen to me. Do not make the mistake a second time. The Belt is Deltora's only protection. The people depend upon you to guard it. And I think that it is in danger. Grave danger."

As Endon stood motionless, still hesitating, Sharn put her arm through his. "You are the king, Endon," she said quietly. "Your duty to Deltora is far greater than your duty to obey the Rule. Let us go together to the tower."

And, at last, Endon nodded. "Very well," he said. "We will go. Together."

✳

They ran up the great stairs — past the first floor, the second, the third, and on towards the tower room. They took care to move quietly, but they saw no one. It was still very early, and though the cooks had begun to move around in the kitchens downstairs, few others in the palace were stirring.

By the time they reached the last flight of stairs, Jarred had begun to think that all was going to be well. He climbed eagerly, with Endon and Sharn close behind him. He reached the top — then stopped abruptly.

The tower room door was gaping open, its three gold locks broken. On the floor outside, the three guards lay dead where they had fallen, their swords still clutched in their hands.

Jarred heard a sobbing gasp behind him. Then Endon ran past him into the tower room. There was a single, anguished cry. Then silence.

Jarred's heart seemed to turn over in his chest. Slowly he and Sharn followed the king.

The small, round room was very still and a foul smell hung in the air. The sky outside the open windows was filled with angry red light as the newly risen sun glared through a smothering blanket of cloud. The glass case that sheltered the Belt of Deltora had been shattered into a thousand pieces.

Endon was on his knees among the glittering fragments. The Belt — or what remained of it — lay on the floor in front of him. He picked it up. It hung limply between his hands — a tangled, useless chain of grey steel. Its medallions were torn and twisted. The seven gems were gone.

7 - Treachery

With a cry, Sharn hurried to her husband's side, gently helping him to rise. He stood, swaying, the empty, ruined Belt clutched in his hands.

Dull despair settled over Jarred. What he had feared had come to pass. The enemy had triumphed.

There was a low, mocking laugh behind him. Prandine was standing in the doorway. In his long black robe he looked as tall and bony as ever, but it was as if a mask had fallen from his face. The grave, serious expression had gone. Now, greed and triumph lit his eyes and cruelty twisted his thin mouth.

"So, Jarred, you have risen from the dead to try to interfere once more," he snarled. "But you are too late. Soon, very soon, Deltora will bow beneath my Lord's shadow."

Wild anger surged through Jarred. He lunged

forward, his sword aimed at Prandine's heart. In an instant, the sword burned white hot. He dropped it with a cry of agony, his hand seared and blistered.

"You were a fool to come here," spat Prandine. "If you had not, I would have gone on believing you safely dead. Now you are doomed, like your idiot king, his little painted doll bride, and the brat she carries."

From his robe he drew a long, thin dagger, its wicked tip glowing sickly green.

Jarred backed away from him, fighting back the pain from his injured hand, trying desperately to think. He had no wish to die, but he knew that at all costs he must save Endon, Sharn, and their unborn child, the heir to the throne of Deltora.

"We are too many for you, Prandine," he said loudly. "While you struggle with one, the others can escape." He wondered if Prandine would realize that this was not just a challenge to him, but a message for Endon. *While I distract him, take Sharn and run!*

But Prandine was laughing again, kicking the door shut behind him. "There will be no struggle," he jeered, moving forward. "The poison on this blade is deadly. One tiny scratch and the end comes quickly. As it did for your mother and father, King Endon."

"Murderer! Traitor!" breathed Endon, pushing Sharn behind him. "You have betrayed your king, and your land."

"This is not my land," sneered Prandine. "My

loyalty, like the loyalty of the chief advisors before me, has always been to another place and to a far greater master."

He looked at Endon with contempt. "You are the last in a line of royal buffoons, King Endon. Little by little we robbed your family of power until you were nothing but puppets moving as we pulled the strings. And then, at last, the time was right to take your last protection from you."

He pointed a bony finger at the tangled chain in Endon's hands. "Finally, the blacksmith Adin's accursed work has been undone. The Belt of Deltora is no more."

"The gems cannot be destroyed," Endon said through pale lips. "And it is death to take them beyond Deltora's borders."

Prandine smiled cruelly. "The gems have been scattered far and wide, hidden where no one would dare to find them. And when you and your unborn brat are dead, finding them would be no use in any case."

The room darkened and thunder growled outside the tower. Prandine's eyes glowed with triumph. "The Shadow Lord comes," he hissed.

Cowering against the wall, Sharn moaned softly. Then she seemed to hear something. She sidled to the open window and looked out — not up to the black sky but down to the ground below the tower. The next moment she had jumped back, covering her mouth with her hand as if to smother a shriek.

"What is it?" snarled Prandine, suddenly alert.

Sharn shook her head. "Nothing," she stammered. "I was mistaken. There is no one there."

Oh, Sharn, even a child could tell that you are lying! thought Jarred desperately. Thanks to you, whoever has come to help us is doomed.

"Stay where you are or she dies at once!" barked Prandine to the two men as he crossed the room.

Sharn shrank away from him as he reached her. "Do not look out! There is no one there!" she cried again.

"So you say," Prandine sneered. He thrust his head and shoulders out of the open window.

And in the next instant Sharn had crouched behind him, thrown her arms around his knees, jerked his legs back and upwards, and tipped him over the sill.

Jarred and Endon, frozen with shock, listened to their enemy's screams as he plunged to the hard earth far below. They both stared, astounded, at the small figure turning from the window to face them.

"Often, in the great hall, I have watched little clowns upset big ones from below," Sharn said calmly. "I did not see why the trick should not work for me."

"What — what did you see from the window?" Jarred stammered.

"Nothing. As I told him. But I knew he would not trust my word." Sharn tossed her head. "And I knew he would lean out. Why should he fear a little painted doll like me?"

Jarred gazed at her in frank admiration, then turned to Endon. "You are as fortunate in your bride as I am in mine," he said.

Endon nodded slowly. He seemed dazed.

Thunder growled outside, threatening as an angry beast. Black clouds edged with scarlet were tumbling towards the tower.

"We must hurry to the tunnel," Jarred said urgently. "Come quickly!"

✳

The palace was echoing with frightened voices as they ran down the stairs. The people were waking to darkness and terror.

"I have brought them to this," moaned Endon, as they reached the chapel door. "How can I leave them?"

"You have no choice, Endon," panted Jarred. "Your family must survive or Deltora will be lost to the Shadow Lord forever."

He pushed Endon and Sharn into the chapel and closed the door behind them. "We will go straight to the forge," he said, hurrying towards the tunnel entrance. "There we will think what we should do."

"We must flee the city and find a place to hide," said Sharn.

But Endon's hands tightened on the tangled handful of steel that had once been the Belt of Deltora.

"I cannot run and hide!" he burst out. "I must find the gems and restore them to the Belt. Without them I am helpless and Deltora is doomed."

Glancing at Sharn's worried face, Jarred took his friend's arm. "The gems must be found, but you cannot be the one to find them, Endon," he said firmly. "The Shadow Lord will be searching for you. You must stay in hiding and wait."

"But what if I die before the Belt is whole again?" Endon argued desperately. "It will only recognize Adin's true heir. It will only shine for me!"

Jarred opened his mouth to speak, then thought better of it. Soon enough Endon would realize for himself that he had lost the last trust his people had in him. The Belt of Deltora would never shine for him again.

But Sharn had moved quietly to her husband's side. "Do not forget, my dear," she murmured. "Our child will also be Adin's heir."

Endon stared at her, open-mouthed. She lifted her chin proudly.

"If the Shadow Lord can be patient, so can we," she said. "We will hide ourselves away from him for now. But it will not be for fear of our own lives, as he will think. It will be to keep our child safe, and to prepare for the future."

She stroked his arm lovingly. "Years will pass and we may die, Endon," she said. "But our child will live after us, to reclaim the kingdom and lift this evil from our land."

Jarred's heart swelled at her courage. And at that moment he himself found the courage to face what he must do.

Endon had gathered Sharn close to him. "You are indeed a precious gift," he was murmuring. "But you do not understand. Without the Belt our child cannot defeat the Shadow Lord. The gems — "

"One day the gems will be found," Jarred broke in.

They turned from each other to look at him. "We will discuss this further at the forge," he said rapidly. "For the moment, remember that now that Prandine is dead, no one knows that you have a friend outside the palace. The Shadow Lord will not suspect that a humble blacksmith could be a threat to him."

"*You* will go now, to find the gems?" whispered Endon.

Jarred shook his head. "I would not succeed now, any more than you would do, Endon. Our enemy's servants will be watching the gems' hiding places for signs that they are in danger. But in years to come the Shadow Lord will begin to believe that he is safe and the watching will become less. Then, and only then, the quest can begin."

He held out his uninjured hand to Endon. "After this day we may not meet again in this life, my friend," he said in a low voice. "We will be far apart, and who can tell what will become of us in the dangerous times ahead? But one day the gems will be found and the Belt will be restored. It will be done."

Endon took the hand in both his own and bowed his head. Then, suddenly, the walls of the chapel trembled as though the palace had been struck by a great wind.

"We must go!" Sharn cried in alarm.

As he helped her climb into the tunnel entrance, Endon turned to Jarred. "You say we must run, that we must hide, but where can we go?" he asked in a trembling voice.

"With the Shadow Lord will come a time of confusion and darkness," Jarred answered grimly. "Many people will be roaming the countryside, neighbor will lose sight of neighbor, and life will not be as it was before. The confusion will aid us."

"You have thought of a place?" whispered Endon.

"Perhaps," muttered Jarred. "It will be dangerous, but if you are willing, the chance is worth taking."

Endon asked no more, but followed his wife into the tunnel. Jarred climbed after him, pulling the marble tile back into place over his head so that no one could tell where they had gone.

As the last of the light from the chapel was shut

out and blackness enfolded him, he thought of Anna and his heart ached.

The life they had known had been hard, but they had been happy. Now all this was ended. Fear and trouble were coming — long years of waiting while Deltora groaned under the yoke of the Shadow Lord.

And only time could tell what would happen then.

8 ~ Lief

L ief ran for home down the dark, winding back-streets of Del, past lighted houses closed tightly for the night. He ran as fast and silently as a cat, his heart hammering in his chest.

He was late. Very late. He had to hurry, but he knew that the smallest sound could betray him.

It was forbidden to be on the streets after sunset. That was one of the Shadow Lord's strictest laws. It had been put into force on the day he took possession of Del, just over sixteen years ago. The penalty for breaking it was death.

Lief slipped into a long, narrow street that ran through the ruined part of the city. It smelt of damp and decay. The stones under his feet were slimy and treacherous.

He had been out after sunset before, but not for so long and never so far from home. He wished with all his heart that he had been more careful. It flashed through his mind that his father and mother would be waiting for him, worried for him.

"You are free for the afternoon, my son," his father had said when their midday meal was over. "Your sixteenth birthday is a special day. Your mother and I want you to be glad and to celebrate with your friends."

Lief was overjoyed. Never before had he been granted leave in the middle of the working day. Usually he had to study in the afternoons.

He had always felt that this was unfair. He was the only one of his friends who had lessons to do. Why learn to read and write? Why learn figures and history and worry at mind games? Of what use were these things to a blacksmith?

But his parents had insisted that the lessons go on, and, grumbling, Lief had obeyed. Now he was used to the way things were. But this did not mean that he liked them any better. A free afternoon was the best birthday gift he could imagine.

"Tonight, there will be another gift. And — things we must discuss together," his father said, exchanging looks with his mother.

Lief glanced at their grave faces with quick curiosity. "What things?" he asked.

His mother smiled and shook her head. "We will talk of them tonight, Lief," she said, pushing him gently towards the door. "For now, enjoy your holiday. But stay out of trouble. And keep track of the time, I beg you. Be home well before sunset."

Lief promised gladly and ran — out of the house, through the hot forge where he helped his father each morning, past Barda, the tattered, half-wit beggar who sat all day at the gate and slept in the forge yard by night. He crossed the road that led to the palace on the hill and waded through the weed-filled fields beyond. Then he ran joyfully on till he reached the market, where he could lose himself in the smells and sounds of the noisy, crowded city.

He found one of his friends, then another, then three more. Happily they roamed their favorite haunts together. They had no money to spend but they found fun anyway — teasing the stall-holders in the mar-kets, running up and down the grimy alleyways, dodging the Grey Guards, looking for silver coins in the choked and overflowing gutters. Then, in a de-serted and overgrown patch of ground not far from the palace walls, they found something better than sil-ver — a twisted old tree covered in small, round red fruits.

"Apples!" Lief knew what the fruits were. He had even tasted an apple, once. It was when he was very young. In those days there were still some large orchards in the city. Apples and other fruits could be bought in the markets, though they were costly. But years ago it had been declared that all fruits of Del were the property of the Shadow Lord, wherever the trees that bore them grew.

This tree had somehow been forgotten, and there were no Guards to be seen.

Lief and his friends picked as many of the apples as they could carry and went down into the drain-tunnels under the city to eat them in secret. The fruits were small and spotted, but they were sweet. It was a feast, enjoyed all the better for knowing that it was stolen from the hated Shadow Lord.

An hour before sunset, Lief's friends left him and hurried home. Lief, however, was unwilling to waste his last hour of freedom. He stayed in the silence and dimness of the drains, exploring and thinking.

He meant to stay only a little while, but then he discovered a small drain-tunnel branching off the main, leading, he was sure, towards the palace on the hill. He crept along this new tunnel as far as he dared, then turned back, promising himself that he would follow it further another day. But when, finally, he crawled up to the surface, he found that time had rushed by. Night had fallen.

So now he was in danger.

Lief skidded to a stop as two Grey Guards turned a corner in front of him and began pacing in his direction. They were talking and had not yet heard him, seen him, or caught his scent. But when they did . . .

He held his breath, desperately looking this way and that, seeking a way of escape. High walls rose on either side of him, dripping with slimy water and slippery with moss. He could never climb them unaided. He could not turn and run, either. To do so would mean certain death.

Lief had prowled Del's streets all his life, and often met with danger. He prided himself on his many lucky escapes in the past. He was fast, agile, and daring. But he had sense, too — sense enough to know that he could not run the length of this street without being cut down.

Each Guard carried a sling and a supply of what the people of Del called "blisters." The blisters were silver eggs filled with burning poison. They burst on contact with a target and the Guards could hurl them with deadly strength and accuracy, even in darkness. Lief had seen enough blister victims fall, writhing in agony, to know that he did not want to risk the same fate.

Yet if he stayed where he was the Guards would come upon him and he would die in any case. By blister or by dagger, he would die.

Lief flattened himself against the wall, still as a shadow, not daring to move a muscle. The Guards paced on towards him. Closer, closer . . .

If only they would turn around! he thought feverishly. If only something would distract them! Then I would have a chance.

He was not praying for a miracle, because he did not believe in miracles. Few citizens of Del did these days. So he was astounded when a moment later there was a clatter from the corner behind the Guards. They spun around and began running towards the sound.

Hardly able to believe his luck, Lief turned to run. Then, with a shock, he felt something hit his shoulder. To his amazement he saw that it was a rope — a rope dangling from the top of the wall. Who had thrown it?

There was no time to think or wonder. In seconds, he was climbing for his life. He did not pause for breath until he had reached the top of the wall and swung himself into a great tree on the other side. Panting, he huddled in a fork between two branches and looked around him.

He was alone. The rope had been tied securely around the tree's trunk, but there was no sign of whoever had thrown it over the wall.

The Guards had still not come back into view, but Lief could hear them nearby, arguing as they searched for whatever had made the sound they had heard. He was fairly certain that they would find nothing. He was sure that the person who had thrown the rope had also hurled a stone to distract them. That was what he himself would have done if he had been trying to save a friend.

A friend? Lief bit his lip as he swiftly pulled the

rope up after him. As far as he knew, all his friends were safely in their homes. Who could have known that he was in trouble?

He puzzled about it for a moment, then shook his head. This is not important now, he told himself. The important thing is to reach home before anything else happens.

He untied the rope, coiled it, and slung it over his shoulder. Ropes such as these were valuable.

He climbed silently to the ground and strained his eyes to see through the darkness. Slowly he recognized the shape nearest to him. It was an old potter's wheel, broken and lying on its side in the grass.

With a chill he realized that he was in the backyard of what had been the city's biggest pottery. A thousand times he had walked past its burned-out shell, its gaping front windows, and its door branded with the Shadow Lord's sign.

The brand meant that the Shadow Lord's hand had been laid upon the pottery. Now it was a dead place, never again to be used, or even entered. There were many such buildings, and many such signs, in this part of the city. A group here had tried to resist the Shadow Lord. They had plotted to overthrow him. But he had found out, as he found out all such secrets.

Lief threaded his way through the huge piles of smashed pots, overgrown with weeds. He passed the two great ovens where the pots had been baked, now just ruined heaps of bricks. He nearly tripped on something buried in the grass — a child's wooden horse, crushed under the foot of a Grey Guard long ago.

By the time he reached the front of the building he was trembling and breathing hard. Not with fear now, but with a sudden, terrible anger.

Why should his people suffer this? Why should he have to creep around in his own city like a criminal, in fear of branding, imprisonment, or death?

He moved out onto the deserted road and looked up at the palace on the hill, sick with loathing. For as long as he could remember the palace had been the headquarters of the Shadow Lord. Before that, his friends had told him, the king of Deltora had lived there, in luxury, and the palace was almost hidden by a pale, shimmering mist. But when the Shadow Lord came, the mist completely disappeared. Now the palace could be seen clearly.

Though Lief's parents had made him study the history of Deltora from its earliest days, they had told him little of the time just before he was born. They seemed to fear speaking of it. They said the Shadow Lord had spies everywhere, and it was best to keep silence. But Lief's friends were not afraid, and they had told him a great deal.

They had told him that the last king, like the rulers before him, had cared nothing for the people, and done nothing to serve them. King Endon's only task had been to guard the magic Belt of Deltora. But he had been weak, lazy, and careless. He had allowed the Belt to be stolen. He had opened the way to the Shadow Lord.

The king was dead, Lief's friends said. And a good thing, too, Lief thought savagely, as again he hurried for home. The king deserved to die for the suffering he had brought to his people.

He reached the fields and began to run, crouching low, hiding himself in the long grass. A few minutes more and he would be safe. Already he could see the lights of home winking dimly in the distance.

He knew he would be in trouble for being so late and that there would be questions asked about the rope he carried. With luck, though, his mother and father would be so relieved to see him that they would forgive him quickly.

They cannot send me to bed without food, at least, Lief thought with satisfaction, scuttling across the road and plunging on towards the forge. They said they wanted to talk to me about something tonight.

Briefly he wondered what that something was, and smiled at the memory of how serious his parents had looked when they had spoken of it.

He loved them both very much, but no two people could be more ordinary, timid, and quiet than Jarred and Anna of the forge. Jarred had limped badly ever since he was injured by a falling tree when Lief was ten. But even before that, he and Anna had kept very much to themselves. They seemed content to listen to the tales of wandering travelers who stopped at the forge, rather than seeing life for themselves.

Lief had not been born until after the time of darkness and terror that had marked the coming of the Shadow Lord. But he knew that many in the city had fought and died and many others had fled in terror.

Jarred and Anna had done neither of these things. While all around them confusion and panic reigned, they stayed in their cottage, obeying every order given to them, doing nothing to attract the anger of the enemy. And when the panic was ended and dull misery had taken its place in the city, they re-opened the forge gates and began work again, struggling only to survive in their new, ruined world.

It was something that Lief himself could never have done. He could not understand it. He was convinced that all his parents had ever wanted in their lives was to stay out of trouble, whatever the cost. He was certain, absolutely certain, that nothing they had to say could surprise him.

So it was only with relief that he ran through the forge gates, dodged the beggar Barda, who was making his slow way to his shelter in the corner of the yard, and rushed through the cottage door. Excuses were ready on his tongue and thoughts of dinner were filling his head.

Little did he know that before another hour had passed everything was going to change for him.

Little did he know that he was about to receive the shock of his life.

9 - The Secret

Stunned by what he had just heard, Lief stared at his father. It was as if he were seeing him with new eyes. "*You* once lived in the palace? *You* were the king's friend? You — I cannot believe this! I will *not* believe it!"

His father smiled grimly. "You must believe it, my son." His fists clenched. "Why else do you think we have lived so quietly all these years, tamely obeying every order given to us, never rebelling? Many, many times I have been tempted to do otherwise. But I knew that we had to avoid drawing the enemy's attention to us."

"But — but why have you never told me before?" Lief stammered.

"We thought it best to keep silent until now, Lief." It was his mother who had spoken. She stood by the fire looking at him gravely.

"It was so important, you see, that no word reached the ears of the Shadow Lord," she went on. "And until you were ten your father believed that he himself would be the one who would go to seek the gems of Deltora, when the time came. But then — "

She broke off, glancing at her husband sitting in his armchair, his injured leg stuck stiffly out in front of him.

He smiled grimly. "Then the tree fell, and I had to accept that this could not be," he finished for her. "I can still work in the forge — enough to earn our bread — but I cannot travel. And so, Lief, the task is left to you. If you are willing."

Lief's head was spinning. So much that he had believed had been overturned in one short hour.

"The king was not killed after all," he mumbled, trying to take it in. "He escaped, with the queen. But why did the Shadow Lord not find them?"

"When we reached the forge the king and queen made themselves look like ordinary working people," his father said. "In haste we discussed the plan for escape while outside the wind howled and the darkness of the Shadow Lord deepened over the land. And then we parted."

His face was furrowed with grief and memory. "We knew that we might never meet again. Endon had realized by then that by his foolishness and blindness the people's last trust in him had been destroyed.

The Belt would never again shine for him. All our hopes rested with his unborn child."

"But — how do you know that the child was born safely and is still alive, Father?" Lief blurted out.

His father heaved himself to his feet. He took off the old brown belt that he always wore at his work. It was strong and heavy, made of two lengths of leather stitched together. He cut the stitching at one end with his knife and pulled out what was hidden inside.

Lief caught his breath. Sliding from the leather tube was a fine steel chain linking seven steel medallions. Even plain and without ornament, it was still the most beautiful thing he had ever seen.

He longed to touch it. Eagerly he held out his hands.

"I mended it, making it ready to receive the gems once more, before I hid it away," his father said, handing it to him. "But so closely is it bound to the blood of Adin that it would have crumbled into pieces if the heir was no more. As you see, it is still whole. So we can be sure that the heir lives."

In wonder, Lief gazed at the marvelous thing in his hands — the dream Belt made by the great Adin himself. How many times had he read of it in *The Belt of Deltora*, the small, pale blue book his father had given him to study? He could hardly believe that he was actually holding it.

"If you agree to go on the quest, my son, you

must put the Belt on and never let it out of your sight until it is complete," he heard his mother say. "Are you willing? Think carefully before you answer."

But Lief had already made his decision. He looked up at his waiting parents, his eyes sparkling.

"I am willing," he said firmly. Without hesitation he clasped the Belt around his waist, under his shirt. It felt cool against his skin. "Where must I go to find the gems?" he asked.

His father, suddenly drawn and pale, sat down again and stared at the fire. "Preparing for this moment we have listened to many travelers' tales," he said at last. "I will tell you what we know. Prandine said that the gems were scattered, hidden in places no one would dare to find them."

"That means, I suppose, that they lie in places people would be afraid to go," Lief said.

"So I fear." His father picked up a parchment from the table beside his chair and began slowly to unfold it. "Seven Ak-Baba were flying together around the palace tower on the day the gems were taken," he went on. "They separated and flew off in different directions. We believe that each was carrying one of the gems, and each was going to one particular place to hide it. See here. I have drawn a map."

His heart beating like a drum in his chest, Lief leaned over to look as his father pointed out one name after the other.

"The Lake of Tears," Lief read. "City of the Rats.

76

The Shifting Sands. Dread Mountain. The Maze of the Beast. The Valley of the Lost. The Forests of Silence . . ." His voice faltered. The very names filled him with fear, particularly the last.

The terrible tales he had heard of the Forests not far to the east of Del flooded Lief's mind, and for a moment the map blurred before his eyes.

"Over the years, different travelers have told of seeing a lone Ak-Baba hovering above one or another of these seven places on the day the Shadow Lord came," his father was saying. "They are where you must search for the gems, we are sure of it. Little is known of them, but all of them have evil reputations. The task will be long and perilous, Lief. Are you still willing?"

Lief's mouth felt dry. He swallowed, and nodded.

"He is so young!" his mother burst out. She bent her head and hid it in her hands. "Oh, I cannot bear it!"

Lief spun around to her and threw his arm around her neck. "I *want* to go, Mother!" he exclaimed. "Do not weep for me."

"You do not know what you are promising!" she cried.

"Perhaps I do not," Lief admitted. "But I know that I would do anything — anything in my power — to rid our land of the Shadow Lord."

He turned from her to look back at his father.

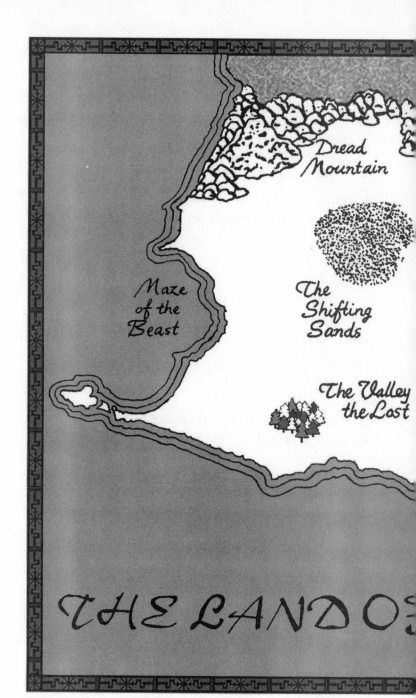

Dread
Mountain

Maze
of the
Beast

The
Shifting
Sands

The Valley
the Lost

THE LAND O?

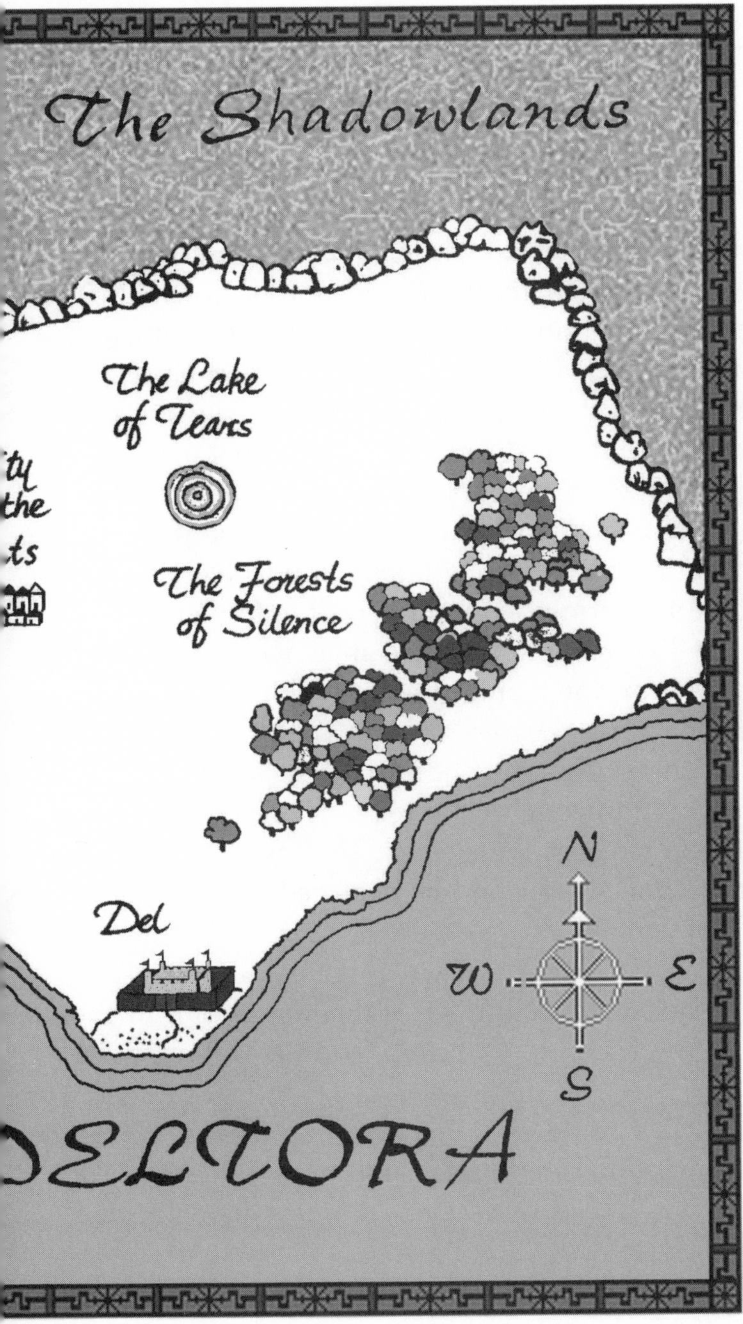
The Shadowlands
The Lake of Tears
The Forests of Silence
Del
N
W
E
S

"Where is the heir?" he demanded excitedly. "That, at least, you know for certain, Father, for you suggested the hiding place."

"Perhaps I did," his father said quietly. "But I must not endanger our cause by telling you of it. The heir is powerless without the Belt, and must remain in deepest hiding until it is complete. You are young and impatient, Lief, and the road ahead of you is hard. You might give way to temptation and seek out the heir before your quest is done. I cannot risk that."

Lief opened his mouth to argue, but his father held up his hand, shaking his head. "When the gems are all in place the Belt will lead you to the heir, my son," he said firmly. "You must wait until then."

He half smiled as Lief sighed with frustration. Then he bent down and drew something from under his chair.

"Perhaps this will cheer you," he said. "It is my birthday gift to you."

Lief stared at the slender, shining sword in his father's hand. Never had he expected to own such a blade.

"I made it on our own forge," his father said, giving the sword to him. "It is the finest work I have ever done. Care for it well, and it will care for you."

As Lief nodded, spluttering his thanks, he became aware that his mother, too, was holding out a gift. It was a finely woven cloak — soft, light, and warm. Its color seemed to change as it moved so that it was hard to tell if it was brown, green, or grey. Somewhere between all three, Lief decided at last. Like river-water in autumn.

"This, too, will care for you, wherever you may go," his mother whispered, pressing the cloak into his hands and kissing him. "The fabric is — special. I used every art I knew in its making, and wove much love and many memories into it, as well as strength and warmth."

Her husband stood up and put his arm around her. She leaned against him lovingly, but tears shone in her eyes.

Lief looked at them both. "You never doubted that I would agree to go on this quest," he said quietly.

"We knew you too well to doubt it," his mother answered, trying to smile. "I was sure, as well, that you would want to start at once. Food and water for the first few days of your journey are already packed and waiting. You can leave within the hour, if you wish."

"Tonight?" gasped Lief. His stomach turned over. He had not thought it would be so soon. And yet almost immediately he realized that his mother was right. Now that the decision had been made, he wanted nothing more than to begin.

"There is one thing more," his father said, limping to the door. "You will not be alone on your quest. You will have a companion."

Lief's jaw dropped. Were the surprises of this night never to end?

"Who — ?" he began.

"A good friend. The one man we know we can trust," his father answered gruffly. He swung the door open.

And, to Lief's horror, into the room shuffled Barda, the beggar.

10 - Decisions

S o, Lief," Barda mumbled. "Are you not pleased with your companion?"

Lief could only stand gaping at him.

"Do not tease him, Barda." Smiling, Lief's mother moved to her son's side and gently touched his shoulder. "How could Lief know you are other than you appear to be? Explain yourself!"

Barda pulled off the ragged cloak he wore, letting it fall to the floor at his feet. Underneath the cloak his garments were rough, but clean. He straightened his shoulders, pushed back his tousled hair from his face, tightened his jaw, and lifted his head. Suddenly he looked completely different — tall, strong, and many years younger.

"I also lived in the palace, when your father and King Endon were young, Lief," he said, in quite a different voice. "I was the grown son of their nursemaid,

Min, but they did not know me, or I them. While they were at their lessons I was already in training as a palace guard."

"But — but all my life you have lived outside the forge," Lief stammered.

Barda's face darkened. "I left the palace on the night my mother was killed. I knew that I would suffer the same fate if I stayed. My guard's uniform helped me to trick my way through the gates, and I came here."

Lief swallowed. "Why here?"

"Fate guided me, I believe, as it had guided Jarred before me," Barda answered quietly. "It was deepest night. The cottage was in darkness. I hid myself in the forge and slept. When at last I stirred, many hours later, it was day, though it did not seem so. A terrible wind was howling. Only half awake, I stumbled outside and saw four strangers by the gate. I know now that they were Jarred and Anna hurrying the king and queen away, but then I knew nothing."

He glanced at Lief's father. "Jarred was rather startled to see a palace guard lurching towards him," he added dryly. "He greeted me with a blow that put me back to sleep for quite some time."

Lief shook his head, hardly able to believe that his gentle father would strike anyone.

"When I woke again I found that Jarred and Anna no longer feared me," Barda went on. "While I was unconscious I had rambled aloud of my grief and fear, so they knew who I was and well understood the danger that threatened me. They knew I was a friend."

"So we did," murmured Lief's mother. She turned to Lief. "We told Barda who our visitors had been. We asked for his help in seeking the lost gems of Deltora when the time came."

Barda frowned grimly. "I agreed willingly. I had already decided that I would do anything to overthrow the Shadow Lord, and avenge my mother's death."

"It — it is incredible!" Lief spluttered. "All this time you . . ."

Barda shrugged. "All this time I have been safe, hidden in my beggar's disguise. Jarred and Anna have given me food and shelter, and helped me to play my part without too much suffering. In return, I have watched over you since you were ten years old — "

"Watched over me?" Lief gasped.

"Oh, yes," drawled Barda. "After your father was injured I said that I would go alone on the quest for the gems, when the time came. But Jarred and Anna — felt differently. They believed that you should be given the chance to fulfil your father's pledge."

He glanced at Lief's parents as he spoke. They

remained expressionless, but it was clear to Lief that there had been many arguments on this subject in the past. Barda would plainly have preferred to travel alone.

He thinks that I will be a burden to him, Lief thought angrily. But before he could say anything, Barda went on.

"I agreed to your company, on the condition that you be allowed to sharpen your wits and learn of life by roaming free in the city. I believed that this was as important as your book-learning and your swordplay in fitting you for the time ahead. But of course you had to be protected from real harm, without your knowledge."

His lips twitched into a smile. "It has not been easy, young Lief, keeping you out of trouble. And this reminds me. You have my rope, I believe?" He held out his hand.

Not daring to look at his parents, Lief passed over the coil of rope he had thrown down in a corner. His face had grown hot as he remembered how he had prided himself on his many lucky escapes over the years, and boasted of them to his friends. So they had not been a matter of luck, or skill. Barda had been his bodyguard all along.

He looked down at the floor, his stomach churning with furious shame. What a fool he must think me! he raged silently. This — this *child* he had to mind like a nurse! How he must have laughed at me!

He became aware that Barda was speaking again, and forced himself to look up.

"My beggar's rags have been useful in other ways," the man was saying, calmly fastening the rope to his belt. "Grey Guards talk freely to one another in front of me. Why should they care what a half-wit beggar hears?"

"It is because of news Barda has gathered in the past year, Lief, that we know it is time to make our move," Lief's father added, eyeing his son's grim face anxiously. "Hungry for further conquest, the Shadow Lord has at last turned his eyes away from us, to lands across the sea. Warships are being launched from our coast."

"There are still many Grey Guards in the city, but few now patrol the countryside, it seems," Barda added. "They have left it to the bands of robbers and to the other horrors that now run wild there. There have always been terrors and evil beings in Deltora, but once they were balanced by the good. With the coming of the Shadow Lord, the balance ended. Evil has become much more powerful."

A chill ran through Lief, quenching his anger. But Barda's eyes were upon him, and he would rather have died than show his fear. He snatched up the map. "Have you decided on our route?" he asked abruptly.

His father seemed about to speak, but Barda answered first, pointing to a spot on the map with a blunt finger. "I believe we should move east, directly to the Forests of Silence."

Three gasps of shock sounded in the small room.

Lief's father cleared his throat. "We had decided that the Forests should be your final ordeal, not your first, Barda," he said huskily.

Barda shrugged. "I heard something today that changed my mind. The Grey Guards have always feared the Forests, as we have. But now, it seems, no Guard will even approach them, because of the losses they have suffered. The roads around them are completely clear — of Guards, at least."

Stiff with shock, Lief stared at the map with glazed eyes. To face the Forests of Silence, that place of childhood nightmare, at some time in the future was one thing. To face it so soon, in a matter of days, was another.

"What think you, Lief?" he heard Barda say.

His voice was casual, but Lief was sure that the question was a test. He wet his lips and looked up from the map, meeting the tall man's gaze steadily. "Your plan seems to me a good one, Barda," he said. "With no Guards to trouble us, we will make good time. And if we can find one gem quickly, it will give us good heart to go on."

Barda's eyes flickered. I was right, thought Lief. He thought I would refuse to go with him. He thought to be rid of me. Well, he was wrong.

"So, Jarred?" Barda asked gruffly.

The blacksmith bowed his head. "It seems fate has taken a hand to alter my plans," he murmured. "I must bow to it. Do as you will. Our thoughts and hopes go with you."

11 ~ Beware!

Many hours later, feeling as though he were living in a dream, Lief was marching east along the road leading away from Del. Barda strode beside him, silent, upright, and strong — a completely different person from the shambling, mumbling wreck who had haunted the gates of the forge for as long as Lief could remember.

They had left Del unnoticed by creeping through a hole in the wall that Lief had not known existed, so cleverly was it disguised. Now the city, his parents, and everything he knew were far behind him, and with every step he was moving towards a place whose very name made him sweat with fear.

He told himself, The Forests of Silence strike a special terror in my heart, for they are near, and I have heard tales of them all my life. But it is certain that the other places on the map are just as deadly in their own way.

This idea did not comfort him in the least.

For the first hour after leaving the city he had walked with his hand on his sword, his heart thumping. But they met no one, and for a long time now he had been concentrating only on moving quickly, keeping up with Barda's long strides. He was determined not to be the one to call for rest. Determined, too, not to be the first to speak, though his head was teeming with questions.

They came to a place where a small road branched off the main one to the right, crossing a little wooden bridge and then winding away into the darkness. Barda stopped.

"I believe that this is the path to Wenn Del — and the shortest way to the Forests," he said. "The turning fits the description I was given. But there should be a signpost, and there is none."

Tall trees rose around them, but no leaves rustled. The silence was heavy and complete. It was as if the land was holding its breath, waiting for them to decide what to do.

The clouds parted for a moment, and the moon's ghostly light beamed down on them. Looking around, Lief saw a tiny glimmer of white on the ground by the side of the road. He moved to it quickly, knelt down, then beckoned to Barda.

"It is here," he called excitedly, scrabbling among the dead leaves. "Someone has pushed it over, to keep the way secret."

The signpost lay flat on the ground, almost covered by leaves and small plants. Lief brushed away the last of the leaves, then sat back on his heels with a gasp as he saw what was underneath.

"Someone has tried to warn other travelers of danger along this path. No doubt the sign was not pushed over to hide the way, but to hide the warning," Barda muttered.

Lief stood up slowly, glancing behind him. Suddenly the silence seemed thick and heavy, pressing in on him.

He became aware that his companion was watching him, frowning. "This path will save us a day and a half, if we take it," Barda said. "But perhaps I should not lead you into certain peril when we have just begun."

All at once, Lief was very angry. With Barda for

seeing his fear, with himself for showing that fear, and, most of all, with the unknown enemy who had so craftily hidden the warning sign.

"You do not have to guard my safety any longer, Barda," he said loudly, kicking at the dead leaves. "A short cut is too precious to waste. We are prepared for trouble, now. We will watch for danger as we go."

"Very well," said Barda, turning away. "As you wish." His voice was as calm and level as always. Lief could not tell if he was pleased or sorry.

They turned to the right, crossed the little bridge, and went on. The road twisted, narrowed, and became darker. Tall, thick bushes lined it on both sides. Their leaves were large, smooth, and stiff, with strange, pale veins showing almost white against the dark green.

They had not gone far before the back of Lief's neck began to prickle. He turned his head slightly and, from the corner of his eye, caught a glimpse of something gleaming through the leaves. It was a pair of red eyes, glinting in the moonlight. Controlling his urge to shout, he touched Barda's arm.

"I see them," Barda muttered. "Draw your sword, but keep walking. Look to the front. Be ready."

Lief did as he was told, his whole body tingling with alarm. He saw another pair of eyes, and another. And soon it seemed that the whole path was lined with burning points of light. But still there was no sound.

He gritted his teeth. The hand that held the sword was slippery with sweat. "What are they? What are they waiting for?" he hissed to Barda.

As he spoke something skittered across the road behind him. He swung around just in time to see a creature disappearing into the bushes — a bent, pale, scuttling thing that seemed all legs and arms. His skin crawled.

"Look ahead!" hissed Barda, furiously dragging on his arm to make him move again. "Didn't I tell you — "

And then the humming began.

The sound was soft, at first. It came from all around them, filling the air — a high, whining hum, as if a great swarm of flying insects had suddenly invaded the road.

But no insects were to be seen. Only the dark green of the leaves. And the eyes, watching. And the sound, which grew louder and louder with every step they took, so that soon their heads were filled with it, and their ears began to ache and ring.

And still the sound rose — high, piercing, unbearable. Desperate to shut it out, they clapped their hands to their ears and bent their heads against it, walking fast, faster — breaking into a run. Their feet thudded on the endless path, their breath came hard and panting, their hearts beat like thunder. But they were aware of nothing — nothing but the pain of the

sound that rose and rose, piercing their brains, driving
out every thought.

They ran, weaving and stumbling, desperate to
escape it. But there was no escape. They cried out for
help. But they could not even hear their own voices.
Finally they fell, exhausted, to lie writhing, helpless in
the dust.

The sound rose to an agonizing wail of triumph.
The leaves thrashed and rustled. A host of pale, lanky
creatures with hot red eyes scuttled towards them.

And, in moments, they were covered.

✳

Lief woke slowly, with no idea of where he was, or
how much time had passed. There was a dull ringing
in his ears. His throat was raw. Every muscle in his
body was aching.

I am alive, he thought, with dull surprise. How
is it that I am alive?

He struggled to think, though his brain seemed
clouded by a thick fog.

The last he remembered was running with Barda
along the Wenn Del path, his head almost bursting
with sound. After that there was only blankness.

Or was there? He seemed to remember a dream.
A dream of needle-sharp, stinging pains all over his
body. A dream of being poked and prodded by thin,
hard fingers. A dream of being carried, jolting, on
bony shoulders. A dream of shrill tittering and mut-

tering, while night turned into day and day to night again.

A terrible dream. But . . . had it been a dream? Or had it been real? Had it all been real?

He was lying on his back. Light slanted through branches high above him. It is day now, then, Lief thought drowsily. Late afternoon, by the look of it. But which afternoon? How long have I been unconscious? And where am I?

He heard a groan nearby. He tried to turn his head. And it was only then that he realized that he could not move.

Panic seized him. He tried to lift his hands, move his feet. But he could not even twitch a finger.

How could they have bound me so completely? he thought stupidly.

And slowly, horribly the answer came to him. He was not tied up at all. His body was simply refusing to move at his will.

"What — has happened?" he cried aloud in terror.

"They stung us — as wasps sting caterpillars, as spiders sting flies." Barda's voice was thick and slow, but Lief recognized it. He realized that it was Barda who had groaned. Barda was lying near to him. Barda was as helpless as he was.

"The creatures have paralyzed us so that we still live, but cannot move," Barda's voice went on. "They will be back, and then they will feast."

Again he groaned. "We were fools to ignore the warning sign. I am to blame. I could not imagine a weapon we could not fight. But that sound! No one could stand against it. I cannot understand why the Guards in Del did not speak of it."

"Perhaps they did not know. Perhaps no one who has ever heard the sound has lived to tell of it," said Lief.

"Lief — I have led you to your death!"

Lief licked his dry lips. "It is not your fault. We took the road together. And we are not dead yet! Barda — where are we?"

The answer came even more slowly than before, and when it came it filled Lief's heart with dread. "They carried us a long way," Barda said weakly. "I think — I think we are in the Forests of Silence."

Lief closed his eyes, trying to fight the wave of despair that was sweeping over him. And then a thought came to him.

"Why?" he asked. "Why bring us here, to a place so far from their home?"

"Because," called a new voice, "you are too great a prize for the Wenn alone. They have brought you as an offering for their god. The Wennbar likes fresh meat. It will come when the sun goes down."

There was a rustle from the tree above. And, as lightly as a butterfly, a wild-haired girl landed on the ground right beside Lief's head.

12 - The Wennbar

Astounded, Lief blinked up at the girl. She was about his own age, elfin-faced, with black hair, slanting black brows, and green eyes. She was dressed in ragged grey clothes that seemed strangely familiar. She was bending over him, unfastening the ties of his cloak.

"Thank heavens you have come!" he whispered.

"This will be useful, Filli," the girl said.

With a shock, Lief realized that she was not speaking to him, but to a small, furry, wide-eyed creature that was clinging to her shoulder.

"How lucky that we came this way today," she went on. "If we had left it until tomorrow the cloth would have been quite spoiled."

With a single push of her slim, sun-browned arm, she rolled Lief onto his side so that she could pull the cloak from beneath him. Then she let him roll back and stood up, the cloak draped carelessly over her arm.

A harsh cry came from overhead. Lief raised his eyes and saw a black bird, a raven, perched in the tree from which the girl had leapt. Its head on one side, it was watching them carefully with one sharp yellow eye.

The girl grinned and held up the cloak. "See what I have found, Kree!" she called. "A fine new blanket for the nest. But we are coming back now. Do not fear."

She turned to go.

"No!" shouted Lief in panic. "Do not leave us!"

"You cannot leave us here to die!" Barda roared at the same moment. But already the girl had disappeared from sight, taking the cloak with her. And suddenly, in the midst of his despair, Lief thought of his mother's hands, patiently weaving the cloth by candlelight.

"Bring back my cloak!" he bellowed.

Even as he shouted, he knew how foolish it was. He was going to die, horribly, very soon. What did it matter if the cloak was gone?

But somehow it *did* matter. "You have no right to take it!" he shouted furiously to the empty air. "My mother made it for me. My mother!"

There was a moment's silence. Then, to Lief's astonishment, the girl was back, staring down at him suspiciously through the tangled mass of her hair.

"How could your mother have made this cloak?" she demanded. "Grey Guards do not know their mothers. They are raised in groups of ten, in houses with — "

"I am not a Grey Guard!" shouted Lief. "My friend and I are — travelers, from Del. Can you not see by our garments?"

The girl laughed scornfully. "Your disguise does not fool me. Only Grey Guards take the Wenn Del path, for it leads nowhere but to the Forests."

She raised her hand to caress the little animal clinging to her shoulder, and her voice hardened. "Many of your fellows have been here before you, seeking living things to take or destroy. They have learned painfully of their mistake."

"We are not Guards," Barda called out. "My name is Barda. My companion is Lief. We came to the Forests for good reason."

"What reason?" the girl demanded disbelievingly.

"We — we cannot tell you," said Lief.

She turned away, shrugging. With a surge of panic Lief shouted after her. "What is your name? Where is your family? Can you bring them here?"

The girl paused and turned back to look at him again. She seemed puzzled, as though no one had ever asked her such things before. "My name is Jasmine," she said at last. "Kree and Filli are my family. Grey Guards took my mother and father long ago."

Lief's heart sank. So there was no one to help her

carry them to safety. But still . . . she was strong. Perhaps even now there was some way . . .

"The Grey Guards are our deadly enemies, as they are yours," he said, as calmly and forcefully as he could. "Our quest to the forest is part of a plan to defeat them — to rid Deltora of the Shadow Lord. Help us, we beg you!"

He held his breath as the girl hesitated, fingering the cloak she still held over her arm. Then, above their heads, the black bird screeched again. Jasmine glanced up at it, threw the cloak down onto Lief's chest, and darted away without another word.

"Come back!" cried Lief, with all his strength. "Jasmine!" But there was no reply, and when he looked up to the tree again, even the bird had gone.

Lief heard Barda moan once, in helpless anger. Then there was utter silence. No bird sang. No small creature rustled in the grass. It was the silence of waiting. The silence of despair. The silence of death.

The sun sank lower in the sky. Long, dark shadows striped the place where they lay. Soon, very soon, it would be dark. And then, thought Lief, then the Wennbar will come.

The cloak felt warm on his chest. He could not lift a hand to touch it, but still it gave him comfort. He was glad that it was with him. He closed his eyes . . .

Something gripped his shoulder. He cried out in terror and opened his eyes to see Jasmine's face close to his.

"Open your mouth!" the girl ordered. "Make haste!" She pushed a tiny bottle towards his lips.

Confused, Lief did as he was told. He felt two cold drops fall on his tongue. A horrible taste filled his mouth.

"What — ?" he spluttered.

But Jasmine had already turned away from him. "Open your mouth!" he heard her hissing to Barda.

A moment later Barda made a choking, disgusted sound. Lief realized that he, too, had been given some of the vile-tasting liquid.

"Poison!" Barda rasped. "You — "

Lief's heart gave a great thud. Then, suddenly, his body grew hot and began to prickle all over. With every instant the feeling grew stronger and more frightening. The heat became burning. The prickles became needle-sharp jabs of pain. It was as though he was caught in a flaming thorn bush.

The warning screech of the bird sounded far above them. The sky was red through the leaves of the tree. Barda was crying out. But now Lief could hear nothing, see nothing, feel nothing but his own pain and fear. He began to writhe and thrash on the ground.

Then, dimly, he realized that Jasmine was bending over him. She was pulling at his arms, kicking at him with hard, bare feet. "Get up!" she was urging. "Listen to me! Do you not see what you are doing? You are moving! You can move!"

You can move! Gasping, hardly able to believe it, Lief fought back the pain and struggled to his hands and knees. Blindly he felt for his cloak. He was not going to leave it now.

"The tree!" Jasmine shouted. "Crawl to the tree and climb! The Wennbar is almost upon us!" She had already turned to Barda. He was rolling on his bed of ferns, groaning in agony.

Lief hauled himself towards them, dragging his cloak behind him, but the girl waved him back. "Go!" she cried furiously. "I will see to him! Go! Climb!"

Lief knew she was right. He could not help her, or Barda. It was as much as he could do to help himself. He began to crawl towards the trunk of the great tree. His legs and arms were trembling. His whole body shuddered, swept by waves of heat.

He reached the tree and pulled himself upright. There was a low branch near his hand. He grasped it, panting, and with the other hand pulled his cloak around him.

Only a day or two ago he had climbed a rope to the top of a high wall without a thought. Now he doubted that he could even haul himself onto this branch.

The clearing dimmed. The sun had slipped below the horizon.

High above Lief there was a clatter of wings as the black bird left its perch. Calling harshly, urgently, it soared down to where Jasmine staggered towards the tree with Barda leaning on her shoulder.

"I know, Kree!" Jasmine gasped, as the bird flapped anxiously around her head. "I can smell it."

As she said the words, Lief smelt something, too. A faint, sickening odor of decay was stealing through the clearing.

His stomach turned over. He tied the strings of the cloak, grasped the branch with both hands, and managed to pull himself up. He clung to the rough bark, panting and shaking, afraid that even now he might fall.

Jasmine and Barda had reached the tree now, the bird still swooping above them. "Higher!" Jasmine shouted to Lief. "As high as you can. It cannot climb, but it will try to claw us down."

Lief gritted his teeth, lifted his arms, and hauled himself to a higher branch. He heard Barda grunting with effort as he struggled to climb after him. The evil smell was stronger now. And there was a sound — a heavy, stealthy sliding, the snapping of twigs, the rustling of leaves and the cracking of branches as something moved towards the clearing.

"Make haste!" Jasmine had leapt up beside Lief. The tiny creature she called Filli was chattering on her shoulder, its eyes wide with fear.

"Barda — " Lief managed to say.

"He knows what he must do. You can help him only by moving out of his way!" the girl snapped.

"Climb, you fool! Do you not understand? The sun has set. The Wennbar is — "

Filli screamed, the black bird screeched. The bushes on the other side of the clearing thrashed and bent. The air thickened with a smell so vile that Lief choked and gagged. Then a huge, hideous creature, like nothing he had ever seen, crawled into view.

Four stubby legs bent under the weight of a swollen body that was as round, blotched, and bloated as some gigantic rotten fruit. Vast, flat feet crushed the twigs beneath them to powder. Folds of wrinkled, green-grey flesh hung from the neck. The head was nothing but two tiny eyes set above long, wicked jaws. The jaws gaped open, showing rows of dripping black teeth and releasing gusts of foul air with every breath.

Choking back a cry of disgust and terror, Lief scrambled higher into the tree, forcing his trembling legs and arms to obey his will. One branch. Then another. And another.

A terrible growl sounded in the clearing. He looked down. Barda and Jasmine were just below him, and they, too, were looking down. The Wennbar had reached the fern bed. It was snapping its jaws together, jerking its head from side to side, growling with anger at finding its prize gone.

We are safe! thought Lief, his heart pounding. Safe! It cannot reach us up here. He closed his eyes, almost dizzy with relief.

105

"Lief!" shrieked Jasmine.

And Lief opened his eyes just in time to see the Wennbar rear up, its front legs clawing at the air, its pale grey belly gleaming through the dimness. The creature roared, and the folds of skin hanging from its neck disappeared as the neck swelled and grew, raising its head higher, higher . . .

And then it was leaping forward, hurling itself at the tree, its jaws snapping, its tiny eyes burning with rage and hunger.

13 - The Nest

Terror drove Lief upwards. Afterwards, he could not remember climbing for his life while the Wennbar's huge body crashed against the trunk of the tree and its cruel jaws snapped at his heels. He had not had time to draw his sword. He had had no time for anything but escape.

When he came to himself he was clinging to a high branch, with Jasmine and Barda beside him. The Wennbar's foul breath filled the air. Its roars filled their ears.

They were at last too high for it to reach them, even with its neck fully extended. But it was not giving up. It was dashing itself against the tree, raking the bark with its claws, trying to make them fall.

It was still not completely dark, but it was growing very cold. Lief's cloak kept his body warm but his hands, clinging to the tree, were numb. Beside him,

Barda was shivering violently, and his teeth were chattering.

If this goes on, he will fall, Lief thought. He drew as near as he could to Barda and Jasmine. With cold, clumsy fingers he gathered up his cloak and threw it around them so that they could share its warmth.

For a moment they huddled together. And then, Lief realized that something had changed.

The beast had stopped beating itself against the tree. The roars had given way to a low, rumbling growl. Lief felt a movement and realized that Jasmine was peeping through the folds of the cloak to see what was happening.

"It is moving away," she breathed in wonder. "It is as though it cannot see us any longer, and thinks we have somehow escaped. But why?"

"The cloak," whispered Barda feebly. "The cloak — must be hiding us."

Lief's heart leapt as he remembered what his mother had said when she gave him the cloak. *This, too, will protect you wherever you go . . . The fabric is — special.*

Just how special?

He heard Jasmine draw a sharp breath. "What is it?" he hissed.

"The Wenn are coming," she said. "I see their eyes. They have heard the roaring cease. They think that the Wennbar has finished with you. They have come for the scraps that remain."

Lief shuddered. Carefully he moved the cloak aside and peered down to the clearing.

Red eyes were glowing in the bushes, near to where the Wennbar prowled. The creature lifted its head, glared, and gave a loud, sharp barking call. It sounded like an order of some kind.

The bushes rustled. The Wennbar called again, even more loudly. And finally two pale, bent shapes crept, quivering, into the clearing to kneel before it.

The Wennbar grunted. Carelessly it seized the kneeling shapes, tossed them into the air, caught them in its hideous jaws and swallowed them whole.

Sickened, Lief turned away from the horrible sight.

Jasmine pushed away the cloak and stood up. "We are safe, now," she said. "See? The Wenn have run away, and the creature is going back to its cave."

Lief and Barda exchanged glances. "The cave must be the hiding place," Barda said in a low voice. "Tomorrow night, when the creature comes out to feed, we will search it."

"There is nothing in the Wennbar's cave but bones and stink," Jasmine snorted. "What is it you are looking for?"

"We cannot tell you," said Barda, stiffly hauling himself to his feet. "But we know that it has been hidden in the most secret place in the Forests of Silence, and that it has a terrible Guardian. Where else could that be but here?"

To their surprise, Jasmine burst out laughing. "How little you know!" she cried. "Why, this is only a tiny corner at the very edge of this one Forest. There are three Forests in all, and each has a hundred places more dangerous and more secret than this!"

Lief and Barda glanced at each other again as her laughter rang out in the clearing. And then, suddenly, the sound stopped. When they turned to look at her again, she was frowning.

"What is it?" asked Lief.

"It is just . . ." Jasmine broke off and shook her head. "We will not speak of it now. I will take you to my nest. There we will be safe. There we can talk."

✳

They travelled as fast as Lief and Barda were able. As the forest thickened they kept to the treetops almost all the way, climbing from one branch to another, using vines to help them. Above were patches of star-studded sky. Below there was silent darkness. Kree flew ahead of them, stopping to wait when they fell behind. Filli clung to Jasmine's shoulder, his eyes wide and bright.

With every moment, Lief felt his strength returning. But still he was glad when they at last reached Jasmine's home. It was indeed a sort of nest — a big saucer of woven branches and twigs perched high in a huge, twisted tree that grew by itself in a mossy clearing. The moon shone down through the leaves above, flooding the nest with soft, white light.

Jasmine did not speak at once. She made Lief and Barda sit while she brought out berries, fruits, nuts, and the hard shell of some sort of melon filled to the brim with sweet, cool water.

Lief rested, looking around in wonder. Jasmine had few possessions. Some of them — like a broken-toothed comb, a tattered sleeping blanket, an old shawl, two tiny bottles, and a small, carved wooden doll — were sad reminders of the parents she had lost. Others — a belt, two daggers, several flints to make fire, and many gold and silver coins — had come from the bodies of Grey Guards who had been sacrificed to the Wennbar.

Jasmine was carefully dividing the food and drink into five equal parts, setting out Filli's and Kree's places as if they were indeed part of her family. Watching her, Lief realized with a shock that her tattered grey clothes had also come from Grey Guards. She had cut and tied the cloth to fit her.

It made him squirm to think of her robbing helpless victims and leaving them to die. He tried to remember that Guards had taken Jasmine's parents — killed them, probably, or at least enslaved them — and left her alone in this wild forest. But still, her ruthlessness chilled him.

"Eat!"

Jasmine's voice broke into his thoughts. He looked up as she sat down beside him. "Food will help you to recover," she said. "And this food is good." She helped herself to a strange, pink-colored fruit and bit into it greedily, the juice running down her chin.

I am a fool to judge her, Lief thought. She lives as best she can. And it is thanks to her that we are alive. She put herself in grave danger for us, when she could have turned her back. Now she has brought us to her home and shares her food and drink with us.

He saw that Barda had begun to eat, and he did the same. He had never eaten a stranger meal. Not just because the food was different from what he was used to at home, but because it was being eaten so high above the ground, beneath a white moon, on a platform that swayed gently with every breeze. And because a black bird called Kree and a small, furred creature called Filli shared the meal with him.

"How long have you lived here alone, Jasmine?" he asked at last.

"I was seven years old when the Grey Guards came," the girl answered, licking her fingers and reaching for another fruit. "They must have come the long way from Del, for the Wenn had not seized them. I was filling the water bags at the stream. My parents were searching for food and carrying it up to our house in the treetops. The Guards saw them and caught them, burned the house, and took them away."

"But the Guards did not find you?" asked Barda. "How was that?"

"My mother looked back to me and made a sign for me to hide in the ferns and to be silent," answered Jasmine. "So I did as I was told. I thought that if I did that, if I was good, my mother and father would come back. But they did not come back."

Her mouth tightened and turned down at the corners, but she did not cry. Jasmine, thought Lief, had probably not cried for a very long time.

"So you grew up alone, in this Forest?" he asked.

She nodded. "The good trees and the birds helped me," she said, as though this was the most normal thing in the world. "And I remembered things my parents had taught me. I collected what I could from our old house — what had not been burned. I made this nest and slept in it at night, and so was safe from the things that roam the forest floor in the darkness. And so I have lived ever since."

"That potion you gave us to help us move again," said Barda, making a face at the memory. "What was it?"

"My mother made it long ago, from leaves like the ones that grow along the Wenn path," Jasmine said. "It cured father when he was stung. I used it on Filli, too, when I found him caught by the Wenn as a baby. That was how he came to live with me, wasn't it, Filli?"

The little creature nibbling berries beside her chattered in agreement. She grinned, but her smile

113

quickly faded as she turned back to Barda and Lief. "There were only a few drops left when I found you," she said quietly. "The bottle is empty now."

"Can you not make more?" asked Barda.

She shook her head. "The Guards' fire killed the leaves that grew here in the Forest. The only others are on the Wenn path."

So, Lief thought. She is unprotected now. Because of us.

"We are deeply grateful, Jasmine," he murmured. "We owe you our lives."

She shrugged, brushing the last of the fruit stones from her lap.

"And Deltora owes you a great debt," Barda added. "For now we can continue our quest."

Jasmine looked up. "If your quest to the Forests leads you to the place I think it will, you will not survive in any case," she said bluntly. "I might as well have left you to the Wennbar."

There was a short, unpleasant silence. Then the girl shrugged again. "But I suppose you will go on, whatever I say," she sighed, climbing to her feet. "So I will show you the way. Are you ready?"

14 - The Dark

They traveled through the night, keeping to the treetops, while below them unseen things rustled, growled, and hissed. Their path was winding, because Jasmine would move only through certain trees. "The good trees," she called them.

Every now and then she would bend her head to the trunk of one such tree and seem to listen. "They tell me what is ahead," she said, when Barda asked her about this. "They warn me of danger." And when he raised his eyebrows at her in surprise, she stared back at him as though she did not see why he should not believe her.

She told them little about the place to which she was taking them. She said there was little she could tell.

"I only know that it is in the center of the middle Forest, the smallest one," she said. "The birds will not

115

venture into that Forest, but they say that at its heart is an evil, forbidden place. They call this place 'The Dark.' It has a terrible Guardian. Those who go there never leave it, and even the trees fear it."

She turned to Lief, with the ghost of a smile. "Does it not sound like the place you seek?" she asked.

He nodded, and touched his sword for comfort.

※

Day was breaking when they crossed a small clearing and entered the middle Forest.

The trees hid all but a few rays of the sun here, and there was no sound at all. Not a bird called. Not an insect moved. Even the trees and vines through which they climbed were still, as though no breeze dared to disturb the dim, damp air.

Jasmine had begun to move more slowly and carefully. Filli huddled against her neck, his head hidden in her hair. Kree no longer flew ahead, but hopped and fluttered with them from one branch to the next.

"The trees tell us to go back," Jasmine whispered. "They say that we will die."

There was fear in her voice, but she did not stop. Lief and Barda followed her through the thickening Forest, their ears and eyes straining for any sound or sight of danger. Yet there was nothing but green all around them, and the silence was broken only by the sounds of their own movement.

Finally they reached a place where they could go no further. Heavy, twisting vines criss-crossed and tangled together, smothering the huge trees, making a barrier like a huge, living net. The three companions searched to left and to right, and found that the vine net made a full circle, enclosing whatever was inside.

"It is the center," breathed Jasmine. She put up her arm to Kree, who flew to her at once.

"We must go down to the ground," said Barda.

Jasmine shook her head. "There is terrible danger here," she murmured. "The trees are silent, and will not answer me."

"Perhaps they are dead," Lief whispered. "Strangled by the vines."

Jasmine shook her head again. Her eyes were filled with grief, pity, and anger. "They are not dead. But they are bound. They are prisoners. They are — in torment."

"Lief, we must go down," Barda muttered again. Plainly, this talk of trees having feelings made him uncomfortable. He thought Jasmine was more than a little mad. He turned to her. "We thank you for all you have done for us," he said politely. "But you can do no more. We must go on alone."

Leaving the girl crouching in the treetops, they began to half-climb, half-slide towards the forest floor. Lief looked up once and caught a glimpse of her. She was still watching them, the raven perched on her arm. With her other hand she was stroking Filli, sheltering under her hair.

They slipped lower, lower. And suddenly, Lief felt something that made his heart leap with fearful excitement. The steel Belt, hidden beneath his clothes, was warming, tingling on his skin.

"We are in the right place," he hissed to Barda. "One of the gems is nearby. The Belt feels it."

He saw Barda's lips tighten. He thought he knew what the big man was thinking. If the gem was near, a terrible enemy was also near. How much easier, Barda must be thinking, if he were alone, with no one else to think about.

"Do not worry about me," Lief whispered, trying to keep his voice steady and calm. "Nothing matters but that we seize the gem. If I die in the attempt, it will not be your fault. You must take the Belt from my body and go on alone, as you have always wished."

Barda glanced at him quickly, and seemed about to reply but then shut his lips and nodded.

They reached the floor of the forest and sank almost knee-deep in dead leaves. Here it was quite dark, and still there was utter silence. Spiderwebs frosted the trunks of the trees, and everywhere fungus clustered in ugly lumps. The air was thick with the smell of damp and decay.

Lief and Barda drew their swords and began slowly to move around the vine-walled circle.

The Belt grew warmer around Lief's waist. Warmer, warmer . . . hot! "Soon . . ." he breathed.

And then he felt Barda clutch his arm.

Before them was an opening in the wall of vines. And standing in the middle of the opening was a hulking, terrifying figure.

It was a knight. A knight in golden battle armor. His breastplate glimmered in the dimness. His helmet was crowned with golden horns. He stood, motionless, on guard, a great sword in his hand. Lief drew a sharp breath when he saw what was set into the sword's hilt.

A huge, yellow stone. The topaz.

"WHO GOES THERE?"

Lief and Barda froze as the hollow, echoing voice rang out. The knight had not turned his head, had not moved at all. Yet they knew that it was he who had challenged them. They knew, too, that it was useless to refuse to answer, or to try to hide now.

"We are travelers, from the city of Del," called Barda. "Who is it who wants to know?"

"I am Gorl, guardian of this place and owner of its treasure," said the hollow voice. "You are trespassers. Go, now, and you may live. Stay, and you will die."

"It is two against one," Lief whispered in Barda's ear. "Surely we can overpower him, if we take him by surprise. We can pretend to leave, and then — "

Gorl's head slowly turned towards them. Through the eye-slit of his helmet they could see only blackness. Lief's spine prickled.

"So, you plot against me," the voice boomed. "Very well. The choice is made."

The armor-clad arm lifted and beckoned, and, to his horror, Lief found himself stumbling forward, as though he were being dragged by an invisible string. Desperately he struggled to hold back, but the force that was pulling him was too strong. He heard Barda cursing as he, too, lurched towards the beckoning arm.

Finally they stood before the knight. He towered above them. "Thieves! Fools!" he growled. "You dare to try to steal my treasure. Now you will join the others who have tried, and your bodies will feed my vines, as theirs have done."

He stepped aside, and Lief stared with fascinated horror through the gap in the vines.

The wall of twisted stems was far thicker than he had realized, made up of hundreds of separate vines locked together. Many, many great trees were held within the vines' net. The wall must have been gradually thickening for centuries, spreading outward from the center as more and more vines grew, and more and more trees were taken.

High above the ground, the vines reached from treetop to treetop, joining together to form a roof over the small, round space they protected. Only a tiny patch of blue sky could still be seen between the thickening leaves. Only a few beams of sunlight reached down to show dimly what lay inside the circle.

Ringing the walls, overgrown by gnarled roots, were the ancient, crumbling bodies and bones of countless dead — the knight's victims, whose bodies had fed the vines. In the center of the circle there was a round patch of thick black mud from which rose three glimmering objects that looked like golden arrows.

"What are they?" Lief gasped.

"You know well what they are, thief," thundered the knight. "They are the Lilies of Life, the treasures you have come to steal."

"We have not come to steal them!" Barda exclaimed.

The knight turned his terrible head to look at him. "You lie!" he said. "You want them for yourselves, as I did, long ago. You wish to have their nectar so that you may live forever. But you shall not! I have protected my prize too well."

He raised his armored fist. "When the Lilies bloom at last, and the nectar flows, only I shall drink of it. Then I shall be ruler of all the seven tribes, for no one will be able to stand against me, and I shall live forever."

"He is mad," breathed Barda. "He speaks as

though the seven tribes were never united under Adin. As though the kingdom of Deltora has never existed!"

Lief felt sick. "I think — I think he came here before that happened," he whispered back. "He came here to find these — these Lilies of which he speaks. And they enchanted him. He has been here ever since."

Gorl lifted his sword. "Move into the circle," he ordered. "I must kill you there, so that your blood will feed the vines."

Again they found that their legs would not do their will, but only his. They staggered through the gap in the vines. Gorl followed them, raising his sword.

15 - The Lilies of Life

It was dim inside the circle. The golden arrowheads of the budding Lilies were the only glimmer of warm color. Everything else was dark brown, or dull green.

Lief and Barda stood, helpless, before the knight. They could not move. They could not fight or run.

Gorl raised his sword higher.

I must prepare for death, Lief thought. But he could only think of the Belt around his waist. If he was killed here, the Belt would lie forgotten with his bones. The gems would never be restored to it. The heir to the throne of Deltora would never be found. The land would remain under the Shadow forever.

It must not be! he thought wildly. But what can I do?

Then he heard Barda begin to speak.

"You wear the armor of a knight, Gorl," Barda

said. "But you are not a true knight. You do not fight your enemies with honor."

Are things not bad enough, Barda? thought Lief, in terror. Why do you risk making him even more angry than he is?

But Gorl hesitated, his great sword wavering in his hand. "I must protect the Lilies of Life," he said sullenly. "I knew my destiny the moment I saw their golden nectar dropping from their petals, long ago."

"But you were not alone when you saw this, were you, Gorl?" Barda demanded, his voice strong and bold. "You would not have come alone on a quest to the Forests of Silence. You had companions."

He is trying to turn Gorl's mind from us, Lief thought, suddenly understanding. He hopes that Gorl's hold over us will weaken, if he begins to think of other things.

"Gorl, what happened to your companions?" Barda demanded.

The knight's head jerked aside, as if Barda had dealt him a blow. "My companions — my two brothers — ran towards the Lilies," he muttered. "And . . ."

"And you killed them!"

Gorl's voice rose to a loud, high whine. "I had to do it!" he wailed. "I could not share with them! I needed a whole cup of the nectar for myself. They should have known that."

He lowered his head and began pacing the circle,

mumbling to himself. "While my brothers fought me, trying to save themselves, the Lilies wilted, and the nectar fell to waste in the mud. But I did not despair. The Lilies were mine, and mine alone. All I had to do was wait until they bloomed again."

Lief's heart leapt as he felt the iron bands of the knight's will loosening, letting him move freely again. Barda's idea was working. Gorl's mind was now far away from them. He glanced at his companion and saw that Barda was reaching for his sword.

Gorl had his back to them now, and was stroking the leaves and stems of the twisting vines with his armored hand. He seemed almost to have forgotten that anyone was with him. "As the new buds rose from the mud, I raised my wall around them, to protect them from intruders," he was muttering. "I did my work well. Never would the vines have grown so strong without my care."

Barda made a silent signal to Lief, and together they began to creep towards Gorl, their swords at the ready. They both knew that they would only have one chance. It could not be a fair fight. They had to take the knight by surprise and kill him, before he could bind them to his will again. Otherwise they were lost, as so many had been lost before them.

Gorl was still talking to himself, stroking the vine leaves. "I have cut the branches from the trees that dared to resist my vines," he mumbled. "I have fed the vines with the bodies of the enemies — man, woman, bird, or beast — who dared to approach them. And I have kept my treasures safe. I have waited long for them to bloom. But surely my time has nearly come."

Barda lunged forward with a mighty shout. His sword found its mark — the thin, dark gap between the knight's helmet and body armor — and he pushed it home.

But to Lief's horror, the knight did not fall. With a low growl, he turned, pulling Barda's sword from the back of his neck and throwing it aside. And then, as Lief cried out in shock and fear, slashing uselessly at his armor, his metal-clad hand darted out like a striking snake, catching Barda by the neck and forcing him to his knees.

"Die, thief!" he hissed. "Die slowly!" And he plunged his sword into Barda's chest.

"NO!" Lief shouted. Through a red haze of grief and terror, he saw Gorl pull his sword free and kick Barda to the ground with a grunt of contempt. He saw the big man groaning in agony, his life ebbing away into the roots of the vines. And then he saw Gorl turn to him and felt the iron grip of the knight's will clamp his very bones.

Frozen to the spot, he waited for death as Gorl raised the bloodstained sword again.

And then . . .

"GORL! GORL!"

From high above them came the cry — as high and wild as a bird's.

Gorl's head jerked backwards as he looked up with a growl of startled fury.

Lief, too, looked up, and with a shock saw that it was Jasmine who was calling. She was swinging from the very top of one of the great trees, peering down at them through the gap in the roof of vines. Kree hovered above her head, his black wings spread over her head as if to protect her.

"You have made good into evil in this place, with your jealousy and spite, Gorl!" Jasmine shouted. "You have bound and enslaved the trees and killed the birds — and all to guard something that is not yours!" With her dagger she began slashing at the vines that covered the clearing. Tattered leaves began to fall like green snow.

With a roar of rage Gorl raised his arms. Lief felt his limbs freed as the knight turned all his power upwards — towards the new intruder.

"Run, Lief!" Jasmine shrieked. "To the center! Now!"

There was a great cracking, tearing sound from above. Lief leapt for safety, flinging himself into the mud at the center of the clearing just as the earth behind him shuddered with a mighty crash that echoed like rolling thunder.

For what seemed a long time he lay still, his eyes tightly closed, his head spinning, his heart hammering in his chest. Then at last he became aware of a soft, pattering on his back, and a feeling of warmth. Gasping, he crawled to his knees and turned.

His eyes, so long accustomed to the dimness, squinted against the bright sunlight that poured into the clearing from the open sky above. The roof of vines had been torn through, and leaves and stems still pattered down like rain. Where he and Gorl had stood together only minutes before lay the reason for the damage — a great fallen branch. And beneath the branch was a mass of crushed golden armor.

Lief stared, unable to believe what had happened so suddenly. The Belt grew hot against his skin. He looked down and saw Gorl's sword, lying right in front of him. Almost absent-mindedly, he picked it up. The topaz in the hilt shone clear gold. So, he thought dreamily, the first gem to be found was the topaz — the symbol of faithfulness.

Suddenly his mind cleared. His eyes searched for, and then found, the still, pale figure of Barda, lying at the edge of the clearing. He jumped up and ran to him, kneeling down beside him, calling his name.

Barda did not stir. He still breathed, but very weakly. The terrible wound in his chest was still bleeding. Lief opened the jacket and shirt, tried to clean the wound, tried to stop the blood with his cloak. He had to do something. But he knew it was useless. It was too late.

He barely looked up as Jasmine leapt lightly

down beside him. "Barda is dying," he said drearily. There was a terrible pain in his chest. A terrible sense of loss and loneliness and waste.

"Lief!" he heard Jasmine gasp. But still he did not move.

"Lief! Look!"

She was pulling at his arm. Reluctantly he raised his head.

Jasmine was staring at the center of the clearing. Her face was filled with awe. Lief spun around to see what she was looking at.

The Lilies of Life were blooming. The golden arrows that were their buds had opened in the sunlight so long denied them. Now they were golden trumpets, their petals spread joyously, drinking in the light. And from the center of the trumpets a rich gold nectar was welling, overflowing, pouring in a sweet-smelling stream down to the black mud.

16 - The Topaz

With a cry, Lief threw down the sword and leapt up. He ran to the patch of mud and thrust his cupped hands under the nectar flow. When they were full to the brim he ran back to Barda, pouring the nectar onto the wound in his chest, smearing what was left on his pale lips.

Then he waited breathlessly. One minute passed. Two —

"Perhaps he has gone too far away already," Jasmine murmured.

"Barda!" Lief begged. "Come back! Come back!"

The big man's eyelids fluttered. His eyes opened. They were dazed, as though he had been dreaming. "What — is it?" he mumbled. As color began to steal back into his cheeks, his hand fumbled towards the wound on his chest. He licked his lips. "Hurts," he said.

"But the cut is healing!" Jasmine hissed in wonder. "See? It is closing of itself! Never have I seen such a thing."

Overjoyed, Lief saw that indeed the wound was repairing itself. Already it was just a raw, red scar. And as he watched the scar itself began to fade, till it was nothing but a thin white line.

"Barda! You are well!" he shouted.

"Of course I am!" With a grunt, Barda sat up, running his hands through his tangled hair. He stared around, astounded, but quite himself again. "What happened?" he demanded, climbing to his feet. "Did I faint? Where is Gorl?"

Lief pointed wordlessly at the crumpled armor beneath the fallen branch. Barda strode over to the branch, frowning.

"This is his armor," he said, kicking at it. "But there is no body inside it."

"I think Gorl's body crumbled to dust long ago," Lief said. "All that was left inside that armor shell was darkness and . . . will. But once the armor was destroyed, even that will could not survive. It could not survive in the light."

Barda grimaced with distaste. He looked up. "So a tree branch fell and finished him," he said. "That was a piece of luck."

"It was not luck!" exclaimed Jasmine indignantly. "I told the tallest tree what must be done, and at last it listened. I promised that it and the others would be rid of the vines, if it did what I asked. The sacrifice of one limb was small in return for freedom."

Barda's eyebrows shot up in disbelief, but Lief put a warning hand on his arm. "Believe me, what Jasmine says is true," he said. "She saved both our lives."

"*You* saved Barda's life." Jasmine objected again. "The sun made the Lilies bloom, and — "

She broke off and turned quickly to look at the Lilies of Life. Lief looked, too, and saw that already they were fading. Only a few drops of nectar still dropped from their wilting petals.

Jasmine rapidly pulled at a chain that hung around her neck, bringing out from under her clothes a tiny white jar capped with silver. She ran to the patch of mud and held the jar under the nectar flow so that the last few golden drops dripped into it. Then she watched as the Lilies bent their heads and slowly collapsed into the mud.

"Who knows how long it will be till they bloom again," she said calmly, when at last she moved back to the others. "But at least they *will* bloom, because the sun will shine on them after this. And in the mean-time, I have at least some of the nectar. It is indeed a great prize."

"Will you drink of it, and live forever?" asked Lief. But he smiled, for he already knew the answer.

Jasmine tossed her head. "Only a fool would want such a thing," she snorted. "And these few drops would not do the work in any case, according to Gorl. But the nectar will still be useful — as we have proved already today."

"How?" asked Barda, bewildered.

"It brought you back from the brink of death, as it happens," Lief murmured. "I will tell you. But first. . ."

He picked up Gorl's sword. The giant topaz seemed to wink, then fell cleanly from the hilt of the sword into his hand. He laughed joyously as he held it up and the sunbeams lit its yellow surface, turning it to gold.

"What is it?" exclaimed Jasmine. "Is this what you have been seeking?"

Lief realized, too late, that in his excitement he had betrayed their secret. He saw Barda grimace, then nod slightly. *Tell her a little but not all*, Barda's nod said.

"It is a topaz, symbol of faithfulness." Lief put the gem into Jasmine's eager hand.

"Some say that a topaz can — " Barda began.

He broke off, startled. The clearing had abruptly dimmed, as though the sun had gone behind a cloud. At the same moment a thick, billowing mist began to form. Kree screeched, Filli chattered nervously. The three companions froze.

Out of the mist, a wavering white figure appeared. It was a woman, sweet-faced and smiling.

"It is a spirit," breathed Barda. "The topaz . . ."

The mist swirled. Then there was a voice.

"Jasmine!" the voice called. "Jasmine, my dearest!"

Lief looked quickly at Jasmine. The girl was standing rigidly, holding the topaz out in front of her. Her face was as white as the mist itself. Her lips moved as she stared at the figure before her. "Mama!" she breathed. "Is — is it you? *Can* it be you?"

"Yes, Jasmine. How wonderful it is to be able to speak to you at last. Jasmine — listen to me carefully. I do not have much time. You have done well, very well, since your father and I were taken from you. But now you must do more."

"What?" Jasmine whispered. "What, Mama?"

The spirit stretched out her hands. "The boy Lief and the man Barda are friends, and their quest is just," she said, her voice as soft as the sighing of the wind. "It is a quest that will free our land from the Shadow Lord. But they still have much to do, and far to travel. You must join them — leave the Forests and go with them — and help them as much as you are able. It is your destiny. Do you understand?"

"Yes," Jasmine whispered. "But Mama — "

"I must leave you now," breathed the sighing voice. "But I will be watching over you, as I always have, Jasmine. And I love you, as I have always done. Be of good heart, my dearest."

Jasmine stood, motionless, as the mist slowly disappeared. When she turned to Lief and handed the topaz back to him, her eyes were wet with tears.

"What is this magic?" she hissed, almost angrily. "What is this stone, that it can show my mother to me?"

"It is said that the topaz has the power to bring the living into contact with the spirit world," Barda said gruffly. "I did not believe it, but — "

"So, my mother is dead," Jasmine murmured. "I thought it was so — I felt it. But still I hoped . . ." Her lips tightened. Then she took a deep breath, raised her chin, and looked at them squarely.

"It seems I am to go with you when you leave here," she said. "If you will have me." She put up her hand to the small, furry creature clinging to her shoulder. "But I could not leave Filli behind. And Kree goes everywhere I go. That would have to be understood."

"Of course!" Lief exclaimed. Then, suddenly realizing that he was not the only one who had to agree, he glanced quickly at Barda. His heart sank when he saw that Barda was slowly shaking his head. But then Barda spoke.

"I must be growing old," he sighed. "Or perhaps I cracked my skull when I fell. Things are moving too fast for me." Slowly a grin spread over his face. "But not so fast that I cannot recognize a good idea when I hear one," he added.

He put his strong hand on Lief's shoulder and turned to Jasmine. "I did not want Lief with me when we began — I confess it," he said cheerfully. "But if he had stayed at home, as I wished, I would by now be dead, and the quest lost. I will not make the mistake a second time. If Fate has decreed that we are to be three, so be it."

The Belt burned around Lief's waist. He unfastened it, laying it on the ground before him. He crouched over it and fitted the topaz into the first medallion. It slid into place and glowed there, as pure and golden as the nectar of the Lilies of Life, as warm and golden as the sun.

Jasmine stared curiously at the Belt. "There are seven medallions," she pointed out. "Six are still empty."

"But one is filled," said Lief with satisfaction.

"The longest journey begins with the first step," said Barda. "And the first step we have taken. Whatever the next may bring, we have cause to celebrate now."

"I am going to celebrate by beginning to rid the trees of these accursed vines," Lief said, putting his hand to his sword.

But Jasmine smiled. "There is no need," she said. "The word has spread that The Dark is no more."

She pointed upward and, to his amazement, Lief saw that the vine-shrouded trees were thick with birds. He had not heard them because they were too busy to call or sing. They were gladly tearing at the vines with their beaks and claws, working furiously. And more birds were coming every moment — birds of every kind.

"The beasts are on their way," Jasmine murmured. "The little gnawing creatures that like roots and stems. They will be here within the hour and they, too, will relish the vines. In a day or two the trees will be free."

The three stood for a moment, watching the amazing scene above them. Already some branches were clear of vines. No longer bound and weighed down, they were stretching gladly towards the sky.

"This must have been a beautiful place, once," Lief said softly.

"And will be again," Jasmine murmured. "Because of you. It was fortunate that you came here."

Barda grinned. "I must confess that for a while I doubted it," he said. "But all has ended well. Very well." He stretched his great arms wearily. "We should stay a day or two, I think. To rest, and eat, and watch the freeing of the trees."

"And then?" Jasmine asked. "What then?"

"And then," Barda said simply, "we will go on."

Lief slowly clipped the Belt around his waist once more. His heart was very full. He felt wonder and a kind of triumph when he thought of what had just passed. He felt excitement, eagerness, and a thrill of fear at the thought of what was ahead.

But most of all he felt relief, and a deep, deep happiness.

The first gem had been found.

The quest to save Deltora had truly begun.

DELTORA QUEST

The Lake of Tears

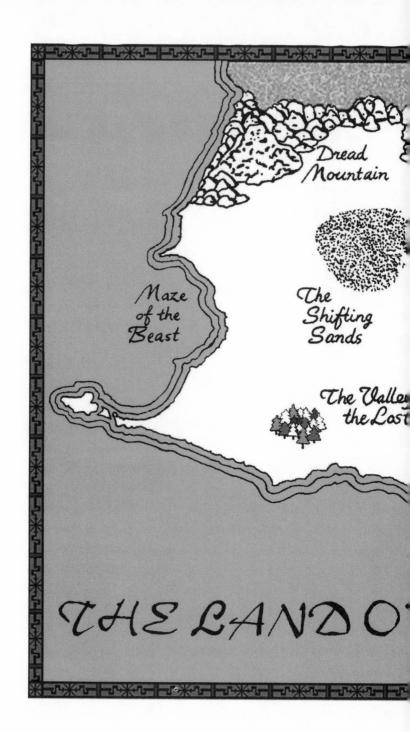

Dread
Mountain

Maze
of the
Beast

The
Shifting
Sands

The Valle
the Lost

THE LAND O

The Shadowlands

The Lake
of Tears

The Forests
of Silence

ity
the
ats

Del

DELTORA

N
W E
S

Contents

1 The Bridge 147

2 Three Questions 152

3 Truth and Lies 158

4 Rescue 167

5 Terror 174

6 Nij and Doj 184

7 Shocks 192

8 Eyes Wide Open 200

9 Stepping Stones 208

10 Quick Thinking 217

11 To Raladin 226

12 Music 235

13 The Lake of Tears 243

14 Soldeen 252

15 The Sorceress 259

16 Fight for Freedom 268

The story so far . . .

Sixteen-year-old Lief, fulfilling a pledge made by his father before he was born, has set out on a great quest to find the seven gems of the magic Belt of Deltora. The Belt is all that can save the kingdom from the tyranny of the evil Shadow Lord, who, only months before Lief's birth, invaded Deltora and enslaved its people with the help of sorcery and his fearsome Grey Guards.

The gems — an amethyst, a topaz, a diamond, a ruby, an opal, a lapis lazuli, and an emerald — were stolen to open the way for the evil Shadow Lord to invade the kingdom. Now they lie hidden in dark and terrible places throughout the land. Only when they have been restored to the Belt can the heir to Deltora's throne be found, and the Shadow Lord's tyranny ended.

Lief set out with one companion — the man Barda, who was once a Palace guard. Now they have been joined by Jasmine — a wild, orphaned girl of Lief's own age, who they met during their first adventure in the fearful Forests of Silence.

In the Forests they discovered the amazing healing powers of the nectar of the Lilies of Life. They also succeeded in finding the first gem — the golden topaz, symbol of faithfulness, which has the power to bring the living into contact with the spirit world, as well as other powers they do not yet understand.

Now read on . . .

1 - The Bridge

Lief, Barda, and Jasmine walked through the crisp, bright morning. The sky was palest blue. The sun slanted between the trees, lighting with bars of gold the winding path they trod. The dark terrors of the Forests of Silence were far behind them.

On such a day, Lief thought, striding along behind Barda, it would be easy to believe that all was well in Deltora. Away from the crowded, ruined city of Del, away from the sight of patroling Grey Guards and the misery of people living in hunger and fear, you could almost forget that the Shadow Lord ruled in the land.

But it would be foolish to forget. The countryside was beautiful, but danger lurked everywhere on the road to the Lake of Tears.

Lief glanced behind him and met Jasmine's eyes.

147

Jasmine had not wanted to come this way. She had argued against it with all her strength.

Now she walked as lightly and silently as always, but her body was stiff and her mouth was set in a straight, hard line. This morning she had tied her long hair back with a strip of cloth torn from her ragged clothes. Without its usual frame of wild brown curls her face seemed very small and pale and her green eyes looked huge.

The little furry creature she called Filli was clinging to her shoulder, chattering nervously. Kree, the raven, was fluttering clumsily through the trees beside her as if unwilling to keep to the ground but also unwilling to fly too far ahead.

And in that moment Lief realized, with a shock, just how afraid they were.

But Jasmine was so brave in the Forests, he thought, turning quickly back to face the front. She risked her life to save us. This part of Deltora is dangerous, certainly. But then, in these days of the Shadow Lord there is danger everywhere. What is so special about this place? Is there something she has not told us?

He remembered the argument that had taken place as the three companions had discussed where they would go after they left the Forests of Silence.

"It is madness to go through the land to the north!" Jasmine had insisted, her eyes flashing. "The sorceress Thaegan rules there."

"It has always been her stronghold, Jasmine," Barda pointed out patiently. "Yet in the past many travelers passed through it and survived to tell the tale."

"Thaegan is ten times more powerful now than she ever was!" exclaimed Jasmine. "Evil loves evil, and the Shadow Lord has increased her strength so that now she is swollen with vanity as well as wickedness. If we travel through the north we are doomed!"

Lief and Barda glanced at each other. Both had been glad when Jasmine decided to leave the Forests of Silence and join them on their quest to find the lost gems of the Belt of Deltora. It was thanks to her that they had not perished in the Forests. It was thanks to her that the first stone, the golden topaz, was now fixed to the Belt Lief wore hidden under his shirt. They knew that Jasmine's talents would be of great use as they moved on to find the six remaining stones.

But for a long time Jasmine had lived by her wits, with no one to please but herself. She was not used to following the plans of others, and had no fear of speaking her feelings plainly. Now Lief was realizing, with some annoyance, that there were going to be times when Jasmine was an uncomfortable, unruly companion.

"We are sure that one of the gems is hidden at the Lake of Tears, Jasmine," he said sharply. "So we must go there."

Jasmine stamped her foot impatiently. "Of

course!" she exclaimed. "But we do not have to travel all the way through Thaegan's territory to do it. Why are you so stubborn and foolish, Lief? The Lake is at the edge of Thaegan's lands. If we approach it from the south, making a wide circle, we can avoid her notice till the very end."

"Such a journey would force us to cross the Os-Mine Hills, so would take five times as long," growled Barda, before Lief could answer. "And who knows what dangers the Hills themselves might hold? No. I believe we should go the way we have planned."

"I, too," Lief agreed. "So it is two against one."

"It is not!" Jasmine retorted. "Kree and Filli vote with me."

"Kree and Filli do not have a vote," growled Barda, finally losing patience. "Jasmine — come with us or return to the Forests. The decision is yours."

With that, he strode away, with Lief close behind him. Jasmine, after a long minute, walked slowly after them. But she was frowning, and in the days that followed, she had grown more and more grave and silent.

✳

Lief was thinking so deeply that he almost cannoned into Barda, who had stopped abruptly just around a bend in the track. He started to apologize, but Barda waved his arm for silence, and pointed.

They had reached the end of the tree-lined pathway, and directly ahead of them yawned a great chasm, its bare, rocky cliffs gleaming pink in the sun-light. Over the terrible drop swayed a narrow bridge made of rope and wooden planks. And in front of the bridge stood a huge, golden-eyed, dark-skinned man holding a wickedly curved sword.

Like a gaping wound in the earth, the chasm stretched away to left and right as far as the eye could see. Wind blew through it, making a soft, eerie sound, and great brown birds swooped on the gusts like enormous kites, wings spread wide.

There was no way across except the swaying bridge. But the way to the bridge was barred by the golden-eyed giant, who stood unmoving and unblink-ing, on guard.

2 - Three Questions

Lief stood stiffly, his heart beating fast, as Jasmine followed him around the bend. He heard her take a sharp breath as she, too, saw what was ahead.

The golden-eyed man had noticed them, but he made no move. He just stood, waiting. He wore nothing but a loincloth, yet he did not shiver in the wind. He was so still you could have thought him a statue, except that he breathed.

"He is bewitched," Jasmine whispered, and Kree made a small, moaning sound.

They walked cautiously forward. The man watched them silently. But when finally they stood before him, at the very edge of the terrible drop, he raised his sword warningly.

"We wish to pass, friend," Barda said. "Stand aside."

"You must answer my question," replied the man in a low, rasping voice. "If you answer correctly, you may pass. If you answer wrongly, I must kill you."

"By whose order?" Jasmine demanded.

"By the order of the sorceress Thaegan," rasped the man. At the sound of the name his skin seemed to quiver. "Once, I tried to deceive her, to save a friend from death. Now it is my doom to guard this bridge until truth and lies are one."

He looked from one to the other. "Who will meet my challenge?"

"I will," Jasmine said, shaking off Barda's restraining hand and stepping forward.

The look of fear had disappeared from her face. It had been replaced by an expression that for a moment Lief did not recognize. And then, with amazement, he realized that it was pity.

"Very well." The huge man looked down at his feet. A row of sticks lay there in the dust.

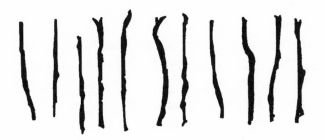

"Change eleven to nine, without removing any sticks," he said harshly.

Lief felt his stomach turn over.

"This is not a fair question," exclaimed Barda. "We are not magicians!"

"The question has been asked," said the man, his golden eyes unblinking. "It must be answered."

Jasmine had been staring at the sticks. Suddenly she crouched and began moving them around. Her body hid what she was doing, but when she stood up again Lief gasped. There were still eleven sticks, but now they read:

"Very good," said the man, with no change of tone. "You may pass."

He stood aside and Jasmine moved onto the bridge. But when Lief and Barda tried to follow her, he barred their way.

"Only the one who answers may cross," he said.

Jasmine had turned and was watching them.

Black wings spread wide, Kree hovered above her head. The bridge swayed dangerously.

"Go on!" Barda called. "We will follow."

Jasmine nodded slightly, turned again, and began walking lightly across the bridge, as carelessly as if it were a tree branch in the Forests of Silence.

"You spoke, so your question is next," said the man with the golden eyes, turning to Barda. "Here it is — what is it that a beggar has, that a rich man needs, and that the dead eat?"

There was silence. Then —

"Nothing," said Barda quietly. "The answer is, 'Nothing.' "

"Very good," said the man. "You may pass."

He stood aside.

"I would like to wait until my companion has answered his question," Barda said, without moving. "Then we can cross the bridge together."

"That is not permitted," said the man. The powerful muscles of his arms tightened slightly on the curved sword.

"Go, Barda," whispered Lief. His skin was tingling with nerves, but he was sure he could answer the question, whatever it was. Jasmine and Barda had succeeded, and he had far more learning than either of them.

Barda frowned, but did not argue further. Lief watched as he stepped onto the bridge and began walking slowly across it, holding tightly to the rails of rope. The rope creaked under his weight. The great birds swooped around him, riding the wind. Far below, there was the thin, snake-like trail of a gleaming river. But Barda did not look down.

"Here is the third question," rasped the man with the golden eyes, stepping back into his place. "It is long, so to be fair I will ask it twice. Listen well."

Lief paid close attention as the man began to speak. The question was in the form of a rhyme:

Thaegan gulps her favorite food
In her cave with all her brood:
Hot, Tot, Jin, Jod,
Fie, Fly, Zan, Zod,
Pik, Snik, Lun, Lod
And the dreaded Ichabod.
Each child holds a slimy toad.
On each toad squirm two fat grubs.
On each grub ride two fleas brave.
How many living in Thaegan's cave?

Lief almost smiled with relief. How many long afternoons had he spent doing sums under the watchful eye of his mother? He could meet this test easily!

He knelt on the ground and as the rhyme was repeated he counted carefully, writing numbers in the dust with his finger.

There were thirteen of Thaegan's children altogether. Plus thirteen toads. Plus twenty-six grubs. Plus fifty-two fleas. That made . . . one hundred and four. Lief checked the sum twice and opened his mouth to speak. Then his heart thudded painfully as, just in time, he realized that he had nearly made a mistake. He had forgotten to add Thaegan herself!

Almost panting at the near disaster, he scrambled to his feet.

"One hundred and five," he gasped.

The man's strange eyes seemed to flash. "You have not answered well," he said. His hand shot out and grabbed Lief's arm with a grip of iron.

Lief gaped at him, feeling the heat of panic rise into his cheeks. "But — the sum is correct!" he stammered. "The children, the toads, the grubs, and the fleas — and Thaegan herself — add up to one hundred and five!"

"Yes," said the man. "But you have forgotten Thaegan's favorite food. A raven, swallowed alive. It was in the cave also, alive in her belly. The answer is one hundred and six."

He lifted his curved sword. "You have not answered well," he repeated. "Prepare to die."

3 ~ Truth and Lies

L ief struggled to free himself. "The question was not fair!" he shouted. "You tricked me! How could I know what Thaegan likes to eat?"

"What you know or do not know is not my concern," said the guardian of the bridge. He raised the sword higher, till its curved blade was level with Lief's neck.

"No!" cried Lief. "Wait!" At this moment of terror, his one thought was for the Belt of Deltora and the topaz fixed to it. If he did nothing to prevent it, this golden-eyed giant would surely find the Belt after he was dead, take it from his body — and perhaps give it to Thaegan. Then Deltora would be lost to the Shadow Lord forever.

I must throw the Belt over the cliff, he thought desperately. I must make sure that Barda and Jasmine see me do it. Then they will have some chance of finding it again. If only I can delay him until I can do it . . .

"You are a trickster and a deceiver!" he cried, slipping his hands under his shirt, feeling for the Belt's fastening. "No wonder you are doomed to guard this bridge until truth and lies are one!"

As he had hoped, the man paused. Anger brightened his golden eyes.

"My suffering was not justly earned," he spat. "It was for pure spite that Thaegan took my freedom and cursed me to be tied to this piece of earth. If you are so interested in truth and lies, we will play another game."

Lief's fingers froze on the Belt. But the flicker of hope that had flared in his heart faded and died with his enemy's next words.

"We will play a game to decide which way you will die," said the man. "You may say one thing, and one thing only. If what you say is true, I will strangle you with my bare hands. If what you say is false, I will cut off your head."

Lief bent his head, pretending to consider, while his fingers secretly struggled with the Belt's catch. The fastening was stiff, and would not open. His hand pressed against the topaz — so hard-won, so soon to be lost, if he did not hurry.

"I am waiting," said the guardian of the bridge. "Make your statement."

True statement, or false? Was it better to be beheaded or strangled? Better to be neither, thought Lief grimly. And then, in a blinding flash, the most wonderful idea came to him.

He looked up boldly at the waiting man. "My head will be cut off," he said clearly.

The man hesitated.

"Well?" cried Lief. "Did you not hear my statement? Is it true or false?"

But he knew that his enemy would have no answer. For if the statement was true, the man was bound to strangle him, thus making it false. And if the statement was false, the man was bound to cut off his head, thus making it true.

And even as he wondered how in his panic he had managed to think of this, the tall figure before him gave a deep, shuddering sigh. Then Lief's eyes widened and he cried out in shock. For the man's flesh had begun rippling, melting — changing shape.

Brown feathers were sprouting from his skin. His legs were shrinking and his feet were spreading, becoming talons. His powerful arms and shoulders were dissolving and re-forming themselves into great wings. His curved sword was becoming a fierce, hooked beak.

And in moments the man was gone, and a huge, proud bird with golden eyes stood on the cliff in his place. With a triumphant cry it spread its wings and soared into the air, joining the other birds swooping and gliding on the wind.

It is my doom to guard this bridge until truth and lies are one.

Lief stared, trembling all over. He could hardly believe what had happened. The guardian of the bridge had been a bird, forced by Thaegan's magic into human form. It had been bound to the earth by her spite as surely as if it had been chained.

And his trick answer had broken Thaegan's spell. He had thought only of saving his own life, but he had broken Thaegan's spell. The bird was free at last.

A sound broke through his racing thoughts. He glanced at the bridge and to his horror saw that it was starting to crumble. Without thinking further, he leapt for it, seizing the rope railings with both hands and running, as he had never imagined he could, over the fearful gap.

He could see Barda and Jasmine standing on the edge of the cliff ahead of him, holding out their arms. He could hear their voices shrieking to him. Behind him, planks rattled together as they slipped from their rope ties and plunged to the river far below.

Soon the rope itself would give way. He knew it. Already it was growing slack. The bridge was sagging, swinging sickeningly as he ran.

All he could think of was to run faster. But he was only halfway across, and he could not run fast enough. Now the planks under his feet were slipping — slipping away! He was stumbling, dropping, the ropes burning his clutching hands. He was dangling in midair, with nowhere to put his feet. And as he hung there, helpless and buffeted by the wind, the planks in front of him — the planks that were his only pathway to safety — began slithering sideways, falling to the river far below.

Painfully, hand over hand, he began swinging himself along the sagging ropes that were all that remained of the bridge, trying not to think of what was below him, what would happen if he lost his grip.

I am playing a game in Del, he told himself feverishly, ignoring the pain of his straining wrists. There is a muddy ditch just below my feet. My friends are watching me, and will laugh at me if I fall. All I have to do is to keep going — hand over hand —

And then he felt a jolt and knew that the ropes had come loose from the cliff-face behind him. Instantly he was swinging forward, hurtling towards the bare, hard face of the cliff in front. In seconds he would slam against it, his bones shattering on the pink rock. He heard his own scream, and the screams of Barda and Jasmine, floating on the wind. He screwed his eyes shut . . .

With a rush something huge swooped under him, and the sickening swing stopped as he felt a warm softness on his face, against his arms. He was being lifted up — up — and the beating of mighty wings was louder in his ears than the wind.

Then he was being clutched by eager hands, and

tumbled onto the dust of solid ground. His ears were ringing. He could hear shouting, laughing voices that seemed very far away. But when he opened his eyes he saw that Jasmine and Barda were leaning over him, and it was they who were shouting, with relief and joy.

He sat up, weak and dizzy, clutching at the ground. His eyes met the golden eyes of the great bird that, but for him, would still be the earthbound guardian of the bridge.

You gave me back my life, the eyes seemed to say. *Now I have returned yours. My debt to you is paid.* Before he could speak, the bird nodded once, spread its wings, and soared away. Lief watched as it joined its companions once more and flew with them, wheeling and shrieking, away along the chasm, into the distance and out of sight.

✳

"You knew that he was a bird," Lief said to Jasmine later, as they moved slowly on. Though he still felt sore and weak, he had refused to rest for long. The very sight of the cliffs made him feel ill. He wanted to get away from them as fast as he could.

Jasmine nodded, glancing at Kree, who was perched on her shoulder with Filli. "I felt it," she said. "And I felt such pity for him when I saw the pain and longing in his eyes."

"In torment he may have been," snorted Barda. "But he would have killed us, without question."

The girl frowned. "He cannot be blamed for that. He was doomed to carry out Thaegan's will. And Thaegan — is a monster."

Her eyes were dark with loathing. And, remembering the riddle that had almost led to his death, Lief thought that now he knew why. He waited until Barda had moved ahead, then spoke to Jasmine again.

"You are not afraid of Thaegan for yourself, but for Kree," he said softly. "Is that not so?"

"Yes," she said, staring straight ahead. "Kree fled to the Forests of Silence after he escaped from her long ago. He was just out of the nest when she took his family. So, in a way, he is like me. I, too, was very young when the Grey Guards took my mother and father."

Her lips tightened. "Kree and I have been together for many years. But I think it is time for us to part. I am leading him into danger. Perhaps to the terrible death he fears more than any other. I cannot bear it."

Kree made a low, trilling sound, and she lifted her arm to him, taking him onto her wrist.

"I know you are willing, Kree," she said. "But I am not. We have talked of this. Now I have truly made up my mind. Please go home to the Forests. If I survive, I will come back for you. If I do not — at least you will be safe."

She stopped, lifted her wrist into the air, and shook it slightly. "Go!" she ordered. "Go home!"

Flapping his wings to steady himself, Kree squawked protestingly.

"Go!" shouted Jasmine. She jerked her hand roughly and Kree was shaken off her wrist. He soared screeching into the air, circled above them once, then flew away.

Jasmine bit her lip and strode on without looking back, Filli chittering miserably on her shoulder.

Lief searched for something comforting to say, but could not find it.

They reached a grove of trees and began following a narrow path that led through the green shade.

"Thaegan hates anything that is beautiful, alive, and free," Jasmine said at last, as they entered a clearing where green ferns clustered and the branches of the trees arched overhead. "The birds say that in the land around the Lake of Tears there was once a town called D'Or — a town like a garden, with golden towers, happy people, and lush flowers and trees. Now it is a dead, sad place."

She waved her hand around her. "As will be all this, when Thaegan and her children have finished their evil work."

Again, there was silence between them, and in the silence they became aware of the rustling of the trees around the clearing.

Jasmine stiffened. "Enemies!" she hissed. "Enemies approach!"

Lief could hear nothing, but by now he knew

better than to ignore one of Jasmine's warnings. The trees here were strange to her, but still she understood their whispering.

He sprinted ahead and caught Barda's arm. Barda stopped and looked around in surprise.

Jasmine's face was pale. "Grey Guards," she whispered. "A whole troop of them. Coming this way."

4 ~ Rescue

Lief and Barda followed Jasmine up into the trees. After their experience in the Forests of Silence it seemed natural to hide above the ground. They climbed as high as they could, while the sound of tramping feet at last came to their ears. They found a safe, comfortable place to cling as the sound grew louder. Wrapped in Lief's disguising cloak, and further hidden by a thick canopy of leaves, they watched as grey-clad figures began marching into the clearing.

They held themselves very still, flattened against the branches. They thought it would be for only a little time, while the Guards passed. So their hearts sank as they saw the men below them halt, drop their weapons, and throw themselves to the ground.

The troop had chosen the clearing as a resting place it seemed. The three companions exchanged despairing glances. What ill fortune! Now they would have to remain where they were — perhaps for hours.

More and more Guards entered the clearing. Soon it was crowded with grey uniforms and ringing with harsh voices. And then, as the last of the troop came into view, there was the clinking sound of chains to go with the sound of marching boots.

The Guards were escorting a prisoner.

Lief craned his neck to look. The captive looked very different from anyone he had ever seen before. He was very small, with wrinkled blue-grey skin, thin legs and arms, small black eyes like buttons, and a tuft of red hair sticking up from the top of his head. There was a tight leather collar around his neck, with a fastening for a chain or rope dangling from it. He looked exhausted, and the chains that weighed down his wrists and ankles had made raw marks on his skin.

"They have captured a Ralad," breathed Barda, moving to see more clearly.

"What is a Ralad?" asked Lief. He thought he had heard or read the name before, but could not think where.

"The Ralads are a race of builders. They were beloved of Adin and all the kings and queens of Deltora's early times," Barda whispered back. "Their buildings were famous for their strength and cleverness."

Now Lief remembered where he had seen the name — in *The Belt of Deltora*, the little blue book his parents had made him study. He gazed in fascination at the drooping figure below them. "It was the Ralads who built the palace of Del," he murmured. "But he is so small!"

"An ant is tiny," muttered Barda. "Yet an ant can carry twenty times its own weight. It is not size that is important, but heart."

"Be silent!" hissed Jasmine. "The Guards will hear you! As it is, they may catch our scent at any time."

But the Guards had plainly walked a long way, and were tired. They were interested in nothing but the food and drink now being unpacked from baskets the leaders had placed in the middle of the clearing.

Two of them pushed the prisoner roughly to the ground at the side of the clearing and threw him a bottle of water. Then they turned their attention to their meal.

Jasmine stared with disgust as the guards tore at their food and splashed drink into their mouths so that it ran down their chins and spilt on the ground.

But Lief was watching the Ralad man, whose eyes were fixed on the scraps of food that were being scattered on the grass of the clearing. Clearly, he was starving.

"The scrag is hungry!" sniggered one of the Guards, pointing a half-gnawed bone in the Ralad man's direction. "Here, scrag!"

He crawled across to where the prisoner was sitting and held out the bone. The starving man cringed, then, unable to resist the food, leaned forward. The Guard hit him hard on the nose with the bone and snatched it away. The other Guards roared with laughter.

"Beasts!" hissed Jasmine, completely forgetting, in her anger, her own warning about being heard.

"Be still," whispered Barda grimly. "There are too many of them. There is nothing we can do. Yet."

The Guards ate and drank till they could eat and drink no more. Then, sprawled carelessly together like a mass of grey grubs, they lay back, closed their eyes, and began to snore.

As quietly as they could, the three companions climbed from branch to branch until they were directly above the Ralad prisoner. He was sitting perfectly still, his shoulders hunched and his head bowed.

Was he, too, asleep? They knew they could not risk startling him awake. If he cried out, all was lost.

Jasmine dug into her pocket and brought out a stem of dried berries. Carefully she leaned out from the tree and threw the stem so that it fell just in front of the motionless captive.

They heard him take a sharp breath. He looked up to the clear sky above where the stem lay, but, of course, saw nothing. His long grey fingers stretched out cautiously and grabbed the prize. He glanced around to make sure that this was not another

Guards' cruel joke, then crushed the stem to his mouth and began tearing at the berries ravenously.

His chains clinked faintly, but the snoring figures around him did not stir.

"Very well," Jasmine breathed. Taking careful aim, she dropped another stem of berries squarely into the prisoner's lap. This time he looked straight up, and his button eyes widened with shock as he saw the three faces looking down at him.

Lief, Barda, and Jasmine quickly pressed their fingers to their lips, warning him to be silent. He did not make a sound and crammed berries into his mouth as he watched the strangers edging carefully down the tree towards him.

They already knew that they had no chance of freeing him from his chains without waking the Guards. They had another plan. It was dangerous, but it would have to do. Jasmine and Lief had refused to leave the prisoner to the mercy of his captors, and Barda had not needed much persuading. He was the only one of them who knew of the Ralad people, and the thought of one being held prisoner by the Grey Guards was horrible to him.

While Jasmine kept watch from the tree, Lief and Barda slipped to the ground beside the little man and made signs to him not to fear. Trembling, the prisoner nodded. Then he did something surprising. With the tip of one thin finger he made a strange mark upon the ground and looked up at them inquiringly.

171

Baffled, Lief and Barda glanced at one another, and then back to him. He saw that they did not understand his meaning. His black eyes grew fearful and he quickly brushed the mark away. But still he seemed to trust the newcomers — or perhaps he thought that no situation could be worse than the one he was in. As the Guards slept on, snoring like beasts, he allowed himself to be quickly and quietly wrapped in Lief's cloak.

They had decided that their only hope was to carry him away, chains and all. They hoped that the tightly wrapped cloak would stop the chains from clinking together, alerting his enemies.

The chains made the little man heavier than he would otherwise have been, but Barda had no difficulty in picking him up and putting him over one shoulder. They knew that to return to the trees, carrying such a burden, would be clumsy and dangerous. But the prisoner had been lying very near the mouth of the path. All they had to do was reach it and creep silently away.

It was a risk they were all prepared to take. And all would have been well if one of the Guards, dreaming, perhaps, had not, right at that moment, rolled over and flung out his arm, hitting his neighbor on the chin.

The Guard who had been struck woke with a roar, looked wildly around to see who had hit him, and caught sight of Lief and Barda running away down the path.

He shouted the alarm. In seconds, the clearing was alive with angry Guards, roused from their sleep and furious to find their prisoner gone.

5 - Terror

Howling like beasts, the Guards thundered down the path after Lief and Barda. All of them carried slings and a supply of the poisonous bubbles they called "blisters." All were fitting blisters to their slings as they ran. They knew that as soon as they had clear aim and could hurl the blisters, the running figures ahead of them would fall, helpless and screaming in pain.

Lief and Barda knew it, too. And so, perhaps, did the Ralad man, for he moaned in despair as he bumped on Barda's shoulder. But the path was winding, so there was no clear aim, and fear gave Lief and Barda's feet wings. They were staying well ahead.

But Lief knew this could not last. Already, he was panting. Weakened from his ordeal in the chasm,

174

he did not have the strength he needed to outrun the enemy. Grey Guards could run for days and nights without rest, and could smell out their prey wherever it was hiding.

Far behind he heard thumping, clattering sounds and the angry shouts of falling men. With a thrill of gratitude, he guessed that Jasmine had been following through the trees, dropping dead branches across the path to trip and delay their pursuers.

Be careful, Jasmine, he thought. Do not let them see you.

Jasmine could have remained hidden and safe with Filli. The Guards would never have known that there had been three strangers in the clearing, not just two. But it was not her way to see friends in trouble and do nothing.

With a start, Lief saw her leap lightly to the ground just ahead. He had not realized how close to them she was.

"I have set them an obstacle course," she said gleefully, as they reached her. "Thorny vine twined round dead branches in six places along the path. That will slow them down!" Her eyes were sparkling with pleasure.

"Keep moving!" grunted Barda. "Their anger will only make them run faster!"

They rounded a bend and to his horror Lief saw that ahead was a long stretch of path with no curves at all. It seemed to go on and on, straight as an arrow, vanishing into the distance.

The Guards could not ask for clearer aim than this. As soon as they reached this spot, the blisters would start flying, for they would see their enemies clearly, however far ahead they were. Lief's heart pounded in his aching chest as he fought down despair.

"Off to the side!" hissed Barda, abruptly swerving from the path. "It is our only chance!"

The trees here were slender, with delicate trailing branches — useless for climbing. A carpet of springy grass spread between them, and wild sweetplum bushes were dotted here and there, plump, purple fruits glistening among fresh green leaves.

Lief had never seen sweetplums growing wild before. He had a sudden vision of how pleasant it would have been to wander here peacefully, picking the rich-smelling fruit and eating it straight from the bush. That, no doubt, was what he, Barda, and Jasmine would have done — if they had not met the troop of Guards and their prisoner on the way.

But they *had* met the Guards, and the prisoner. So instead of enjoying the afternoon, they were running for their lives.

Lief glanced at the bundle bobbing on Barda's shoulder. The Ralad man was no longer groaning, and there was no movement within the folds of the cloak. Perhaps he had fainted. Perhaps he was dead of starvation and terror, and all this had been for nothing.

Abruptly, the ground began to slope away, and Lief saw that their steps were taking them into a little valley that had not been visible from the path. Here the sweetplum bushes were larger, and growing more thickly. The air was filled with their rich perfume.

Jasmine sniffed as she ran. "This is a perfect place to hide!" she muttered excitedly. "The smell of these fruits will mask our scent."

Lief glanced behind him. Already the grass bent by their running feet had sprung back into place. There was no sign of the way they had taken. For the first time since they left the path he felt a flicker of hope.

He followed Barda and Jasmine to the bottom of the valley. They pushed into the midst of the bushes, which rose above their heads, hiding them completely. In silence, they crept through the dim, green shade. The ground was damp underfoot, and somewhere there was the gurgling of running water. Sweetplums hung everywhere like tiny, glowing lanterns.

They had been under cover for only a few minutes when Jasmine stopped and raised her hand warningly. "I hear them," she breathed. "They are nearing the place where we left the path."

Crouching very still, listening carefully, Lief finally heard what her sharper ears had heard before him — the sound of running feet. The sound became louder, louder — and then the feet faltered. The first of the Guards had come to the straight section of the path. Lief imagined the leaders peering ahead and seeing no one.

There was a moment's silence. He held his breath at the thought of them sniffing the air, muttering to each other. There was a loud, harsh sound that could have been a laugh or a curse. And then, to his overwhelming relief and joy, he heard an order barked, and the sound of the whole troop turning. In seconds the Guards were marching back the way they had come.

"They have given up," he breathed. "They think we have outrun them."

"It may be a trap," Barda muttered grimly.

The sound of marching feet gradually faded away and though the three companions waited, motionless, for several long minutes, nothing disturbed the silence. Finally, at a whisper from Jasmine, Filli skittered away to the nearest tree and ran up the trunk. In moments he was back, chattering softly.

"All is well," Jasmine said, standing up and stretching. "Filli cannot see them. They have truly gone."

Lief stood up beside her, easing his cramped muscles with relief. He pulled a sweetplum from the bush beside him and bit into it, sighing with pleasure as the sweet, delicious juice cooled his parched throat.

"There are better fruits further along," said Jasmine, pointing ahead.

"First I must see how my poor piece of baggage is faring," said Barda. He unwrapped the cloak and was soon cradling the Ralad man in his arms.

"Is he dead?" asked Lief quietly.

Barda shook his head. "He is unconscious — and no wonder. The Ralad are a strong people, but no one can resist starvation, exhaustion, and fear forever. Who knows how long our friend has been a prisoner of the Guards, or how far he has walked in heavy chains without being given any food or rest?"

Lief looked at the small man curiously. "I have never seen anyone like him before," he said. "What was that sign he drew upon the ground?"

"I do not know. When he awakes, we will ask him." Barda groaned as he lifted the Ralad man up again. "He has caused us some trouble, but still the meeting was fortunate," he added. "He can guide us from here. The village of Raladin, where he comes from, is very near the Lake of Tears. Let us find a place where we can sit in more comfort and remove these chains."

They pushed on through the bushes. The further they moved into the little valley, the more enchanting it seemed. Soft moss covered the ground like a thick green carpet and nodding flowers clustered every-where. Brightly colored butterflies fluttered around the sweetplum bushes, and the sun, filtering through the delicate leaves of the slender trees, shed a gentle, green-gold light over everything it touched.

Never had Lief seen such beauty. He could tell from Barda's face that he felt the same. Even Jasmine was soon looking around with warm pleasure.

They reached a small clearing and gratefully sank down onto the moss. There Barda used Jasmine's dagger to cut the tight leather collar from the Ralad man's neck and break the locks on his chains. As he pulled the chains away he frowned at the rubbed, raw patches on the man's wrists and ankles.

"They are not so bad." Jasmine inspected the wounds casually. She pulled a small jar from her pocket and unscrewed the lid. "This is of my own making, from my mother's recipe," she said, lightly spreading a pale green cream onto the raw places. "It heals skin quickly. It was often useful . . . in the Forests of Silence."

Lief glanced at her. She was looking down, frowning fiercely as she screwed the lid back on the jar.

She is homesick, Lief thought suddenly. She misses Kree, and the Forests, and the life she had there. Just as I miss my home, and my friends, and my mother and father.

Not for the first time he felt a stab in his heart as he thought of all he had left behind in Del. He thought of his room — tiny, but safe and full of his own treasures. He thought of evenings in front of the fire. Running wild in the streets with his friends. Even working with his father at the forge.

Suddenly he longed for a hot, home-cooked meal. He longed for a warm bed and a comforting voice bidding him good night.

He jumped up, furious with himself. How could he be so weak, so childish? "I am going to explore," he said loudly. "I will collect some sweetplums for us to eat, and wood for a fire."

He did not wait for an answer from Barda and Jasmine, but strode to the edge of the clearing and through a gap between two trees.

The sweetplum bushes here were even more heavily laden than the ones he had already seen. He walked between them, using his cloak as a pouch to hold the fragrant fruits he picked. There were few dead sticks, but those there were he collected. Even a small fire would be welcome when night came.

His eyes fixed to the ground, he walked on. At last he stumbled on a good piece of flat wood, far bigger than anything else he had seen. It was damp, and moss had grown over it, but he knew it would soon dry and burn once the fire was well alight.

Pleased, he picked it up and, straightening his back, looked around to see where he was. And it was then that he saw something very surprising, right in front of his nose. It was a sign — old, broken, and battered, but plainly made by human hands:

RING AND ENTER

Beside the sign, hanging from a tree branch, was a metal bell.

How strange, Lief thought. He peered through the bushes beyond the sign and jumped with surprise. Directly ahead was a strip of smooth, bright green lawn. And beyond the lawn, in the distance, was what looked like a small white house. Smoke was drifting from the chimney.

"Barda!" he cried, his voice cracking. "Jasmine!"

He heard them exclaiming and running towards him, but he could not tear his eyes away from the little house. As they reached him, he pointed and they gasped in amazement.

"I never thought to find people living here!" exclaimed Barda. "What a piece of good fortune!"

"A bath!" cried Lief happily. "Hot food! And perhaps a bed for the night!"

" 'Ring and Enter,' " said Jasmine, reading the sign. "Very well, then. Let us obey!"

Lief stretched out his hand and rang the bell. It made a cheery, welcoming sound, and together the friends ran through the bushes and onto the green lawn.

They had taken only a few steps before they realized that something was terribly wrong. Desperately they tried to turn back. But it was too late. Already they were sinking — to their knees . . . their thighs . . . their waists . . .

Beneath the green-covered surface of what they had thought was a fine flat lawn — was quicksand.

6 - Nij and Doj

Floundering, terrified, they screamed for help as the quicksand sucked them down. Already they had sunk nearly to their chests. Soon — soon they would disappear under the treacherous green surface that they now knew was simply a thin layer of some slimy water plant.

The fruit and sticks that Lief had been carrying had scattered and sunk without trace, but the big piece of wood he had found was still lying on the surface of the quicksand between the three struggling friends. It floats because it is flat and wide, Lief thought through his panic. It is floating where nothing else will.

There was a shout, and he saw, hurrying from the little white cottage, two plump, grey-haired figures carrying a long pole between them. Help was coming. But by the time it arrived it would be too late. Too late. Unless . . .

184

Lief reached out for the flat piece of wood and just managed to touch its edge with the tips of his fingers.

"Jasmine! Barda!" he shouted. "Hold on to this wood. At the edges. Gently. Try to — to stretch out and spread yourselves flat, as though you were swimming."

They heard him. They did as he asked. In moments the three companions were spread out around the piece of wood like the petals of a giant flower or the spokes of a wheel. High on Jasmine's shoulder, Filli chattered with fear, clutching her hair with his tiny hands.

They were no longer sinking. The wood was holding them almost steady. But for how long could their balance last? If one of them panicked — if the wood tipped one way or the other, it would slide under the quicksand and they would go with it and be lost.

"Help is coming!" gasped Lief. "Hold on!"

He did not dare to raise his head to look for the two old people in case the movement disturbed his balance. But he could hear their gasping cries. They were very close now.

Oh, quickly, he begged them in his mind. Please hurry!

He heard them reach the edge of the quicksand. He could not understand their words, because they were speaking in a strange tongue. But their voices were urgent. It was clear that they wanted to help.

185

"Taem hserf!" the man was panting.

"Knis ti tel ton od!" the woman exclaimed in answer. *"Tou ti teg!"*

There was a splash. The quicksand surged and rippled. Lief clutched at his piece of wood and cried out. Green slime and sand covered his mouth, his nose . . . Then he felt something catch him around the back, curving under his arms, holding him up, pulling him forward.

Choking and spluttering, he opened his eyes. Whatever was holding him — a large metal hook, perhaps — was attached to the end of a long wooden pole. Jasmine and Barda had caught hold of the pole itself. Like him, they were being towed slowly towards firm ground by the two old people who heaved together, grunting with the effort.

There was nothing the three friends could do to help themselves. Progress was agonizingly slow. The quicksand sucked at their bodies, holding them back. But the two old people would not give up. Red-faced, they sweated and puffed, pulling at the pole with all their might.

And at last, Lief saw Jasmine and Barda pulled out of the sand's grip. With a horrible, sucking sound it released them and they flopped together onto dry land — wet, filthy, and covered in slime.

Moments later it was his turn. His body popped from the ooze and onto the bank like a cork from a bottle — so suddenly that the two old people tumbled

backwards and sat down hard. They gasped, clutching each other and laughing.

Lief lay, panting on the ground, gabbling his relief and thanks. Hard against his back was the hook
that had saved his life, but he did not care. He found
that he was still clutching the piece of wood, and
laughed. Rough and rubbishy as it was, it, too, had
played its part. He was glad it had not been lost in the
sand. He sat up and looked around.

The two old people were picking themselves up,
chattering excitedly to one another.

"*Efas era yeht!*" cried the old woman.

"*Egamad on!*" her companion agreed.

"What are they talking about?" muttered Jasmine. "I cannot understand a word they say."

Lief glanced at her. Her face was thunderous.

"Do not frown at them so, Jasmine," he whispered urgently. "They saved our lives!"

"They nearly *took* our lives, with their foolish
'Ring and Enter' sign," she snapped. "I do not see
why I should be grateful to them!"

"They may not have put the sign there," Barda
pointed out calmly. "It may have been here longer than
they have. It looked very old — broken and battered."

Suddenly, Lief had a terrible thought. He looked
down at the piece of wood he held in his hand. It, too,
looked very old. And it, too, had a jagged edge, as
though it had been broken away from something
larger, a long time ago.

Slowly he rubbed away the moss that still clung to one side. His face began to burn as faded words and letters became visible.

In his mind's eye he fitted this piece of wood to the sign on the other side of the quicksand.

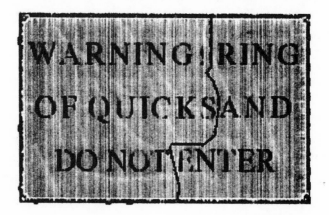

Silently, he held up the piece of wood so that Jasmine and Barda could see the words. Their eyes widened and they groaned as they realized how they had made the mistake that had nearly been their death.

The two old people were bustling up to them. When they in their turn saw the piece of broken sign, they exclaimed and looked shocked.

"*Ti was yeht!*" cried the woman.

"*Ti wonk ton did yeht. Sloof!*" growled the man. He took the piece of sign from Lief's hand and shook his head. Then he pointed across to the other side of the quicksand and made breaking movements with his hands.

Lief nodded. "Yes, the warning sign was broken," he said, though he knew they could not understand him. "We were fools for not realizing that, and for rushing forward as we did."

"The sign has been broken for years!" muttered Jasmine, still angry. "The piece that has fallen off is covered in moss. They must have known. And why is there a bell hanging from the tree?"

"If a ring of quicksand surrounds their land, perhaps they rarely leave it," Barda murmured. "If that is so, how could they know what is beyond?"

The old woman smiled at Lief. Her smile was sweet and merry. She was pink-cheeked, with twinkling blue eyes, and she was wearing a long blue dress. Her apron was white and her grey hair was tied in a knot on the back of her neck.

Lief smiled back at her. She reminded him of a picture in one of the old storybooks in the bookshelf at home. It made him feel warm and safe just looking at her. The old man was also comforting to look at. He had a kind, cheery face, a fringe of grey hair around a bald patch on his head, and a bushy white mustache.

"Nij," the woman said, patting her chest and bowing slightly. Then she pulled the old man forward. *"Doj,"* she said, tapping him.

Lief realized that she was telling him their names. "Lief," he said in return, pointing at himself. Then he held out his hand to Jasmine and Barda and said their names as well.

With each introduction, Nij and Doj bowed and smiled. Then they pointed to the little white house, mimed washing and drinking, and looked at the three companions questioningly.

"Certainly," beamed Barda, nodding vigorously. "Thank you. You are kind."

"Yrgnuh era ew," said Doj, patting him on the back. He and Nij both roared with laughter as if at some great joke, and began walking together towards the house.

"Are you forgetting the Ralad man?" asked Jasmine in a low voice, as the three companions followed. "He will wake and find us gone. He may look for us. What if he falls into the quicksand, too?"

Barda shrugged. "I doubt that he will try to find us," he said comfortably. "He will be too eager to make his way home again. Though Ralads have always traveled to do their building work, they hate to be away from Raladin for too long."

As the girl lingered, looking back over her shoulder, his voice sharpened. "Come along, Jasmine!" he complained. "Anyone would think that you enjoyed being wet and covered in slime!"

Lief was hardly listening. His feet were quickening as he approached the little white house with the smoking chimney and the flower gardens. *Home*, his heart was telling him. *Friends. Here you can rest. Here you will be safe.*

Barda strode beside him, as eager as Lief was to reach the welcoming house and to enjoy the comforts inside.

Jasmine trailed behind, with Filli nestled against her hair. She was still frowning. If either Lief or Barda had paid attention to her, had listened to her doubts and suspicions, they might have slowed their steps.

But neither of them did. And they did not realize their mistake until long after the green door had shut behind them.

7 ~ Shocks

Nij and Doj led the three companions into a large, bright kitchen with a stone floor. Polished pots and pans hung from hooks above the big fuel stove and a large table stood in the center of the room. It reminded Lief of the kitchen in the forge, and he would have been happy to stay there — especially as, like Barda and Jasmine, he was wet and muddy.

But Nij and Doj seemed shocked at the idea of their guests sitting in the kitchen, and bustled them into a cosy sitting room beyond. Here an open fire burned, and there were comfortable-looking easy chairs and a woven carpet on the floor.

With many nods and smiles, Nij gave Jasmine, Lief, and Barda rugs to wrap themselves in, and made them sit by the fire. Then she and Doj rushed away again, making signs to say they would return.

Soon Lief could hear clattering and murmuring in the kitchen. He guessed that the two old people were heating water for baths and perhaps preparing a meal. *"Retaw liob,"* Nij was saying busily. And Doj was laughing as he worked. *"Noos taem hserf! Noos taem hserf!"* he was chanting in a singsong voice.

Lief's heart warmed. Whatever these people had, they would give to help the strangers in trouble.

"They are very kind," he said lazily. He felt relaxed for the first time in days. The fire was cheery, and the rug around his shoulders was comforting. The room, too, made him feel at home. There was a jug of yellow daisies on the mantelpiece — daisies exactly like the ones that grew wild by the forge gate. Over the fireplace hung a framed piece of embroidery, no doubt made by Nij's own hands.

"Yes, they are very good," murmured Barda. "It is for people such as these that we wish to save Deltora."

Jasmine sniffed. Lief glanced at her and wondered at the restless look on her face. Then he realized that, of course, she had never been inside a house like this, never met ordinary people like Nij and Doj before. She had spent her life in the Forests, among trees, under the sky. No wonder she felt uncomfortable here, instead of at peace as he and Barda did.

Filli was hunched on Jasmine's shoulder with his paws over his eyes. He was not happy, either, though Nij and Doj had made him welcome, smiling and trying to stroke him.

"Lief," Jasmine whispered, as she saw him looking at her. "Is the Belt safe? Is the topaz still in place?"

Lief realized with a small shock that he had forgotten all about the Belt until this moment. He felt for it, and was relieved to find that it was still securely fixed around his waist.

He lifted up his filthy shirt to look at it. Its steel links were clogged with mud and slime. The topaz was thickly coated, its golden lights hidden. With his fingers he began to clean the gem of the worst of the murky grime. It seemed wrong that it should be so fouled.

His work stopped abruptly as Doj hurried in from the kitchen, carrying a tray. Lief cursed his own carelessness. The rug which was wrapped around him hid the Belt from the doorway, but this was just a fortunate chance. Nij and Doj were kind and good, but it was vital that the quest for the Belt of Deltora was revealed to as few people as possible. He should have taken more care.

He sat perfectly still, his head bent and his hands clasped over the topaz, while Doj set down the tray, which was loaded with drinks and a plate of small cakes.

"Here, scum!" said Doj. *"Enjoy your last meal on earth."*

Lief's scalp prickled with shock. Was he hearing things? Was he dreaming? He stole a look at Barda and saw that he was smiling pleasantly. Jasmine, too, seemed undisturbed.

He felt a nudge on his arm and looked up. Doj was smiling at him, handing him a cup of what looked like sweetplum juice. But with a thrill of horror Lief saw that the old man's face was horribly changed. The skin was mottled and covered in lumps and sores. The eyes were yellow, flat, and cold, like snake's eyes, over a nose that was just two flaring black holes. The grinning mouth was greedy and cruel, with crooked metal spikes for teeth and a fat blue tongue that crept out and licked at swollen lips.

Lief shrieked aloud and cowered back.

"Lief, what is the matter?" cried Jasmine, alarmed.

"What are you thinking of?" growled Barda at the same moment, glancing in an embarrassed way at the horrible monster who was still holding out the cup.

The blood was pounding in Lief's head. He could hardly breathe, but his mind was racing.

Plainly, his friends were not seeing what he was seeing. To them, Doj was still the kindly old man that Lief had once believed him to be.

But that vision had been a lie — an illusion, created by some evil magic. Lief knew that now. He also knew that at all costs the hideous being must not find out that for him, at least, the spell had been broken.

He clutched at the topaz beneath his shirt and forced himself to smile and nod. "I — was dozing," he stammered. "I — woke with a shock. I am sorry." He mimed sleeping and waking suddenly, and pretended to laugh at himself.

Doj laughed, too. And it was horrible to see his bared, shining teeth, and his dripping mouth gaping wide.

He handed the cup to Lief and walked back towards the kitchen. *"Reverof peels nac uoy noos,"* he said, at the door. Again he licked his lips. And again Lief heard the words for what they really were: *"Soon you can sleep forever."*

The words were not a strange language, but ordinary words turned backwards! His head whirling, phrases and comments coming back to him, Lief saw that every sentence Doj and Nij had said had been turned backwards.

In a daze of horror he watched Doj leave the room. He heard him begin clattering round in the kitchen with Nij, raising his voice in the same singsong chant: *"Noos taem hserf, noos taem hserf!"*

"Fresh meat soon, fresh meat soon!"

Lief's whole body shuddered as if blasted by an icy wind. He swung round to Jasmine and Barda, and as he did he saw the living room as it really was.

It was a grim, dark cell. The walls were stone, dripping with greasy water. The soft carpet was made of the skins of small animals, roughly sewn together. But the embroidery over the mantelpiece was still complete. For the first time he stared at it with clear eyes:

"Lief, what is the matter?"

He tore his eyes away from the terrible words and looked at Jasmine. She was watching him in puzzlement, a cup halfway to her lips.

"Do — do not drink that!" Lief managed to say.

Jasmine frowned. "I am thirsty!" she protested, and lifted the cup.

Desperately, Lief struck it from her hand and it fell to the floor. Jasmine sprang up with a cry of anger.

"Be still!" he hissed. "You do not understand. There is danger here. The drink — who knows what is in it!"

197

"Are you mad, Lief?" yawned Barda. "It is delicious!" He was leaning back on the stinking animal skins. His eyes were partly closed.

Lief shook his arm frantically, realizing with a sinking heart that the big man had already drunk half of his drink. "Barda, get up!" he begged. "They are trying to drug us! Already you feel the drug's effects."

"Nonsense," drawled Barda. "Never have I seen such kindly people as Nij and Doj. Are they husband and wife, do you think, or brother and sister?"

Nij. Doj . . . Suddenly the names turned themselves around in Lief's head and he saw them, too, for what they really were.

"They are brother and sister," he said grimly. "Their names are not Nij and Doj, but Jin and Jod. They are two of the sorceress Thaegan's children. They were named in that rhyme the guardian of the bridge repeated to me. They are monsters! When we are asleep they will kill us — and then eat us!"

"That is a poor joke, Lief," Jasmine frowned.

And Barda just blinked in concern. He looked around the room, and Lief knew that all he was seeing was homely comfort. Barda's own eyes were telling him that fear had turned his companion's wits.

"Noos taem hserf, noos taem hserf!" chanted the monster Jod in the kitchen. And his sister joined in, her voice raised over the sound of a sharpening knife. *"Wets ylevol! Wets ylevol!"*

Barda smiled sleepily. "Hear how they sing at

their work?" he said, leaning over and patting Lief's arm. "How could you think they were anything other than what they seem? Rest, now. You will be feeling better soon."

Lief shook his head desperately. What was he going to do?

8 - Eyes Wide Open

L ief knew that he had to break the spell that was
blinding Barda and Jasmine.

But how was he to do it? He did not understand how he himself had come to understand the
truth. It had happened so suddenly. He had been
cleaning the topaz when Doj came in and —

The topaz!

Some half-remembered sentences from his fa-
ther's little blue book, *The Belt of Deltora*, drifted into
his head.

He closed his eyes, concentrating hard, till he
saw the page of the book in his mind.

✝ **The topaz is a powerful gem, and its strength
increases as the moon grows full. The topaz protects its
wearer from the terrors of the night. It has the power to**

200

open doors into the spirit world. It strengthens and clears the mind . . .

It strengthens and clears the mind!

Lief grasped the topaz tightly as his thoughts raced. He remembered that his hand had been on the topaz when he managed to meet the last test set by the guardian of the bridge. He had been cleaning the topaz when he realized Doj was not what he seemed.

The golden gem was the key!

Without bothering to explain, he grabbed Barda's hand, and Jasmine's, and pulled them forward until they touched the topaz.

Their gasps of astonishment and annoyance changed almost instantly to smothered shrieks of horror. Their eyes bulged as they looked around the room — saw, at last, what Lief was seeing, and heard the words floating from the kitchen.

"Fresh meat soon! Fresh meat soon!"

"Lovely stew! Lovely stew!"

"I did not like them, or their house," hissed Jasmine. "And Filli felt the same. But I thought it was because we had grown up in the Forests, and did not know how people in the world behaved."

"I — " Barda swallowed, and brushed his hand over his forehead. "How could I have been so blind?"

"We were all blinded by magic," Lief whispered.

"But the topaz has strengthened and cleared our minds so that we can resist the spell."

Barda shook his head. "I thought it was strange that the Grey Guards did not search for us after they lost sight of us on the trail," he muttered. "Now I understand it. They must have guessed where we were hiding. They knew we would at last wander to the quicksand and be caught by Jin and Jod. No wonder they laughed as they went away."

"Jin and Jod are clumsy and slow," said Lief. "If they were not, they would not need magic or a sleeping drug to catch their victims. We have a chance . . ."

"If we can find a way out." Jasmine darted away and began searching the walls of the cell, running her fingers over the dripping stones.

Barda staggered to his feet and tried to follow, but stumbled and caught Lief's arm to steady himself. The big man was swaying and very pale.

"It is their accursed drink," he mumbled. "I did not take enough to put me to sleep, but it has weakened me, I fear."

They heard Jasmine hissing their names. She was beckoning from the other side of the room. As quickly as they could, Barda and Lief hurried over to her.

She had found a door. It had been made to look like part of the wall. Only a narrow crack showed its outline. Filled with frantic hope, they pushed their fingers into the crack and tugged.

The door swung open without noise. They looked beyond it, and their hopes died.

The door did not lead to a way out, but to a storeroom piled to the roof with a tangled mass of possessions. There were clothes of every size and type, musty and stained with damp. There were rusted pieces of armor, helmets, and shields. There were swords and daggers, dull with neglect and cluttered together in a towering pile. There were two chests overflowing with jewels, and two more heaped with gold and silver coins.

The three companions stared in horror, realizing that these were the possessions of all the travelers trapped and killed by Jin and Jod in the past. No weapon had been strong enough, no fighter clever enough, to defeat them.

"The broken sign has lured many into the quicksand," breathed Jasmine.

Lief nodded grimly. "It is a neat trap. The monsters hear the bell ring, and run down to pull out whoever has fallen in. Their victims are grateful, and also see only what Jin and Jod want them to see. So they do not fight them, but come tamely up to the house . . ."

"To be drugged, killed, and eaten," said Barda, gritting his teeth. "As nearly happened to us."

"And as still might," Jasmine reminded him, "if we do not find a way out of here!"

203

And at that moment, they heard the faint clanging of the bell. Someone else had read the broken sign. Someone else was about to be caught in the quicksand trap.

For a single moment they stood, frozen. Then Lief's mind began to work again. "Back to the fireplace!" he hissed. "Lie down! Pretend to be — "

He did not have to finish. His companions understood and were already hurrying back to their places, emptying the drugged juice from their cups and throwing themselves down on the floor.

"*Doj, team erom!*" they heard Jin screech from the kitchen. "*Kooh eht teg!*"

"*Tsaef a!*" gibbered her brother excitedly. "*Tey peelsa srehto eht era?*" There was the clatter of a lid being thrown back on a pot and the sound of running footsteps.

Like Jasmine and Barda, Lief was pretending to be unconscious when Jin came in to check on them. He did not stir when he felt her foot nudge him. But as she grunted with satisfaction and moved away he opened his eyes to slits and looked at her through his eyelashes.

She had turned and was lumbering quickly towards the door. He could only see a humped mass of sickly green-white flesh covered in black bristles, and the back of a bald head from which sprouted three stubby horns. He could not see her face, but of that he was very glad.

"Efink eht rof ydaer era yeht!" she bellowed as she left the cell, slamming the door after her. Shuddering, Lief heard her footsteps in the kitchen and the sound of another slamming door. Then there was silence. She and her brother had both left the house.

"So we are ready for the knife, are we? And now they have caught another poor wretch in their trap!" muttered Barda, clambering unsteadily to his feet and hurrying to the door with the others.

"It must be the Ralad man," hissed Jasmine. She ran into the kitchen, with the others close behind.

Now that the spell had been broken, they saw the kitchen with new eyes. It was dark, stinking, and filthy. The stone floor was caked with ancient grime. Old bones lay scattered everywhere. In the darkest corner there was a small bed of moldy straw. By the look of the frayed rope attached to a ring on the wall above it, some sort of pet had slept there until quite recently, when it had chewed its way to freedom.

The companions only glanced at all these things. Their attention was fixed on the great pot of water bubbling under its lid on the stove, the huge pile of roughly sliced onions, and the two long, sharpened knives lying ready on the greasy table.

Lief stared, his stomach churning. Then he jumped as his ears, sharpened by fear, picked up a small, stealthy sound from deep within the house. Someone — or something — was moving.

205

His companions had heard it, too. "Out!" hissed Barda. "Make haste!"

They crept into the open, gasping with relief as finally they were able to breathe in fresh, clean air. They looked around cautiously.

The sweet little cottage they thought they had seen was in fact a grim, hulking square of white stones with no windows. The flower gardens were nothing but beds of onions and thistles. Rough grass stretched on all sides, leading always to the bright green band that marked the quicksand.

In the distance, they could see Jin and Jod. Shouting angrily at one another, they were digging their long pole into a patch of quicksand where something had fallen in, disturbing the green slime before sinking out of sight.

A wave of sadness swept over Lief.

"They were not in time to save him. He has gone under," said Barda, his face showing his pain.

"Very well, then," snapped Jasmine. "We have nothing to stay for. So why are we standing here, when at any moment they could turn and see us?"

Lief glanced at her. She returned his gaze defiantly, her lips pressed tightly together and her chin raised. Then she turned and began walking quickly around the house, out of sight.

Lief helped Barda to follow her.

The back of the house was just the same as the front, with a single door and no windows. On all sides, bare grass stretched away, ending in the same band of bright green. Beyond, there was forest. But the quicksand circled the whole of Jin and Jod's domain like a moat.

"There must be a way across!" muttered Lief. "I cannot believe that they never leave this place."

Jasmine was scanning the green band with narrowed eyes. Suddenly, she pointed to a slightly mottled-looking section almost opposite the house. The place was marked by a huge rock on the bank. "There!" she exclaimed, and began running.

9 - Stepping Stones

As quickly as he could, with Barda leaning on his shoulder, Lief hurried after Jasmine. When finally they reached her, she was standing beside the rock at the edge of the quicksand. Now Lief could see what had made the green slime look mottled in this spot. In the middle of the moat floated a cluster of pale green leaves marked with red — the leaves of some swamp plant, perhaps.

The edges of the leaves were straight, so that where they touched they fitted together like a puzzle. Where there were gaps between them, the bright green of the quicksand slime showed ominously.

Lief looked more closely and realized that the red markings on the leaves were even stranger than they had first appeared. They were numbers, letters, and symbols.

He clutched Jasmine's arm.

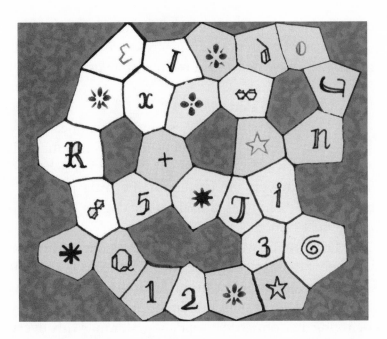

"There is a pathway hidden here, I am sure of it!" he whispered in excitement. "There are stepping stones under some of those leaves."

"But which ones?" muttered Jasmine. "We would have to be very sure. The cluster is in the middle of the quicksand. We have nothing long enough to test which leaves are solid and which are not. We would have to leap, and trust that there is no mistake."

"The topaz, Lief," Barda urged. "Perhaps it will help you — "

There was a muffled roar of rage from the house. They spun around just in time to see the back door burst open and crash against the wall. Someone hurtled out and began pounding across the grass towards them. Lief cried out in astonishment as he saw who it was.

It was the Ralad man!

"He is not drowned!" shouted Jasmine. "They saved him after all!" The relief in her voice made it clear that, however uncaring she had seemed, she had in fact cared, very much, about the little prisoner's fate. Already she was drawing her dagger and rushing to help him.

For now he needed help more than ever. Jin and Jod were after him, bursting through the door, screaming with rage. Jin had caught up an axe, and Jod was holding the long pole out in front of him, savagely swinging it from side to side as he ran. With every swing, the hook at the end, still dripping with slime from its dunking in the quicksand, missed the fleeing Ralad man by a hair. Any moment it might reach its mark.

Lief drew his sword and ran forward, leaving Barda standing, swaying, by the rock. He did not spare a thought for his own danger. The Ralad man's danger was too clear and urgent for that.

Jasmine's darting attacks were not slowing Jin and Jod down at all. The point of her dagger seemed to bounce off their leathery skin, and they were barely glancing at her. They were spitting with fury, and plainly far more interested in killing the Ralad man than in fighting anyone else.

It was as if the very sight of him filled them with rage. As if they knew him.

The little man was closer now. Panting in terror, he was desperately waving Lief back, pointing towards the leaves on the quicksand by the big rock and then to his own legs.

Lief realized that they had been wrong in thinking that he had fallen into the quicksand. Mud and slime coated his legs to the knees, but above that he was perfectly dry and clean. Somehow he had crossed the moat — perhaps at this exact spot.

He knows this place, Lief thought. He has been here before.

Two clear pictures flew into his mind. The cruel collar around the Ralad man's neck. The bed of moldy straw and the frayed rope in the monsters' kitchen.

And suddenly he was sure that the Ralad man had once slept on that straw, and that the collar he wore was once attached to that rope. Not long ago, he had been a prisoner of Jin and Jod. He was too small to be worth eating, so they had made him their slave. But at last he had escaped, only to be caught by the Grey Guards.

Lief, Jasmine, and Barda had left him asleep among the sweetplum bushes. He must have awoken, found himself alone, and guessed what had happened. Or perhaps he had even been roused by the shouting, and watched their capture from the bushes.

He rang the bell and threw a heavy rock into the quicksand, to lure Jin and Jod away from the house. Then he ran around to the other side of the house and crossed the moat. He returned to this terrible place, when he could have run away to safety. Why?

There could be no reason except to try to save the friends who had saved him.

Lief was only a few steps away from the running figures now. He sprang to one side, signalling to Jasmine to do the same. His mind was racing. His plan was to wait his chance, then leap between the monsters and their victim. He doubted that he and Jasmine could do more than wound them — but that, at least, would give the little man a chance to escape.

For that was the most important thing now. Not just for the Ralad man, but for them all. The small, running man with the muddy feet was the only one who could save them. Only he could tell them the way across the quicksand. Only he could tell them which of the floating leaves were safe to tread upon, and which were not.

Lief thought of the leaves as he had seen them, their strange red markings showing clearly against the shining, pale green background. Then, suddenly, he gasped.

"But he has already told us!" he exclaimed aloud.

Startled, the Ralad man glanced in his direction and stumbled. The great curved hook caught him around the waist, stopping him short and driving all the breath from his body. Jod screamed in triumph and began to pull him in.

But at the same moment Lief's sword came crashing down on the pole, cutting it through. Off balance and taken by surprise, Jod fell backwards, crashing into Jin. They went down in a tangle of lumpy, heaving flesh.

Jasmine sprang for them, her dagger raised.

"No, Jasmine!" shouted Lief, snatching the Ralad man from the ground and heaving him over his shoulder. "Leave them!"

He knew that now that he had discovered the secret of the stepping stones, speed would be far more likely to save them than fighting would.

Jin and Jod were clumsy, but very strong. If either Lief or Jasmine were wounded, it would be disastrous. The Ralad man was helpless, and Barda nearly so. They would both need help if they were to survive.

He began running back towards the rock, where Barda was anxiously waiting. After a moment's hesitation, Jasmine followed, shouting after him. He ignored her until they had reached Barda's side. Then he turned to her, panting.

"You are mad, Lief!" she cried angrily. "Now we are trapped with our backs to the quicksand! It is the worst possible place to stand and fight!"

"We are not going to stand and fight," gasped Lief, pulling the Ralad man more firmly onto his shoulder. "We are going to cross to the other side."

"But which leaves are we to trust?" Barda demanded. "Which mark the path?"

"None of them," panted Lief. "The spaces between them are the path."

He peered over Jasmine's head and his heart thumped as he saw that Jin and Jod were already scrambling to their feet. "Jasmine, you go first!" he urged. "Then you can help Barda. I will follow with the Ralad man. Make haste! They will be upon us at any moment!"

But Barda and Jasmine just gaped at him.

"The spaces between the leaves are quicksand!" Jasmine shrilled. "You can see it. If we leap upon it we will sink and die!"

"You will not die!" Lief panted desperately. "You will die if you leap anywhere else! Do as I say! Trust me!"

"But how do you know it is safe?" mumbled Barda, rubbing his hand over his brow as he tried to clear his head.

"The Ralad man told me."

"He has not said a word!" Jasmine protested.

"He pointed to this spot and then to his legs," shouted Lief. "His legs are muddy to the knees. But the leaves have not been trodden down into the mud in the last hour. They are quite clean and dry."

214

Still Barda and Jasmine hesitated.

Jin and Jod were coming. Jin's green-white, bristled face was so swollen with rage that her tiny eyes had almost disappeared. Yellow tusks jutted from her open, shrieking mouth. She was rushing towards them, the axe raised high, ready to strike.

Lief knew there was only one thing he could do. He took a breath and, holding the Ralad man tightly, jumped straight for the first gap between the leaves.

He plunged straight through the green slime. With a stab of panic he wondered if he had been wrong. He heard Jasmine and Barda crying out in horror. But then, at last, his feet touched flat rock. He had sunk only to his ankles.

With an effort he wrenched his right foot free and stepped to the next gap. Again he sank to his ankles. But again he touched firm ground.

"Come on!" he shouted over his shoulder, and with relief heard Barda and Jasmine leaping after him.

Jin and Jod squealed in fury. Lief did not turn to look. The muscles of his legs strained as he wrenched each foot free of the sucking quicksand to move on. Another step. Another . . .

And finally there was only the opposite bank ahead of him. Grass. Trees towering above. With a final, huge effort, he jumped. His feet hit solid earth and, sobbing with relief, he fell forward, feeling the weight of the Ralad man rolling from his shoulder.

He crawled to his hands and knees and turned to

look. Barda was close behind him. He was about to make the jump for the shore.

But Jasmine had stopped just behind him. She was crouching, slashing at something with her dagger. Had her foot become caught in a plant root? What was she doing?

The monster had not yet reached the edge of the moat, but Jin had raised the axe over her head. In terror, Lief realized that she was going to throw it.

"Jasmine!" he screamed.

Jasmine looked around and saw her danger. Like lightning, she stood, twisted, and jumped for the next stepping stone. The axe hurtled, spinning, towards her. It caught her on the shoulder just as she landed. With a cry she fell to her knees, slipping off the stone hidden under the green slime, toppling into the quicksand beyond. Greedily, it began to suck her down.

10 - Quick Thinking

Barda turned, swaying. He bent and caught Jasmine's arm, trying to haul her up beside him. But he was too weak to do more than stop her sinking further.

Howling in triumph, Jin and Jod lumbered forward. Any moment they would reach the big rock. And then . . .

"Leave me!" Lief heard Jasmine scream to Barda. "Take Filli — and leave me."

But Barda shook his head, and Filli clung grimly to her shoulder, refusing to move.

Desperately, Lief looked around for something he could hold out to them, to pull them in.

A tree branch, a vine . . . but there were no vines, and the branches of the trees here were thick and grew high off the ground. Never could he cut one in time. If only they had not lost their rope in the Forests of Silence! They had lost everything there. All they had were the clothes they wore . . .

Their clothes!

With a gasp of anger at his own slow wits, Lief tore off his cloak. He ran to the edge of the quicksand, twisting and knotting the soft fabric so that it made a thick cord.

"Barda!" he shouted.

Barda turned a white, strained face to look at him. Holding tightly to one end of the twisted cloak, Lief threw the other. Barda caught it.

"Give it to Jasmine!" shouted Lief. "I will pull her in!"

Even as he spoke, he knew the task was almost hopeless. Jin and Jod had reached the big rock. They were jeering, gathering themselves to spring. In moments they would be on the stepping stones, reaching for Jasmine, pulling her back towards them, tearing the cloak from Lief's hands. He would not be able to resist them.

Then, suddenly, like a miracle, a shrieking black shape plunged from the sky, straight for the monsters' heads.

Kree!

Jin and Jod shouted in shock as the black bird attacked them, its sharp beak snapping viciously. It wheeled away from their flailing arms and dived again.

Lief heaved on the cloak with all his might. He felt Jasmine's body move slowly towards him through the quicksand. Too slowly. Kree's attack was continuing, but Jod was hitting at him with the broken pole now. Surely the bird could not survive for long.

Desperately, Lief pulled again, and then felt two hands close over his own. Barda had reached the bank and was adding his strength to the task. Together they heaved on the cloak, digging their heels into the soft ground. And as they heaved, Jasmine's body moved, coming closer and closer to the bank.

She was beyond the last of the pale leaves and almost within reach of the bank when Kree shrieked. The lashing pole had caught him on the wing. He was fluttering crazily in the air, losing height.

Howling like beasts, free from the bird's attacks at last, Jin and Jod leaped together onto the first stepping stone. Lief caught a glimpse of Jod's metal teeth, gnashing in furious triumph.

Soon they will have Jasmine, he thought in despair. They will have her, and they will have us, too. They know we could not leave her. They know we will come after her, if they drag her away . . .

But Jasmine had twisted her head to look over her shoulder. It seemed she was thinking only of Kree. "Kree!" she called. "Get to the other side! Make haste!"

The bird was dazed and in pain, but he obeyed

the call. He fluttered across the moat, one wing barely moving, his feet almost touching the green slime. He reached the bank and fell to the ground.

Lief and Barda hauled on the cloak, their arms straining. One more pull and Jasmine would be near enough for them to reach her. One more pull . . .

But Jin and Jod were charging across the moat towards them. The bright patches of green slime between the pale leaves marked their path clearly. They did not hesitate. Already they were almost in the center.

As Lief watched in horror they lunged forward once more, roaring savagely, their clawed hands reaching for their prey.

And then their faces changed, and they shrieked. Their feet had plunged through the green slime — but found no safe ground beneath. Bellowing in shock and terror, they sank like stones, their arms thrashing frantically as their great weight drove them down.

And in seconds it was all over. The horrible screams were smothered. They were gone.

Dazed and trembling, Lief reached out and grasped Jasmine's wrist. Barda took the other, and together they dragged her up onto the bank. Her injured shoulder must have given her great pain, for she was white to the lips, but she did not murmur.

"What happened?" Barda gasped. "How did they sink? There were stepping stones there — we trod on them ourselves! How could they vanish?"

Jasmine managed a grim smile. "The stepping stones did not vanish," she muttered. "They are under the leaves I cut and moved. The monsters trod in the wrong places — the places where the leaves were floating before. I knew they would be too stupid, and too angry, to notice that the pattern had changed. They just went from one bright green patch to the next, as they always had."

Lief stared at the moat. He had not noticed the change to the leaf pattern, either. Even now he could not quite remember exactly how it had been.

Wincing with pain, Jasmine pulled out the tiny jar that she wore attached to a chain around her neck. Lief knew what the jar held: a little of the Nectar of Life that had cured Barda when he was injured in the Forests of Silence.

He thought that Jasmine was going to use it on her gashed shoulder, but instead she crawled to where Kree lay. The black bird struggled feebly on a patch of bare, sandy earth, his beak gaping and his eyes closed. One wing was spread out uselessly.

"You did not go home, wicked Kree," Jasmine crooned. "You followed me. Did I not tell you there would be danger? Now your poor wing is hurt. But do not fear. Soon you will be well."

She unscrewed the lid of the jar and shook one drop of the golden liquid onto the broken wing.

Kree made a harsh, croaking sound and blinked his eyes. He moved a little. Then, all at once, he stood

221

up on his feet, fluffed his feathers, and spread both wings wide, flapping them vigorously and squawking loudly.

Lief and Barda laughed with pleasure at the sight. It was so good to see Kree well and strong again — and just as good to see Jasmine's radiant face.

There was a muffled sound behind them and they turned to see the Ralad man sitting up, blinking in confusion. His patch of red hair stood up like a crest. His eyes stared wildly around him.

"Do not fear, my friend!" cried Barda. "They are gone. Gone forever!"

Lief left them and went to Jasmine. She was sitting on the grass beside the sandy patch of earth, with Filli chattering in her ear. They were both watching Kree soaring and diving above them, testing his wings.

"Let me use the nectar on your shoulder, Jasmine," Lief said, sitting down beside her.

The girl shook her head. "We must save the nectar for important things," she said briefly. She dug in her pocket and brought out the jar of cream with which she had treated the Ralad man's wrists and ankles. "This will do for me," she said. "The wound is not serious."

Lief wanted to argue with her, but decided he would not. He was beginning to learn that it was best to allow Jasmine to do things her own way.

The shoulder was badly bruised. Now it was

swollen and angry red. Soon it would be deep purple. The wound in the center of the bruise was small, but deep. The corner of the axe blade must have struck there.

As gently as he could, Lief smeared the wound with the strong-smelling green cream. Jasmine sat very still and did not utter a sound, though the pain must have been great.

Barda came up to them with the Ralad man, who nodded and smiled at them, then put the palms of his hands together and bowed.

"His name is Manus. He wishes to thank you for saving him from the Guards, and from Jin and Jod," Barda said. "He says he owes us a great debt."

"You owe us nothing, Manus," said Lief, smiling back at the little man. "You risked your life for us, too."

Manus bent and, with his long, thin finger, rapidly made a row of marks in the sand beside him.

" 'You saved me twice from death,' " Barda translated slowly. " 'My life is yours.' "

Manus nodded vigorously, and it was only then that Lief realized that he was unable to speak.

Barda saw his surprise. "None of the Ralads

have voices, Lief," he said gruffly. "Thaegan saw to that, long ago. It was when, out of spite and jealousy, she created the Lake of Tears from the beauty of D'Or. The Ralads of that time raised their voices against her. She — put a stop to it. Not just for them, but for all who came after them. There have been no words spoken in Raladin for a hundred years."

Lief felt a chill. What sort of mad, evil being was this sorceress? Then he thought of something else, and glanced at the silent quicksand. Somewhere in those depths lay Jin and Jod, their wickedness stifled forever.

How long would it be before Thaegan found out? A month? A week? A day? An hour? Or was she flying towards them, filled with rage, at this very moment?

Thaegan had stolen the voices of a whole people because they had dared to speak against her. What sort of horrible revenge would she take on Barda, Jasmine, and Lief, who had caused the deaths of two of her children?

Run! whispered a small, shuddering voice in his head. *Run home, crawl into your bed and pull the covers over your head. Hide. Be safe.*

He felt a hand touch his arm, and looked up to see Manus beckoning to him urgently.

"Manus is anxious to be well away from here before the sun goes down," Barda said. "He fears that Thaegan may come. We all need rest, but I have agreed that we will walk as far as we can before making camp. Are you ready?"

Lief took a deep breath, banished the whispering voice from his mind, and nodded. "Yes," he said. "I am ready."

11 ~ To Raladin

That night they slept under a cluster of sweet-plum bushes far away from any stream or path. None of them wanted to be seen by anyone who might tell Thaegan where they were.

They were cold and uncomfortable, for their clothes were still damp and stiff with mud and they could not risk lighting a fire. But still they fell asleep at once, exhausted by all that had befallen them.

Sometime after midnight, Lief stirred. Moonlight shone palely through the leaves of the bushes, making shadows and patches of light on the ground. Everything was very silent. He turned over and tried to settle to rest once more. But, though his body still ached with weariness, thoughts had begun chasing one another through his mind, and sleep would not come.

Beside him, Manus was sighing and twitching — tormented, no doubt, by dreams.

It was not surprising that it should be so. Using signs and the strange picture-writing of his people, Manus had told them that he had been a prisoner of Jin and Jod for five long years. He had been making his way from Raladin to Del when, lured from the path by the tempting scent of the sweetplum bushes, he had fallen into the quicksand and been captured.

Lief could not bear to think of the long misery that the little man had suffered since then. Barda's understanding of Ralad's writing was not complete — but still he could translate enough to tell the terrible story.

Manus had been forced to work like a slave, beaten, starved, and treated with terrible cruelty. Tied to the wall of the kitchen, he had been forced to watch helplessly as Jin and Jod trapped, killed, and ate victim after helpless victim. Finally he had escaped — only to be seized by the troop of Grey Guards when he was almost home, and forced to march back the way he had come.

For five years he had lived with fear and loathing in the company of wickedness.

No wonder his sleep was haunted by nightmares.

When Lief asked him how long the journey to Raladin would take, he had answered quickly, scribbling on the earth with his finger.

"Three days," Barda said heavily, looking at the marks. "If Thaegan does not catch us first."

If Thaegan does not catch us first . . .

Lief lay hunched on the ground and shivered as he thought of the letter "T" and the question mark. Where was Thaegan now? What was she doing? What orders was she giving?

The darkness of the night seemed to press in on him. The silence was heavy and menacing. Perhaps, even now, Thaegan's demons were stealing towards him like flickering shadows. Perhaps they were stretching out long, thin hands to clutch feet and ankles and drag him, screaming, away . . .

Sweat broke out on his forehead. A gasp of terror caught in his throat. He fought to stay still, not to wake the others. But the fear grew in him until he felt as though he must scream aloud.

The topaz protects its wearer from the terrors of the night . . .

He scrabbled under his shirt and pressed his shaking fingers against the golden gem. Almost at once the shadows seemed to shrink, and the terrible beating of his heart slowed.

Panting, he rolled onto his back and stared up through the leaves of the sweetplum bush. The moon was three-quarters of the way to full. Black against the starry sky was the proud shape of Kree, perched on the branch of a dead tree above them. The bird's head was up, and his yellow eyes shone in the moonlight.

He was not sleeping. He was alert. He was on guard.

Strangely comforted, Lief turned onto his side again. Only three days, he thought. Only three days to Raladin. And Thaegan will not catch us. She will not.

He closed his eyes and, still clutching the topaz, let his mind slowly relax into sleep.

In the morning they set off again. At first they kept to small, well-hidden paths, but little by little they were forced into the open as the trees and bushes became less and the ground grew more parched.

They met no one. Now and again they passed houses and larger buildings where once grain had been stored or animals tended. All were deserted and falling into ruins. Some were marked with the Shadow Lord's brand.

At evening, as the light began to fail, they chose an empty house and set up camp there for the night. They filled their waterbags at the well and helped themselves to any food they found that was not spoiled.

They took other supplies, too, collecting rope, blankets, clothes, a small digging tool, a pot to boil water, candles, and a lantern.

Lief felt uneasy about taking things that belonged to others. But Manus, grieving at every sign of fear, destruction, and despair in the house, shook his head and pointed to a small mark scratched on the wall beside the window. It was the same mark he had made in the dust when he first saw them in the clearing.

He trusted them enough, now, to tell them what the mark meant. It was the Ralad sign both for a bird and for freedom. But it had spread far beyond Raladin, and had taken on a special meaning throughout Deltora. Carefully, Manus explained what the meaning was:

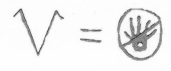

The freedom mark had become a secret signal used between those who had sworn to resist the tyranny of the Shadow Lord. By it they recognized one another — and told enemies from friends.

Before the owners of this deserted house had died or fled, they had left the mark for any future traveler of their kind to find. It was the only way they had of showing their defiance in defeat, and their hope for the future. It made Lief understand that they would have been glad to give anything they had to help the cause.

It was indeed fortunate that we found Manus, he thought. It is almost as if fate has brought us together for a purpose. As if our steps are being guided by an unseen hand.

He was half ashamed of the thought. Like his friends in Del, he had always jeered at such talk. But his journey had taught him that there were many things of which his friends in Del knew nothing, and many mysteries he was still to understand.

※

They moved on the next morning, and now that they knew what to look for they saw the freedom mark everywhere. It was chalked on crumbling walls and fences, marked out with pebbles on the ground, scratched into the trunks of trees.

Every time he saw it, hope rose in Lief. The sign was evidence that, however things were in the city of Del, in the countryside there were still people who were as willing as he was to defy the Shadow Lord.

Manus himself, however, was growing more and more serious and worried. The sight of the deserted countryside, the ruined houses, made his fears for his own village grow stronger with every step he took.

He had first left home, it seemed, when his people heard that the Shadow Lord wanted more slaves, and that his eyes were fixed on Raladin. The Shadow Lord had heard that the Ralads were hard workers of great strength and builders beyond compare.

Manus was to seek help from the resistance groups that the Ralads thought must exist in Del. They did not know that resistance in the city had been crushed long ago, and that their hopes of help were in vain.

Manus had been away over five years — years in which Thaegan had laid the land further to waste. He had no idea what he might find in Raladin.

But doggedly he moved on, hurrying despite his exhaustion. By the end of the third day it was all they could do to persuade him to rest for the night.

Lief would long remember what happened the next morning.

They rose as dawn broke and left the cottage where they had taken shelter. Almost running, Manus led them across an open field and plunged into a patch of scrubby bushes beyond.

There was a small, deep pool there, fed by a little

stream that bubbled down from some gentle hills. Manus moved up the stream, sometimes splashing through the water, sometimes trotting along the bank. They followed, keeping up with difficulty, trying to keep his bobbing red top-knot in sight when he drew ahead.

He did not speak a word. All of them could feel his tension as he neared the place he had missed for so long. But when at last they reached a waterfall that cascaded in a fine veil from a sheet of rock, he stopped.

He turned and waited for them, his small face completely without expression. But even when they reached him, he did not move.

We have arrived, thought Lief. But Manus is afraid to go the last step. He is afraid of what he will find.

The silence grew long. Finally, Jasmine spoke.

"It is best to know," she said quietly.

Manus stared at her for a moment. Then abruptly he turned and plunged through the water-fall.

One by one the three companions went after him, shivering as icy water drenched them. There was darkness beyond — first the darkness of a cave, and then the greater darkness of a tunnel. And finally there was a soft glow in the distance that grew brighter and brighter as they moved towards it.

Then they were climbing through an opening on

the other side of the hill, blinking in the sunlight. A pebbled path ran down from the opening to a beautiful village of small, round houses, workshops, and halls, all simply but craftily made of curved, baked earth bricks. The buildings surrounded a square paved with large, flat stones. In the center of the square a fountain splashed, its clear, running water sparkling in the sunlight.

But there were no lights in the houses. Spiders had spun thick webs over the windows. The doors hung open, creaking as they swung to and fro in the gentle breeze.

And there was no other movement. None at all.

12 - Music

They trudged down the pebbled path to the village and began searching for signs of life. Lief and Jasmine looked carefully and slowly, their hearts growing heavier by the moment. Manus ran desperately into one house after another, with Barda pacing grimly behind him.

Every house was deserted. What had not been taken from inside had been destroyed.

When finally they met by the fountain in the square, the Ralad man's face was lined with grief.

"Manus thinks that his people have been taken to the Shadowlands, or are dead," Barda murmured.

"They may simply have moved away from here, Manus," said Lief. "They may have escaped."

The Ralad man shook his head vigorously.

"They would never have left Raladin willingly," said Barda. "It has always been their place."

He pointed at the piles of rubbish and the ashes of fires that dotted the streets and the square. "Grey Guards' leavings," he said, curling his lip in disgust. "They must have been using the village as a resting place for some time. And see how thickly the spider-web coats the windows. I would say that Raladin has been empty for a year or more."

Manus slumped onto the edge of the fountain. His feet kicked against something caught between a paving stone and the fountain edge. He bent and picked it up. It was a long flute, carved from wood. He cradled it in his arms and bowed his head.

"What are we to do?" whispered Lief, watching him.

Jasmine shrugged. "Rest for a day, then move on," she said. "We are not far now from the Lake of Tears. Manus will guide us the rest of the way, I am sure. There is nothing to keep him here."

Her voice was flat and cold, but this time Lief was not deceived into thinking that she cared nothing for the Ralad man. He knew now how well she cloaked her feelings.

Suddenly, a beautiful, clear sound filled the air. Startled, Lief looked up.

Manus had put the flute to his lips and was playing. His eyes were closed, and he was swaying from side to side.

Lief stood, spellbound, as the pure, running notes filled his ears and his mind. It was the most exquisite music he had ever heard, and the most heart-breaking. It was as though all the feelings of grief and loss that Manus could not speak aloud were pouring through the flute, straight from his heart.

Lief's eyes stung with tears. In Del he had never cried, fearing to be thought unmanly. But here and now, he felt no shame.

He could feel Barda, motionless beside him. He could see Jasmine nearby, her green eyes dark with pity. Filli was sitting bolt upright in Jasmine's arms, staring at Manus in wonder, and Kree was perched on her shoulder, still as a statue. All of them were caught and held, as he was, by the sound of Manus mourning his lost people.

Just then, behind Jasmine, in the corner of the square, Lief saw something move. He blinked furiously, thinking at first that his wet eyes were playing tricks. But there was no mistake. One of the huge paving stones was tilting!

He made a choking sound as a cry of alarm stuck in his throat. He saw Jasmine glance at him, startled, and turn to look behind her.

The stone was moving noiselessly from its place. Beneath it was a deep space glowing with warm light. Something was moving there!

Lief caught a single glimpse of a red-tufted head, and peering black button eyes. And then, with one, quick movement of a long-fingered, blue-grey hand, the stone was thrust completely aside. In moments, dozens of Ralads were clambering out into the open and rushing towards Manus.

Gaping in amazement, Lief turned and saw that exactly the same thing was happening at the other three corners of the square. Stones were sliding open and Ralad people were popping out of the holes beneath like corn from a hot pan.

There were dozens of them . . . hundreds! Adults and children of all ages. All of them were clapping, laughing, rushing to greet Manus, who had sprung up, dropping the flute, his face alight with joy.

※

Hours later, bathed, filled with good food, and resting on soft couches of bracken fern and blankets, Lief, Barda, and Jasmine looked with wonder at what the Ralads had made in a few short years.

The cavern was huge. Lanterns filled it with soft light. There was a stream of water at one side, running into a deep, clear pool. Fresh, sweet air blew softly through pipes that ran through the chimneys of the houses above and opened to the sky. On the ground were cottages, storehouses, and a meeting hall. There were even streets and a central square like the one above their heads.

"What labor it must have been, to hollow out this cavern and make a hidden village here," Lief murmured. "It is like the secret tunnel their ancestors dug under the palace in Del. But so much larger!"

Barda nodded sleepily. "I told you the Ralads

were tireless workers and clever builders," he said. "And I told you they would never abandon Raladin. But even I did not suspect this!"

"And, plainly, Thaegan and the Grey Guards do not suspect it either," yawned Jasmine, who was lying back with her eyes closed. "The Guards camp above this very spot, with no idea that the Ralads are below."

"*We* had no idea, until they showed themselves," said Lief. "And they only did that because they heard the sound of the flute."

Jasmine laughed. She looked more peaceful than Lief had ever seen her. "It is good. The Shadow Lord must be very angry because the Ralads have slipped through his fingers. The more time the Guards take searching for them, the less time they will have to trouble us."

Lief watched Manus, who, surrounded by his friends, was still describing his adventures and the dangers he had faced since last seeing them. He was scribbling on a wall of the cavern with some sort of chalk, rubbing marks out almost as soon as he had written them.

"Do you think Manus will still lead us to the Lake of Tears?" he asked.

"He will," Barda murmured. "But not for a few days, I suspect. And that is good. It will force us to rest, and it is rest that we need, more than anything." He stretched lazily. "I am going to sleep," he announced. "It is still day, but who can tell down here?"

Lief nodded, but Jasmine made no reply. She was already asleep.

Soon afterwards, Manus turned away from the wall and went with his friends to the square in the middle of the cavern. All the Ralads seemed to be going there. Lazily, Lief wondered what they were doing, but in moments he understood.

Soft music filled the air — the sound of hundreds of flutes singing together of thankfulness, happiness, friends, and peace. The Ralads were celebrating the return of one they thought was lost. And Manus was among them, pouring into his own flute his heart's joy.

Lief lay still and let the music wash over him in waves of sweetness. He felt his eyelids drooping and did not fight it. He knew that Barda was right. For the first time in days they could sleep peacefully, knowing they were safe from harm and surprise. They should take all the rest they could while they had the chance.

✳

They passed three more days in Raladin. In that time they learned much about the Ralads and their life.

They learned, for example, that the little people did not stay below ground all the time. When it was safe, they spent their days outside. They tended the food gardens hidden nearby. They checked and repaired the pipes that brought air to the cavern and the alarms that alerted them when people approached the village. They taught the children to build and mend, and simply enjoyed the sunlight.

One thing they never did in the open was to play their music. They could not risk being heard. They played only underground, stopping immediately if the alarms warned them of intruders. It was a miracle that Manus had found the flute by the fountain. It had been lost and forgotten years ago, while the Ralads were still digging their hiding place in secret. It had lain in its place ever since, as if waiting for him.

On their fourth morning, the companions knew that it was time to leave. They were much stronger, well fed and well rested. Jasmine's wound had almost healed. Their clothes were clean and dry, and the Ralads had given each of them a bag of supplies.

They climbed to the surface with heavy hearts. They had no further reason to stay, but none of them wanted to go. This time of safety and peace had made the task ahead of them seem even more grim and terrifying.

Now, at last, they told the Ralads where they planned to go. Manus had told them to keep this secret for as long as they could, and now they found out why.

The people were horrified. They clustered around the travelers, refusing to let them pass, clutching Manus with all their strength. Then they began scribbling on the ground so fast that even Barda could not understand what they had written.

"We know the Lake of Tears is bewitched and forbidden," Lief told them. "We know we will face danger there. But we have faced danger before."

The people shook their heads in despair at their foolishness. Again they began scribbling on the ground — many, many signs of wickedness and death, with one sign larger than any other and repeated many times.

"What does that mean? What is it they especially fear?" whispered Lief to Manus.

Manus grimaced and wrote a single, clear word in the dust.

SOLDEEN

13 - The Lake of Tears

Jasmine frowned. "What is Soldeen?" she asked. But Manus could not, or would not, explain.

"Whatever this Soldeen is, we must face it," growled Barda. "As we must face Thaegan, if she pursues us."

The Ralads drew together at the mention of Thaegan's name. Their faces were very grave. Plainly, they thought the travelers did not understand their peril, and that meant that Manus was doomed to die with them, for he was determined to be their guide.

"Do not fear," Lief said grimly. "We have weapons. If Thaegan tries her tricks on us, we will kill her!"

The people shook their heads and scribbled again. Barda bent, frowning over the lines.

"They say she cannot be killed," he said at last, reluctantly. "The only way to kill a witch is to draw

243

blood. And Thaegan's whole body is armored by magic. Many have tried to pierce it. All have failed, and died."

Lief glanced at Jasmine. Her eyes were fixed on Kree, who was flying high above them, stretching his wings.

Lief bit his lip and looked back at the Ralads. "Then we will hide from her," he told them. "We will hide, we will creep, we will do everything we can to avoid her notice. But we must go to the Lake of Tears. We must."

The tallest of the Ralads, a woman called Simone, stepped forward and scrawled on the ground.

"We cannot tell you why," said Barda. "But please believe that we do not go into danger out of reckless foolishness. We are pledged to a quest that is for the good of Deltora and all its people."

Simone looked at him keenly, then slowly nodded. And after that the Ralads stood aside and let the travelers walk down the narrow path that wound away from the village.

Manus led the way, his head high. He did not look back, but Lief did.

The people were standing very still, crowded together, watching them. Their hands were pressed to their hearts. And they did not move until the travelers were out of sight.

✳

By mid-afternoon the way had grown rough and the hills more rugged. Dead trees held bleached, white branches up to the pale sky. The grass crackled under the travelers' feet, and the low-growing bushes were dusty and dry.

There were scuttlings in the bushes, and rustlings in dark holes beneath the tree roots, but they saw no living creature. The air was heavy and still, and it seemed hard to breathe. They stopped for food and water, but sat only for a short time before moving on. The scuttling sounds were not pleasant, and they had the feeling that they were being watched.

As the sun sank lower in the sky, Manus began to walk more and more slowly, his feet dragging as though he was forcing them to move. His companions trudged behind him in single file, watching the ground which had become treacherous, filled with cracks and holes and littered with stones. They all knew, without being told, that they were nearing the end of their journey.

Finally, they came upon a place where the bases

245

of two steep, rocky hills met, making a narrow "V" shape. Through the gap they could see the red-stained sky and the fiery ball of the setting sun, glowing like a danger sign.

The Ralad man stumbled to a stop and leaned against one of the rocks. His skin was as grey as dust, his small black eyes were blank with fear.

"Manus, is the Lake — " Lief had not spoken for so long that his voice sounded like a croak. He swallowed, and began again. "Is the Lake just beyond these rocks?"

Manus nodded.

"Then there is no need for you to come any farther," said Barda. "You have guided us here, and that is all we ask of you. Go home now to your friends. They will be waiting anxiously for your return."

But Manus firmed his lips and shook his head. He took a stone and wrote on the rock.

This time Lief did not have to wait for Barda to read what the Ralad man had written. He had seen this message before. "You saved me twice from death. My life is yours."

He, Jasmine, and Barda all began to speak at once, but nothing they could say would change

Manus's mind. In fact, their arguments seemed to strengthen him. His breathing slowed, his color returned, and his dull eyes began to shine with determination.

At last, he decided to take action. He turned abruptly and almost ran to the gap between the rocks. In moments he had disappeared from view. They had no choice but to run after him.

They stumbled through the narrow passage in single file, keeping as close to the Ralad man, and to one another, as they could. So intent were they on their task that they were not prepared for what they saw when finally they reached the end of the pass.

Not far below them was a murky lake ringed by banks of thick, grey mud riddled with what looked like worm holes. In its center a slimy rock oozed water which dripped ceaselessly into the pool, causing slow, oily ripples to creep across its surface.

Twisted, barren peaks of clay rose beyond the lake like haunted things. There was not one green, growing thing to be seen. There was no sound but the dripping of water and the faint, squelching movements of mud. There were no smells but damp and decay. It was a place of bitterness, ugliness, misery, and death.

Lief's stomach churned. The Lake of Tears was well named. This, then, was what the sorceress Thaegan had made of the town of D'Or — the town that Jasmine had said was "like a garden." He heard Barda cursing softly beside him, and Jasmine hissing to Filli and Kree.

Manus simply stared, shivering, at the horror he had heard of all his life, but never seen. The demonstration of Thaegan's jealousy and wickedness. The evil that had caused his people to speak out, and receive a terrible punishment.

"Is the Belt warm?" Barda murmured in Lief's ear. "Does it feel the presence of a gem?"

Lief shook his head. "We must go closer," he whispered back.

Manus glanced at him curiously. They had spoken in low voices, but he had heard what they had said.

He has come this far with us, Lief thought. We must tell him something of what we are trying to do, at least. He will certainly find out in the end, if we are successful.

"We are searching for a special stone that we believe is hidden here," he told the Ralad man carefully. "But the matter is a deadly secret. If we find what we seek, you must tell no one, whatever happens."

Manus nodded, his hand on his heart.

Slowly they scrambled down the last of the rocks until they reached the mud that circled the Lake.

"This mud may not be safe," murmured Jasmine, remembering the quicksand.

"There is only one way to find out," Barda said,

and stepped forward. He sank to his ankles in the fine, grey ooze, but that was all.

Cautiously, the others joined him. Dropping the bags from their backs, they walked together to the edge of the Lake, their feet leaving deep holes where they trod. Lief crouched and touched the water with the tips of his fingers.

Immediately, the Belt around his waist warmed. His heart gave a great thud.

"The gem is here," he said in a low voice. "It must be somewhere under the water."

His ankle itched and absent-mindedly he put down his hand to scratch it. His fingers touched something that felt like slimy jelly. He glanced down and cried out with disgusted horror. His ankle was covered with huge, pale worms. Already they were swelling and darkening as they sucked his blood. He leapt up and kicked wildly, trying to shake them off.

"Be still!" shouted Jasmine. She sprang forward and caught Lief's foot in her hand. Her mouth twisted with distaste, she began pulling the squirming things off one by one, flicking them aside.

The swollen bodies scattered onto the grey mud and into the water, and Lief's stomach heaved as other mouths, other crawling hungers of every shape and size, coiled out of the ooze to snatch them up as they fell.

Suddenly the mud was alive with slimy things

twisting, creeping, slithering out of hiding. They fought for the worms, tearing them to shreds, and in seconds were winding around the travelers' feet and legs, wriggling eagerly upwards to find warm, bare flesh on which to feast.

Jasmine could help Lief no longer. Now his ears were ringing with her panic-stricken cries, and Barda's, as well as his own. Manus could not cry out. He was staggering, nearly covered by coiling shapes — shapes with no eyes, shapes that made no sound.

There was no hope. Soon they would be overwhelmed — eaten alive . . .

Filli screamed piteously. Kree, attacking from the air, tore at the beasts on Jasmine's arms, fighting as they coiled around his feet and wings, pulling him down.

Then, abruptly, as though on some sort of signal, the creatures froze. In their hundreds they began dropping to the ground and burrowing beneath the surface of the mud. In moments, they had all disappeared.

An eerie silence fell.

Shuddering all over, Jasmine began brushing frantically at her legs, arms, and clothes as if she still felt slimy things crawling over her body.

But Lief stood, dazed. "What happened?" he asked huskily. "Why . . . ?"

"Perhaps they do not like how we taste," said Barda, with a shaky laugh. He turned to give his hand to Manus, who had fallen to his knees in the churned mud.

It was then that Lief saw a trail of bubbles moving from the center of the Lake towards them. Moving fast.

"Barda! Jasmine!" he shrieked. But the warnings had no sooner left his mouth than the oily water beside them heaved and a huge, hideous creature rose from the depths.

Slime dripped from its skin. Its gaping mouth, lined with needle-sharp teeth, swirled with water, worms, and mud. Wicked spines sprouted, gleaming, from its back and sides and sprang like narrow spears from the flesh under its eyes, which burned with ravenous, endless hunger.

It lunged for them, throwing its body onto the shore with a hissing roar that chilled Lief's blood.

He knew that this was Soldeen.

14 ~ Soldeen

L ief stumbled back, frantically drawing his
sword. Then he saw that Barda and Manus were
the monster's chosen victims. They had fallen,
and were frantically scrabbling in the mud, trying to
escape. But Soldeen was almost upon them, his terrible jaws snapping shut and opening wide in an instant, like a huge, cruel trap.

Barely knowing what he was doing, Lief darted
forward, shouting at the creature, plunging his sword
into the vast, spiny neck.

The sword was torn from his hand as Soldeen
swung around, the weapon still hanging, quivering,
from his slimy hide. The blade was like a thorn to him
— no more than a stinging irritation — but he was not
used to defiance. He was angry now, as well as hungry.

He lunged at Lief, mouth agape. Lief leapt away — and sprawled heavily over the bags still lying on the mud where they had been dropped only minutes before.

He lay flat on his back, stunned. He heard Barda and Jasmine shrieking to him in terror, screaming at him to get up, to run!

But it was too late to run. And he had no weapon. He had nothing to protect himself from those terrible jaws, those needle teeth. Except . . .

He twisted and seized two of the bags by their straps. With all his strength he swung and threw them, straight into that gaping mouth, right to the back of the throat.

Soldeen reared back, choking for breath, shaking his great head from side to side. His tail lashed, churning the water to muddy foam. The sword flew out of his neck, turned in the air, and speared into the mud by Lief's foot.

Lief grasped it, sprang to his feet, and ran, ran for his life, shrieking for his companions to follow. He knew they had only moments to escape. Soldeen would swallow the bags, or cough them up, in no time.

Only when he reached the rocks did he look back. Barda was clambering up beside him with Manus in his arms. Jasmine, Filli, and Kree were close behind.

And Soldeen was sliding back into the Lake of Tears. He was sliding back into the murky depths, and disappearing from sight.

✳

Darkness came. They stayed upon the rocks, unwilling to move away from the Lake, though fearing another attack from the dark water at any moment.

Jasmine's supplies were gone, and Barda's also, for by chance it was their packs that Lief had thrown at Soldeen. The four companions huddled miserably together, sharing the blankets that remained and a damp meal that tasted of mud and worms. Slitherings, squelchings, and the sound of dripping water from the weeping rock set their nerves on edge.

As the full moon rose, flooding the Lake with its ghostly light, they tried to talk, to plan, to decide what they should do. If a gem was somewhere in the mud beneath that murky water, how could it ever be found?

They could return to Raladin for the proper tools and try to drain the Lake. But the work would take months, and none of them really believed that they would survive to complete it. Soldeen, the creatures of the mud, and Thaegan herself would see to that.

Two of them could try to lure Soldeen to the water's edge at one side of the Lake, while the other two dived for the gem on the other side. But in their hearts they all knew that such a scheme was doomed to failure. Soldeen would feel the movement in his waters, turn, and attack.

Gradually, as the hours crept by, they fell silent. Their cause seemed hopeless. The heavy sadness of the place had seeped into their very souls.

Remembering that the topaz was at its strongest at full moon, Lief put his hand upon it. Hope swelled in him as his mind cleared. But no great idea or wonderful knowledge came into his mind — only one fixed thought. They must at all costs fight this sadness. They must fight the feeling that they could never win, or defeat was certain.

They needed something that would lift them from their despair. Something to give them hope.

He turned to the Ralad man, who was sitting with his head bowed, his hands clasped between his knees.

"Play your flute, Manus," he begged. "Make us think of times and places other than this."

Manus looked at him in surprise, then fumbled in his bag and brought out the wooden flute. He hesitated for a moment, then put it to his lips and began to play.

Music rose in lilting waves, filling the dead air with beauty. The flute spoke of crystal-clear water trickling in cool shade, of birds singing in leafy green, of children playing and friends laughing, of flowers lifting their faces to the sun.

Lief felt as if a deadening weight was falling from his shoulders. He saw in the faces of Barda and Jasmine, and even in Manus himself, a dawning hope. Now they remembered what they were fighting for.

He closed his eyes, the better to feel the music. So he did not see the trail of bubbles breaking sluggishly on the surface of the Lake as something surged silently towards the shore.

But then, suddenly, the music stopped. Lief opened his eyes and looked in surprise at Manus. The Ralad man was rigid, the flute still held to his lips. His eyes, wide and glazed with fear, were staring straight ahead. Slowly, Lief turned to see what he was looking at.

It was Soldeen.

Muddy water poured from his back and slime dripped from the holes and lumps in his mottled skin as he slid onto the shore, forcing a great trough in the ooze. He was huge — far larger than they had realized. If he lunged for them now, he could reach them. He could crush them all with one snap of his terrible jaws.

And yet he did not attack. He watched them, waiting.

"Back!" Barda muttered under his breath. "Back away. Slowly . . ."

"DO NOT MOVE!" the hollow, growling command lashed out at them, freezing them to the spot.

Shocked, terrified, and confused, they stared, unable to believe that it was the monster who had spoken. And yet already he was turning his burning eyes to the trembling Manus, and was speaking again.

"PLAY!" he ordered.

Manus forced his lips and fingers to move. At last, the music began again, hesitating and feeble at first, but gaining in strength.

Soldeen closed his eyes. He was utterly still, poised half in and half out of the water. Like a hideous statue he faced them, while mingled mud and slime slowly dried on his skin in lumpy streaks.

Lief felt a light touch on his leg. Manus was nudging him with his foot, making signals with his eyes. *This is your chance to escape*, Manus's eyes were saying. *Climb up the rocks, move back through the pass, while he is distracted.*

Lief hesitated. Jasmine jerked her head at him impatiently. *Go!* her frown told him. *You have the Belt. You, at least, must survive, or all is lost.*

But it was too late. Soldeen's eyes had opened once more, and this time they were fixed on Lief.

"Why have you come to this forbidden place?" he growled.

Lief wet his lips. What should he say?

"Do not try to lie," Soldeen warned. "For I will know if you do, and I will kill you."

The music of the flute fluttered and stopped as if Manus had suddenly lost his breath.

"PLAY!" roared Soldeen, without moving his

gaze from Lief. Tremblingly, the Ralad man obeyed.

Lief made his decision. He lifted his chin. "We have come to seek a certain stone, which has special meaning for us," he said clearly, over the soft, wavering sound of the flute. "It was dropped from the sky, into this Lake, over sixteen years ago."

"I know nothing of time," hissed the beast. "But . . . I know of the stone. I knew that one day someone would seek it."

Lief forced himself to continue, though his throat seemed choked. "Do you know where it is?" he asked.

"It is in my keeping," growled Soldeen. "It is my prize — the only thing in this bitter and lonely place that comforts me in my misery. Do you think that I would let you take it, with nothing in return?"

"Name your price!" called Barda. "If it is within our power, we will pay it. We will go from here and find whatever — "

Soldeen hissed, and seemed to smile. "There is no need for you to search for my price," he said softly. "I will give you the stone in return for — a companion." He turned his great head to look at Manus.

15 - The Sorceress

Lief felt a chill run through him. He swallowed.

"We cannot — " he began.

"Give the little man to me," hissed Soldeen. "I like his face, and the music he makes. He will come into the Lake with me and sit upon the weeping stone. He will play to me through the endless days, the lonely nights. He will ease my pain, for as long as he lives."

Lief heard Jasmine draw a sharp breath and looked around. Manus had risen, and was stepping forward.

"No, Manus!" cried Barda, catching his arm.

Manus was very pale, but his head was high. He strained against Barda's grip.

"He wishes to join me," hissed Soldeen. "Let him come."

"We will not!" shrieked Jasmine, catching Manus

by the other arm. "He would sacrifice himself for us, but we will not allow it!"

"Give him to me, or I will kill you," growled Soldeen, the spines rising on his back. "I will tear you apart, and your flesh will be devoured by the creatures of the mud until there is nothing left but bones."

A wave of anger rose in Lief, burning like fire. He jumped up and threw himself in front of Manus, protecting him from the front, as Barda and Jasmine were protecting him at the sides. "Then do it!" he shouted, drawing his sword. "But if you do you will kill your companion, too, for you are too large to take one of us without the others!"

"WE SHALL SEE!" roared Soldeen, lunging forward. Lief braced himself for the attack, but at the last moment the beast twisted like a serpent, and three of the swordlike spines beneath his eyes ran under Lief's arm, tearing his shirt to ribbons and running through the folds of his cloak.

One easy toss of Soldeen's head, and Lief was jerked away from Manus and swung off his feet. For two terrifying seconds he dangled in midair, fighting for breath as the strangling ties of the cloak bit into his throat.

There was a roaring in his ears and a red haze before his eyes. He knew that in moments he would be unconscious. The cloak was double-tied, and he could not unfasten it. There was only one thing he could do. With the last of his strength he twisted, swung himself up, and caught one of the spines in his hands.

Immediately, the choking band around his neck loosened. Panting, he pulled himself up until he was sitting on the spine. He edged along it until he was just under the beast's eye.

His shirt had been torn away, and he shuddered at the feel of Soldeen's slippery, ridged hide on his bare skin. But still he clung there, pressing himself close, his sword steady in his hand.

"Drag me down into the mud and slime and drown me, if you will, Soldeen," he muttered. "But while we are gone my friends will escape. And I will plunge my sword into your eye before I die, I promise you. Will you enjoy life half-blind in this dank place? Or does your sight mean nothing to you?"

The monster was very still.

"Let our friend go, Soldeen," Lief urged. "He has suffered long, and only now is free. He came here for our sake. Make up your mind that we will not give him up. You shall not have him, whatever the cost!"

"You . . . would die for him," the beast growled, finally. "He . . . would die for you. And all of you would give up — everything — for your cause. I remember — I seem to remember — a time when I, too . . . long ago. So long ago . . ."

His eyes had narrowed. He had begun to sway, groaning and shaking his head.

"Something — is — happening   to   me,"   he

moaned. "My mind is — burning . . . clearing. I see — pictures of another time, another place. What have you done to me? What sorcery — ?"

And only then did Lief realize that the Belt of Deltora, and the topaz that it held, were pressing against the creature's skin.

"It is no sorcery, but the truth you see," he whispered. "Whatever you see — is real."

Soldeen's eyes gleamed in the moonlight, no longer the eyes of a ravenous beast, but those of a creature filled with unbearable suffering. And suddenly Lief remembered the golden eyes of the guardian of the bridge, and understood.

"Help us, Soldeen," he whispered. "Let Manus go free, and give us the stone. For the sake of what you once were. For the sake of what you have lost."

The tortured eyes darkened, then seemed to flash.

Lief held his breath. Confused and afraid, Barda, Jasmine, and Manus pressed together on the rocks, not daring to move.

"I will," said Soldeen.

Lief felt the eyes of his friends upon him as Soldeen slid back into the Lake and moved away from the shore. He knew that his life hung by a thread. At any moment Soldeen might change his mind, grow impatient or angry, toss him into the oily water, tear at him in rage.

Then he felt something that made him forget fear

and doubt. The Belt of Deltora was warming on his skin. It sensed that another gem was near — very near.

Soldeen had almost reached the weeping rock. The water had worn deep cracks and holes in its smooth surface. Under the gentle light of the moon it looked like a woman with her head bent in sorrow, tears falling from between her hands. Lief's heart thudded as he saw, cupped in one of the hands, something that did not belong there.

It was a huge, dark pink gem. The dripping flow of water hid it completely from the shore. Even here, so close, it was very hard to see.

"Take it," hissed Soldeen.

Perhaps he was already regretting his promise, for he turned his head aside, as if he could not bear to watch, while Lief stretched out his hand and plucked the gem from its hiding place.

Lief drew his hand back from the rock, opened it, and stared at his prize. Then, slowly, his excitement changed to confusion. He had no doubt that this was one of the gems they had been seeking, for the Belt around his waist was so warm that his damp clothes were steaming.

But he could not remember that any of the gems in the Belt of Deltora were pink. Yet this stone was pink, indeed, and seemed to be growing paler in color as he looked at it.

Or was it just that the light had changed? A thin

cloud had covered the moon, so that it shone through a smoky veil. Even the stars had dimmed. Lief shivered.

"What is the matter?" growled Soldeen.

"Nothing!" Lief said hastily, closing his hand again. "I have the stone. We can go back."

He twisted and signaled to Barda, Jasmine, and Manus, clustered together on the rocks. He saw them raise their arms, and heard their shouts of triumph.

The emerald is green, thought Lief, as Soldeen turned to swim back to the shore. The amethyst is purple. The lapis lazuli is deep blue with silver dots like stars, the opal is all the colors of the rainbow, the diamond is clear as ice, the ruby is red . . .

The ruby . . .

Some words leapt into his mind. He could see them as clearly as if the page from *The Belt of Deltora* was open before him.

✝ **The great ruby, symbol of happiness, red as blood, grows pale in the presence of evil, or when misfortune threatens . . .**

The ruby is red, Lief thought. The ruby grows pale in the presence of evil. And when red pales, what is it but pink?

The gem in his hand was the ruby, its rich color drained away by the evil of the Lake. But surely it had faded even more in the last few moments. Now it was no darker than the palm of his hand.

A terrible fear seized him. "Soldeen!" he cried. "We must — "

But at that moment, the sky seemed to split open with a jagged streak of light. With a fearful, rushing sound, a cloud of foul-smelling, yellow smoke belched through the crack, churning the Lake to mud and filling the air above it with thick, choking fumes.

And in the midst of the smoke, hovering above the water, was a towering figure, shining green, with wild, silver hair that crackled and flew around her beautiful, sneering face as though it was itself alive.

"Thaegan!" It was as though the whole Lake moaned the name. As though every creature, and even the rocks themselves, shrank and trembled.

The sorceress jeered.

She pointed the little finger of her left hand at Soldeen, and a spear of yellow light flew at him, hitting him between the eyes.

The beast cried out, twisting and rolling in agony. Lief was pitched violently sideways, and the great ruby flew from his hand, high into the air. He shouted in horror, snatching at it vainly even as he plunged towards the churning water of the Lake.

The gem made a great half-circle and began to fall. Gasping, struggling in the muddy foam, Lief watched in horror as it dropped into a deep crack in the weeping rock and disappeared from sight.

"You shall never have it!" cried Thaegan, her voice cracking with fury. "You — who have dared to enter my lands! You who have freed one of my creatures and made another do your will! You who have killed two of my children and mocked my power! I have followed you. I have smelt you out. Now, you will see!"

Again she raised her hand, and Lief felt himself being swept towards the edge of the Lake. Foul-smelling water rushed into his eyes, nose, and mouth. Nameless things, fighting for life as he was, battered against his face and body and were crushed.

Half-drowned, he was cast up on the shore. He crawled, coughing and choking, through the oozing mud and foam, only half aware that Barda, Jasmine, and Manus were running towards him.

They hauled him to his feet and began dragging him to the rocks.

But Thaegan was already there, barring their way, her silver hair flying in the smoke, her body shining green. "You cannot escape me," she hissed. "You will never escape."

Barda flung himself at her, his sword pointed straight at her heart. "One drop of your blood, Thaegan!" he shouted. "One drop, and you are destroyed!" But the sorceress laughed shrilly as the blade swerved aside before it touched her and Barda was flung back, sprawling, into the mud. Kree screeched as Jasmine leapt forward to take the big man's place, only to be thrown back with even greater force, tumbling over Lief and Manus, taking them both down with her.

They wallowed helplessly in the ooze, struggling to rise.

Thaegan grinned, and Lief's stomach heaved as her beautiful face shifted like a mask and he glimpsed the evil horror beneath.

"Now you are where you belong!" she spat. "At my feet, crawling in the mud."

Kree screeched again and flew at her, trying to beat at her with his wings. She turned to him, as if noticing him for the first time, and her eyes lit with greed.

"Kree!" screamed Jasmine. "Get away from her!"

Thaegan laughed, and turned back to face them. "The black bird I will save for my own delight," she snarled. "But you — you will know nothing of his pain."

Baring her teeth, she raked her victims with eyes full of hate and triumph. "You are to become part of my creation. Soon you will forget everything you have ever held dear. Sick with loathing at your own ugliness, feeding on worms in the cold and the dark, you will creep in the ooze and slime with Soldeen, forever."

16 - Fight for Freedom

Thaegan raised her left hand high above her head, fist tightly clenched. It gleamed, green and hard as glass. The yellow smoke swirled as Kree dived wildly, uselessly, around her head. Lief, Barda, Jasmine, and Manus staggered together, trying to run. Laughing at their terror, she lifted the little finger, ready to strike. Its tip, white as bone, gleamed through the dimness.

Like a black arrow, Kree hurtled from the smoke. With a vicious snap his sharp beak stabbed and stabbed again at the death-pale fingertip.

The sorceress shrieked in rage, shock, and pain, shaking the bird off, hurling him aside. But red-black blood was already welling from the wound on her fingertip and slowly dripping to the ground.

Her eyes widened, unbelieving. Her body shuddered and writhed and turned as yellow as the smoke that still hung about her. Her face became a hideous blur, melting and re-forming before her victims' horrified eyes.

And then, with a high, whistling hiss, she began to shrivel, to crumple, to collapse in upon herself like a rotting fruit left in the sun.

Face down in the mud, Lief wrapped his arms around his head to hide the ghastly sight, smother the terrible sound. He heard Soldeen bellowing in the Lake behind him, crying out in triumph or terror. Then, with a low, terrifying rumble, the earth began to shudder and heave. Icy waves pounded on his back as the waters of the Lake swelled and crashed upon the shore.

Terrified at the thought of being sucked back into the deep, he threw himself forward, dragging himself blindly through the spray. Dimly he could hear Jasmine and Barda calling to each other, calling to Manus and to him. His fingertips touched rock, and with a last, desperate effort he heaved himself out of the swirling mud onto firm ground. He clung there, the breath sobbing in his aching throat.

Then, suddenly, everything stilled.

His skin prickling, Lief lifted his head. Barda and Manus were lying near him, pale but alive. Jasmine crouched a little further away, with Kree on her wrist and Filli, soaked and bedraggled, in her arms. Where Thaegan had stood there was nothing but a yellow stain on the rock.

The sorceress was dead. Trying only to stop her from casting her spell, Kree had wounded her in the one place on her body that was not armored — the fingertip she used to work her evil magic.

But it was not the end. Something was about to happen — Lief could feel it. The clouds had disappeared, and the full moon flooded the earth with radiant white light. The very air seemed to shimmer.

And the silence! It was as though the earth had caught its breath. Waiting . . .

Slowly, Lief turned to look behind him.

The tempest had almost emptied the Lake. Now it was just a broad sweep of shallow water gleaming in the moonlight. A multitude of slimy creatures lay stranded in heaps around its edges and on its flattened banks.

Soldeen was in the center, by the weeping rock. He was motionless, his head upraised. He was staring at the moon as though he had never seen it before. As Lief watched, there was a long, whispering sigh. Then Soldeen simply — vanished, and standing in his place was a tall, golden man with a mane of tawny hair.

The weeping rock quivered, and cracked from top to bottom. The two halves crumbled away in a cloud of fine, glittering dust. A woman stepped from the shining cloud. She was golden, like the man, but her hair was black as night. In her hand, held high, was a huge, red gem.

Lief staggered to his feet. He wanted to shout, to

exclaim, to cry out in shock, disbelief, and joy. But he could not make a sound. He could only stare as the man and woman joined hands and together began to walk towards him, across the water.

And as they walked, looking around them with the wondering eyes of those who still cannot believe their happiness, everything began to change.

The earth dried and bloomed with grass and flowers under their feet. Color and life spread from their footsteps, carpeting the dead earth as far as the eye could see. Twisted stumps and bare rocks became trees of every kind. Clay fell in sheets from the ragged peaks, revealing shining towers, beautiful houses, and spraying fountains. The pure, sweet sound of bells rang through the air.

All around the margins of the Lake, creatures were dissolving and re-forming. Golden people were rising from the ground, dazed from their long sleep, murmuring, weeping, laughing. Birds were fluffing their feathers and taking flight, singing their joy. Insects were chirruping. Furred animals were looking about them and hopping, bounding, or scurrying into the grass.

Lief felt Barda, Jasmine, and Manus move to stand behind him. The man who had been Soldeen, and the woman who had shared his long, long suffering, were not far from them now, but still Lief could hardly believe his own eyes.

"Can it be true?" he murmured.

"If it is not, we are all dreaming the same dream," said a chirpy voice he did not know. He swung around to see Manus, grinning at him.

"Manus — you can speak!" His own voice cracked and squeaked in his astonishment.

"Of course! With Thaegan's death, all her spells have been undone," said Manus cheerfully. "The people of Raladin and D'Or will not be the only ones in these parts with reason to be grateful to your gallant black bird, believe me."

Perched proudly on Jasmine's wrist, Kree squawked and puffed out his chest.

"And grateful to you." The deep, quiet voice was new to Lief, yet there was something familiar in it. He turned to meet the steady, deep grey eyes of the man who had been Soldeen.

"We have met before as enemies," the man said. "Now, at last, we meet as friends." His grey eyes warmed. "I am Nanion. This — is my lady, Ethena. We are the chiefs of D'Or, and we owe you our freedom."

The woman smiled, and her beauty was like the beauty of a radiant summer sky. Lief blinked, dazzled. Then he realized that she was holding out her hand to him. Balanced in the palm was the ruby — richly glowing, deepest red.

"You have need of this, I think," she said.

Lief nodded, swallowing, and took the gem from

her hand. It warmed his fingers, and the Belt around his waist grew hot. Quickly he moved to unfasten it, then hesitated, for Manus, Nanion, and Ethena were watching.

"Your secret, if it is a secret, will be safe with us," Manus chirped. He cleared his throat, as if still amazed and startled by the sound of his own voice.

"It will," said Ethena. "For a hundred years we have lived a half-life that was worse than death, our land laid waste and our souls imprisoned. Because of you, we are free. Our debt to you will never be repaid."

Barda smiled grimly. "Perhaps it will," he said. "For if our quest succeeds, we will have need of you."

He nodded to Lief, and Lief took off the Belt and put it on the ground in front of him.

Manus gasped, his button eyes wide. But it was Nanion who spoke.

"The Belt of Deltora!" he breathed. "But — how do you have it, so far from Del? And where are the seven gems? There is only one!"

"Two, now," said Lief. He fitted the ruby into the medallion beside the topaz. It glowed there, scarlet against the shining steel. The ruby, symbol of happiness. Greedily, he drank in the sight.

But Ethena and Nanion had drawn close together, and their tawny faces were pale under the moon. "It has happened, then," Ethena murmured.

"What we feared. What Thaegan promised, before she sent us into darkness. The Shadow Lord has come. Deltora is lost forever."

"No! Not forever!" cried Jasmine fiercely. "Any more than D'Or was lost forever. Or you!"

Nanion stared at her, startled by her anger. Then, slowly, he smiled. "You are right," he said softly. "No cause is lost while brave souls live and do not despair."

Lief lifted the Belt and put it on. It felt heavier than before. Only a little — but enough to make his heart swell with happiness.

A clamor of shouting and singing arose from the valley. The people had seen Nanion and Ethena from afar and were running towards them.

Ethena put a gentle hand on Lief's arm. "Stay with us a while," she urged. "Here you can rest, and feast, and be at peace. Here you can regain your strength for the journey ahead."

Lief glanced at Barda, Jasmine, and Manus and read in their faces what he knew he would. D'Or was beautiful, and the air was sweet. But —

"Thank you," he said. "But we are expected — in Raladin."

They said their farewells and left Ethena and Nanion turning to greet their people. The sound of bells ringing in their ears, they climbed up the rocks, pushed their way through the gap, and began to trudge back the way they had come.

Happiness was behind them, and happiness was before them. They could only guess at the Ralads' joy.

A few days' rest, thought Lief. A few days of storytelling, laughing, and music, with friends. And then — another journey, another adventure.

Two gems were found. The third awaited them.

City of the Rats

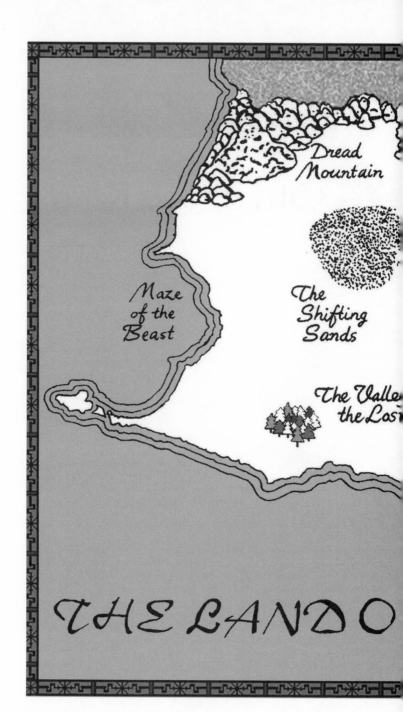

Dread
Mountain

Maze
of the
Beast

The
Shifting
Sands

The Valle
the Los

THE LAND O

The Shadowlands

The Lake
of Tears

ty
the
ts

The Forests
of Silence

Del

DELTORA

N
W E
S

Contents

1 The Trap 285

2 Roast Meat 293

3 Everything for the Traveller 300

4 Money Matters 308

5 The Bargain 316

6 Noradz 323

7 Strange Customs 331

8 The Trial 339

9 The Kitchens 348

10 The Hole 356

11 The Price of Freedom 364

12 A Matter of Business 373

13 Broad River and Beyond 381

14 Night of the Rats 389

15 The City 396

16 Reeah 404

17 Hope 411

The story so far . . .

Sixteen-year-old Lief, fulfilling a pledge made by his father before he was born, has set out on a great quest to find the seven gems of the magic Belt of Deltora. The Belt is all that can save the kingdom from the tyranny of the evil Shadow Lord, who, only months before Lief's birth, invaded Deltora and enslaved its people with the help of sorcery and his fearsome Grey Guards.

The gems — an amethyst, a topaz, a diamond, a ruby, an opal, a lapis lazuli, and an emerald — were stolen to open the way for the Shadow Lord to invade the kingdom. Now they lie hidden in dark and terrible places throughout the land. Only when they have been restored to the Belt can the heir to Deltora's throne be found, and the Shadow Lord defeated.

Lief's companions are the man Barda, who was once a Palace guard, and Jasmine, a wild, orphaned girl of Lief's own age who they met in the fearful Forests of Silence.

In the Forests they discovered the amazing healing powers of the nectar of the Lilies of Life. There they also won the first gem — the golden topaz, symbol of faith, which has the power to bring the living into contact with the spirit world, and to clear and sharpen the mind. At the Lake of Tears, they broke the evil enchantment of the sorceress Thaegan, released the peoples of Raladin and D'Or from her curse, and won the second gem — the great ruby, symbol of happiness, which pales when misfortune threatens its wearer.

Now read on . . .

1 - The Trap

Footsore and weary, Lief, Barda, and Jasmine moved west, towards the fabled City of the Rats. They knew little about their goal except that it was a place of evil, deserted by its people long ago. But they were almost sure that one of the seven lost gems of the Belt of Deltora lay hidden there.

They had been walking steadily all day and now, as the glowing sun slipped towards the horizon, they longed to stop for rest. But the road on which they walked, deeply rutted with the tracks of wagons, threaded through a plain where thornbushes had taken hold and spread, covering the land. The thorns lined the road without break, and extended as far as the eye could see.

Lief sighed, and for comfort touched the Belt hidden under his shirt. It held two gems now: the golden topaz and the scarlet ruby. Both had been won

285

against great odds, and in the process of winning them, great things had been done.

The people of Raladin, with whom they had stayed for the last two weeks, did not know of their quest to find the lost gems. Manus, the Ralad man who had shared the search for the ruby, was sworn to silence. But it was no secret that the companions had caused the death of the evil sorceress Thaegan, ally of the evil Shadow Lord. It was no secret, either, that two of Thaegan's thirteen children had gone the way of their mother. The Ralads, freed at last from Thaegan's curse, had made many songs of joy, praising the companions for their deeds.

It had been hard to leave them. Hard to leave Manus, and the happiness, safety, good food, and warm, soft beds of the hidden village. But five gems were still to be found, and until they were restored to the Belt, the Shadow Lord's tyranny over Deltora could not be broken. The three companions had to move on.

"These thorns are never-ending," Jasmine complained, her voice breaking into Lief's thoughts. He turned to look at her. As usual, the little furred creature called Filli was nestled on her shoulder, blinking through Jasmine's mass of black hair. Kree, the raven, who was never far out of her sight, was swooping over the thorns nearby, catching insects. He, at least, was filling his belly.

"There is something ahead!" called Barda. He

pointed to a glimmer of white on the side of the road.

Curious and hopeful, they hurried to the place. There, sticking out of the thorns, was a strange signpost.

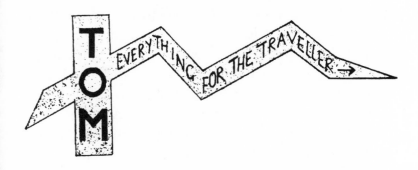

"What does it mean?" Jasmine murmured.

"It seems to point the way to some sort of shop," said Lief.

"What is a shop?"

Lief glanced at the girl in surprise, then remembered that she had spent her life in the Forests of Silence, and had never seen many of the things he took for granted.

"A shop is a place for buying and selling goods," Barda explained. "In the city of Del, these days, the shops are poor, and many are closed. But once, before the Shadow Lord, there were many, selling food and drink and clothes and other things to the people."

Jasmine looked at him with her head to one side. Lief realized that even now she did not understand. For her, food grew on trees and drink ran in the streams. Other things were found or made — and what you could not find or make, you did without.

They tramped on up the road, talking in low voices, trying to forget their tiredness. But soon it was too dark to see, and they had to light a torch to guide their way. Barda held the flickering flame low, but all of them knew that it could still be seen from the air.

The idea that their progress could be followed so easily was not pleasant. The Shadow Lord's spies might even now be patrolling the skies. Also, they had not yet reached the end of Thaegan's territory. Though she was dead, they knew well that where wickedness had held sway for so long, danger threatened everywhere.

About an hour after they had lit the torch, Jasmine stopped, and glanced behind her. "We are being followed," she breathed. "Not just by one, but by many."

Though they themselves could hear nothing, Lief and Barda did not bother asking her how she knew. They had learned that Jasmine's senses were far keener and sharper than their own. She might not know what shops were, she might not be able to read and write more than a little, but in other ways her knowledge was vast.

"They know we are ahead," she whispered. "They stop when we stop, and move when we move."

Silently Lief pulled up his shirt and looked down at the ruby in the Belt around his waist. His heart thudded as he saw, by the flickering light of the torch, that the deep red gem had faded to a dull pink.

Barda and Jasmine were looking at the stone also. They knew, as Lief did, that the ruby paled when danger threatened its wearer. Its message, now, was clear.

"So," Barda muttered. "Our followers have evil intent. Who are they? Could Kree fly back, and — ?"

"Kree is not an owl!" snapped Jasmine. "He cannot see in the dark, any more than we can." She crouched, put her ear to the ground, and frowned, listening intently. "The followers are not Grey Guards, at least," she said at last. "They move too quietly for that, and they are not marching in time."

"It is a band of robbers, perhaps, thinking to ambush us when we stop to sleep or rest. We must turn and fight!" Lief's hand was already on the hilt of his sword. The songs of the Ralad people were ringing in his ears. What was a ragged crew of robbers compared to the monsters he, Barda, and Jasmine had faced and defeated?

"The middle of a road hemmed in by thorns is no good place to make a stand, Lief," said Barda grimly. "And there is nowhere here that we could hide, to take enemies by surprise. We should move on, to try to find a better place."

They began to walk again, faster now. Lief kept glancing behind him, but there was nothing to be seen in the shadows at his back.

They came to a dead tree that stood like a ghost at the side of the road, its white trunk rising out of the thornbushes. Moments after they had passed it, Lief sensed a change in the air. The back of his neck began to prickle.

"They are gaining speed," Jasmine panted.

Then they heard it. A long, low howl that chilled the blood.

Filli, clutching Jasmine's shoulder, made a small, frightened sound. Lief saw that the fur was standing up all over his tiny body.

There was another howl, and another.

"Wolves!" hissed Jasmine. "We cannot outrun them. They are almost upon us!"

She tore two more torches from her pack and thrust them into the flame of the one she already held. "They will fear the fire," she said, pushing the newly burning sticks into Lief's and Barda's hands. "But we must face them. We must not turn our backs."

"We are to walk backwards all the way to Tom's shop?" Lief joked feebly, gripping his torch. But Jasmine did not smile, and neither did Barda. He was staring back at the dead tree glimmering white in the distance.

"They did not make their move until we were past that tree," he muttered. "They wished to prevent us climbing it, and escaping them. These are no ordinary wolves."

"Be ready," Jasmine warned.

She already had her dagger in her hand. Lief and Barda drew their swords. They stood together, the torches held high, waiting.

And with another chorus of bloodcurdling howls, out of the darkness surged what seemed a sea of moving pinpoints of yellow light — the eyes of the wolves.

Jasmine lashed her torch from side to side in front of her. Lief and Barda did the same, so that the road in front of them was blocked by a moving line of flame.

The beasts slowed, but still moved forward, growling. As they came closer to the light, Lief could see that, indeed, they were no ordinary wolves. They were huge, covered with shaggy, matted fur striped with brown and yellow. Their lips curled back from their snarling jaws and their open, dripping mouths were not red inside, but black.

He counted them quickly. There were eleven. For some reason, that number meant something to him, but he could not think why. In any case, there was no time to worry about such things. With Barda and Jasmine he began to back away, keeping his torch moving. But for every step the companions took, the beasts took one, too.

Lief remembered his weak joke. "We are to walk

backwards all the way to Tom's shop?" he had asked.

Now it looked as though they might be forced to do just that. The beasts are driving us, he thought.

The beasts are driving us . . . They are not ordinary wolves . . . There are eleven . . .

His stomach lurched. "Barda! Jasmine!" he hissed. "These are not wolves. They are . . ."

But he never finished. For at that moment he and his companions took another step back, the great net trap that had been set for them was sprung, and they were swung, shrieking, into the air.

2 - Roast Meat

Crushed together in the net, bundled so tightly that they could hardly move, Lief, Barda, and Jasmine swung sickeningly in midair. They were helpless. Their torches and weapons had flown from their hands as they were whipped off their feet. Kree swooped around them, screeching in despair.

The net was hanging from a tree growing by the side of the track. Unlike the other tree they had seen, it was alive. The branch that supported the net was thick and strong — too strong to break.

Below, wolf howls were changing to bellows of triumph. Lief looked down. In the light of the fallen torches he could see that the beasts' bodies were bulging, transforming into humanlike forms.

In moments, eleven hideous, grinning creatures were capering on the track below the tree. Some were large, some were small. Some were covered in hair,

293

others were completely bald. They were green, brown, yellow, sickly white — even slimy red. One had six stumpy legs. But Lief knew who they were.

They were the sorceress Thaegan's children. He remembered the rhyme that listed their names.

Hot, Tot, Jin, Jod,
Fie, Fly, Zan, Zod,
Pik, Snik, Lun, Lod,
And the dreaded Ichabod.

Jin and Jod were dead — smothered in their own quicksand trap. Now only eleven of the thirteen remained. But they were all here. They had gathered together to hunt the enemies who had caused the deaths of their mother, brother, and sister. They wanted revenge.

Grunting and snuffling, some of the monsters were tearing thornbushes up by the roots and piling them beneath the swinging net. Others were picking up the torches and dancing around, chanting:

More heat, more heat,
Tender, juicy roast meat!
Watch the fun,
Till it's done.
Hear its groans,
Crack its bones!
More heat, more heat,
Tender, juicy roast meat!

"They are going to burn us!" groaned Barda,

struggling vainly. "Jasmine, your second dagger. Can you reach it?"

"Do you think that I would still be hanging here if I could?" Jasmine whispered back furiously.

The monsters below were cheering as they threw the torches onto the pile of thorns. Already Lief could feel warmth below him, and smell smoke. He knew that soon the green bushes would dry and catch alight. Then he and his friends would roast in the heat, and when the net burned through they would fall into the fire.

Something soft moved against Lief's cheek. It was Filli. The little creature had managed to work his way off Jasmine's shoulder and now was squeezing through the net right beside Lief's ear.

He, at least, was free. But he did not run up the ropes and into the tree above, as Lief expected. Instead, he remained clinging to the net, nibbling at it desperately. Lief realized that he was going to try to make a hole big enough for them to climb through.

It was a brave effort, but how much time would it take for those tiny teeth to gnaw through such thick, strong netting? Too much time. Long before Filli had made even a small gap, the monsters below would notice what he was doing. Then they would drive him away, or kill him.

There was a howl of rage from the ground. Lief looked down in panic. Had their enemies caught sight of Filli already? No — they were not looking up. Instead, they were glaring at one another.

"Two legs for Ichabod!" the biggest one was roaring, beating his lumpy red chest. "Two legs *and* a head."

"No! No!" two green creatures snarled, baring dripping brown teeth. "Not fair! Fie and Fly say no!"

"They are fighting over which parts of us they will eat!" exclaimed Barda. "Can you believe it?"

"Let them fight," muttered Jasmine. "The more they fight, the more time Filli has to do his work."

"We share the meat!" shrieked the two smallest monsters, their piercing voices rising above the noise of the others. "Hot and Tot say equal shares."

Their brothers and sisters growled and muttered.

"Are they not stupid?" Lief shouted suddenly, pretending that he was talking to Barda and Jasmine. "Do they not know that they cannot have equal shares!"

"Lief, are you mad?" hissed Jasmine.

But Lief went on shouting. He could see that the monsters had grown still, and were listening. "There are three of us, and eleven of them!" he roared. "You cannot divide three fairly into eleven parts. It is impossible!"

He knew as well as Jasmine did that he was taking a risk. The monsters could look up at him, and see Filli at the same time. But he was gambling on the hope that suspicion and anger would make them keep their eyes fixed on one another.

And, to his relief, he saw that his gamble had succeeded. The monsters had begun muttering together in small groups, glancing slyly at one another.

"If they were nine only, they could cut each of us into three parts and have one part each," he shouted. "But as it is . . ."

"Equal shares!" shrieked Hot and Tot. "Hot and Tot say — "

Ichabod pounced upon them and knocked their heads together with a sharp crack. They fell senseless to the ground.

"Now," he snarled. "Now there be equal shares, like you want. Now we be nine."

The fire had begun to blaze and crackle. Smoke billowed upwards, making Lief cough. He looked sideways and saw that Filli had already succeeded in making a small hole in the net. Now he was working on enlarging it. But he needed more time.

"There is something they have forgotten, Lief," Barda said loudly. "If we are each divided into three, the shares will still not be equal. Why, I am twice the size of Jasmine! Whoever gets a third part of her will not do well at all. Really, she should be divided in half!"

"Yes," agreed Lief, just as loudly, ignoring Jasmine's cries of rage. "But that would only make eight pieces, Barda. And there are nine to feed!"

He watched out of the corner of his eye as Zan, the six-legged monster, nodded thoughtfully, then swung around and clubbed his neighbor, who happened to be Fie, felling her to the ground.

Fly, furious at the attack on his twin, leaped onto Zan's back, screeching and biting. Zan roared, lurched around, and knocked over the hairy brother on his other side, who in turn fell over the sister in front of him, stabbing himself on her horns.

And then, suddenly, they were all fighting — shrieking, biting, and bashing — crashing into the thornbushes, tumbling into the fire, rolling on the ground.

The fight went on, and on. And by the time Filli had finished his work, and the three companions had escaped from the net and climbed into the tree above, there was only one monster left standing. Ichabod.

Surrounded by the bodies of his fallen brothers and sisters, he stood by the fire, bellowing and beating his chest in triumph. Any moment he would look up and see that the net was empty, and that the food he had fought for was in the tree — with nowhere to go.

"We must take him by surprise," whispered Jasmine, pulling her second dagger from her leggings and checking that Filli was safely on her shoulder again. "It is the only way."

Without another word, she jumped, striking Ichabod on the back with both feet. Knocked off balance, he fell into the fire, landing with a crash and a roar.

298

Gathering their wits, Barda and Lief slid down the tree as quickly as they could and ran to where Jasmine was snatching up her dagger and their swords.

"Why did you wait?" she demanded, thrusting their swords at them. "Make haste!"

With Kree soaring above, they ran like the wind along the track, careless of the ruts in the road and the darkness. Behind them, Ichabod was howling in rage and pain as he crawled from the fire and began stumbling after them.

3 - Everything for the Traveller

Panting, chests aching, ears straining for the sound of howls behind them, they ran on. They all knew that if Ichabod changed into a wolf or other beast, he could catch them easily. But they heard nothing.

It is possible that he cannot transform when he is injured, thought Lief. If so, we are safe. But, like his companions, he did not dare to stop or slow.

Finally they came to a place where the track crossed a shallow stream.

"I am sure that this marks the border of Thaegan's lands," gasped Barda. "See? There are no thorn-bushes on the other side. Ichabod will not follow us across."

Legs trembling with weariness, they splashed through the cold water. On the other side of the stream the track continued, but soft, green grass and small trees grew beside it, and they could see the shapes of wildflowers.

They staggered on for a little, then turned from the track and fell down in the shelter of a grove of the small trees. Leaves whispering overhead, grass soft under their heads, they slept.

※

When they woke, the sun was high, and Kree was calling them. Lief stretched and yawned. His muscles were stiff and aching after the long run, and his feet were sore.

"We should have slept in turns," Barda groaned, sitting up and easing his back. "It was dangerous to trust in our safety, so close to the border."

"We were all tired. And Kree was watching." Jasmine had jumped up, and was already prowling around the grove. She felt no stiffness, it seemed.

She put her hand to the rough trunk of one of the trees. Above her, leaves stirred faintly. She put her head to one side, and seemed to listen.

"The trees say that carts still use this road quite often," she announced finally. "Heavy carts, drawn by horses. But there is nothing ahead today."

Before starting off again, they ate a little of the bread, honey, and fruit that the Ralads had given them. Filli had his share, as well as a piece of honey-comb, his favorite treat.

Then they moved on slowly. After a time, they saw another of the signs directing them to Tom's shop.

"I hope Tom sells something for sore feet," muttered Lief.

"The sign says, 'Everything for the Traveller,' " Barda said. "So no doubt he does. But we must choose only what we really need. We have little money."

Jasmine glanced at them. She said nothing, but Lief noticed that she began to walk a little faster. Plainly, she was curious to see exactly what a shop was like.

An hour later they rounded a bend and saw, sticking up from the middle of a grove of trees, a long, jagged metal shape, like a lightning bolt. Huge metal letters stuck out from the side of the shape.

Wondering, they walked on. As they moved closer to the place they saw that the trees were in the shape of a horseshoe, clustering around the sides and back of a strange little stone building. The jagged shape supporting the metal letters plunged right into the middle of its peaked roof, as though the building were being struck by lightning.

Plainly, this was Tom's shop, though at first glance it looked rather more like an inn than a place where things could be bought. There was a flat, cleared space between the building and the road — space enough for several carts to stop — and here and there stood great stone troughs filled with water for animals to drink. But a large shop window shone on one side of the door, and on the glass the shop owner's name had been painted in bright red letters — arranged from top to bottom, like they were on the chimney sign and the signposts the travellers had passed.

"This Tom certainly likes to let people know his name." Barda grinned. "Very well, then. Let us see what he has for us."

They crossed the cleared space and peered into the shop window. It was filled with packs, hats, belts, boots, socks, waterbags, coats, ropes, pots and pans, and many, many other things, including some that Lief did not recognize. Strangely, there were no prices or labels, but right in the middle was a yellow sign.

A bell fastened to the door tinkled as they entered the shop, but no one came forward to greet them. They looked around, blinking in the gloom. The crowded room seemed very dim after the bright sunlight outside. Narrow corridors ran between shelves that rose from the floor to the low ceiling. The shelves were crammed with goods. At the far end was a dusty counter cluttered with account books, a set of scales, and what looked like a money tin. Behind the counter were more shelves, a door, and another sign:

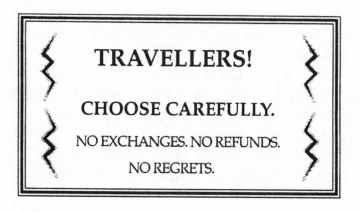

TRAVELLERS!

CHOOSE CAREFULLY.

NO EXCHANGES. NO REFUNDS.

NO REGRETS.

"Tom is a trusting fellow," Barda said, looking around. "Why, we could have come in here, stolen whatever we liked, and walked out again, by now."

To prove his point, he reached for a small lantern on the shelf closest to him. When he tried to pick it up, however, the lantern would not move.

Barda's jaw dropped in astonishment. He tugged, but without success. Finally, as Lief doubled up with laughter and Jasmine stared, he gave up. But when he tried to take his hand away from the lantern, he could not. He heaved, cursing, but his fingers were stuck fast.

"You want a lantern, friend?"

They all jumped violently and spun around. A tall, lean man with a hat on the back of his head was standing behind the counter, his arms folded and his wide mouth curved in a mocking smile.

"What *is* this?" shouted Barda angrily, jabbing his free hand at the lantern.

"It is proof that Tom is *not* a trusting fellow," the man behind the counter said, his smile broadening. He put a long finger below the counter, and perhaps he pressed a button there, because suddenly Barda's hand was released. He jerked backwards, bumping into Lief and Jasmine with some force.

"Now," said the man behind the counter. "What can Tom show you? And more to the point, what can Tom *sell* you?" He rubbed his hands.

"We need a good length of strong rope," said

Lief, seeing that Barda was going to say nothing. "And also, something for sore feet, if you have it."

"Have it?" cried Tom. "Of course I have it. Everything for the traveller. Did you not see the sign?"

He eased himself out from behind the counter and selected a coil of thin rope from a shelf.

"This is my very best," he said. "Light, and very strong. Three silver coins, and it is yours."

"Three silver coins for a piece of rope?" Barda exploded. "That is robbery!"

Tom's smile did not waver. "Not robbery, friend, but business," he said calmly. "For where else will you find a rope like this?"

Holding one end of the rope, he threw the rest upwards with a flick of his wrist. The rope uncoiled like a snake and wound itself tightly around one of the ceiling rafters. Tom pulled at it, to show its strength. Then he flicked his wrist again, and the rope unwrapped itself from the rafter and dropped back into his hands, winding itself up into a neat coil as it fell.

"Trickery," growled Barda, glowering.

But Lief was fascinated. "We will take it," he said excitedly, ignoring Barda's elbow in his ribs, and Jasmine's suspicious frown.

Tom rubbed his hands. "I knew you were a man who understood a bargain," he said. "Now. What else might I show you? No obligation to buy!"

Lief looked around excitedly. If this shop had

rope that acted as though it were alive, what other wonders might it hold?

"Everything!" he exclaimed. "We want to see everything!"

Tom beamed.

Jasmine moved uncomfortably. It was clear that she did not like the crowded shop, with its low ceiling, and she did not much like Tom, either. "Filli and I will wait outside with Kree," she announced. She turned on her heel and left.

The next hour flew by as Tom showed Lief cushioned socks for sore feet, telescopes that saw around corners, plates that cleaned themselves, and pipes that blew bubbles of light. He showed machines to predict the weather, little white circles that looked like paper but swelled up to full-size loaves of bread when water was added, an axe that never blunted, a bedroll that floated off the ground, tiny beads that made fire, and a hundred more amazing inventions.

Slowly, Barda forgot his suspicion and began to watch, ask questions, and join in. By the time Tom had finished, he was quite won over, and as eager as Lief was to have as many of these marvels as they could afford. There were such wonderful things . . . things that would make their travels easier, safer, and more comfortable.

At last, Tom folded his arms and stood back, smiling at them. "So," he said. "Tom has shown you. Now, what can he sell you?"

4 - Money Matters

Some of Tom's goods, like the floating bedroll, cost more by themselves than all the money Lief and Barda had. But other things they could afford, and it was difficult to decide between them.

In the end, as well as the self-coiling rope, they chose a packet of "No Bakes" — the white rounds that expanded into loaves of bread — a jar of "Pure and Clear" — a powder that made any water fit to drink — and some cushioned socks. The pile was disappointingly small, and they had had to put aside many far more interesting things, including a jar of the fire-making beads and the pipe that blew bubbles of light.

"If only we had more money!" Lief exclaimed.

"Ah!" said Tom, pushing his hat a little back on his head. "Well, perhaps we can make a bargain. I buy as well as sell." He cast a sly glance at Lief's sword.

But Lief shook his head firmly. Much as he

wanted Tom's goods, he would not give up the sword his father had made for him on their own forge.

Tom shrugged. "Your cloak is a little stained," he said casually. "But still, I could perhaps give you something for it."

This time Lief smiled. However uncaring Tom appeared to be, he plainly knew very well that the cloak Lief's mother had woven for him had special powers.

"This cloak can make its wearer almost invisible," he said. "It has saved our lives more than once. I fear it is not for sale either."

Tom sighed. "A pity," he said. "Ah, well." He began to pack the fire beads and the light pipe away.

At that moment the bell on the shop door tinkled, and a stranger walked in. He was as tall as Barda, and as powerful, with long, tangled black hair and a shaggy black beard. A jagged scar ran down one cheek, showing pale against his brown skin.

Lief saw Jasmine slipping inside after him. She stood against the door, her hand on the dagger at her belt. Clearly, she was ready for trouble.

The stranger nodded briefly to Lief and Barda, snatched up a length of the self-coiling rope from a shelf, and strode past them to lean over the dusty counter.

"How much?" he asked Tom abruptly.

"One silver coin to you, good sir," said Tom.

Lief's eyes widened. Tom had told them that the

price of the rope was *three* silver coins. He opened his mouth to protest, then felt Barda's warning hand on his wrist. He glanced up and saw that his companion's eyes were fixed on the counter, near to where the stranger's hands were resting. There was a mark there. The stranger had drawn it in the dust.

The secret sign of resistance to the Shadow Lord! The sign that they had seen scratched on walls so many times on their way to the Lake of Tears! By drawing it on the counter, the stranger had signalled to Tom. And Tom had responded by lowering the price of the rope.

The man threw a silver coin into Tom's hand and as he did his sleeve casually wiped the mark away. It all happened very quickly. If Lief had not seen the mark with his own eyes, he would not have believed it was ever there.

"I have heard rumors of strange happenings at the Lake of Tears, and indeed all through the territory across the stream," the stranger said carelessly, as he turned to go. "I have heard that Thaegan is no more."

"Indeed?" said Tom smoothly. "I cannot tell you. I am but a poor shopkeeper, and know nothing of these things. The thorns by the road, I understand, are as wild as ever."

The other man snorted. "The thorns are not the result of sorcery, but of a hundred years of poverty and neglect. The Del King's thorns, I call them, as do many others."

Lief's heart sank. By making the secret sign, this stranger had proved that he was dedicated to resisting the Shadow Lord. But plainly he hated the memory of the kings and queens of Deltora as much as Lief himself had once done, and blamed them for the kingdom's misfortune.

He knew he could say nothing, but could not help staring at the man as he passed. The man returned his gaze, unsmiling, and left the shop, brushing past Jasmine as he went through the door.

"Who was that?" Barda whispered to Tom.

The shopkeeper settled his hat on his head more firmly before replying. "No names are mentioned in Tom's shop but Tom's own, sir," he said calmly. "It is better so, in these hard times."

Lief heard the door tinkle again and turned to see Jasmine leaving. Now that the possibility of danger had passed, she had become restless, and had decided to go out into the fresh air once more.

Perhaps Tom realized that Barda and Lief had

seen and understood the mark the stranger had made on the counter, for suddenly he picked up the fire beads and the light pipe, and added them to their little pile of goods.

"No extra charge," he said, as they glanced at him in surprise. "Tom is always happy to help a traveller — as you have seen."

"A traveller who is on the right side." Barda smiled.

But Tom merely raised his eyebrows, as if he had no idea what the big man meant, and held out his hand for payment.

"A pleasure to serve you, sirs," he said, as they handed over their money. He counted the coins rapidly, nodded, and put them away in his cash box.

"And what of our free gift?" asked Lief cheekily. "The sign in the window says — "

"Ah, of course," said Tom. "The gift." He bent and fumbled under the counter. When he stood up, he was holding a small, flat tin box. He handed it to Lief.

"If you do not ask, you do not get. Is that your motto, young sir?" he asked. "Well, it is my motto too."

Lief looked at the box. It fitted easily into the palm of his hand, and looked quite old. The faded lettering on the label said simply:

"What is it?" Lief asked, bewildered.

"The instructions are on the back," said Tom.

Suddenly, he paused, listening. Then he slipped out from behind the counter and darted through the shop's back door.

In his haste he had left the door open, and Lief and Barda followed him. To their surprise, the door led directly into a small field enclosed by a white fence and completely hidden from the road by the tall trees that surrounded it. Three grey horses were standing by the fence, and sitting upon it, patting them, was Jasmine, with Kree perched on her shoulder.

Tom strode towards the fence, waving his arms. "Do not touch the animals, if you please!" he shouted. "They are valuable."

"I am not hurting them!" exclaimed Jasmine indignantly, but she took her hand away. The beasts snuffled in disappointment.

"Horses!" Barda muttered to Lief. "If only we

had horses to ride! How much faster would our journey be then?"

Lief nodded slowly. He had never ridden before, and he was sure that Jasmine had not, either. But surely they could soon learn. On horseback they would be able to outrun any enemy — even Grey Guards.

"Will you sell us the beasts?" he asked, as they caught up with Tom. "For example, if we were to return to you all the things we have bought, would that be enough — ?"

Tom looked at him sharply. "No exchanges!" he snapped. "No refunds! No regrets!"

Lief's stomach lurched with disappointment.

"What are you talking about?" demanded Jasmine. "What is this 'buy' and 'sell'?"

Tom stared at her in surprise. "Your friends would like to have some beasts to ride, little miss," he explained, as though Jasmine were a small child. "But they no longer have anything to give me in exchange for them. They have spent their money on other things. And" — he glanced at Lief's cloak and sword — "they do not choose to trade anything else."

Jasmine nodded slowly, taking it in. "Perhaps, then, I have something to trade," she said. "I have many treasures."

She began to feel in her pockets, bringing out in turn a feather, a length of plaited twine, some stones, her second dagger, and the broken-toothed comb from

314

her nest in the Forests of Silence. Tom watched her, smiling and shaking his head.

"Jasmine!" Lief called, feeling a little ashamed. "None of those things is — "

Then his jaw dropped. Barda gasped. And Tom's eyes bulged.

For Jasmine had pulled out a small bag and was carelessly upending it. Gold coins were pouring out, making a shining heap on her lap.

5 - The Bargain

Of course, Lief thought, after his first astonishment had passed. Jasmine had robbed many Grey Guards who had fallen victim to the horrors of the Forests of Silence. He had actually seen a mass of gold and silver coins among the treasures she kept in her treetop nest. But he had not realized that she had brought some of them with her when she left the Forests to join their quest. He had quite forgotten about them till now, and, because to her they were just pretty keepsakes, she had not mentioned them.

A few coins bounced away onto the ground. Barda hurried to pick them up, but Jasmine barely looked at them. She was looking at Tom — at his glittering eyes. Perhaps she did not understand about buying and selling, but she recognized greed when she saw it.

"You like this?" she asked, holding up a handful of the gold.

"Indeed I do, little miss," said Tom, recovering a little. "I like it very much."

"Then, will you exchange the horses for it?"

A strange expression crossed Tom's face — a pained expression, as though his desire for the gold was struggling with another feeling. As if he was calculating, weighing up risks.

Finally, he seemed to come to a decision.

"I cannot sell the horses," he said regretfully. "They — are promised to others. But — I have something better. If you will come this way . . ."

He led them to a shed at one side of the field. He opened the shed door and beckoned them inside.

Standing together in one corner, munching hay, were three creatures of very odd appearance. They were about the same size as horses, but had long necks, very small heads with narrow, drooping ears, and, most surprising of all, only three legs — one thick one at the front and two thinner ones at the back. They were unevenly splodged all over with black, brown, and white, as though they had been splashed with paint, and instead of hooves they had large, flat, hairy feet, each with two broad toes.

"What are they?" asked Barda, astonished.

"Why, they are muddlets," cried Tom, striding forward to turn one of the beasts towards them. "And very fine examples of the breed. Steeds fit for a king, sir. The very thing for you and your companions."

Barda, Lief, and Jasmine glanced at one another uncertainly. The idea of being able to ride instead of walk was very appealing. But the muddlets looked extremely strange.

"Their names are Noodle, Zanzee, and Pip," said Tom. Affectionately, he slapped each of the muddlets' broad rumps in turn. The beasts went on chewing hay, completely undisturbed.

"They seem gentle enough," Barda said, after a moment. "But can they run? Are they swift?"

"Swift?" exclaimed Tom, holding up his hands and rolling his eyes. "My friend, they are swift as the wind! They are strong, too — far stronger than any horse. And loyal — oh, their loyalty is famous. In addition, they eat almost anything, and thrive on hard work. Muddlets are everyone's steeds of choice, in these parts. But they are hard to get. Very hard."

"How much do you want for them?" asked Lief abruptly.

Tom rubbed his hands. "Shall we say, twenty-one gold coins for the three?" he suggested.

"Shall we say, fifteen?" growled Barda.

Tom looked shocked. "Fifteen? For these superb beasts that are as dear to me as my own children? Would you rob poor Tom? Would you make him a beggar?"

Jasmine looked concerned, but Barda's face did not quiver. "Fifteen," he repeated.

Tom threw up his hands. "Eighteen!" he said. "With saddles and bridles thrown in. Now — can I say fairer than that?"

Barda glanced at Lief and Jasmine, who both nodded vigorously.

"Very well," he said.

And so the bargain was struck. Tom fetched saddles and bridles and helped Lief, Barda, and Jasmine load the muddlets with their packs. Then he led the beasts out of the shed. They moved with a strange, rocking motion, the one front leg stepping forward first, and the two hind legs swinging together after it.

Tom opened a gate in the fence and they walked out of the field. The three grey horses watched them go. Lief felt a pang of regret. In the excitement of bargaining with Tom, he had forgotten the horses. But how nice it would have been to ride them away, instead of these other strange, lolloping creatures.

Never mind, he told himself, patting Noodle's splodgy back. We will become used to these beasts in time. By the end of our journey, no doubt, we will have grown very fond of them.

Later, he was to remember that thought — remember it bitterly.

When they reached the front of the shop, Tom held the reins while the three companions climbed up on their mounts' backs. After some discussion, Jasmine took Zanzee, Lief took Noodle, and Barda took

Pip, though in fact there was little to choose between the beasts, who looked very alike.

The saddles fitted just behind the muddlets' necks, where their bodies were narrowest. The baggage was strapped behind, across the broad expanse of the rump. It was quite a comfortable arrangement, but, all the same, Lief felt a little anxious. The ground seemed very far away, and the reins felt awkward in his hands. Suddenly he was wondering if this had been a good idea after all, though, of course, he did his best not to show it.

The muddlets were making glad, snuffling sounds. They were clearly very pleased to be out in the fresh air, and were looking forward to exercise.

"Hold the reins tightly," said Tom. "They may be a little lively at first. Call, 'Brix' when you want them to go, and 'Snuff' when you want them to stop. Call loudly, as their hearing is not sharp. Tie them up well when you stop, so they will not stray. That is all there is to it."

Lief, Barda, and Jasmine nodded.

"One more thing," Tom murmured, inspecting his fingernails. "I have not asked you where you are going, for I do not want to know. Knowledge is dangerous, in these hard times. But I am going to give you a piece of advice. It is excellent advice, and I suggest you follow it. About half an hour from here you will come to a place where the road divides. At all costs take the left path, however tempted you may be to do otherwise. Now — travel well!"

With that, he lifted a hand and slapped Noodle's rump. "Brix!" he shouted. And, with a lurching jerk, Noodle started forward, with Pip and Zanzee following close behind. Kree squawked, flapping above them.

"Remember!" Tom's voice called after them. "Keep tight reins! Be sure to take the left path!"

Lief would have liked to wave, to show that he had heard, but he did not dare lift a hand. Noodle was picking up speed, her floppy ears blowing backwards in the breeze, her powerful legs bounding forward.

Lief had never been to sea, for before he was born, the Shadow Lord had forbidden the coast to the citizens of Del. But he imagined that clinging to a lively muddlet must be very like sailing a boat in stormy weather. It required all his attention.

❉

After about ten minutes, the muddlets' excitement wore off and they slowed to a steady, lolloping pace. Noodle began to remind Lief of a rocking horse he had had as a child, rather than making him think of a pitching boat.

This is not so hard, he thought. In fact, it is easy! He was filled with pride and satisfaction. What would his friends say, if they could see him now?

The road was wide, and the companions were able to ride beside one another. Lulled by the rocking movement, Filli settled down to sleep inside Jasmine's jacket, and now that he was sure that all was well, Kree flew ahead, dipping now and then to catch an insect. Jasmine herself rode silently, her eyes thoughtful. Barda and Lief talked.

"We are making very good time," said Barda with satisfaction. "These muddlets are certainly excellent steeds. I am surprised that we have not heard of them before. I never saw one in Del."

"Tom said they were hard to get," answered Lief. "The people in this part of Deltora keep them to themselves, no doubt. And Del has had little news from the countryside since long before the Shadow Lord came."

Jasmine glanced at him, and seemed about to speak, but then she closed her mouth firmly, and said nothing. Her brows were knitted in a frown.

They rode on without speaking for a moment, and then, at last, Jasmine opened her lips.

"This place we are to go — the City of the Rats. We know nothing of it, do we?"

"Only that it is walled, appears deserted, and stands alone in the bend of a river called the Broad," said Barda. "It has been seen by travellers from afar, but I have heard not a whisper of anyone who has been inside its walls."

"Perhaps no one who has been inside has lived to tell the tale," said Jasmine grimly. "Have you considered that?"

6 ~ Noradz

Barda shrugged. "The City of the Rats has an evil reputation, and an Ak-Baba was seen in the skies above it on the morning the Shadow Lord invaded. We can be almost sure that one of the Belt's gems has been hidden there."

"So," said Jasmine, still in that hard voice, "we must go to the place, but we know little of what we will find there. We cannot prepare or plan."

"We could not prepare or plan for the Lake of Tears or the Forests of Silence," Lief put in stoutly. "But still we succeeded in both. As we will succeed in this."

Jasmine tossed her head. "Brave words!" she retorted. "Perhaps you have forgotten that in the Forests you had me to help you, and at the Lake of Tears we had Manus to guide our way. This time, it is different. We are alone, without advice or help."

Her plain speaking irritated Lief, and he could see that it irritated Barda also. Perhaps she was right in what she said, but why lower their spirits?

He turned away from her and stared straight ahead. They rode on in silence.

Shortly afterwards the road ahead of them split into two, as Tom had told them it would. There was a signpost in the middle of the fork, one arm pointing to the left, the other to the right.

"Broad River!" exclaimed Lief. "That is the river on which the City of the Rats stands! Why, what a piece of good fortune!"

Excitedly, he began turning Noodle's head to the right.

"Lief, what are you doing?" protested Jasmine. "We must take the left-hand path. Remember what the man Tom said."

"Don't you see, Jasmine? Tom would never have dreamed that we would go willingly to the City of the Rats," called Lief over his shoulder, as he urged Noodle on. "So of course he warned us against this path. But, as it happens, it is the very path we want. Come on!"

324

Barda and Pip were already following Lief. Still unsure, Jasmine let Zanzee carry her after them.

The track was as wide as the other, and a good, strong road, though showing the marks of cart wheels. As they moved on, the land on either side became more and more rich and green. There were no parched spaces or dead trees here. Fruits and berries grew wild everywhere, and bees hummed around the flowers, their legs weighed down by golden bags of pollen.

Far to the right there were hazy purple hills, and to the left, the green of a forest. Ahead, the road wound like a pale ribbon into the distance. The air was fresh and sweet.

The muddlets snuffled eagerly and began to pick up speed.

"They are enjoying this," laughed Lief, patting Noodle's neck.

"And so am I," called Barda in answer. "How good to ride through fertile country at last. This land, at least, has not been spoiled."

They bounded past a grove of trees and saw that not far ahead a side road branched off the main track and led away towards the purple hills. Idly, Lief wondered where it led.

Suddenly, Noodle made a strange, excited barking sound and stretched out her neck, straining against the reins. Pip and Zanzee were calling out, also. They began leaping ahead, covering great distances with every bound. Lief tossed and bounced on the saddle. It was taking all his strength just to hold on.

"What is the matter with them?" he shouted, as the wind beat against his face.

"I do not know!" gasped Barda. He was trying to slow Pip down, but the muddlet was taking not the slightest notice. "Snuff!" he bellowed. But Pip only ran faster, neck outstretched, mouth wide and eager.

Jasmine shrieked as Zanzee thrust his head forward, ripping the reins violently from her hands. She slipped sideways, and for a terrifying moment Lief thought she was going to fall, but she managed to throw her arms around her mount's neck, and pull herself up on the saddle once more. She clung there grimly, her head bent against the wind, as Zanzee bolted on, the stones of the road scattering under his flying feet.

There was nothing any of them could do. The muddlets were strong — far too strong for them. They thundered to the place where the side road branched, swerved off the main road in a cloud of dust, and bolted on up, up towards the hazy purple hills.

His eyes streaming, his voice hoarse from shouting, Lief saw the hills rushing towards them in a purple blur. There was something black in the midst of the purple. Lief blinked, squinted, tried to see what it was. It was coming closer, closer . . .

And then, without warning, Noodle pulled up short. Lief shot over her head, his own cry of shock ringing in his ears. Dimly he was aware of Jasmine and Barda shouting as they, too, were thrown from their mounts. Then the ground rushed up to meet him, and he knew no more.

✳

There were pains in Lief's legs and back, and his head ached. Something was nudging at his shoulder. He tried to open his eyes. At first they seemed gummed shut, but then he managed to force them open. A face-less red shape was looming over him. He tried to scream, but all that came from his throat was a stran-gled moan.

The red shape drew back. "This one is awake," a voice said.

A hand came down, holding a cup of water. Lief lifted his head and drank thirstily. Slowly he realized that he was lying with Barda and Jasmine on the floor of a large hall. Many torches burned around the stone walls, lighting the room and casting flickering shad-ows, but they did little to warm the cold air. There was a huge fireplace in one corner. It was filled with great logs, but unlit.

An overpowering smell of strong soap mingled with the smell of the burning torches. Perhaps the floor had been recently scrubbed, for the stones on which Lief lay were damp, and there was not a speck of dust anywhere.

The room was full of people. Their heads were shaved, and they were strangely dressed in close-fitting suits of black, with high boots. They were all staring intently at the companions on the floor, fascinated and fearful.

The one with the water backed away, and the towering red figure that had so frightened Lief as he returned to consciousness moved once more into his view. Now he could see that it was a man, dressed entirely in red. Even his boots were red. Gloves covered his hands, and his head was swathed in tight-fitting cloth that covered his mouth and nose, leaving a space only for the eyes. A long whip made of plaited leather hung from his wrist. It trailed behind him, swishing on the ground as he moved.

He saw that Lief had regained his senses, and was watching him. "Noradzeer," he murmured, brushing his hands down his body, from shoulders to hips. It was plainly a greeting of some kind.

Lief wanted to make sure that, whoever these strange people were, they knew he was friendly. He struggled into a sitting position and tried to copy the gesture, and the word.

The black-clad people murmured, then they too swept their hands from their shoulders to their hips and whispered, "Noradzeer, noradzeer, noradzeer . . ." till the great room was echoing with their voices.

Lief stared, his head swimming. "What — what is this place?"

"This is Noradz," said the scarlet figure, his voice muffled by the cloth that covered his mouth and nose. "Visitors are not welcome here. Why have you come?"

"We — did not mean to," Lief said. "Our mounts bolted, and carried us out of our way. We fell . . ." He winced as pain stabbed behind his eyes.

Jasmine and Barda were stirring now, and being given water in their turn. The red figure turned to them and greeted them as he had greeted Lief. Then he spoke again.

"You were lying outside our gates, with your goods scattered about you," he said, his voice cold with suspicion. "There were no mounts to be seen."

"Then they must have run away," exclaimed Jasmine impatiently. "We certainly did not throw ourselves upon the ground with such force as to knock ourselves senseless!"

The man in red drew himself up, lifting the coiling whip menacingly. "Guard your tongue, unclean one," he hissed. "Speak with respect! Do you not know that I am Reece, First Ra-Kachar of the Nine?"

Jasmine began to speak again, but Barda raised his voice, drowning her words.

"We are deeply sorry, my Lord Ra-Kachar," he

said loudly. "We are strangers, and ignorant of your ways."

"The Nine Ra-Kacharz keep the people to the holy laws of cleanliness, watchfulness, and duty," droned Reece. "Thus is the city safe. Noradzeer."

"Noradzeer," murmured the people, bending their bare heads and brushing their bodies from shoulder to thigh.

Barda and Lief glanced at each other. Both were thinking that the sooner they could leave this strange place, the happier they would be.

7 - Strange Customs

Jasmine was clambering to her feet, looking fretfully around the great room. The black-clad people murmured, drawing back from her as though her tattered clothing and tangled hair could somehow contaminate them.

"Where is Kree?" she demanded.

Reece turned his face towards her. "There is another of you?" he asked sharply.

"Kree is a bird," Lief explained hurriedly, as he and Barda stood up also. "A black bird."

"Kree will be waiting for you outside, Jasmine," Barda muttered under his breath. "Be still, now. Filli is safe, isn't he?"

"Yes. But he is hiding under my coat and will not come out," Jasmine hissed sullenly. "He does not like it here, and neither do I."

Barda turned to Reece and bowed. "We are most

grateful for your care of us," he said loudly. "But with your kind permission we will be on our way."

"It is our time to eat, and a platter has been prepared for you," said Reece, his dark eyes sweeping their faces as if daring them to object. "The food has already been blessed by the Nine. When food has been blessed, it must be eaten within the hour. Noradzeer."

"Noradzeer," echoed the people reverently.

Before Barda could say anything else, gongs began to sound, and two great doors at one end of the room opened to reveal a dining hall beyond. Eight tall figures, dressed in red as Reece was, stood at the opening, four on each side. The eight other Ra-Kacharz, thought Lief.

Long, leather whips hung from the Ra-Kacharz' wrists. They watched sternly as the black-clad people began shuffling past them.

Lief's head ached. He had never felt less hungry in his life. He wanted more than anything to be out of this place, but it was clear that he, Barda, and Jasmine were not to be allowed to leave until they had eaten.

Unwillingly, they walked through to the dining hall. It was as clean and scrubbed as the other room had been, and so brightly lit that every corner was visible. It was filled with bare tables, arranged in long rows. The tables were very high, with tall, slender metal legs. A plain cup and plate stood at every place, but there were no tools for eating, and no chairs. The people of Noradz, it seemed, ate with their fingers, standing up.

At the far end of the hall, a set of steps led to a raised platform. There another table stood alone. Lief guessed that this was where the Ra-Kacharz would eat, their high position giving them a good view of all that went on below.

Reece showed Lief, Barda, and Jasmine to their table, which was set a little apart from the others. Then he went to join the other Ra-Kacharz, who, as Lief had expected, were all standing at the table on the platform, facing the crowd.

When he had taken his place in the center, Reece lifted his gloved hands and surveyed the room. "Noradzeer!" he called. He swept his hands from shoulders to hips.

"Noradzeer!" echoed the people.

With one movement, all the Ra-Kacharz pulled away the cloth that swathed their mouths and noses. Immediately, gongs sounded once more, and more people in black began entering the hall, carrying huge, covered serving platters.

"I cannot think of a more uncomfortable way to eat!" Jasmine whispered. She was the smallest person in the room, and the tabletop barely reached her chin.

A serving girl came to their table and put down her burden, her hands trembling. Her light blue eyes were scared. Serving the strangers was plainly frightening for her.

333

"Are there no children in Noradz?" Lief asked her. "The tables are so high."

"Children eat only in the training room," the servant said in a low voice. "Children must learn the holy ways before they can grow to take their places in the hall. Noradzeer."

She removed the cover from the serving platter and Lief, Jasmine, and Barda gasped. The platter was divided into three parts. The largest held an array of tiny sausages and other meats, threaded on wooden sticks with many vegetables of every shape and color. The second was piled with golden, savory pastries and soft, white rolls. The third and smallest was filled with preserved fruits, little pink-iced cakes covered with sugar flowers, and strange-looking round, brown sweets.

Barda picked up one of the sweets and stared at it, as if amazed. "Can this be — chocolate?" he exclaimed. He popped the sweet into his mouth and closed his eyes. "It is!" he murmured blissfully. "Why, I have not tasted chocolate since I was a Palace guard! Over sixteen years!"

Lief had never seen such luxurious food in his life, and suddenly, despite everything, he felt ravenous. He picked up one of the sticks and began chewing at the meat and vegetables. The food was so delicious! Like nothing he had ever tasted before.

"This is so good!" he murmured to the serving girl, with his mouth full. She gazed at him, pleased but a little confused. Plainly, she was used to the food of Noradz, and did not know any other way of eating.

Nervously she stretched out her hand to take the heavy cover from the table. As she lifted it over the serving platter, her fingers trembled and the cover's edge caught one of the bread rolls, and knocked it from its place. The bread rolled onto the table and, before she or Lief could catch it, bounced onto the floor.

The girl screamed — a high, piercing scream of terror. At the same moment there was a cry of rage from the high table. Everyone in the room froze.

"Food is spilled!" roared the Ra-Kacharz as one. "Pick it up! Seize the offender! Seize Tira!"

Several people from the table nearest the guests spun around. One of them darted to the fallen bread and picked it up, holding it high. The others seized the serving girl. She screamed again as they began to drag her towards the high table.

Reece moved towards the steps, uncoiling his whip. "Tira spilled food upon the ground," he droned. "Spilt food is evil. Noradzeer. The evil must be driven out by one hundred strokes of the whip. Noradzeer."

"Noradzeer!" echoed the black-clad people around the tables. They watched as Tira, sobbing in fear, was cast down at Reece's feet. He raised the whip . . .

"No!" Lief darted out from his table. "Do not punish her! It was me! I did it!"

"You?" thundered Reece, lowering the whip.

335

"Yes!" called Lief. "I caused the food to fall. I am sorry." He knew that it was foolhardy to take the blame. But whatever the strange customs of these people, he could not bear for the girl to be punished for a simple accident.

The other Ra-Kacharz were muttering together. The one nearest Reece moved to his side and said something to him. There was a moment's stillness, broken only by the sobbing of the fallen girl. Then Reece faced Lief once more.

"You are a stranger, and unclean," he said. "You do not know our ways. The Nine have decided that you are to be spared punishment."

His voice was harsh. Clearly, he did not approve of this decision, but had been outvoted by the rest.

Breathing a sigh of relief, Lief sidled back to his table as Tira scrambled from the ground and ran, stumbling, from the room.

Barda and Jasmine greeted him with raised eyebrows. "That was a near thing," Barda muttered.

"It was a risk worth taking," Lief answered lightly, though his heart was still thudding at his near escape. "It was a fair chance that they would not punish a stranger as they would punish one of their own — at least on the first occasion."

Jasmine shrugged. She had taken vegetables from one of the sticks, and was holding them up to her shoulder, trying to coax Filli out to eat. "We should leave here as soon as we are able," she said. "These people are very strange. Who knows what other odd laws — ah, Filli, there you are!"

Tempted by the smell of the tidbits, the little creature had at last ventured to poke his nose from under the collar of Jasmine's jacket. Cautiously he crawled out onto her shoulder, took a piece of golden vegetable in his tiny paws, and began to nibble at it.

There was a sudden, strangled sound from the high table. Lief glanced up and was startled to see all the Ra-Kacharz pointing at Jasmine, their faces masks of horror.

The other people in the room turned to look. There was a moment's shocked silence. Then, suddenly, shrieking with terror, they stampeded for the doors.

"Evil!" Reece's voice thundered from the platform. "The unclean ones have brought evil to our halls. They try to destroy us! See! The creature crawls there, on her body! Kill it! Kill it!"

As one, the Nine Ra-Kacharz ran from the platform and plunged towards Jasmine, using their whips freely to slice their way through the panic-stricken crowd.

"It is Filli!" gasped Barda. "They are afraid of Filli."

"Kill it!" howled the Ra-Kacharz. They were very close now.

Barda, Lief, and Jasmine looked around desperately. There was nowhere to run. A press of people struggled at every door, trying to get through.

"Run, Filli!" Jasmine cried in fear. "Run! Hide!"

She threw Filli to the floor and he darted away. The people screamed at the sight of him, stumbling back, falling and trampling one another in their terror. He scampered through the gap in the crowd and was gone.

But Lief, Barda, and Jasmine were trapped. And the Ra-Kacharz were upon them.

8 - The Trial

The great logs in the meeting hall fireplace had been lit, and the blaze threw a ghastly red light over the faces of the prisoners.

For hours they had stood there, while a useless search was made for Filli. The Ra-Kacharz guarded them grimly, their eyes growing darker and more stern as the minutes ticked by.

Exhausted and silent, Lief, Barda, and Jasmine awaited their fate. They had learned by now that it was useless to argue, rage, or plead. In bringing a furred animal into Noradz they had committed the most hideous of crimes.

Finally, Reece spoke.

"We can wait no longer. The trial must begin."

A gong sounded, and black-clad people began to file into the hall. They arranged themselves in rows, facing the prisoners. Lief saw that Tira, the serving girl he had saved from punishment, was in the first row, very near to him. He tried to meet her eyes, but she looked quickly at the ground.

Reece raised his voice so all could hear.

"Because of these unclean ones, evil is abroad in Noradz. They have broken our most sacred law. They claim it was done out of ignorance. I think they lie, and deserve death. Others of the Nine believe them, and think imprisonment should be their fate. Therefore, it will be left to the sacred Cup to decide."

Barda, Jasmine, and Lief stole glances at one another. What new madness was this?

Reece took from the shelf above the fireplace a shining silver goblet — once used for drinking wine, perhaps.

"The Cup reveals the truth," he droned. "Noradzeer."

"Noradzeer," murmured the watching people.

Next, Reece showed two small cards. Each card had one word printed upon it.

LIFE	DEATH

340

He turned to the prisoners. "One among you will draw a card from the Cup," he said, his dark eyes gleaming. "Who will be that person?"

The companions hesitated. Then Lief stepped forward. "I will," he said reluctantly.

Reece nodded. "Face the front," he said briefly.

Lief did as he was told. Reece turned away from him, and from his fellow Ra-Kacharz. He put his gloved hand over the Cup.

Lief saw that Tira was watching Reece with close attention. Suddenly, her blue eyes widened with astonishment and horror. She glanced quickly at Lief, and her lips moved soundlessly.

Lief's face began to burn as he made out the mouthed words.

Both cards say "Death."

Tira must have seen Reece replace the "Life" card with a second "Death" card hidden in his sleeve or his glove. Reece was determined that the strangers would die.

The tall red figure turned back to him, the Cup held high. "Choose!" Reece sneered.

Lief did not know what to do. If he cried out that the Cup held only two "Death" cards, no one would believe him. Everyone would think that he was simply afraid to face the trial. No one would take his word, or Tira's, against the word the First Ra-Kachar of Noradz. And Reece could easily change the cards around again if challenged.

341

Lief slipped his fingers under his shirt and gripped the topaz fixed to the Belt. It had helped him find answers before. Could it help him now? The fire roared behind him, lighting the tall figure in front of him with an eerie glow. The silver cup shone red like solid flame.

Flame. Fire . . .

His heart thudding, Lief stretched up his hand, dipped his fingers into the Cup, and chose a card. Then, like lightning, he whirled, seemed to stumble backwards, and dropped the card into the roaring flames. It flared for a moment, and was consumed.

"I beg pardon for my clumsiness," cried Lief, over the horrified gasps of the crowd. "But you can easily tell which card I drew. Simply look at the one remaining in the Cup."

Reece stood perfectly still, seething with baffled rage, as one of the other Ra-Kacharz took the Cup from his hand and plucked out the card that still lay within it. She held it up.

"The card that remains is 'Death,' " she droned. "The prisoner drew the 'Life' card. The Cup has spoken."

Lief felt Barda's hand grip his shoulder. Weak at the knees, he turned to face his friends. Their eyes were relieved, but full of questions. They suspected that he had burned the card on purpose, and wondered why.

"Take them to the dungeons," Reece thundered.

"There they will live out their lives, repenting of the evil they have done."

The eight other Ra-Kacharz surrounded Lief, Barda, and Jasmine and began marching them from the hall. The whispering crowd parted to let them through. Lief twisted his head, looking for Tira among the black-clad figures, but could not see her.

As they left the hall, they heard Reece's voice raised once more as he spoke to the people. "Continue the search for the creature who has befouled our city," he ordered. "It must be found and killed before night-fall."

Lief glanced at Jasmine. She did not open her lips, but her face was pale and set. He knew that she was thinking of Filli — hunted and afraid.

The Ra-Kacharz pushed their prisoners through a maze of brightly lit hallways and down some wind-ing stone steps. The smell of soap hung everywhere, and the stones under their feet were scrubbed smooth.

At the bottom of the steps was a large space lined with metal doors, each with a narrow flap through which a tray of food could be passed. The leading Ra-Kachar threw one of the doors open, and her companions pulled Lief, Barda, and Jasmine to-wards it.

Jasmine took one look at the grim, windowless cell beyond the door and began to struggle wildly. Lief and Barda, too, fought grimly for their freedom. But it was no use. They had no weapons, no protection against the whips of the Ra-Kacharz, cracking around their faces, stinging their legs and arms. They were driven back into the cell. Then the door was slammed behind them and a heavy bolt was driven home.

They threw themselves at the door, beating on it with their fists. But the footsteps of the Ra-Kacharz were already fading into the distance.

Frantically, they searched the cell, looking for weaknesses. But the narrow wooden bunks fixed to one wall could not be moved. The empty water trough fixed to another wall was solid as rock.

"They will come back," Barda said grimly. "We were condemned to life, not death. They will have to give us food, and fill the water trough. They cannot leave us here to starve or die of thirst."

But miserable hours passed, and no one came.

※

They had all drifted into an uneasy sleep when the scratching came at the door. Even when Lief woke, he thought he had dreamed the timid sound. But then it came again. He jumped from his bunk and ran to the door with Jasmine and Barda close behind him. The food flap had been pushed open. Through it, they could see the blue eyes of Tira.

"The First Ra-Kachar gave orders that he and he alone would bring you food and water," she whispered. "But — I feared that he may have . . . forgotten. Have you eaten? Has the water trough been filled?"

344

"No!" Lief whispered back. "And you know that he did not just forget, Tira. That is why you came. Reece intends us to die here."

"It cannot be!" Her voice was agonized. "The Cup gave you Life."

"Reece cares nothing for the Cup!" hissed Barda. "He cares only for his own will. Tira, unbolt the door! Let us out!"

"I cannot! I dare not! You brought evil to our halls, and it has still not been found. All except the night cooks are sleeping now. That is why I could slip away and not be missed. But the people are afraid, and many are crying out in their sleep. In the morning, the search will begin again." Through the narrow slit, the girl's eyes were dark with fear.

"Where we come from, animals like Filli are not evil," Lief said. "We meant no harm in bringing him here. He is Jasmine's friend. But if you do not let us out of this cell, we are doomed. Reece will see to it that we die of hunger and thirst and no one will ever know. No one but you."

There was no reply but a soft groan.

"Please help us!" begged Lief. "Tira, please!"

There was a moment's silence. Then the eyes disappeared and they heard the sliding of the bolt.

The door swung open and they crowded out of the cell. White-faced in the light of the torches, Tira gave them water and they drank thirstily. She said nothing as they thanked her, and when they bolted

345

the door behind them to disguise their escape, she shivered and covered her face with her hands. Plainly, she felt as though she was doing something very wrong.

But when they discovered their packs hidden in a crevice beside the stone steps, she gasped with surprise. "We were told that these had been put into your cell with you!" she said. "So that you would have bedding, and some comforts."

"Who told you that?" asked Barda grimly.

"The First Ra-Kachar," she whispered. "He said he had brought them to you himself."

"Well, he did not, as you can see," snapped Jasmine, pulling her bag onto her back.

They crept up the steps. The passage above was empty, but they could hear a few distant voices.

"We must escape the city," Barda whispered. "Which way should we go?"

"There is no way out." Tira shook her head hopelessly. "The gate in the hill is locked and barred. Those who work in the fields are taken out each morning and brought back at night. No one else may leave, on pain of death."

"There must be another way!" hissed Lief.

She hesitated, then shook her head. But Jasmine had seen the hesitation, and pounced.

"What did you think of, just then? Tell us what is in your mind!" she urged.

Tira licked her lips. "It is said . . . it is said that

the Hole leads, in the end, to the outside world. But — "

"What is the Hole?" demanded Barda. "Where is it?"

"It is near the kitchens," shuddered Tira. "It is where they throw the food that has not passed inspection. But it is — forbidden."

"Take us there!" hissed Jasmine fiercely. "Take us there now!"

9 - The Kitchens

They crept like thieves through the corridors, darting into side passages whenever they heard someone approaching. Finally they reached a small metal door.

"This leads to the walkways above the kitchens," Tira whispered. "The walkways are used by the Ra-Kacharz, to watch the work below, and by those whose task it is to wash the kitchen walls."

She opened the door a crack. From the space beyond poured the smell of cooking, and a muffled clattering.

"Be very silent," the girl breathed. "Tread softly. Then we will not be noticed. The night cooks work at speed. They have much to do before dawn."

She slipped through the door, and the companions followed her. The sight that met their eyes astonished them.

They were standing on a narrow metal walkway. Far below lay the great kitchens of Noradz, clattering with sound and blazing with light. The kitchens were huge — as big as a small village — and filled with working people dressed as Tira was, but all in gleaming white.

Some were peeling vegetables or preparing fruits. Others were mixing, baking, stirring pots that bubbled on the huge stoves. Thousands of cakes cooled on racks, waiting to be iced and decorated. Hundreds of pies and tarts were being lifted from the great ovens. At one side, a team was packing prepared foods into boxes and glass or stone jars.

"But — surely this does not go on every day and every night?" gasped Lief in amazement. "How much food can the people of Noradz eat?"

"Only a small amount of the food prepared is eaten," Tira whispered back. "Much of what is cooked does not pass the inspection and is wasted." She sighed. "The cooks are valued, trained from their youngest days, but I would not like to be one of them. It makes them sad to try so hard, and to fail so often."

They crept along the walkway, looking down, fascinated, at the activity below. They had been moving for about five minutes when Tira stopped and crouched.

"Ra-Kachaz!" she breathed.

Sure enough, two red-clad figures were striding into the kitchens.

349

"It is an inspection," whispered Tira.

The Ra-Kacharz moved quickly to a place where four cooks stood, their hands behind their backs. Hundreds of jars of sugared fruits, bright as jewels, were lined up on a counter, awaiting inspection.

The Ra-Kacharz paced along the line of jars, staring at them closely. When they had reached the end, they turned and paced back again. This time they pointed at certain jars, and these the cooks picked up and put on another bench.

When finally the inspection was finished, six jars of fruit had been separated from the rest.

"Those are the jars that will be blessed, and eaten by the people," said Tira. "The rest have been rejected." She gazed with sympathy at the cooks, who, shoulders sagging with disappointment, had begun packing the rejected jars into a huge metal bin.

Lief, Barda, and Jasmine stared, horrified. The fruit all looked delicious and wholesome to them. "This is wicked!" Lief muttered angrily, as the Ra-Kacharz turned and strode away to another part of the kitchens. "In Del, people are starving, scrabbling for scraps. And here, good food is wasted!"

Tira shook her head. "It is not good food," she insisted earnestly. "The Ra-Kacharz know when food is unclean. By their inspections the Ra-Kacharz protect the people from disease and illness. Noradzeer."

Lief would have liked to argue. Jasmine, too, was

red with anger. But Barda shook his head at them, warning them to be silent. Lief bit his lips. He knew that Barda was right. They needed Tira's help. There was no point in upsetting her. She was not to understand how things were in the rest of Deltora. She knew only her place, and the laws with which she had grown up.

In silence they moved on along the walkway and at last came to the end of the kitchens. Steep metal steps led down to the ground just in front of a door.

"The Hole is through that door," Tira said in a low voice. "But — "

She broke off and crouched once more, gesturing to her companions to do the same. The four cooks who had made the sugared fruits walked into view below, carrying the bin of rejected jars between them. The bin was now sealed tightly with a metal lid. They carried it through the door, and disappeared from sight.

"They are going to put the bin into the Hole," Tira whispered.

A few moments later the cooks came back and walked off to their part of the kitchens to begin the task of preparing food all over again. Tira, Lief, Barda, and Jasmine crept down the steps, passed shelves lined with pots and pans, and slipped through the door.

They found themselves in a small, bare room. To

their left was a red-painted door. Facing them, on the wall opposite the kitchens, a metal grille barred the round, dark entrance to the Hole.

"Where does the red door lead?" asked Barda.

"To the sleeping quarters of the Nine," Tira whispered. "They sleep in turns, it is said, coming through this door when inspections are due."

She glanced nervously over her shoulder. "Let us leave here, now. I brought you here because you demanded it. But at any moment we may be surprised."

The companions crept closer to the Hole and peered through the grille. Dimly they saw the beginning of a tunnel lined with stone that seemed to gleam red. The tunnel's roof and sides were rounded. It was very narrow, and sloped down into blackness. Deep within it, something growled, long and low.

"What is inside?" murmured Lief.

"We do not know," answered Tira. "Only the Ra-Kacharz can enter the Hole and survive."

"So they tell you!" said Lief scornfully.

But Tira shook her head. "In my life I have seen two people try to escape the city through the Hole," she said softly. "Both were brought out stiff and dead. Their eyes were open and staring. Their hands were torn and blistered. There was foam on their lips." She shuddered. "It is said that they died of terror."

The dull roar sounded again from the tunnel. They peered into its darkness, but could see nothing.

"Tira, do you know where our weapons are?"

352

asked Barda urgently. "The swords — and the daggers?"

Tira nodded warily. "They are waiting at the furnace," she whispered. "Tomorrow they will be melted down, to be made into new things for the kitchen."

"Get them for us!" Barda urged.

She shook her head. "I cannot!" she hissed desperately. "It is forbidden to touch them, and already I have committed terrible crimes for you."

"All we want is to leave here!" exclaimed Lief. "How can that hurt your people? And no one will ever know that it was you who helped us."

"Reece is the First of the Nine," murmured Tira. "His word is law."

"Reece does not deserve your loyalty," hissed Barda furiously. "You have seen for yourself that he lies and cheats, and makes a mockery of your laws! If anyone deserves to die, it is he!"

But in saying this, he had gone too far. Tira's cheeks flushed, her eyes widened, and she turned and ran back into the kitchen. The door swung closed behind her.

Barda sighed impatiently. "I frightened her," he muttered. "I should have guarded my tongue! What will we do now?"

"We will make the best of it." Determinedly, Lief lifted the grille from the tunnel entrance. "If the Ra-Kacharz can enter the Hole and live, so can we — with weapons or without."

He turned and beckoned to Jasmine. She backed away, shaking her head.

"I cannot go," she said loudly. "I thought Filli might be here, waiting for me. But he is not. He would not leave Noradz without me, and I will not leave without him."

Lief felt like shaking her. "Jasmine! There is no time to waste!" he urged. "Stop this foolishness!"

She turned her clear green gaze to him. "I am not asking you and Barda to remain," she said calmly. "You began this quest without me, and so you can continue." She looked away. "Perhaps — it may be better, in any case," she added.

"What do you mean?" Lief demanded. "Why would it be better?"

She shrugged. "We do not agree on — some things," she said. "I am not sure — "

But she never finished what she had to say, for at that moment the red door behind her burst open and Reece strode in, his black eyes glistening with triumphant fury. Before she could move he had grabbed her with one powerful arm and lifted her off her feet.

"So, girl!" he snarled in her ear. "My ears did not deceive me. By what witchcraft did you escape from your cell?"

Lief and Barda started towards him but he lashed out at them with his whip, holding them back.

"Spies!" he growled. "Now your wickedness is proved. Now you invade our kitchens — to guide your evil creature to them, no doubt. When the people hear this, they will be happy for you to die a thousand deaths."

Jasmine struggled, but his grip was like iron.

"You cannot escape, girl," he sneered. "Even now, others of the Nine are stirring beyond this door. Your friends will die before you. I trust you will enjoy hearing their screams."

He lashed at Lief and Barda with his whip, driving them back, slowly but surely, towards the Hole.

10 ~ The Hole

One thought burned in Lief's mind more strongly than all the rest. Some terrible danger really did lurk within the darkness of the Hole. Otherwise Reece would not be smiling so triumphantly as he drove his prisoners towards it.

Barda and Jasmine had plainly come to the same conclusion. Jasmine was shrieking, vainly tearing at the Ra-Kacharz' thick garments with her nails. Barda was struggling to hold his ground, his arms wrapped around his head to protect it.

The leather whip flicked viciously around Lief's ears. He staggered back, turning away, the stinging pain bringing tears to his eyes. Again the whip cracked, and now the warm blood was running down his neck and shoulders. The blackness of the Hole yawned just in front of him . . .

Then there was a dull, ringing thump. And suddenly there was no more cracking of the whip, no more stinging pain.

Lief spun around.

Tira was standing over Reece's crumpled body. The kitchen door gaped wide behind her. Her eyes were glazed with fear. In her left hand she clutched the companions' weapons. In her right was the frying pan she had snatched from the kitchen shelf and used to hit Reece over the head.

With a gasp of horror at what she had done, she threw the pan violently away from her. It struck the stones with a ringing crash.

Lief, Barda, and Jasmine raced to the girl's side and took their weapons from her. She seemed paralyzed with shock. She had sprung to their defense without thinking, but plainly in attacking a Ra-Kachar she had committed a terrible crime.

"Barda!" hissed Jasmine urgently. She pointed. The handle of the red door was turning.

Barda flung himself against the door and leaned against it with all his strength. Jasmine added her weight to his. An angry thumping began and the door shuddered.

"Run, Tira!" hissed Lief. "Go! Forget this ever happened."

She stared at him, wild-eyed. He hurried her towards the kitchen door, pushed her through, and shot the bolt behind her. Now the Ra-Kacharz trying to beat their way through the red door would have no help from the people in the kitchen, and, with luck, Tira would be able to reach the stairs and climb to the walkway unseen.

He spun around again just in time to see Barda and Jasmine knocked sprawling and the red door flying open. He sprang to his friends' aid, and, at the same moment, three Ra-Kacharz charged through the opening. Though they had been roused from sleep, they were fully dressed in their red suits, gloves, and boots, and their heads and faces were covered.

Their eyes were already burning with rage as they burst into the little room. But when they saw their leader lying on the floor, and the three prisoners standing over him, they roared and lunged forward, cracking their whips without mercy.

Barda, Lief, and Jasmine were driven back, their blades slashing uselessly at the empty air. Lief cried out in frustration as a whip curled around his sword and tore it out of his hand.

Now he was helpless. In moments he heard with horror the sound of Barda's sword, too, clattering to the ground. Now Jasmine's two daggers were their only defense. But the Ra-Kacharz were pushing forward, driving them into a corner, the lashing whips whirling together in the air like a terrible, cutting machine.

"Stop!" cried Jasmine piercingly. "We mean you no harm! We want only to leave this place!"

Her voice echoed against the stone walls, soaring above the cracking of the whips. The Ra-Kacharz did not falter. They made no sign that they had even heard.

But someone had heard. Through the red door hurtled a scrap of grey fur, chattering and squeaking with joy.

"Filli!" exclaimed Jasmine.

The Ra-Kacharz shouted in horror and disgust, lurching out of the way as the little animal scuttled between them, leaping for Jasmine's shoulder.

It was just a moment's distraction, but it was all that Barda needed. With a roar he hurled himself at the two nearest red-clad figures, throwing them against the wall with all his strength. Their heads hit the stones and they slumped together to the ground.

Lief twisted and kicked at the third Ra-Kachar, feeling his foot connect with the leg just above the boot. The man howled and stumbled. Lief snatched up the frying pan and felled him with a single blow.

Panting above the bodies of their fallen enemies, the friends glanced over to where Jasmine stood, crooning to Filli.

"Filli saved us," Jasmine said happily. "How brave he is! He was lost, but he heard my voice and came running to me. Poor Filli. He has been so afraid, and in such danger!"

"*He* has been afraid and in danger!" exploded Barda. "And what of us?"

But Jasmine simply shrugged and went back to stroking Filli's fur.

"What are we to do now?" muttered Lief. "There are four Ra-Kacharz here, counting Reece. And we know that there are two in the kitchens. But three of the Nine are still missing. Where are they? Where should we go for safety?"

"We must take our chances with the tunnel," said Barda grimly, looking around for his sword. "There is no other way out for us."

Lief glanced at the Hole. "Reece thought that whatever is in there would kill us," he said.

"If the Ra-Kacharz can survive it, so can we," snapped Barda. "They are strong, and good fighters, but they do not have magic powers."

"We should put on their garments," said Jasmine from her place by the wall. "Surely it is not by chance that they dress differently from the others in this place, and it is only they who can use the Hole. Perhaps the creature that dwells in the darkness is trained to attack all colors but red."

Barda nodded slowly. "It could be. In any case, to wear the Ra-Kacharz garments is a good idea," he said. "Our own clothes mark us as strangers. We could never bluff our way out of the city through the front entrance. But perhaps the back way . . ."

They wasted no more time, but began to strip the three Ra-Kacharz they had just defeated. Jasmine was quick and deft at the work. Lief could not help remembering, with a chill, how many times she had stripped the bodies of Grey Guards in the Forests of

Silence. She had done it to obtain clothes and other things she needed, and she had done it efficiently and without a moment's pity, as she was doing now.

They dressed quickly, pulling the red garments over their own clothes, the boots over their own shoes. The Ra-Kacharz lay still. Tight white underclothes covered them from wrist to ankle. Their heads, like those of the other people in the city, were shaved bald.

"They do not look so dangerous now," said Jasmine grimly, winding red cloth around her head and making sure that Filli was buttoned securely under the collar of her clothes.

Despite his haste and worry, Lief had to smile as he glanced at her. She looked very strange. The Ra-Kacharz garments were too big for him and even for Barda, but on Jasmine they hung in vast, baggy folds. The gloves were not a problem, for they were made of a clinging material that fitted all sizes. But he doubted that she would be able to walk in the huge red boots.

Jasmine had thought of that. Carrying the boots in her hand, she ran over to where Reece lay. She pulled off his gloves, crumpled them, and stuffed them into the toe of one boot. Then she unwound the cloth that bound his head and face and used it in the second boot.

Reece mumbled, his shaven head rolling on the hard floor.

"He is waking," Jasmine said, pulling on the

boots. She drew the dagger from her belt.

"Do not kill him!" exclaimed Lief in panic.

Jasmine glanced at him in surprise. "Why not?" she demanded. "He would kill me, if our places were reversed. And when he was attacking you, you would have killed him, if you could."

Lief could not explain. He knew she would never agree that to kill in the heat of the moment, in defense of your life, was very different from killing a man, even an enemy, in cold blood.

But Barda had suddenly exclaimed, striding to Jasmine's side. He crouched beside Reece's body. "Look at this!" he muttered, pushing the man's head to one side.

Lief knelt beside him. On the side of Reece's neck was the ugly scar of an old burn. The scar was in a shape he knew only too well.

"He has been branded," he hissed, looking at the dull red mark with horror. "Branded with the mark of the Shadow Lord. Yet he lives here, free and powerful. What does this mean?"

"It means that things in Noradz are not what they seem," said Barda grimly. Quickly he moved to the bodies of the other Ra-Kacharz. The Shadow Lord's brand was on every one.

They looked up sharply as the handle of the door that led into the kitchen shook and rattled. There was a loud knock. Someone was trying to get in.

"Another inspection must have been completed," muttered Jasmine. "The cooks have a bin of food to throw away."

Finding that their way was barred, the people behind the door began shouting and thumping with their fists. Reece mumbled and groaned. His eyelids fluttered. He was about to wake.

Barda sprang to his feet. "We will take him with us. We will force him to tell us how to save ourselves from whatever is inside the passage. And, in any case, a hostage will be useful."

Hastily they pulled their packs onto their backs and dragged Reece to the Hole entrance. They pushed him into the darkness. Then, one by one, they crawled after him. There was no time, now, to think of what might await them below.

11 - The Price of Freedom

Lief slithered cautiously down the slope, holding Reece's ankles with one gloved hand, and with the other catching at the sides and roof of the passage to stop himself from moving too quickly. It was not easy, for the rock was covered with a thin layer of fungus that slipped and smeared under his fingers. Gradually the passage narrowed until it was just wide enough for one of the big bins to move through without sticking.

Lief's pack kept catching on the roof. With a shout of warning to Barda, who was behind him, he wriggled till the straps slipped from his shoulders, and let himself slide away from underneath the bag. He knew that it would keep moving after him. The slope had become steeper, and it was all he could do to stop himself from slipping down out of control.

Other things had changed, too. The growling was louder, a ceaseless rumbling that seemed to fill Lief's ears and his mind. It was harder to hold Reece, who was still not quite awake, but was starting to move his legs, to catch at the walls with his hands, and to raise his head so that now and then it grazed the roof of the tunnel.

And there was light below — a faint glow, too yellow to be moonlight. It quickly grew brighter and Lief realized that he was reaching the bottom of the slope, that the passage was about to level out.

"Be ready!" he shouted to Barda and Jasmine. And almost at the same moment, without warning, Reece's body began to writhe and twist. He shrieked and kicked. His ankles slipped from Lief's grasp and he slid away, downward towards the light. Gasping with shock, Lief saw his jerking body reach the bottom of the slope.

But it did not stop. Somehow, it kept moving.

Thinking of nothing but keeping his enemy in sight, Lief let go of the walls and let himself slide down the last part of the slope. In moments he had reached level ground.

Ahead of him the passage broadened. Light glowed softly from the roof. The rumbling sound was all about him. The ground beneath him was no longer the smooth, hard rock of the tunnel, but something softer, lumpier — something that trembled slightly under his hands . . . and that moved! Like Reece, he was being carried on — and the ground itself was carrying him!

The red-clad figure was crawling a little further ahead. Lief picked himself up and ran towards it, covering the distance in seconds. He jumped for the writhing man, wrestling with him, trying to hold him still.

Their rolling, struggling bodies hit the wall at the side of the passage. Lief felt rough earth beneath him. Rough earth that did not rumble or move. Reece arched his back, cried out, and lay still.

Then Lief realized two things. The center of the passage was a moving path, driven by some unseen machinery. And Reece was dead. Horribly dead. Lief gazed down at the terrible face, and shuddered, remembering Tira's description of others who had tried to escape through the Hole.

He heard a shout and saw Barda and Jasmine running towards him down the pathway, looming out of the darkness with amazing speed.

"Jump off to the side!" Lief called. "The moving strip is only in the center!"

They did as he told them, stumbling as their feet hit solid ground. When they reached his side, and saw Reece's body, they gasped in horror.

"What — what has happened to him?" muttered Barda, shuddering.

The palms of the man's hands, and the top of his

shaved skull, were smeared with red fungus, and hideously blistered. Foam flecked his lips. His face was blue, twisted into a grimace of agony.

"Poison!" breathed Jasmine. She looked feverishly around her. "In the Forests of Silence there is a spider whose bite can — "

"There are no spiders here," Lief broke in, his stomach churning. His finger shook slightly as he pointed to the dead man's head and hands. "The fungus in the passage — I think — I think one touch on bare skin is deadly. We dragged Reece to his death. He woke, and saw where he was. But already it was too late."

Sickened, they looked down at the crumpled body. "I did not know," Jasmine said, defiantly, at last. "I did not know that to take his gloves and the wrapping from his head would kill him!"

"Of course you did not," said Barda quietly. "How could you? Only the Ra-Kacharz know that it is their gloves and head-coverings that allow them to enter the Hole and live." He grimaced. "Our clothes are smeared all over with the fungus. How will we be able to take them off in safety?"

Lief had been thinking about that.

"I think that the poison is only deadly when it is fresh," he muttered, looking down at his own gloved hands. "I do not see how, otherwise, the Ra-Kacharz could go among their people without harming them."

Barda shrugged. "I pray that you are right."

There was a soft sound behind them. They spun around and saw the gleaming shape of one of the silver drums sliding down the Hole and coming to rest on the moving pathway. It settled gently and began to come towards them.

"I closed the grille after us, hoping that the cooks would not realize that we had escaped into the Hole," said Jasmine. "It seems they have not."

"Not yet," said Barda grimly. "But once the Ra-Kacharz' sleeping quarters have been searched, they will know there was nowhere else for us to go. We must find the way out quickly. If we follow this tunnel, I believe we will find ourselves on the other side of the hill."

Leaving Reece's body where it lay, they jumped back onto the moving pathway and began running along it, soon leaving the silver drum far behind them.

They had not been travelling for long when they saw a gleam ahead of them, felt fresh air on their faces, and heard the sound of clangs and voices. They jumped from the moving pathway again and began creeping along beside it, flattening themselves against the tunnel wall.

It grew lighter. The voices grew louder. There were strange, snuffling sounds, too — sounds that seemed familiar to Lief, though he could not place them. And then, all at once, he saw a gateway ahead. The moving pathway stopped just in front of it, and a small cluster of the silver bins stood in the opening like guards. Beyond them Lief could see the shapes of trees, and grey sky. A night bird called. It was nearly dawn.

As he watched, three tall figures strode into view. Each lifted one of the bins, and carried it out of sight.

"They were Ra-Kacharz!" hissed Jasmine. "Did you see?"

Lief nodded in puzzlement. So the three missing Ra-Kacharz were here. What were they doing with the waste food? And what was that snuffling sound? He had definitely heard it before. But where?

The three companions crept forward, keeping low and close to the wall, craning their necks to see through the gateway. But when at last the scene outside lay before their eyes, they stopped dead, gaping with astonishment.

The Ra-Kacharz were lifting the bins onto a cart, carefully packing straw between them so they would not rattle together. Two other carts stood waiting, already fully loaded. And snuffling happily between the shafts of each cart was — a muddlet!

"They are taking the bins away! And they are using our muddlets to do it!" Lief whispered.

Jasmine shook her head. "I do not think they are our beasts," she breathed. "They look very like them, but their color patches are in different places." She peered around the corner of the gateway and stiffened. "There is a whole field of muddlets just over there," she hissed. "There must be twenty of them!"

Barda shook his head. "Our beasts are probably among them," he said grimly. "But they can stay there. I would not ride a muddlet again if my life depended upon it."

"Well, our lives *do* depend on our getting away from here as fast as we can," muttered Jasmine. "What do you think we should do?"

Barda and Lief exchanged glances. The same thought was in both their minds.

"The straw between the bins is deep," said Lief. "We could hide in it well enough, I think."

Barda nodded. "So, history will repeat itself, Lief." He grinned. "We will escape from here in the same way your father escaped from the palace in Del as a boy. In a rubbish cart!"

"But what of Kree?" Jasmine whispered. "How will he know where I am?"

As if in answer to her question, there was a screech from one of the trees. Jasmine's face brightened.

"He is here!" she hissed.

At that moment the Ra-Kacharz came back to carry away more bins and the companions moved out of sight. But as soon as the red-clad figures had staggered away with their huge burdens, three shadows darted from the shelter of the gateway and climbed into one of the loaded carts. One of them signalled at the trees as she burrowed under the straw between the bins, and a bird cried out in answer.

The friends lay cramped, still, and hidden while the Ra-Kacharz finished their work.

"Was that the last?" they heard a familiar voice ask. It was the woman who had spoken for them at the trial.

"It seems so," said another voice. "I had thought there would be more. There must be a problem in the kitchens. But we can wait no longer, or we will be late."

Late? Lief thought, suddenly alert. Late for what?

There was a creaking sound as the Ra-Kacharz climbed into the carts. Then three voices cried, "Brix!" and with a jolt the carts started to move.

Lying under the straw, the three companions could see nothing but patches of grey sky, and, now and then, the shape of Kree flying high above them. If the Ra-Kacharz thought it strange that a raven should be flying before dawn, they said nothing. Perhaps, Lief thought, they did not even notice Kree, so intent were they on urging the muddlets to greater speed.

Lief, Barda, and Jasmine had planned to jump from the cart when they were a safe distance from the city. But they had not counted upon their cart being in the middle of the three. And they had not counted upon the speed of the muddlets.

371

The carts jolted and bounced upon the rough roads, and the countryside flew by. Even dragging heavy loads, the beasts galloped amazingly fast. It was plain that any attempt to jump would lead to injury and capture.

"We will have to wait until the carts stop," whispered Jasmine. "Surely they cannot be going far."

But the minutes stretched into hours, and dawn had broken, before finally the carts slowed and jolted to a halt. And when, sleepy and confused, Lief peered cautiously through the straw to see where they were, his stomach seemed to turn over.

They were back at Tom's shop. And marching towards them was a troop of Grey Guards.

12 - A Matter of Business

The carts creaked as the drivers climbed from their seats and jumped to the ground. "You are late!" growled the leader of the Grey Guards.

"It could not be helped," said one of the Ra-Kacharz calmly. Lief heard a jingling sound, and guessed that the muddlets were being freed from their harness.

There was the sound of hooves, as though horses were being led towards the carts. The grey horses from the field behind the shop, Lief thought.

"Good morrow, my lords and my lady Ra-Kacharz!" shouted Tom's voice. "A fine day!"

"A fine day to be late!" the Guard grumbled.

"Leave this to me, my friend," said Tom heartily. "I will see to the changing of the beasts. Go and finish your ale. It is a long, dry way back to Del."

Lief's heart lurched. He heard Barda and Jasmine draw quick, horrified breaths.

The food was not to be dumped. The carts were going on to Del!

Lief lay motionless, his mind whirling. He hardly heard the sounds of the Guards' feet marching back to the shop. Suddenly, everything had fallen into place. For centuries carts had trundled up the hill to the palace in Del, loaded with luxurious foods. However scarce food was in the city, the favored people of the palace never went hungry.

No one had ever known where the food came from. But now Lief did.

The food came from Noradz. The people of Noradz labored to grow and gather food in their fertile fields. The cooks of Noradz worked night and day to produce delicious dishes. But only a little of what they made was enjoyed by their people. The rest was taken all the way to the palace in Del. Once it had kept the kings and queens of Deltora in ignorance of their people's misery. Now it fed the servants of the Shadow Lord.

The Ra-Kacharz were traitors to their people. Tom, who had pretended to be against the Shadow Lord, was in fact a friend to the Grey Guards.

A hot wave of anger flooded Lief. But Barda had his mind on more pressing matters.

"We must get out of this cart!" he hissed. "Now, while the Guards are gone. Lief, can you see — ?"

"I can see nothing!" Lief whispered back.

Harness jingled. Kree screeched from some-where nearby.

"It is strange. That black bird has followed us all the way from Noradz," said a Ra-Kachar's voice.

"Indeed," said Tom thoughtfully.

Lief, Barda, and Jasmine stiffened under their covering of straw. Tom had seen Kree before. Would he guess . . . ?

Tom cleared his throat. "By the by, I must give you bad news. You will have to return to Noradz on foot. The fresh beasts kept here for your journey home have been stolen — by some crafty travellers."

"We know it!" said one of the Ra-Kacharz an-grily. "You should have taken more care. We found the beasts trying to get back into their field behind the hill late yesterday. They had bolted for home, and thrown the strangers from their backs outside our front gate."

"The strangers brought evil to our halls," an-other Ra-Kachar droned. "They escaped death by a breath, and even now lie in our dungeons."

"Indeed," said Tom again, very softly. Then his voice became more cheerful. "There! These poor, tired muddlets are free from their bonds. If you will take them to the field, I will finish harnessing the horses. Then, perhaps, you will share a mug of ale with me before you begin your march."

The Ra-Kacharz agreed, and soon Lief, Barda,

and Jasmine heard the sound of the muddlets being led away.

Moments later, Tom spoke again. It seemed he was talking to the horses. "Should anyone wish to leave a cart unobserved, and run to the trees at the side of the shop, this would be the time to do it. Poor Tom is alone here, now."

The message was clear. Clumsily, the three companions wriggled out of the straw and ran, feeling stiff and bruised, to the shelter of the trees. Tom did not look up. He just went on harnessing the horses, whistling softly to himself.

Lief, Barda, and Jasmine lay watching as the shopkeeper walked casually to the back of the cart where they had been hiding and picked up the straw that had fallen to the ground. He pushed it back into place, then strolled towards the trees, his hands in his pockets. He bent down and began pulling grass, as though he was gathering it for the horses.

"You sold us muddlets that did not belong to you!" Barda hissed at him furiously.

"Ah well," murmured Tom, without looking up. "Poor Tom finds it hard to resist gold. He admits it. But what happened was your fault, not mine, my friend. If you had taken the left-hand path, as I advised, the beasts would never have caught the scent of home and bolted. You have only yourselves to blame for your present trouble."

"Perhaps we do," said Lief bitterly. "But at least our only crime is foolishness. You, however, are a liar. You pretend to be on the side of those who would resist the Shadow Lord, and all the time you help to feed his servants. You deal with Grey Guards as friends."

Tom straightened, a clump of sweet grass in his hand, and turned to look at the sign that rose so proudly upon his roof.

"Have you not noticed, my friend?" he said. "Tom's name looks the same, whichever side you are on. It is the same whether you approach from the west

377

or the east. It is the same whether you are inside his shop, or outside it, whether you see it in a mirror, or with your own eyes. And Tom himself is like his name. It is a matter of business."

"Business?" spat Lief.

"Certainly. I am the same Tom to all. I do not take sides. I do not interest myself in things that are not my affair. This is wise, in these hard times. And there is far more money in it."

He smiled, the edges of his wide mouth curving up, creasing his thin face. "Now, I suggest you make haste to leave this place. I will keep my good friends the Ra-Kacharz here for as long as I can, to give you a good start. Take off those glaring red garments first, but do not leave them here, I beg you. I want no trouble."

He turned away and began strolling back towards the carts.

"You are a deceiver!" Lief hissed after him.

Tom paused. "Perhaps," he drawled, without looking back. "But I am a live, rich one. And because of me, you live to fight another day."

He walked on, holding out the grass and clicking his tongue to the horses.

The three friends began pulling off the red garments and boots, and stuffing them into their packs. Lief was simmering with rage. Jasmine glanced at him curiously.

378

"Tom helped us," she pointed out. "Why should you ask any more of him? Many creatures believe in nothing but themselves. He is one of those."

"Tom is not a creature, but a man," Lief snapped. "He should know what is right!"

"Are you so sure *you* know?" Jasmine answered sharply.

Lief stared at her. "What do you mean by that?" he demanded.

"Do not argue," said Barda wearily. "Save your strength for walking. It is a long way to Broad River." He fastened his pack, slung it over his shoulder, and tramped off through the trees.

"We must go back to Noradz first," said Lief, hurrying after him. "We must tell the people that they are being lied to!"

"Indeed?" said Barda wearily. "And if we survived long enough to tell them, which we probably would not, and if they believed us, which I do not think they would, and if by some miracle they broke the pattern of centuries, rebelled against the Ra-Kacharz, and refused to send their food away any longer . . . what do you think would happen?"

"The Shadow Lord's food supply would dry up," said Lief promptly.

"Yes. And then the Shadow Lord would bring down his wrath on Noradz, make the people do his will by force instead of by trickery, and begin scouring the country for us," said Barda bluntly. "Nothing would be gained, and much would be lost. It would be a disaster."

He lengthened his stride, and moved ahead.

Lief and Jasmine went after him, but they did not speak for a long time after that. Lief was too angry, and Jasmine's mind was busy with thoughts she did not wish to share.

13 - Broad River and Beyond

Four days of hard marching followed — four long days in which Lief, Barda, and Jasmine spoke little and then only of moving on and keeping out of sight of any possible enemy. But when, at last, in the afternoon of the fourth day, they stood on the banks of Broad River, they realized that they should have planned their next step more carefully.

The river was deep, and its name described it well. It was so wide that they could only faintly see the land on the other side. The great sheet of water stretched in front of them like a sea. There was no way across.

Bleached white, and hard as stone, the ancient remains of wooden rafts lay half-buried in the sand. Perhaps, long ago, people had crossed the river here, and abandoned the rafts where they came to rest. But there were no trees on this side to provide wood for rafts — only banks of reeds.

Jasmine's eyes narrowed as she peered across the dull sheen of the water. "The land on the other side is very flat," she said slowly. "It is a plain. And I see a dark shape rising from it. If that is the City of the Rats, it is straight ahead of us. All we have to do is — "

"Cross the river," said Lief heavily. He threw himself down on the fine, white sand and began rummaging in his pack, looking for something to eat.

He pulled out the collection of things they had bought from Tom and tipped them onto the ground in a small heap. He had almost forgotten about them, and now he stared at them with distaste.

They had seemed so exciting in the shop. Now they looked like rubbishy novelties. The beads that made fire. The "No Bakes" bread. The powder labelled "Pure and Clear." The little pipe that was supposed to blow bubbles of light. And a small, flat tin box with a faded label . . .

Of course. Tom's free gift. Something completely useless, no doubt, that he could not dispose of any other way. Lief sneered to himself as he turned the tin over.

"It is too far for us to swim. We will have to follow the river until we find a village where there are boats," Barda was saying. "It is a pity to have to go out of our way, but we have no choice."

"Perhaps we do," Lief said slowly.

Jasmine and Barda looked at him in surprise. He held up the box and read aloud the words on the back.

Instructions:
Scatter Water Eaters sparingly
wherever dry land is required.

WARNING!
Effective for 1 hour only.
Handle with care.
Do not eat.
Store in a dry place.

*Note: The makers of 'Water Eaters' are not responsible for
any death, injury , damage or other disaster that may occur
before, during or after the use of this product.

"Are you saying that whatever is in this little tin box can dry up a river?" jeered Jasmine.

Lief shrugged. "I am saying nothing. I am simply reading the instructions."

"There are more warnings than instructions," said Barda. "But we shall see."

They walked together to the river's edge and

Lief pried the lid off the tin box. Inside were some tiny crystals, each not much larger than a grain of sand. Feeling rather foolish, he pinched out a few of the crystals and tossed them into the water. They sank immediately without changing appearance in any way.

And nothing else happened.

Lief waited for a moment, then, fighting his disappointment, he tried to grin. "I should have known better," he shrugged. "As if that Tom would give away anything that actually — "

Then he shouted and jumped back. A huge, colorless, wobbling lump was rising from the river. Beside it was another — and another!

"It is the crystals!" shouted Barda in excitement. "They are sucking up the water!"

So they were. As they grew, spreading as Lief watched, they joined together to make a towering, wobbling wall that held back the river. And the water between them simply dried up, leaving a narrow, winding path of puddled, sandy mud.

Kree squawked in amazement as Jasmine, Lief, and Barda stepped carefully onto the riverbed, squeezing between the jellied lumps and walking on until they came to the end of the dry patch. Then Lief threw another pinch of crystals into the water ahead, and, after a moment, more lumps broke the surface of the river and another path began to clear for them.

✳

The crossing of Broad River was a strange, frightening journey. In all their minds was the thought of what would happen if the trembling walls that held back the river should fail. The great press of water would close over them. There would be no escape.

The swollen Water Eaters blocked their view as they crept along, twisting and turning, their feet sinking into the soft mud. Lief was just beginning to worry that the crystals in the tin box would run out before they reached the shore, when suddenly the shore was before him, and he was clambering up onto a harsh, dry plain.

He stood with Barda and Jasmine, staring.

The plain lay in the bend of the river. It was encircled by water on three sides, and should have been lush and fertile. But not a blade of grass softened its hard, baked clay. As far as the eye could see there was no sign of any living, growing thing.

In the center was a city whose towers shone dark red in the last rays of the setting sun. Though it was so far away, a feeling of evil and menace seemed to stream from it like vapor.

They left the river and began to move over the bare plain. The sky arched over them, red and lowering. From above, thought Lief suddenly, we must look like ants — three tiny, crawling ants. One blow would kill us all. Never had he felt so exposed to danger.

Kree felt it, too. He sat motionless on Jasmine's

shoulder. Filli was huddled inside her jacket, only his small nose visible. But even their company could not help Jasmine. Her feet dragged. She began to walk more and more slowly, and at last, as the sun began to sink below the horizon, she shuddered and stopped.

"I am sorry," she muttered. "The barrenness of this place is death to me. I cannot bear it."

Her face was white and set. Her hands were shaking. Lief and Barda glanced at each other.

"Only now I was thinking that we should soon stop for the night," said Barda, though Lief doubted this was true. "We must rest, and eat. And I do not think the city is a place to enter in darkness."

They sat down together and began unpacking their food, but there were no sticks to make a fire.

"Now is a good time to try Tom's fire-making beads," said Lief, following Barda's lead and trying to be cheerful. In the failing light, he read the instructions on the jar. Then he put one of the beads on the ground and hit it sharply with their digging tool. Immediately, it burst into flames. Lief added another bead and it, too, flared up. Soon there was a merry blaze that apparently needed no other fuel. He pushed the jar into his pocket, well-satisfied.

"Instant comfort. Amazing!" said Barda heartily. "A villain Tom may be, but at least the things he sells are worth their price."

It was still early, but Barda and Lief spread their

supplies around them and made much of deciding what they would eat. They added water to one of the flat white rounds of No Bakes and watched it swell quickly into a loaf of bread. They cut the bread into slices and toasted it, eating it with some of the dried berries, nuts, and honey they had carried from Raladin.

"A feast," said Barda contentedly, and Lief was relieved to see that Jasmine's tense face was beginning to relax. As they had hoped, the warmth, light, and food were giving her comfort.

He gazed over her shoulder at the distant city. The red light was fading from its towers now. Hulked on the plain, it stood silent, grim, deserted. . . .

Lief blinked. The last rays of the sun were playing tricks with his eyes. For a moment it had seemed as though the earth around the city were moving like water.

He looked again, and frowned in puzzlement. The plain *was* moving. Yet there was no grass to bend in the wind. No leaves to blow across the clay. What . . . ?

Then, suddenly, he saw. "Barda!" he said huskily.

He saw Barda look up, surprised by the fear in his voice. He tried to speak, but his breath caught in his throat. Waves of horror flooded through him as he stared wildly at the moving plain.

"What is it?" asked Jasmine, turning to look.

And then she and Barda were crying out together, leaping to their feet.

Spilling from the city, covering the ground, surging towards them like a long, low wave, was a scurrying, seething mass of rats.

14 - Night of the Rats

Rats in the thousands — in the tens of thousands! Suddenly Lief understood why the earth of the plain was bare. The rats had eaten every living thing.

They were creatures of the shadows. They had remained hidden in the ruined city while the sun glared down on the plain. But now they were coming, racing towards the scent of food in a frenzy of hunger.

"The river!" shouted Barda.

They ran for their lives. Lief glanced over his shoulder once only, and the sight he saw was enough to make him run even faster, gasping with fear.

The first rats had reached their campfire. They were huge. They were surging over the food and other belongings left scattered upon the ground, gobbling and tearing with needle-sharp teeth. But their fellows were close behind, leaping on top of them, smothering them, fighting one another for the spoils, tipping into the fire in the haste, squealing and shrieking.

And in the thousands more were scrambling over them, or wheeling around the struggling pile and scuttling on, sharp noses sniffing, black eyes gleaming. They could smell Lief, Barda, and Jasmine ahead — smell their warmth and their life and their fear.

Lief ran, the breath aching in his chest, his eyes fixed on the river. The water gleamed in the last rays of the sun. Nearer . . . nearer . . .

Jasmine was beside him, Barda close behind. Lief plunged into the cold water, gasping, and waded out as far as he dared. He turned to face the land, his cloak swirling around him.

The squealing, dark grey tide that was the rats reached the riverbank. Then it seemed to curl and break like a wave, and surged out into the water.

"They are swimming for us!" Barda shouted, struggling to draw his sword and pull it to the surface. "By the heavens, will nothing stop them?"

Already, Jasmine was slashing with her dagger, shouting fiercely, and dead rats in their dozens were being swept away by the tide. Beside her, Lief and Barda swept their blades across the water, back and forth, gasping with the effort of the task.

The water around them swirled with blood and foam. And still the rats came, clambering with bared teeth over their own sinking dead.

How long will our strength last? thought Lief. How long will it be before they overwhelm us?

His mind raced as he fought, his hands numb on the hilt of his sword. They would be safe on the other side of the river. The water was too wide for the rats to swim. But it was too wide for him, Jasmine, and Barda also. They would never survive if they cast themselves adrift in this cold, deep water.

And the long night was ahead. Until the sun rose again, bringing light to the plain, the rats would attack. Thousands would die, but thousands would take their places. Gradually Lief, Barda, and Jasmine would weaken. And then at last the rats would swarm over them, biting and clawing, till they sank beneath the water and drowned together.

The sun had set, and the plain had darkened. Lief could no longer see the city. All he could see was the campfire, flickering like a beacon.

It was then that he remembered that he had put the jar of fire beads in his pocket.

He took his left hand from his sword, plunged it under the water, and dug deep into his jacket. His fingers closed around the jar and he pulled it up to the surface. Water dripped from it, but the beads still rattled inside.

Shouting to Barda and Jasmine to cover him, he waded forward, unscrewing the jar's tight cap. He dug out a handful of beads with his stiff fingers and threw them at the rats on the bank with all his strength.

There was a huge burst of flame as the beads struck. The light was blinding. Hundreds of rats fell dead, killed by the sudden heat. The horde behind them shrieked, and scattered from the burning bodies. The creatures already in the water scrambled and writhed in terror, leaping towards Lief, Barda, and Jasmine, their long tails switching and coiling. Barda and Jasmine slashed at them, defending Lief and themselves, as Lief threw another handful of beads, and another, moving slowly downstream to lengthen the wall of flame.

And soon a long sheet of fire burned on the river's edge. Behind it the plain seethed. But where Lief, Barda, and Jasmine stood, panting and shuddering with relief, there was only rippling water, alive with red, leaping light. Dead rats were swept away by the tide, but no more took their places.

In a few moments there were splashes up and downstream as the rats began plunging into the river above and below the line of flame. But the distance was too great for them to swim in safety. The swift-running current pulled most of them under before they could reach their prey, and those that remained alive were easily beaten off.

So the three companions stood together, waist-deep in water, trembling with weariness but safe behind their fiery barricade, as the long, cold hours passed.

✳

Dawn broke at last. Dull red tinged the sky. Beyond the line of fire a murmuring, scuffling sound arose, like a forest of leaves rustling. Then it was gone, and a great stillness fell over the plain.

Lief, Barda, and Jasmine waded to the shore. Water streamed from their clothes and hair, hissing as it fell onto the flames of their barricade. They stepped over the flickering embers.

The rats had gone. Between the river and the smoking remains of the campfire there was nothing but a tangled litter of small bones.

"They have eaten their own dead," muttered Barda, looking sick.

"Of course," said Jasmine matter-of-factly.

Shivering with cold, feeling as though his legs were weighed down with stones, Lief began trudging towards the place where they had eaten their food many hours ago. Jasmine and Barda followed him, quiet and watchful. Kree flew overhead, the sound of his beating wings loud in the silent air.

Little remained around the ashes of the fire except for three patches of brilliant red.

Lief laughed shortly. "They have left the Ra-Kachar garments and boots," he said. "They did not like them, it seems. Why would that be?"

"Perhaps the garments still bear the scent of the fungus from the Hole," Jasmine suggested. "We can smell nothing — but we do not have the senses of a rat."

They looked around at the wreckage. Buckles from the packs, the caps of the water bags, the pipe that blew bubbles of light, a button or two, a few coins, and the flat tin box containing the last of the Water Eaters lay strewn on the hard clay among the bones and cinders. Except for the clothes from Noradz, nothing else had survived the rats' hunger. Not a crumb of food, a shred of blanket, or a thread of rope.

"At least we have our lives," said Barda, shivering in the light dawn breeze. "And we have dry garments to put on. They may not be the garments we would like, but who is to see us here?"

Wearily they stripped off their wet clothes and pulled on the red suits and boots of the Ra-Kacharz. Then, warm and dry at last, they sat down to talk.

"The jar of fire beads is almost empty. We will not survive another night on this plain," said Barda heavily. "We must enter the city now, if we are to enter it at all. These strange garments will give us some protection, since the rats do not like them. And we still have the pipe that blows bubbles of light. If it works as we were told, it may be of use."

They bundled up their wet clothes, collected their few remaining possessions from the ground, and began to walk towards the city.

Lief's eyes prickled with weariness, and his feet dragged in the high red boots. The thought of the rat horde, crawling and fighting inside the crumbling towers ahead, filled him with dread. How could they enter the city without being covered and torn to pieces?

Yet enter it they must. For already the Belt of Deltora had begun to grow warm around Lief's waist. One of the lost gems was indeed hidden in the city. The Belt could feel it.

15 - The City

The towers of the city rose dark and forbidding above their heads. Long ago, the great iron entrance gates had fallen and rusted away. Now all that remained was a gaping hole in the wall. The hole led into darkness, and from the darkness drifted a terrible, stealthy, scrabbling sound and the stink of rats. There was something else, too. Something worse. A sense of ancient evil — spiteful, cold, terrifying.

Lief, Barda, and Jasmine began drawing on the Ra-Kachar gloves and covering their faces and heads with the red fabric they had worn during the escape from Noradz.

"I do not understand how the rats became so many," Lief said. "Rats breed quickly, it is true. And they breed faster when there is dark, and dirt, and food is left where they can find it. But why did the

people of this city not see the problem, and put a stop
to it before it became so great that they had to flee?"

"Some evil was at work." Barda stared grimly
at the crumbling walls before them. "The Shadow
Lord — "

"You cannot blame the Shadow Lord for everything!" Jasmine burst out suddenly.

Barda and Lief glanced at her in surprise. Her
brows were knitted in a frown.

"I have kept silent for too long," she muttered.
"But now I will speak, though you will not like what I
say. That stranger we saw in Tom's shop — the man
with the scar on his face — spoke of the thorns on the
plain. He called them the Del King's thorns. And he
was right!"

They were staring. She took a deep breath, and
hurried on.

"The Shadow Lord has ruled Deltora for only
sixteen years. But it has taken far longer than that for
the thorns to cover the plain. The sorceress Thaegan's
enchantment at the Lake of Tears began a *hundred*
years ago. The people of Noradz have been living as
they do for centuries. And this evil place must have
been abandoned by its people for just as long."

She fell silent, staring moodily ahead.

"What are you saying, Jasmine?" asked Barda
impatiently.

The girl's eyes darkened. "The kings and queens

of Deltora betrayed their trust. They shut themselves up in the palace at Del, living in luxury while the land went to ruin and evil prospered."

"That is true," said Lief. "But — "

"I know what you are going to say!" Jasmine snapped. "You have told me before that they were deceived by servants of the Shadow Lord. That they followed stupid rules blindly, thinking that this alone was their duty. But I do not believe that *anyone* could be so blind. I think the whole story is a lie."

Barda and Lief were silent. Both could see why Jasmine would find the truth so hard to believe. She had fended for herself since she was five years old. She was strong and independent. She would never have allowed herself to be a puppet, dancing as a Chief Advisor pulled the strings.

Now she was rushing on. "We are risking our lives to restore the Belt of Deltora. And why? To return power to the royal heir — who even now is hiding, while Deltora suffers and we face danger. But do we really *want* kings and queens back in the palace at Del, lying to us and using us as they did before? I do not think so!"

She glared at them both, and waited.

Barda was angry. To him, what Jasmine was saying was treason. But Lief felt differently.

"I used to think as you do, Jasmine," he said. "I hated the memory of the old King. But questions about whether he and his son were vain and idle or simply foolish, and whether their heir is worthy, are not important now."

"Not *important*?" Jasmine cried. "How can you — ?"

"Jasmine, nothing is more important than ridding our land of the Shadow Lord!" Lief broke in. "However bad things were in Deltora before, at least then the people were free, and not in constant fear."

"Of course!" she exclaimed. "But — "

"We cannot defeat the Shadow Lord by arms. His sorcery is too powerful. Our only hope is the Belt, worn by Adin's true heir. So we are not risking our lives for the royal family, but for our land and all its people! Do you not see that?"

His words struck home. Jasmine paused and blinked. Slowly, the fire in her eyes died. "You are right," she said flatly, at last. "My anger made me lose sight of our main purpose. I am sorry."

She said nothing more, but finished winding the red cloth around her head and face. Then, dagger in hand, she went with them, into the city.

✳

They plunged into a maze of darkness, and the walls were alive with sound. The rats came in the thousands, streaming from cracks in the crumbling stone, their tails lashing like whips, their red eyes gleaming.

Lief took the pipe and blew. Glowing bubbles rose from it, warming and brightening, lighting the darkness like tiny, floating lanterns.

The great rush of rats slowed, became a confused rabble, as most of the creatures scrabbled away from the light, shrieking in panic.

The bravest, darting in the shadows of the ground, tried to cling to the strangers' moving feet, to climb their legs. But the high, slippery boots and smooth, thick red garments defeated all but a few, and these Lief, Barda, and Jasmine could brush off with their gloved hands.

"These garments might have been made for our purpose," muttered Barda, as they struggled along. "It is a fortunate chance that we came by them."

"And a fortunate chance that Tom gave us this pipe," answered Lief. But even as he spoke he wondered. *Were* these things just chance? Or were they — something else? Had he not felt before, on this great journey, that somehow their steps were being guided by an unseen hand?

Brushing, shuddering, they stumbled forward. Now and again Lief blew on the pipe and new bubbles of soft light bloomed. The bubbles they had left behind drifted high above their heads, glowing on the ancient timbers that still supported the roof. The rats had not been able to gnaw through these timbers — or perhaps they knew better than to try, for without them the roof would cave in, exposing the city to the sun.

The whole city was like one huge building — a maze of stone that seemed to have no ending. There was no fresh air, no natural light. This, it seemed, was the way towns were built in these parts, Lief thought. Noradz had been the same.

Everywhere were the signs of vanished grandeur. Carvings, high arches, vast rooms, huge fireplaces filled with ashes, great, echoing kitchens heaped with dust.

And everywhere, rats crawled.

Lief's foot kicked against something that clanged and rolled. The rats caught at his gloves as he bent to pick it up.

It was a carved goblet — silver, he thought, though stained and tarnished with age and neglect. His heart was heavy as he turned it in his hands. It was as though it spoke to him of the people who had fled their home so long ago. He peered at it more closely. Somehow it seemed familiar. But why . . . ?

"Lief!" growled Barda, his voice muffled by the cloth around his mouth and nose. "Keep moving, I beg you. We do not know how long the light pipe will last, and by nightfall we must be in a place of safety."

"Somewhere, at least, where there are no rats," added Jasmine. Furiously, she swept her hands from her shoulders to her hips, so that the rats crawling on her body fell squeaking to the ground.

A vivid memory, and a rush of astonished understanding, jolted Lief to his core. "And if we find such a place, we will say, 'No rats here,' and it will be a blessing," he murmured.

"What?" Jasmine demanded crossly.

There was no time to explain now. Lief made himself move on, pushing the stem of the goblet into his Belt. Later, he would tell Jasmine and Barda. When they were out of danger. When . . .

Come to me, Lief of Del.

Lief started, looking around wildly. What was that? Who had spoken?

"Lief, what is the matter?" Jasmine's voice seemed distant, though she was right beside him. He looked down at her puzzled green eyes. Dimly he realized that she could hear nothing.

Come to me. I am waiting.

The voice hissed and coiled in Lief's mind. Hardly knowing what he was doing, he began to move fast and blindly, following its call.

The bubbles of light floated before him, shining on ruined walls, rusted metal brackets where torches had once burned, fragments of pots piled in heaps. Rats teemed in corners and clawed at his boots.

He stumbled towards the city's heart. The air grew thick and hard to breathe. The Belt around his waist throbbed with heat.

"Lief!" he heard Barda shout. But he could not turn, or answer. He had reached a wide passage. At the end loomed a vast doorway. A sickening, musky smell billowed from whatever was beyond. He faltered, but still he moved on.

He reached the doorway. Inside, something huge moved in darkness.

"Who are you?" he quavered.

And the hissing voice struck at him, piercing and burning.

I am the One. I am Reeah. Come to me.

16 - Reeah

Darkness. Evil. Fear.

Trembling, Lief put the pipe to his mouth, and blew. Glowing bubbles drifted upward, lighting what had once been a vast meeting hall.

A giant snake rose, hissing, in the center of the echoing space. The coils of its shining body, as thick as the trunk of an ancient tree, filled the floor from edge to edge. Its eyes were flat, cold, and filled with ancient wickedness. On its head was a crown. And in the center of the crown was a gem that flashed with all the colors of the rainbow.

The opal.

Lief took a step forward.

Stop!

Lief did not know if the word was in his mind, or if the snake had hissed it aloud. He stood motionless. Barda and Jasmine came up behind him. He heard them draw breath sharply, and felt their arms move as they raised their weapons.

Remove the thing you wear under your clothes. Cast it away.

Lief's fingers slowly moved to the Belt around his waist.

"No, Lief!" he heard Barda whisper urgently.

But still he fumbled with the Belt's fastening, trying to loosen it. Nothing seemed real — nothing but the voice that was commanding him.

"Lief!" Jasmine's hard brown hand gripped his wrist, tugging at it furiously.

Lief struggled to shake her off. And then, all at once, it was as if he had woken from a dream. He looked down, blinking.

The palm of his hand was resting on the golden topaz. So it was this that had cleared his mind, and broken the great snake's power over him. Beside the topaz the ruby glimmered. It was no longer bloodred, but pink, showing danger. Yet still it seemed to glow with strange power.

The giant snake hissed in fury and bared its terrible fangs. Its forked tongue flicked in and out. Lief felt the tug of its will, but pressed his hand onto the topaz even harder, and resisted it.

"Why does it not attack?" breathed Jasmine.

But by now, Lief knew. He had remembered some lines from *The Belt of Deltora* — lines about the powers of the ruby.

✝   **The great ruby, symbol of happiness, red as blood, grows pale in the presence of evil, or when misfortune threatens its wearer. It wards off evil spirits, and is an antidote to snake venom.**

"It feels the power of the ruby," he whispered back. "This is why it is fixing its attention on me."

Your magic is strong, Lief of Del, but not strong enough to save you, hissed the snake.

Lief staggered as again its will struck at his mind.

"The opal is in its crown," he panted to Jasmine and Barda. "Do what you can while I distract it!"

Ignoring their whispered warnings, he began edging away from them. The snake turned its head to follow him with hard, cold eyes.

"How do you know my name?" Lief demanded, holding the topaz tightly.

I have the gem that shows the future. I am all-powerful. I am Reeah, the Master's chosen one.

"And who is your master?"

The one who gave my kingdom to me. The one they call the Shadow Lord.

Lief heard Jasmine make a stifled sound, but did not turn to look at her. Instead, he held Reeah's gaze, trying to keep his mind blank.

"Surely you have been here for a very long time, Reeah," he called. "You are so large, so magnificent!"

406

The snake hissed, raising its head proudly. As Lief had thought, its vanity was as great as its size.

A tender worm I was when first I came into the cellars beneath this city. A race of snivelling humans lived here, then. In their ignorance and fear they would have killed me, had they found me. But the Master had servants among them, and these were awaiting me. They welcomed me, and brought me rats to feed upon, till I grew strong.

Out of the corner of his eye Lief caught a glimpse of Jasmine. She was climbing one of the columns that supported the roof. Gritting his teeth, he forced his mind away from her. It was vital that Reeah's attention remain with him.

"What servants?" he called. "Who were they?"

You know them, hissed Reeah. *They are branded with his mark. They have been promised eternal life and power in his service. You wear their garments, to deceive me. But I am not deceived.*

"Of course you are not!" Lief cried. "I was testing you, to see if you could really see into my mind. Who else would have known where to find rats, what would make them breed, and how to trap them? Who else but the city's rat catchers? It was a clever plan."

Ah, yes, hissed Reeah. *There were few rats, then. My kingdom had not yet achieved the glory of its destiny. But my Master had chosen his servants well. They bred more rats for me — more rats, and more. Until at last the walls teemed with them, and disease spread, and all the food of the city was consumed. And then the people begged the* rat catchers to save them, little knowing that they were the very ones who had caused the plague.

Its wicked eyes glowed with triumph.

"So the rat catchers seized power," said Lief. "They said that the rat plague had come through the people's own wickedness, and that there was nothing left but to flee."

Yes. Across the river to another place where they would build again. When they were gone, I came up from beneath, and claimed my kingdom.

Lief felt, rather than saw, that Jasmine was beginning to walk along the great beam that spanned the hall right beside the great snake's head — walking as easily and lightly as she had walked along branches in the Forests of Silence. But what was her plan? Surely she did not think her daggers could pierce those shining scales? And where was Barda?

The great snake was growing restless. Lief could feel it. Its tongue was flicking in and out. Its head was bending towards him.

"Reeah! The new city is called No Rats — Noradz," he shouted. "I have seen it. The people have forgotten what they once were, and where they came from. Their fear of rats has broken their spirit. The rat catchers are called Ra-Kacharz now, and are like priests, keeping sacred laws. They carry whips like the tails of rats. They are all-powerful. The people live in fear and slavery, serving your Master's purpose."

It is good, hissed Reeah. *It is what they deserve. So*

you have told your story, Lief of Del. Your pitiful magic, your puny weapons, and your smooth tongue have amused me — for a time. But now I am sick of your chatter.

Without warning, it struck. Lief slashed with his sword to protect himself, but the snake's first sweep struck the weapon from his hand as if it were a toy. It spun away from him, circling high into the air.

"Jasmine!" Lief cried. But there was no time to see if Jasmine had caught the sword. The snake was about to strike again. Its huge jaws were open, its fangs dripping with poison.

"Lief! The fire beads!" Barda's voice sounded from the other end of the hall. He must have crept there, to try to attack the monster from behind. The giant snake's tail lashed, and to his horror, Lief saw Barda's body crash into a column and lie still.

The fire beads. Desperately, Lief felt in his pockets, found the jar, and threw it, hard, straight at his enemy's open mouth. But Reeah was too fast for him. The wicked head jerked to one side. The jar sailed past it, smashing uselessly into a column and bursting in a ball of flames.

And then it was only Lief and Reeah.

You are mine, Lief of Del!

The huge head lunged forward with terrifying speed. And the next moment the great snake was raising itself, triumphant, Lief's body dangling from its jaws.

Up, up to the rafters, the hot breath burning . . .

I will swallow you whole. And your magic with you.

There was smoke. There was a crackling sound. Dimly Lief realized that the flames had raced up the column and were licking at the old wood of the rafters.

The fire will not save you. When I have devoured you I will put it out with one gust of my breath. For I am Reeah, the all-powerful. I am Reeah, the One . . .

Through a dizzy haze of terror and pain, through a film of smoke that stung his eyes, Lief saw Jasmine, balancing on a beam beside him. His sword was swinging in her hand. She had torn the red covering from her face. Her teeth were bared in savage fury. She raised her arm . . .

And with a mighty slash she swung the sword, slitting the monster's throat from edge to edge.

Lief heard a hoarse, bubbling cry. He felt the beast's jaws open. He was falling, hurtling towards the ground, the hard stones rushing up to meet him.

And then — there was nothing.

17 - Hope

Groaning, Lief stirred. There was a sweet taste on his lips, and he could hear a crackling sound, a tearing, chewing sound, and shouting, very far away.

He opened his eyes. Jasmine and Barda were leaning over him, calling his name. Jasmine was screwing the top back onto a small jar attached to a chain around her neck. Dimly, Lief realized that he had been given nectar from the Lilies of Life. It had saved him — perhaps brought him back to life as once it had done for Barda.

"I — I am well," he mumbled, struggling to sit up. He looked around. The hall was filled with flickering shadows. Flames, begun and spread by the blazing fire beads, roared in the ancient rafters. The giant snake lay dead on the floor, its body covered by gnawing rats. More rats were streaming from the walls and

411

through the doorway, fighting one another to reach the feast.

For hundreds of years it has eaten them, thought Lief, dazed. Now they are eating it. Even fear of fire will not stop them.

"We must get out! Out!" Barda was shouting.

Lief felt himself pulled to his feet and slung over Barda's shoulder. His head was spinning. He wanted to cry out, "What of the crown? The opal?"

But then he saw that the crown was in Barda's hand.

Limp as a doll, he was carried through burning hallways. Jolting on Barda's back, he closed his stinging eyes against the smoke.

When he looked again, they were staggering through the city gateway onto the dark plain and Kree, squawking anxiously, was soaring to meet them. There was a tremendous crash from behind them. The roof of the city had begun to fall.

On they went, and on, till they had nearly reached the river.

"I can walk," Lief managed to croak. Barda stopped and put him gently on the ground. His legs trembled, but he stood upright, turning to look at the burning city.

"I never thought I'd see you stand on your own two feet again, my friend," Barda said cheerfully. "That fall Jasmine gave you was — "

"It was let him fall or see him disappear into the

412

snake's belly," exclaimed Jasmine. "Which do you think was better?"

She handed Lief's sword to him. It gleamed in the moonlight, its blade still dark with Reeah's blood.

"Jasmine — " Lief began. But she shrugged and turned away, pretending to be busy coaxing Filli out onto her shoulder. He saw that she was embarrassed at the idea that he would try to thank her for saving his life.

"Do you think it is safe to rest here?" he asked instead. "Having recently had every bone in my body broken, I do not think I could face crossing the river yet."

Barda nodded. "Quite safe, I think. For a while, at least, there will be no rats here." Then his teeth gleamed as he grinned and brushed his hands from shoulder to hip. "Noradzeer," he added.

"Lief, how did you know, before the snake told you, that the people of Noradz had once lived in the City of the Rats?" Jasmine demanded.

"There were many clues," Lief said tiredly. "But, perhaps, I would not have seen the connection if I had not found this." He pulled the tarnished goblet from his Belt and held it out to them.

"Why, it is a pair to the goblet that held the Life and Death cards — the sacred Cup of Noradz," said Barda, taking it in his hands and looking at it with wonder. "It must have been dropped and left behind when the people fled the city."

413

Lief smiled as Filli's small black nose peeped over Jasmine's collar to see what was happening.

"No wonder Filli frightened the people in Noradz," he said.

"He looks nothing like a rat!" Jasmine exclaimed indignantly.

"They hate anything small with fur. It must be a fear taught to them from their earliest days," said Barda.

Lief nodded. "Like the fear of dropping food on the ground, or leaving dishes uncovered, because such things once attracted rats in the hundreds. Or the fear of eating food that has been spoiled, as it often was in the days of the plague. The need for such great care passed hundreds of years ago. But the Ra-Kacharz have seen to it that the fear remains, and keeps the people in bondage to them — and to the Shadow Lord."

Lief was speaking lightly and idly, to blot from his mind the horrible things that had just happened to him. But Jasmine looked at him seriously, her head to one side.

"Plainly, then, it is quite possible for a people to forget their history, and to follow foolish rules out of duty, if they are born to it," she said. "I would not have believed it. But now I have seen it with my own eyes."

Lief realized that this was her way of saying that she was beginning to think that the kings and queens

414

of Deltora had been less to blame than she had thought. Of this, he was very glad.

"Mind you," Jasmine added quickly, as he smiled, "there is always a choice, and bonds can be broken. The girl Tira helped us, though she feared." She paused. "One day, I hope, we can go back for her and set her free. Make them all free, if they wish it."

"This is our best chance of doing so." Lief unfastened the Belt and laid it before him on the hard ground of the plain. Then Barda handed him the crown that held the great opal.

As it neared the Belt, the opal fell from the crown into Lief's hand. His mind was suddenly filled with a vision of sandy wastes, of lowering, clouded skies. He saw himself, alone, among rippling dunes that had no ending. And he felt terror lurking, unseen. He gasped in horror.

He looked up and saw Jasmine and Barda watching him anxiously. He closed his trembling hand more tightly around the gem.

"I had forgotten," he said huskily, trying to smile. "The opal gives glimpses of the future. It seems that this may not always be a blessing."

Fearing that they might ask him what he had seen, he bent to fit the stone into the Belt. Under his fingers, its rainbow colors seemed to flash and burn like fire. Abruptly, his racing heart quietened, the fear faded, and a tingling warmth took its place.

415

"The opal is also the symbol of hope," Barda murmured, watching him.

Lief nodded, pressing his hand over the dancing colors, feeling the gem's power flood through him. And when finally he looked up, his face was at peace.

"So now we have the topaz for faith, the ruby for happiness, and the opal for hope," he said quietly. "What will be next?"

Jasmine held up her arm to Kree, who fluttered down to her with a glad screech. "Whatever the fourth stone is, surely it will not lead us into worse danger than the other three."

"And if it does?" Barda teased.

She shrugged. "We will face what comes," she said simply.

Lief lifted the Belt from the ground and fastened it around his waist. It warmed against his skin — solid, safe, and a little heavier than before. Faith, happiness, hope, he thought, and his heart swelled with all three.

"Yes," he said. "We will face what comes. Together."

The Shifting Sands

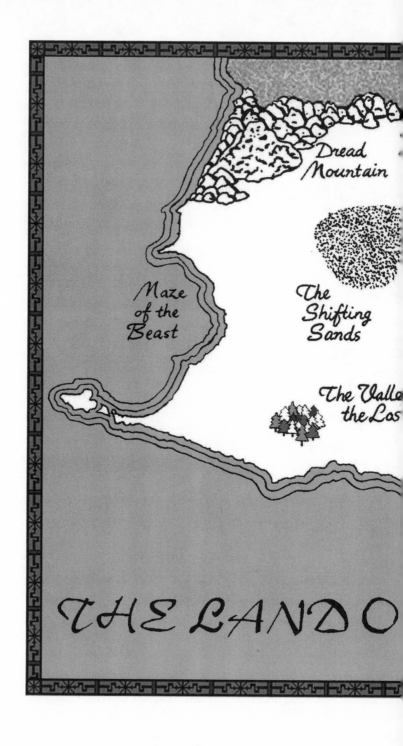

Dread
Mountain

Maze
of the
Beast

The
Shifting
Sands

The Valle
the Los

THE LAND O

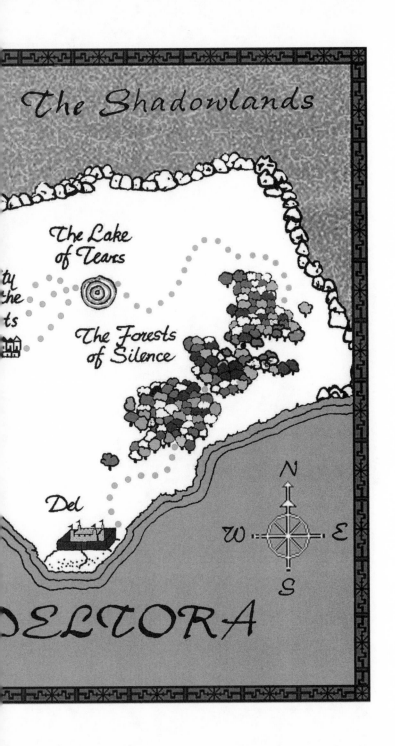

The Shadowlands

The Lake
of Tears

The Forests
of Silence

Del

DELTORA

N
W ·—⊕—· E
S

Contents

1 Flight 425

2 Forbidden Fruit 433

3 The Road to Rithmere 441

4 Lost in the Crowd 449

5 Win and Lose 455

6 Berry, Birdie, and Twig 463

7 Trouble 472

8 The Games 480

9 The Finalists 488

10 The Champion 496

11 Easy as Winking 505

12 No Choice 513

13 The Shifting Sands .521

14 Terror 530

15 The Center 538

16 The Cone 546

The story so far . . .

Sixteen-year-old Lief, fulfilling a pledge made by his father before he was born, is on a great quest to find the seven gems of the magic Belt of Deltora. The gems—an amethyst, a topaz, a diamond, a ruby, an opal, a lapis lazuli, and an emerald—were stolen to open the way for the evil Shadow Lord to invade Deltora. Hidden in fearsome places throughout the land, they must be restored to the Belt before the heir to the throne can be found and the Shadow Lord's tyranny ended.

Lief's companions are the man Barda, who was once a Palace guard, and Jasmine, a wild, orphaned girl of Lief's own age who they met in the fearful Forests of Silence.

So far they have found three gems. The golden topaz, symbol of faith, has the power to contact the spirit world, and to clear the mind. The ruby, symbol of happiness, pales when danger threatens, repels evil spirits, and is an antidote to venom. The opal, gem of hope, gives glimpses of the future.

On their travels, the companions have discovered a secret resistance movement made up of people pledged to defy the Shadow Lord. But servants of the Enemy are everywhere. Some, like his brutal Grey Guards, are easily recognized. Others keep their dark loyalty well hidden.

The three companions are lucky to have escaped the City of the Rats alive. But now they are stranded on the barren plain that surrounds it, having lost all their supplies. The opal has given Lief a terrible vision of their next goal: The Shifting Sands.

Now read on . . .

1 - Flight

It seemed to Lief that they had been walking beside the river forever. Yet only one night and part of a day had passed since he, Barda, and Jasmine had left the City of the Rats in flames. The faint smell of smoke hung in the still air, though the city was now just a blur on the horizon at their backs.

They had long ago discarded the heavy red garments and boots which had saved them from the rats. Walking was easier now. But hunger and exhaustion were making the journey seem endless, and the fact that the landscape never changed did not help. Hour by hour the companions had trudged over bare, baked earth hemmed in on both sides by the waters of Broad River — waters so wide that they could barely see the far banks.

Though all of them badly needed rest, they knew that they had to keep moving. The plume of smoke staining the blue sky at their backs was like a signal to their enemies. It was a sign that something of great importance had happened in the terrible place where the third stone of the Belt of Deltora had been hidden. Should the Shadow Lord become aware that the stone had been taken, his servants would begin searching for the thieves.

And how easily they would find them on this bare plain.

Barda plodded beside Lief, his head lowered. Jasmine walked a little ahead. Now and then she murmured to Filli, who was nestled on her shoulder, but her eyes were fixed on the horizon. She was watching for Kree, the raven. Kree had flown off as dawn broke to survey the land ahead and to look for food.

He had been away for many hours. This boded ill for them. It meant that food and shelter were far distant. But there was nothing to do but keep moving. There was no direction to take but the one they were taking, for the Plain of the Rats lay in a bend of the river, and was bounded on three sides by deep water.

For centuries the rats have been trapped by the river that curves around their plain, thought Lief grimly. And now we are trapped also.

Suddenly Jasmine gave a high, piercing cry. A faint, harsh sound came back in answer.

Lief looked up, and saw a black speck coming towards them through the distant blue. With every

426

moment the speck grew larger, and at last Kree was soaring down, squawking harshly.

He landed on Jasmine's arm and squawked again. Jasmine listened, expressionless. Finally she turned to Lief and Barda.

"Kree says that the plain ends in a broad band of water that is almost as wide as the river itself," she said.

"What?" Appalled, Lief slumped to the ground.

"The plain is an island?" growled Barda. "But it cannot be!" He sat down beside Lief, with a heavy sigh.

Kree ruffled his feathers, and made an annoyed, clucking sound.

"Kree has seen it with his own eyes," snapped Jasmine. "A bar of water joins the two arms of the river. It is very broad, he says, but perhaps not too deep for us to wade. It seemed paler in color than the river, and he could see schools of fish not far from the surface."

"Fish!" Lief's mouth watered at the thought of hot food.

"How far?" he heard Barda ask.

Jasmine shrugged. "Kree thinks that we could reach it by tomorrow, if we move on through the night."

"Then so we will," Barda said grimly, hauling himself to his feet. "At least we cannot easily be seen in the dark. And we have no food, after all. We have no shelter, or anything to sleep upon but the bare earth. So what comfort is there in stopping? We might as well walk till we drop."

✳

So it was that in the pale dawn of the following day they found themselves at the end of the plain, staring, with eyes that prickled with weariness, at a gleaming sheet of water that blocked their path.

"Surely this is not a natural channel," Lief said. "The banks are too straight and even."

"It was dug by human hands," Barda agreed. "Long ago, I would guess, as a barrier against the rats."

Kree soared above them, squawking excitedly.

"On the other side there are trees," murmured Jasmine. "Trees and other growing things."

Without hesitation she stepped into the water, her eyes fixed eagerly on the ragged line of green ahead.

"Jasmine, take care!" Lief called after her. But Jasmine waded on without pausing or turning. The water rose to her waist, then to her chest, but no further. She began moving steadily towards the opposite shore.

Barda and Lief hastened after her, splashing into the cool stream. "When it was my task to keep you out of trouble on the streets of Del, Lief, I thought that you were the most impulsive, troublesome young pest in creation," muttered Barda. "I apologize. Jasmine is just as bad — or worse!"

Lief grinned, then jumped and yelled as something brushed softly against his ankle. He looked down into the water and saw a flurry of sudden movement as several large fish darted away into the shadows.

"They will not hurt you," called Jasmine, without turning around.

"How do you know?" Lief called back. "They could be feeling as hungry as I am. They — "

He broke off as Kree cried out and plummeted towards them, skimming the surface of the water and then soaring up into the air again.

Jasmine stopped, alert, then swung around to face Lief and Barda. "Something is coming from the sky!" she called. "Kree — "

Screeching, the black bird dived towards them once more. Plainly he was terrified.

"What is it?" Frantically, Lief scanned the sky, but could see nothing.

"Something huge! Something very bad!" Jasmine snatched Filli from her shoulder and held him up into the air, a tiny bundle of grey fur, chattering with fear. "Kree!" she shrieked, "Take Filli! Hide him, and yourself!"

And at that moment Lief's straining eyes caught

sight of a black spot on the horizon. It was growing larger by the moment. In seconds Lief could make out a long neck and huge, beating wings.

"Ak-Baba!" hissed Barda. "It has seen the smoke."

Lief's blood seemed to chill in his veins. His father had told him of the Ak-Baba — giant, vulture-like birds that lived a thousand years. Seven of them were the servants of the Shadow Lord. It was they who had carried the gems from the Belt of Deltora to their perilous hiding places.

Obeying Jasmine's command, Kree had snatched up Filli in his claws and was speeding with him to the other side of the band of water. There they could both conceal themselves in the long grass or shelter in a tree.

But Lief, Barda, and Jasmine had nowhere to hide. Behind them was the bare earth of the plain. Before them was a huge sweep of water, glittering in the dawn.

They floundered forward a few steps, but all of them knew it was no use. The Ak-Baba was flying with incredible speed. It would be upon them long before they could reach safety.

Already it could see the smoke of the burning city. When it saw three ragged strangers escaping from the plain it would know at once that they were enemies of the Shadow Lord.

Would it attack them? Or would it simply plunge down, snatch them up in its huge talons, and carry them away to its master? Either way, they were doomed.

The only possible hiding place was under the water. And yet Lief knew that this was no hiding place at all. From the air, the Ak-Baba would be able to see them as clearly as Kree had seen the schools of fish.

"It has not seen us yet," Barda said rapidly. "Its eyes are fixed on the smoke from the city. Lief — your cloak!"

Of course! With wet, clumsy fingers Lief pulled at the strings that fastened his cloak around his throat. At last the cloak floated free.

"Down!" Barda hissed.

All of them took a deep breath and sank below the surface of the stream, holding the cloak over them like a canopy. It drifted above their heads, almost invisible in the water.

They had done their best. But was their best good enough to hide them from the sharp eyes of the Ak-Baba? If it had been dusk, perhaps. But surely, in this bright dawn light, the beast could not fail to notice that one patch of water looked a little different from the rest. Suspicious, it would circle above the place, watching, waiting . . .

And for how long could Lief, Barda, and Jasmine

hold their breath? Sooner or later they would have to rise, gasping, to the surface. Then the monster would strike.

Lief's fingers felt for the clasp of the Belt he wore under his shirt. The Belt of Deltora must not be captured with him. If necessary, he would unloose it and let it fall into the mud at the bottom of the stream. It would be better for it to lie there than for it to fall into the hands of the Shadow Lord again.

Already his lungs felt tight. Already his body was telling him to rise to the surface and breathe. Something nudged at his shoulder and he opened his eyes. Fish were moving all around him — big silver fish, their glassy eyes staring. Their fins and tails buffeted his head and face. They were closing in on him, crowding him.

Then, suddenly, it grew dark. A huge shadow was blocking out the sun.

The Ak-Baba was overhead.

2 - Forbidden Fruit

Lief fought down the panic that threatened to engulf him. The shadow of the Ak-Baba had turned the water black. He could no longer see the fish, but he could feel their weight. Dozens were now swimming above the cloak, cutting the companions off from the surface, pressing them down, down . . .

Lief's head was spinning. He began to struggle, his chest aching with the need to breathe. Desperately he pushed at the cloak above his head, but the fish were clustered together so tightly on top of it that they were like a living, moving ceiling, impossible to break.

His struggles became more and more feeble. He could feel himself losing consciousness, his mind drifting away from his body.

Is this, then, how it ends? he thought. After all

we have faced . . . A picture of his mother and father at home flashed through his mind. They would be breakfasting now, in the forge kitchen. Talking of him, perhaps, and of Barda.

They will never know what became of us, Lief thought. Our bones will lie in this mud forever, and with them the Belt of Deltora.

Dimly he became aware of urgent nudges on his legs and chest. The fish were bumping against him. They seemed to be trying to push him upwards. And — the fish above his head were moving aside.

With the last of his strength he forced his trembling legs to straighten. His head broke the surface and he took huge, grateful gulps of air.

At first he could see nothing. The cloak was still draped over his head, clinging to his face. Then it fell away and he was left blinking at Barda and Jasmine, who were as gasping and bedraggled as he.

In terror he looked up. But the Ak-Baba was well past the channel, flying steadily over the plain towards the plume of smoke on the horizon.

"It did not see us!" he croaked, coughing. "It passed us by." He could not believe it.

"Of course," Jasmine grinned, gathering the drifting cloak into a bundle. "When it looked down at the water it saw nothing but a school of fish. Fish that it had seen a hundred times before."

She patted her hands on the rippling surface.

"Ah, you were clever, fish," she laughed. "You hid us well."

The fish swam about her, lazily blowing bubbles. They seemed pleased with themselves.

"I thought they were trying to drown us," said Barda. "And all the time they were disguising us from the Ak-Baba. Whoever heard of fish coming to anyone's aid?"

"These are no ordinary fish," Jasmine assured him. "They are old and wise. They had no love for the rats who turned the plain on one side of their river into a wasteland. And they have no love for the Shadow Lord or his servants, either."

"They *told* you this?" asked Lief, amazed.

The girl shrugged. "They are no ordinary fish," she repeated. "They would speak to you, too, if only you would listen."

Lief stared at the shapes beneath the water and concentrated with all his strength. But all he could hear was rippling and the sound of bubbles.

"I should have known we would not die in the river," he murmured. "On the plain the opal showed me a vision of myself standing in the Shifting Sands. If I am to die anywhere, it will be there."

He felt Barda and Jasmine's eyes upon him. "Does the opal tell what *will* be? Or only what *might* be?" asked Barda abruptly.

Lief shrugged. He did not know.

Kree called from the other side of the channel.

"We must move on," Jasmine said. "The Ak-Baba may return this way."

With the fish swimming ahead of them to make their way easy, the companions waded on across the channel. When at last they had reached the opposite shore they turned and bowed their thanks.

"We owe our lives to you, fish," Jasmine called softly, as Kree flew down to perch on her arm. "We thank you for your kindness."

The fish ducked their own heads, then slowly swam away, their tails waving as if in farewell.

Kree squawked and took flight once more. Lief, Barda, and Jasmine followed him as he fluttered towards a tree that grew beside the water, its long, feathery green branches bending and sweeping the ground.

They pushed through the greenery and found themselves in a small clear space surrounded on all sides by drooping branches. It was like a little green room with the tree's gnarled trunk in its center. Filli sat there waiting for them. He scuttled over to Jasmine and leaped onto her shoulder, chattering with pleasure.

Groaning with relief, the three companions sank to the ground. A thick layer of soft brown leaves cushioned their aching bones. Above them was a roof of green. Around them were walls that whispered in the gentle breeze.

"Safe," murmured Jasmine. But for once there was no need for her to explain what the tree had said. They all felt its peace.

In moments, they were asleep.

⁕

When Lief woke, he was alone. Birds were calling above his head. It was cool, and the light was dim.

The sun is going down, he thought, shivering. I have slept the whole day through.

Where were Barda and Jasmine, Kree and Filli? Lief crawled over to the hanging branches that curtained his shelter, parted them cautiously and peered out. With a shock he realized that the sun was not setting, but rising. He had slept not just through the day, but through the following night as well!

Jasmine and Barda were coming towards the tree. He guessed they had been searching for food and hoped they had found something. His stomach felt hollow. It seemed a very long time since he had eaten. He pushed through the leaves and ran to meet them.

"Apples!" Barda called, as he approached. "Rather wizened, but sweet enough, and strangely filling."

He threw an apple to Lief, who sank his teeth into it ravenously and soon finished it, core and all.

"It is said that stolen fruit tastes the sweetest," Barda laughed, tossing him another.

"Stolen?" asked Lief, with his mouth full.

"Those trees over there are an orchard," said Barda, pointing behind him. "Jasmine helped herself without troubling to find the owner and ask permission."

Jasmine tossed her head. "The trees are groaning with fruit," she snapped. "They are anxious to be picked. And you can see how withered the apples are. Who could object to us helping ourselves?"

"I am not complaining," said Lief cheerfully. "The last time I had an apple — " He broke off, the sweet fruit suddenly dry in his mouth. The last time he ate an apple he was in Del, feasting with his friends. It had been his sixteenth birthday. It was the day he had said goodbye to childhood, the life he had known, his home, and the parents he loved. How long ago it seemed now.

Jasmine was looking at him curiously. He realized that his expression had grown sad and quickly he turned away. Jasmine had lived alone in the Forests of Silence, with only Filli and Kree for company. She had seen her parents taken away by Grey Guards, and braved terrors without number from her earliest childhood. He was sure that his homesickness would seem a weak and childish thing to her.

He took another bite of his apple, then jumped as a high-pitched voice rang out.

"Thieves!"

Lief squinted against the shimmering dawn light. Something was rolling through the long grass towards them, shrieking. As it drew closer he realized that it was a little old woman. She was so plump, and so wrapped and bundled in shawls, that she seemed completely round. Thin brown hair was screwed up into a tiny topknot on her head. Her face was creased and crinkled all over like a wizened apple, and red with anger. She was frowning furiously, shaking her fist.

"Thieves!" she shrieked. "Vagabonds! Give them back! Give them back!"

The three companions stared at her, open-mouthed.

"You stole my apples!" the old women shrieked. "You stole my beauties while my guards slept. Where are they? Give them to me!"

Silently, Jasmine passed over the three apples that remained in her hands. The woman clasped them to her chest and glared.

"Cheat! Where are the others?" she shouted. "Where are the other six? Every apple is numbered. Every one must be accounted for. How else can I fill my quota? Nine fruit you took, and nine must be returned."

Barda cleared his throat. "I am very sorry, madam, but we cannot return them. I fear they are already eaten."

"*Eaten??*"

The old woman seemed to swell, and went so red that Lief feared she might explode.

"We — we beg your pardon," he stammered. "We were so hungry, and — "

439

The old woman threw back her head, raised her arms, shook her shawls, and gave a terrible, high-pitched cry.

Immediately she was surrounded by a dark, whirling, humming cloud.

Bees. Thousands of bees. They had been riding on her back, clustered under her shawls. Now they were swarming in the air around her, waiting for the order to attack.

3 - The Road to Rithmere

L ief, Barda, and Jasmine stumbled back. The cloud of bees surged this way and that, making patterns in the air behind the old woman's head. Their buzzing was like the threatening growl of a great animal.

"You thought I was unprotected, did you?" screeched the old woman. "You thought you could steal from me without fear. My guards are small, but many, and act with one mind. You will suffer death by a thousand stings for what you have done."

Jasmine was desperately feeling in her pockets. She found what she was looking for and held out her hand. Gold and silver coins gleamed in the sunlight.

"Will you take these for your apples?" she asked.

The old woman gave a start. Her eyes narrowed. "If you have money, why do you steal?" she demanded. But her wrinkled hand shot out and took the coins.

"No!" Lief exclaimed, lunging forward without thinking. "That money is all we have. You cannot take it all for a few dried-up apples!"

The bees surged at him, buzzing dangerously.

"Softly, boy, softly. Gently, gently!" cackled the old woman. "My guards do not like sudden movements, and are easily angered. Why, even I must use smoke to calm them when I take their honey from the hive. Even I."

She made a soft sound and the cloud of bees behind her shrank and disappeared as the creatures returned to the folds of her shawls. She tucked the coins carefully away and scowled at the companions.

"Let this be a lesson to you!" she ordered. "And tell all your fellow vagabonds that the next thieves who come here will receive no mercy."

Lief, Barda, and Jasmine hesitated.

She shook her fist at them. "Go on!" she shrilled. "Get back to the road where you came from."

"We did not come from the road, old woman! And we are not thieves, either!" Jasmine cried.

The woman grew very still. "If you did not come from the road, then where did you come from?" she murmured after a moment. "There is no other way to my orchard. Except . . ."

Suddenly she reached out and grasped the edge of Lief's cloak. Feeling its dampness, she gasped and slowly raised her head to look across the water and away to the horizon where a faint drift of smoke still rose over the Plain of the Rats.

A look of dread crossed her wrinkled face.

"Who are you?" she whispered. Then she held up her hand. "No — do not tell me. Just go! If you are seen here not even my bees will be able to protect me."

"How do we find the road?" asked Lief quickly.

She pointed to the orchard behind her. "Go through the orchard. There is a gate on the far side. Hurry! And forget what I said. Tell no one you were here."

"You can count on that," said Barda. "As I presume we can count on you forgetting you ever saw us?"

She nodded silently. The three companions turned and strode away across the grass. As they reached the trees they heard a shout and looked back. The strange old woman was standing, round as a ball, in a cloud of bees, staring after them.

"Good fortune!" she cried, raising her arm.

They lifted their own arms in reply, and went on.

"It is all very well to wish us good fortune now," complained Jasmine as they threaded their way through the apple trees. "A few moments ago she was threatening to have us stung to death by her bees. And she did not offer to return our money."

Barda shrugged. "Who knows what troubles she has suffered? Perhaps she is right to be suspicious of strangers. Except for the bees she seems all alone here."

"She spoke of a 'quota' that had to be filled," Lief said slowly, as they reached the end of the orchard and let themselves through a gate that led to a winding, tree-lined track. "It sounds as though she has to grow a certain number of apples."

"Or make something from them," said Barda. He closed the gate behind them and nodded towards a sign fixed to the old wood.

Queen Bee Cider
The Champion's Choice
Made from genuine tree-aged cider apples
NO ENTRY
WITHOUT PERMISSION

"Queen Bee Cider was a drink much prized among the guards and acrobats when I was at the palace in Del," Barda went on. "It gave extra strength to anyone who drank it. It seems that it is made here — by our friend back there, who is no doubt Queen Bee herself."

Lief sighed. "I wish that she had given us a glass or two before sending us on our way."

Indeed, all of them were tired and in low spirits as they trudged along the track, talking in low voices. They knew that their next goal must be the Shifting Sands. But how they were to reach it was a mystery.

In all their minds was the thought that they had no money, no food, no blankets, no packs — nothing but the map Lief's father had drawn for him, their weapons, and the ragged clothes on their backs.

And the Belt of Deltora, Lief reminded himself. But the Belt, for all its power, for all that three stones now glimmered in their places along its length, could not fill their bellies or shelter them from the weather.

"The opal gives glimpses of the future," said Jasmine, after a moment. "Surely it can tell us what is ahead?"

But Lief was unwilling to touch the opal. His vision of the Shifting Sands still haunted him. He had no wish to experience it again.

"We do not need to see into the future to know that we need help," he said, staring straight ahead.

"We need supplies and a safe place to rest for a while. Let us think only of that for now."

He expected Jasmine to argue, but when he glanced at her he saw that she had stopped listening to him and was concentrating on something else.

"I hear carts and the sound of feet," she announced finally. "Voices, too. There is a larger road ahead."

Sure enough, in a few more minutes the winding trail met a broad, straight highway. Cautiously they looked both ways along its length. A horse-drawn cart was approaching from the right with several men and women walking beside it.

"It seems there are others going our way," muttered Barda. "They look harmless enough. But still it might be wise to wait until they have passed. We cannot afford too many questions until we are well away from here."

They crouched among the trees and watched while the cart came closer. It was worn and rickety, and the horse that pulled it was old and plodding. But the people — those walking beside it as well as those who jolted along inside — were talking and laughing with one another as though all was well with the world.

Lief heard the name "Rithmere" repeated several times as the cart passed by. It was clear that Rithmere was a town, and that the people were looking forward to reaching it. His spirits rose.

"There must be a festival or fair being held in this Rithmere place," he whispered.

"A festival in these days?" grunted Barda. "I cannot believe it. But still, if Rithmere is to the left along this road, it is on our way to the Shifting Sands. And a town is what we need — the larger the better."

"Why?" hissed Jasmine, who far preferred the open countryside.

"In a town we can lose ourselves in the crowd and earn money for new supplies. Or beg for it."

"*Beg?*" exclaimed Lief, horrified.

Barda glanced at him, a grim smile tweaking the corner of his mouth. "There are times when pride must be put aside in a good cause," he said.

Lief mumbled an apology. How could he have forgotten that Barda had spent years disguised as a beggar in Del?

When the cart was well past, the companions crept out from the trees and began to follow it. They had not gone far before Lief saw something lying on the ground.

It was a notice. Curious, he picked it up:

THE RITHMERE GAMES

Come one, come all!
Test your strength and skill!

*100 GOLD COINS
TO EVERY FINALIST!

*1000 GOLD COINS
TO GRAND WINNER!!!

Lief showed the notice to Barda and Jasmine. His heart was thudding with excitement.

"Here is our answer!" he said. "Here is our chance to earn the money we need, and more. We will enter the Games. And we will win!"

4 ~ Lost in the Crowd

D ays later, when Rithmere was at last in sight, Lief was not feeling so hopeful. The way had been long and weary, and he was very hungry. Berries growing at the side of the road were the only food the companions had been able to find, and they were few. Travellers who had passed along the highway before them had almost stripped the bushes bare.

The longer they had walked, the more crowded the highway had become. Many other people were moving towards Rithmere. Some were as ill-prepared for the journey as Lief, Barda, and Jasmine. Their clothes were tattered and they had little or nothing to eat. A few, famished and exhausted, fell by the roadside in despair.

The companions managed to keep moving, stopping often for rests. They spoke to their fellow travellers as little as possible. Though they were feel-

449

ing safer concealed in a crowd, they still felt it wise to avoid questions about where they had come from.

They kept their ears open, however, and quickly learned that the Games had been held every year for the past ten years. Their fame had grown and spread — now hopeful contestants came from everywhere to seek their fortune at Rithmere. The friends also learned, to their relief, that Grey Guards were seldom seen in the town while the Games were in progress.

"They know better than to interfere with something the people like so much," Lief heard a tall, red-haired woman say to her companion, a giant of a man whose muscles bulged through his ragged shirt as he bent to tighten the laces of his boot.

The man nodded. "A thousand gold coins," he muttered. "Or even a hundred! Think of the difference it would make to us — and to all at home." He finished tying his lace, straightened, and gritted his teeth as he stared at the city ahead. "This year we will be finalists at least, Joanna. I feel it."

"You have never been stronger, Orwen," the woman agreed affectionately. "And I, too, have a good chance. Last year I was not watchful enough. I let that vixen Brianne of Lees trip me. It will not happen again."

Orwen put his great arm around her shoulders. "You cannot blame yourself for losing to Brianne. After all, she went on to become Champion. She is a great fighter. And think how hard the people of Lees worked to prepare her."

"She was treated like a queen, they say," said Joanna bitterly. "Extra food, no duties except her training. Her people thought she would be their salvation. And what did she do? Ran off with the money as soon as she had it in her hand. Can you believe it?"

"Of course," the man said grimly. "A thousand gold pieces is a great fortune, Joanna. Very few Games Champions return to their old homes after their win. Most do not want to share their wealth, so they hurry away with it to start a new life elsewhere."

"But you would never do that, Orwen," Joanna protested fiercely. "And neither would I. I would *never* leave my people in poverty while I could help them. I would rather throw myself into the Shifting Sands."

Lief stiffened at her last words and glanced at Jasmine and Barda to see if they had heard.

Joanna and Orwen strode on, shoulder to shoulder, towering above the rest of the crowd.

"That she mentions the Shifting Sands means nothing, Lief," Barda said in a low voice, looking after them. "The Sands are as familiar a nightmare to folk who live in these parts as the Forests of Silence are to the people of Del."

His face was grim, deeply marked with lines of weariness. "A more important matter is to decide whether we are wasting our time trying to compete with such as Joanna and Orwen. In our present state — "

"We have to try," Lief mumbled, though his own heart was very heavy.

"There is no point in talking of this now!" Jasmine broke in impatiently. "Whether we compete in the Games or not, we must enter the city. We must get some food — even if we have to steal it. What else are we to do?"

✳

Rithmere seethed with people. Stalls lined the narrow streets, packed together, filling every available space, their owners shouting of what they had to sell and watching their goods with eagle-sharp eyes.

The noise was deafening. Musicians, dancers, fire-eaters, and jugglers performed on every corner, their hats set out in front of them to catch coins thrown by passersby. Some had animals — snakes, dogs, even dancing bears, as well as strange creatures the companions had never seen before — to help them attract attention.

The noise, the smells, the bright colors, the confusion, made Lief, already light-headed with hunger, feel faint and sick. Faces in the crowd seemed to loom out at him as he stumbled along. Some he recognized from the highway. Most were strange to him.

Everywhere were the hunched forms of beggars, their gaunt faces turned up pleadingly, their hands outstretched. Some were blind, or had missing limbs. Others were simply starving. Most people paid no attention to them at all, stepping over them as if they were piles of rubbish.

"Hey, girl! You with the black bird! Over here!"

The hoarse shout had come from somewhere very near. They looked around, startled.

A fat man with long, greasy hair was beckoning urgently to Jasmine. The three companions edged through the crowd towards him, wondering what he wanted. As they drew closer they saw that he was sitting at a small table which had been covered by a red cloth that reached the ground. Leaning against the wall behind him was a pair of crutches. On the table stood a perch, a basket of painted wooden birds, and a wheel decorated with brightly colored pictures of birds and coins.

It was plainly some sort of gambling game.

"Like to make some money, little lovely?" the man shouted above the noise of the crowd.

Jasmine frowned and said nothing.

"She cannot play," Lief shouted back. "Unless it costs nothing."

The man snorted. "How would I make my living that way, young fellow-me-lad? No, no. One silver coin for a spin of the wheel, that is my price. But I am not asking your friend to play. No one can play at present. My bird just died on me. See?" He held up a dead pigeon by its feet and swung it in front of their noses.

Jasmine glared at him, stony-faced. The man's mouth turned down mournfully. "Sad, isn't it?" he said. "Sad for Beakie-Boy, sadder for me. I need a bird to turn the wheel. That's the game. Beat the Bird, you see? I have another two pigeons back in my lodgings, but if I go and fetch one now I'll lose my spot. Lose half a day's earnings. Can't afford that, can I?"

His small eyes narrowed as he looked Jasmine up and down. "You and your friends look as if you could do with a good meal inside you," he said slyly. "Well, I will help you out."

He threw the dead pigeon on the ground, kicked it under the table, and pointed at Kree. "I will buy your bird. How much do you want for him?"

5 - Win and Lose

Jasmine shook her head. "Kree is not for sale," she said firmly, and turned to go. The fat man clutched at the sleeve of her jacket.

"Don't turn your back on me, little lovely," he whined. "Don't turn your back on poor old Ferdinand, for pity's sake."

Kree put his head to one side and looked at the man carefully. Then he hopped onto the table and stalked right up to him, inspecting him closely, his head darting this way and that. After a moment he squawked loudly.

Jasmine glanced at Lief and Barda, then back at Ferdinand. "Kree says, how much would you give for his help just for today?" she said.

The fat man laughed. "Talks to you, does he?" he jeered disbelievingly. "Well now, that is something you don't see every day."

He took a small tin from his pocket, opened it, and took out a silver coin. "Tell him from me that I'll give him this if he turns the wheel till sunset. Would that suit him?"

Kree flew back to perch on Jasmine's arm and squawked again. Jasmine nodded slowly. "For one silver coin, Kree will turn the wheel thirty times. If you want him to do more, you pay again."

"That is robbery!" Ferdinand exclaimed.

"It is his price," said Jasmine calmly.

Ferdinand's face crumpled, and he buried it in his hands. "Ah, you are a cruel girl! Cruel to a poor unfortunate trying to make a living," he mumbled. "My last hope is gone. I will starve, and my birds with me." His shoulders shook as he began to sob.

Jasmine shrugged, apparently quite unmoved. Lief, glancing at Ferdinand's crutches propped against the wall, felt very uncomfortable.

"It seems harsh, Jasmine," he whispered in her ear. "Could you not — ?"

"He is acting. He can afford ten times as much," Jasmine hissed back. "Kree says he has a purse at his belt that is bulging with coins. It is hidden from us by the cloth that covers the table. Just wait."

Sure enough, when after a moment the fat man peeped through his fingers and saw that Jasmine was not going to change her mind, he stopped pretending to sob and took his hands away from his face. "Very well," he snapped, in quite a different voice. "For a bird, he drives a hard bargain. Put him on the perch."

"The money first, if you please," Barda put in quickly.

Ferdinand shot him an angry look, then, with much groaning and sighing, passed the silver coin he had taken from the tin to Jasmine.

Satisfied, Kree fluttered onto the perch.

"Stand aside, you three," Ferdinand said sharply. "Make way for the customers."

The companions did as they were told, but remained close by so that they could watch what happened. None of them trusted Ferdinand. The smell of food wafting from a nearby stall made Lief's mouth water, but he knew that they could not buy anything with the silver coin until Kree was safely back on Jasmine's arm.

"Roll up, roll up!" Ferdinand bellowed. "Beat the bird and win! One silver coin for a spin of the wheel! Every player wins a prize!"

A small crowd began to cluster around his table as he began pointing at the numbers on the coins painted around the wheel. "Two silver pieces for one!" he shouted. "Or would you prefer three silver pieces? Or four? Yes, ladies and gentlemen, boys and girls. Four silver pieces for one!"

People began feeling in their pockets for coins.

Ferdinand's pudgy hand moved around the

wheel, his finger stabbing at one number after an-other. "But why stop at four?" he shouted. "This is your lucky day! Why, you could win five, six, or *ten* silver pieces!" He tore at his hair and rolled his eyes. His voice rose to a shriek. "Ten silver coins for one! A prize for every player! Why do I do it? I must be los-ing my wits!"

Several people pressed forward, holding out their money. Lief moved restlessly.

"Perhaps we should use our coin on the game," he muttered to Barda. "We could double our money. Or even better!"

Barda smiled at him pityingly. "Or, which is more likely, we could lose our coin and finish with nothing but a worthless wooden bird," he said. "If the wheel stops at a bird instead of a coin . . ."

Lief was not convinced. Especially when he saw Kree spin the wheel for the first time, hitting it sharply with his beak. The wheel spun smoothly around and around. The player, an eager-looking woman with flowing hair, watched anxiously, then cried out with delight as the wheel stopped and the marker showed that she had won two coins.

"She has beaten the bird!" shrieked Ferdinand, scrabbling in his money tin and handing the woman her prize. "Oh, mercy me!" He turned to Kree and shook his fist. "Try harder!" he scolded. "You will ruin me!"

The crowd laughed. Another player stepped forward. Kree spun the wheel again. The second player was even luckier than the first, winning three coins.

"This bird is hopeless!" Ferdinand howled in despair. "Oh, what will I do?"

After that, he could not take his customers' money fast enough. People crowded in front of his table, eager for their turn to play.

Kree spun the wheel again and again. And, somehow, no one else seemed to have the luck of the first two players. More and more often the wheel would stop at a bird picture, and the disappointed player would creep away clutching a wooden bird. Only rarely did the marker point to a picture of a coin, and when it did it was usually a coin marked "1" or "2."

But whenever that happened Ferdinand would make an enormous fuss, congratulating the winner, saying he was ruined, shouting at Kree for playing badly, and fretting that next time the prize would be even bigger.

But the pile of silver in the money tin was growing. Every few minutes, Ferdinand would quietly take some coins and tuck them away in the purse at his belt. And still the players pressed forward, eager to try their luck.

"No wonder his purse is bulging," Jasmine muttered in disgust. "Why do these people give him their money? Some of them are plainly very poor. Can they not see that he wins far more often than they do?"

"Ferdinand only makes noise when players win," said Barda heavily. "The losers are ignored and quickly forgotten."

Jasmine made a disgusted face. "Kree has made twenty-nine turns," she said. "After one more, we can take him back. I have no wish to go on with this. I do not like Ferdinand, or his wheel. Do you agree?"

Barda nodded, and Lief did also. However much they needed money, neither of them wanted to help Ferdinand any longer.

Barda pointed to a banner fixed high to a building a little way along the road.

OFFICIAL GAMES INN
*Bed and Board *Competitors Only
*Amazing Prices!

"We may find shelter and some food there," he suggested. "They may let us work for our keep. At least we can try."

Kree had spun the wheel for a final time. The player, a thin-faced man with deep shadows under his eyes, watched desperately as it slowed. When it stopped at the picture of a bird, and Ferdinand handed him the little wooden trinket, his mouth quivered and he slunk away, his bony shoulders bowed.

Jasmine stepped to the table and held out her arm for Kree. "The thirty turns have been made, Ferdinand," she said. "We must go now."

But Ferdinand, his plump face glistening with sweat and greed, turned his small eyes towards her and shook his head violently.

"You cannot go," he spat. "I need the bird. He is the best I have ever had. Look at the crowd! You cannot take him!"

His arm shot out, his pudgy hand grasping at Kree's feet. But Kree fluttered from his perch just in time, landing at the edge of the table.

"Come back here!" hissed Ferdinand, reaching for him. Kree bent his head and with his sharp beak tweaked at the red cloth that covered the table. As it was pulled aside, the crowd gasped, then began to roar with anger.

For on the ground under the table was a pedal with some wires that led up through the tabletop to the wheel.

"He can stop and start the wheel as he wills!" someone shouted. "He uses his feet. See? He cheats!"

The crowd pressed forward angrily. Kree hopped hastily onto Jasmine's arm. Ferdinand swept up the wheel and leaped to his feet, tipping over the table.

The wooden birds and the tin of silver coins crashed to the ground as he took to his heels, hurtling down the street with surprising speed, the wheel tucked under his arm, the remains of its cheating wires trailing. Some of his customers stopped to pick up the money which was rolling everywhere. Most sped off in pursuit of the escaping man, shouting in fury.

6 - Berry, Birdie, and Twig

Lief looked after them, open-mouthed. "Why, there is nothing wrong with Ferdinand's legs at all!" he exclaimed. "He has left his crutches behind — and he is running!"

"A cheat in every way," Barda snorted. "I hope his customers catch him. We are fortunate that they did not blame Kree and turn on us."

"Fortunate, too, that you made Ferdinand pay us in advance," murmured Jasmine. She was scanning the roadway, searching for coins. But the crowd had picked the ground clean and all she found was one wooden bird. She picked it up and tucked it away in her pocket with her other treasures. For Jasmine, nothing was too small to be of use.

Guided by the banner billowing high above the heads of the crowd, they made their way to the Champion Inn. They entered the door and to their surprise found themselves in a very small closed room. A plump woman in a bright green dress decorated with many frills and ribbons rose from behind a desk in one corner and bustled towards them, the large bunch of keys at her waist jingling importantly.

"Good-day!" she cried, in a friendly way. "I am Mother Brightly, your hostess. Please forgive me, but before I can welcome you here I must ask if you are competitors in the Games."

"We wish to be," said Barda cautiously. "But we are strangers in these parts, and do not know how to enter."

"Why, then, you have come to the right place!" Mother Brightly beamed. "This is the official Games inn. Here you can register as competitors, and stay until the Games begin tomorrow."

The companions exchanged glances. It sounded wonderful, but . . .

"We have only one silver coin between us," Barda admitted reluctantly. "We were hoping that perhaps we could work for our keep."

The woman flapped her hands at him, shaking her head. "Work? Nonsense!" she exclaimed. "You must rest and eat so that you can do your best in the Games. If one silver coin is all you have, one silver coin is the price you will pay. Competitors pay only what they can afford at the Champion Inn."

Before the companions could say any more she hurried back to the desk, beckoning them to follow.

She sat down, pulled a large open book towards her and took up a pen. "Name and town?" she asked briskly, glancing at Barda.

Lief caught his breath. He, Barda, and Jasmine had decided that it would be unwise to give their real names when they entered the Games. But they had not realized that they would have to think of false names so soon.

Mother Brightly was waiting, pen poised and eyebrows raised.

"Ah . . . my name is — Berry. Of Bushtown," stammered Barda.

The woman wrote, frowning slightly. "I have not heard of Bushtown before," she said.

"It is — to the north," Barda answered. "My friends — Birdie and — and Twig — are also from there."

He glanced nervously at Jasmine and Lief, who were both glaring at him, but Mother Brightly nodded, writing busily and apparently quite satisfied.

"Now," she said, jumping up with the book clutched under her arm. "Follow me, if you please!"

Things were moving very fast. Feeling rather dazed, Lief, Barda, and Jasmine followed her into another room where stood a large set of scales, a long rule, and a big cupboard.

"Please give me your weapons," Mother Brightly said, taking a key from the bunch at her waist and unlocking the cupboard. Then, as the companions hesitated, she clapped her hands sharply and raised her voice. "I must insist! It is forbidden to carry weapons in the Champion Inn."

Unwillingly, Lief and Barda unbuckled their swords, and Jasmine handed over the dagger she wore at her belt. Mother Brightly locked the weapons in the cupboard, nodding approvingly. "Do not fear," she said in a calmer voice. "They will be quite safe here, and returned to you before you leave. Now — your measurements."

She weighed Lief, Barda, and Jasmine in turn, and measured their heights, writing all the details down in her book. She felt their muscles and looked carefully at their hands and feet. Then she nodded, pleased.

"You need food and rest, my dears, but otherwise you are all strong, and should do well," she said. "I thought so, when first I saw you. One last thing. Your special talents. What are they?"

She waited with her head on one side.

Lief, Barda, and Jasmine glanced at one another. They were not quite sure what the woman meant.

"I — can climb," said Jasmine hesitantly at last. "I can balance on high places, swing, jump . . ."

"Excellent, Birdie!" said Mother Brightly, and wrote "AGILITY" beside Jasmine's false name. She turned to Barda. "And you, Berry? Let me guess. Your talent would be strength. Am I right?"

466

Barda shrugged and nodded. The woman beamed, and wrote again. Then she looked at Lief. "And Twig?" she enquired.

Lief felt his face growing hot and knew that he was blushing. What had possessed Barda to give him such an absurd name? And what was his special talent? He was not sure that he had one.

"Speed," Barda said quickly. "My friend is very fast on his feet, and can jump, duck, and dodge with the best."

"Perfect!" cried Mother Brightly, writing "SPEED" beside the name "Twig of Bushtown." "Agility, strength, and speed. Why, together you three must be a fine team. Now, wait here a moment. I will not be long."

She bustled out of the room again. The companions looked at one another. All of them were bewildered at this sudden change in their fortunes.

"No wonder people flock to Rithmere," said Lief in a low voice. "It is surprising that the whole of Deltora is not here. Why, at the very least folk get free food and a bed for a while."

"So long as they are willing to compete," Barda whispered back. "I have a feeling that these Games may be more difficult, or more dangerous, than we expect."

"No running or jumping race could be more dangerous than what we have been through," hissed

Jasmine. "The most difficult thing about this will be remembering to answer to those stupid names you chose for us, Barda."

"Yes," Lief agreed. "Twig! Could you think of nothing better?"

"I was taken by surprise and said the first things that came into my head," Barda growled. "If I had hesitated she would have known I was lying."

At that moment Mother Brightly came rustling into the room again. With her she brought three colored strips of cloth — a red, a green, and a blue. She tied the red band around Barda's wrist, the green band around Lief's wrist, and the blue around Jasmine's. Their false names had been written on their bands, with their heights and weights underneath.

"Do not take your wristbands off, even to sleep," Mother Brightly advised. "They mark you as official competitors, show your special talent, and entitle you to food, drink, and entrance to the Games. Now — you will want to eat, I do not doubt, and rest after your journey. The silver coin, if you please?"

Jasmine handed her the coin and in return received a key labelled with the number 77. "This is the key to your room," Mother Brightly said. "A lucky number indeed. Keep it safe."

As they nodded she hesitated, nibbling at her bottom lip as if trying to make up her mind about something. Then, suddenly, she glanced behind her to make sure they were alone and leaned towards them with a rustle of green frills.

"Now — I do not say this to every competitor, but you are strangers to the Games, and I have taken a liking to you," she whispered. "Trust no one, however friendly. And keep your door locked at all times — especially at night. We do not want any . . . accidents."

She put a finger to her lips, then turned and hurried off again, beckoning them to follow.

Wondering, they followed her down a hallway to a large dining room, where a great number of people wearing red, blue, and green wristbands were eating and drinking with gusto. Many of the diners looked up and stared, their faces alive with curiosity, challenge, suspicion, or menace. Most of them were very large and looked extremely strong, though there were some smaller, leaner men and women as well.

Lief lifted his chin and looked around proudly, determined to show that he was not nervous or afraid. At a center table he saw Joanna and Orwen, the two tall companions he had seen on the highway. Then he gave a start. Sitting near to them, though alone, was another person he knew.

It was the dark, scarred traveller the companions had seen at Tom's shop, on their way to the City of the Rats. The man's hard eyes were fixed on the newcomers, but he gave no sign that he recognized them.

"Help yourselves to anything you fancy, my

dears," Mother Brightly said, pointing to a long bench at the side of the room where dishes stood keeping warm over low flames. "Eat, then rest. Do all you can to be fit for tomorrow. I have great hopes for you three! To me, you have the look of finalists. And I have seen many come and go."

She had not troubled to lower her voice, and Lief fidgeted as the gazes of the other competitors grew even more alert. They had all heard what she had said.

"Now, I must return to my post," Mother Brightly said. "It grows late, but new competitors could arrive even now. A bell will wake you for breakfast tomorrow. A second bell, an hour later, will call you to the Games."

She turned to go. Suddenly unwilling to be left alone in the unfriendly room, Lief spoke to delay her. "Before you go, Mother Brightly, could you advise us on which events we should try for?" he asked.

The woman's eyebrows rose as she stared at him. "But surely you know? You do not choose for yourselves who you will fight."

"Fight?" Lief echoed faintly.

Mother Brightly nodded. "You fight those chosen for you — others who match your height, weight, and special talent," she said. "At least at first. Of course, if you win your early rounds, you will at last fight competitors of all kinds."

She clasped her hands. Her eyes were sparkling.

470

"Those events are always the most exciting of all. Agility against strength. Speed against agility. Wits against weight. Large against small. Sometimes the contests last for many hours. Two years ago there was a final that lasted a day and a night — ah, a bloody battle that was. The loser, poor fellow, lost his leg in the end, for it was smashed to pieces. But of course he had his hundred gold coins as comfort. And it was wonderful entertainment, I assure you!"

She nodded to them happily and trotted off. The door clicked shut behind her.

7 - Trouble

The companions eyed one another in silence. "So," said Barda at last. "Now we know why the whole of Deltora does not enter the Rithmere Games. Most people have no wish to be pounded into the ground for sport."

Lief glanced at the place where the scar-faced man had been sitting, ready to point him out to Jasmine and Barda, but the chair was pushed back and empty. The man had gone.

"I think we should leave here," he said slowly. "We cannot risk serious injury just to make money. We will have to get supplies another way."

Jasmine shook her head. "I am not leaving until I eat," she announced. "I am very hungry, and so is Filli."

Barda and Lief looked at each other. The idea of food was very tempting. "Mother Brightly has our silver coin," Lief murmured. "It will surely pay for one meal."

So it was decided. They helped themselves to food, heaping their plates high. Then they found a place to sit and began to eat gratefully. The food was very good. Jugs of Queen Bee Cider stood on the table, and they drank mug after mug of its bubbling sweetness.

Concentrating on their meal they spoke little to one another at first, and no one spoke to them. But Lief's neck prickled, and he knew that dozens of pairs of eyes were still trained on him. The other competitors were trying to judge how dangerous an opponent he would be. You do not have to worry, he told them silently. Soon I will be gone.

The dining hall had almost emptied by the time they finished their meal. His hunger satisfied at last, Lief found that he was longing for sleep. Barda and Jasmine were also yawning, but they all knew that they could not stay in the inn. Unwillingly they rose to their feet and went to the door through which they had come, aware that their every step was being watched.

"I will be glad to be out of here, but I do not look forward to telling Mother Brightly that we have changed our minds," Lief murmured uncomfortably.

Jasmine laughed. "Because she will be angry with us? What does it matter?"

Barda pushed at the door, but it did not budge. It seemed to be locked from the outside.

"Not that way," a slow, deep voice said behind them. "The sleeping rooms and training areas are through there." They turned and saw the huge figure of Orwen. He was pointing to another door at the end of the room.

"We do not want the sleeping rooms or the training areas," Jasmine answered abruptly. "We want to leave the inn."

Orwen gazed at her blankly for a moment. Then, finally, he shook his head. "You are competitors," he said. "You cannot leave."

Lief decided that the big man must be slow-witted. "We have changed our minds, Orwen," he said gently. "We no longer wish to compete in the Games. We wish to leave Rithmere and go on our way."

But again Orwen shook his head. "You cannot change your minds," he said. "Your names are in the book. You have your wristbands. You have eaten and drunk in the dining hall. They will not let you leave."

"Do you mean we are *prisoners*?" Barda demanded.

Orwen shrugged his great shoulders. "The rest of us wish to be here," he said. "We do not think of ourselves as prisoners. But certainly we are not free to come and go as we please."

With a nod of farewell, he turned and left them.

474

Angrily, Jasmine beat on the door with her fists. It shuddered and its frame rattled, but no one came.

"What shall we do now?" demanded Lief.

"We will go quietly to our room," said Barda evenly. "Our minds are working slowly now, because we are tired. We will sleep, and when we wake we will find a way out, never fear."

The room was silent and everyone was staring as they strode to the door at the back of the dining hall and went out. Signs directed them up some stairs to the sleeping quarters floor. Once there, they began to walk through a maze of door-lined hallways, looking for Room 77.

Rugs cushioned their feet and the hallways were well lit and silent, but as they walked, Lief began to feel more and more uncomfortable. Sudden draughts kept striking chill on his legs. The back of his neck was tingling. He was sure that doors were stealthily opening behind him and that unfriendly eyes were peering after him. Several times he spun around to try to catch the spies, but there was never anything to be seen.

"Just keep walking," said Barda loudly. "Let the fools look. What does it matter to us?"

"Someone is following us, also," Jasmine breathed. "I feel it. That woman should not have said what she did about us. I fear that someone has decided to put us out of the way before the Games even begin."

Automatically, Lief's hand moved to his sword, but of course the weapon was missing — locked away in Mother Brightly's cupboard.

The numbers on the doors beside him were 65 and 66. Ahead there was a turn in the hallway. "Our room cannot be far away now," he whispered. "Once we reach it we will be safe."

They quickened their pace. In moments they had reached the turn in the hallway. They hurried around the corner and found themselves in a short, dead-end corridor. Seeing that Room 77 was right at the end, they began moving towards it.

Then the light went out.

Kree screeched a warning. In the blackness, Lief twisted and leaped sideways, flattening himself against the wall. He felt a glancing blow on his shoulder. He heard Barda shout. He heard a thump and a crash and an angry hiss of pain. There was a scrabbling, scuffling noise and the sound of running feet. Then silence.

"Lief! Barda!" It was Jasmine's voice. "Are you — ?"

Lief answered, and to his relief heard Barda mutter also. Then, as suddenly as it had gone out, the light went on again. Shading his eyes against the sudden glare, Lief blinked at Barda who was staggering to his feet, pulling a crumpled paper from his pocket.

Behind him stood Jasmine, her hair wildly tangled. Her left hand was held up protectively to where

Filli hid under her jacket. In her right hand she held her second dagger — the one she usually kept hidden. Its tip was stained with red. She was frowning fiercely, looking back along the hallway. Lief followed her gaze and saw that a trail of red drops marked the floor all the way to the corner.

"Good! I thought I had drawn blood, but I was not certain. That will teach them that we are not easy marks," Jasmine hissed. "Cowards, to attack us from behind, in the dark!"

"They took our key," said Barda grimly. "And they left this in its place." He showed them the paper he was holding.

The companions looked around them. The hallway was silent. None of the doors had opened.

"Well?" Lief asked, after a moment. "What are we to do about this?"

But he already knew the answer. He could feel himself simmering with anger. He could see the fire in Jasmine's eyes, and the stubborn set of Barda's jaw.

"Whoever attacked us made a mistake," Jasmine said, loudly enough for anyone listening to hear. "Whatever we may have thought before, we will certainly now not be running away from this contest."

"And it will not be *we* who will regret it!" Barda added, just as loudly.

They walked slowly to the door marked 77. It opened when Barda turned the knob and they went into the small, neat room beyond.

It was light and bright, with a gaily colored rug on the floor, but the barred window made it look like a prison cell. The only pieces of furniture were three beds with bright red covers and a small, heavy cupboard.

"Whoever has taken our key thinks, perhaps, to make us lie awake all night, fearing attack," muttered Lief.

"Then he is foolish," Barda snapped. "We will sleep well. We will fear nothing." He put his shoulder against the cupboard and pushed it against the door.

With relief they fell on their beds and slept. As Barda had predicted, they slept soundly. If there were any small sounds outside their door in the darkness of the night, they were not disturbed. They slept on, safe in the knowledge that no one could enter the room without waking them.

But, as Barda had said, they were very tired, and were thinking slowly. Focused on the danger of attack, they had forgotten one thing.

Just as a key can unlock a door, so it can lock it. When the wakening bell rang in the morning and they moved the cupboard aside they found the door locked fast.

Their unknown enemy had found another way of seeing that they did not win in the Games. He had decided to prevent them attending the Games at all.

8 - The Games

For a long time they shouted and beat upon the door, but no one came. Finally Barda charged at the door in fury, trying to burst it with his shoulder, but the wood was thick, the lock was heavy, and his efforts were of no use.

At last they admitted defeat and flung themselves back on their beds.

"We were fools not to expect this," Barda panted.

Jasmine was silent. Lief knew that she was fighting panic. For Jasmine, being imprisoned was the worst sort of torture. After a moment she sprang to her feet and ran to the window, shaking the bars and calling loudly to the blank sky. But the wind snatched her cries and blew them away unheard.

"Could Kree fit through the bars?" asked Lief. Jasmine shook her head, but the question had given her an idea. She snatched the cover from her bed and pushed it halfway through the bars so that it flapped in the breeze like a flag.

The second bell rang. Time dragged on. Lief gritted his teeth. How their enemy must be laughing at the ease with which they had been tricked.

Suddenly there was a sharp knock at the door and the handle rattled. They all shouted and immediately heard the sound of a key in the lock. The door swung open to reveal Mother Brightly, wearing a bright red dress and a sunbonnet tied with green and blue ribbons. Her cheeks were flushed and she was very short of breath.

"I was just leaving for the Games when what did I see but one of my coverlets flapping from a window!" she exclaimed. "I could not believe my eyes, and came running at once."

Quickly Lief, Barda, and Jasmine explained what had happened. The woman listened with many exclamations of horror and dismay.

"Oh, I am ashamed that this has happened at my inn!" she cried. "I hope the upset will not affect your performance. I have told everyone that I think you will be finalists, at least."

"But — is it not too late?" Lief asked.

Mother Brightly shook her head decidedly. "Not at all!" she snapped. "Follow me."

Leaving Kree and Filli behind in the room, Lief, Barda, and Jasmine followed the woman down the stairs to the empty dining hall. There she served them food, and great mugs of foaming Queen Bee Cider. "Eat and be strong," she said fiercely. "We will show your spiteful enemy that Mother Brightly's favorites are not to be trifled with!"

When they had eaten and drunk their fill, she led them through the training rooms at the back of the inn, along a covered walkway, and into an arena. The Games Opening Ceremony was still in progress, and many heads turned to look at the newcomers. Barda, Jasmine, and Lief lifted their chins and ignored the stares and whispers.

"Good fortune!" Mother Brightly whispered, and bustled away, leaving the companions alone.

The arena was a large, round field of sand surrounded by rows of benches that rose, tier after tier, high into the air. The benches were crowded with people, many of them waving red, green, and blue flags bearing the gold medal that was the symbol of the Games.

The competitors, clustered together on the sand, raised their hands, pledging that they would fight as well as they were able. Among them, easily seen because they were so tall, stood Joanna and Orwen. The scar-faced stranger was there also, not far from where Lief was standing. A ragged piece of cloth was knotted around his neck like a scarf.

Was it protection from the sun? Or to hide a wound made by Jasmine's dagger in the hallway last night? Lief's fist clenched as he raised his own hand. All his doubts and fears had disappeared. Now he was only angry, and determined to show that he could not be defeated so easily.

✳

Soon afterwards, pairs of names were read out, and the contests began. The rules were simple. All the pairs fought at one time. Each pair fought until one could no longer stand.

The loser was taken away. The winner, after only a few minutes' rest, was paired with another winner to fight again, for endurance was considered as important as strength, agility, speed, and cunning.

Lief, Barda, and Jasmine soon learned that the idea of a fair contest played no part in the Rithmere Games. Competitors fought with savage fury, biting and clawing, butting with their heads and tearing at their rivals' hair and eyes, as well as punching and kicking. Nothing was forbidden except the use of weapons.

The crowd roared, waving their flags, urging their favorites on, hissing and booing those who did not fight well. Sellers of sweetmeats, hot food, and Queen Bee Cider did a fine trade as they wandered up and down the aisles between the seats, shouting their wares.

As more and more defeated competitors left the arena, disappointed and nursing their injuries, the space between the struggling pairs grew greater. Each fight was harder than the last, but Lief, Barda, and Jasmine managed to survive every round.

Unlike most of their rivals they were used to

fighting for their lives. They had all learned much since they first met in the Forests of Silence. But even their early training helped them now.

Not for nothing had Lief spent his childhood on the dangerous streets of Del. As Barda had told Mother Brightly, he could dodge and run with the best, and use his wits to foil enemies far bigger than himself. He was young, but because of his work with his father in the blacksmith's forge his body was strong, his muscles used to working hard.

From boyhood Barda had trained as a palace guard — and the guards were the most powerful fighters in Deltora, only defeated at last by the sorcery of the Shadow Lord. For many years Barda had wrestled and fought his fellows as part of that training. And even during his time disguised as a beggar outside the forge gates he had kept his strength, following Lief through the city and protecting him from harm.

And Jasmine? Small and slight as she was, no one in that company had faced what she had faced, or lived the life that she had lived. Shrewd Mother Brightly had seen the strength in those slim arms, and the determination in the green eyes. But Jasmine's opponents continually mistook her smallness for weakness, and paid the price.

✳

The sun was low in the sky when the eight finalists, the ones who would fight their last battles on the morrow, were announced.

Barda, Lief, and Jasmine were among them. So were Joanna and Orwen. The other three were a short, heavily muscled man called Glock, a woman, Neridah, whose speed had amazed the crowd, and the scar-faced stranger whose name the companions now learned for the first time — Doom.

"A fitting name for such a dark character," muttered Barda, as Doom stepped forward, unsmiling, and held up his arms to the cheering crowd. "I do not relish the idea of fighting him."

Neither did Lief. But he had thought of something that worried him even more. "I did not expect that we would all be finalists," he whispered. "What if we have to fight each other?"

Jasmine stared at him. "Why, we will decide who is to win, then just pretend to fight," she said. "As, in any case, we must do for all our other bouts tomorrow. We must let our opponents win, and so avoid injury. We are already sure of 100 gold coins each, because we are finalists. That is all the money we need, and more."

Barda moved restlessly. Plainly, the idea of cheating to lose offended him as much as the idea of cheating to win. "It would not be honorable . . ." he began.

"Not *honorable*?" hissed Jasmine. "What has *honor* to do with this?" She spun around to Lief. "Tell him!" she urged.

Lief hesitated. He was not troubled, as Barda was, by the idea of deceiving the organizers of the

Games, or even the crowd. On the streets of Del, honor among friends was all that was required, and survival was the only rule. But part of his mind — the part that still simmered with anger over the warning note and the locked door — rebelled against Jasmine's plan.

"Our rivals will know, if we do not try to win. It will seem that we are at last bowing to their threats," he said in a low voice.

Jasmine snorted in disgust. "You are as foolish as Barda! Will you risk our quest for the sake of your pride? Oh, I have no patience with you!"

She turned her back and stalked away.

✳

That evening the finalists ate together in the dining hall attended by Mother Brightly, smiling and bright in her ruffled red dress. It was a strange meal, for where only the night before the room had been busy and filled with noise, now it was empty and echoing. The defeated competitors, it seemed, had already been sent away. Lief wondered how they were faring, for many of them were injured and almost all without money.

Jasmine was still angry. She ate little and drank only water. "That Queen Bee Cider is too rich for me," she muttered. "The thought of it sickens me. The air in the arena stank of it. The people in the seats were drinking it all day."

Barda frowned. "It should not be sold to them. It

486

is intended for use by fighters, who need massive energy, not for those who simply sit and look on. No wonder they cry for blood."

Just then Mother Brightly rang a small bell.

"One word before you begin retiring to your rooms, my dears," she said, as all the finalists turned to her. "I want no tricks or trouble here tonight, so I plan to take your keys and lock your doors myself. I will unlock them in the morning immediately after the waking bell."

There was complete silence in the room. The woman looked around, her plump face very serious. "So sleep soundly and regain your strength," she went on. "Tomorrow you must show no sign of weakness or lack of purpose. The crowd — well, it is always very excited on the final day. Very excited, indeed. It has been known for finalists who do not perform well to be attacked and torn to pieces. I would not like this to happen to any of you."

Lief's stomach seemed to turn over. He did not dare glance at Jasmine or Barda. So this was how the Games organizers made sure that all the finalists tried their best at the last. The crowd was their weapon — the crowd, swarming, acting with one mind, excited to fever pitch and hungry for blood.

9 - The Finalists

The arena was already growing warm when they reached it in the morning. The sun glared down on one side of the newly raked sand. The other side was in deep shadow. The benches were packed, the crowd simmering with excitement.

The eight finalists raised their hands and repeated their pledge to fight their best. Then they stepped forward one by one to choose a card from the woven basket held up by a smiling Mother Brightly.

Lief looked at his card, his heart in his mouth. The number upon it was 3. He glanced at Barda and Jasmine and to his relief saw that Barda was holding up number 1, and Jasmine number 4. So, for this round at least, they were not to fight each other. But who were their opponents to be?

He looked around and his heart sank as he saw scar-faced Doom walking towards Barda, holding his card high so that all could see the number 1 upon it. The giant Orwen had drawn the second number 4 and was already standing with Jasmine, who looked like a child beside him. Glock and Joanna had both drawn cards marked 2. So the only one who remained was Neridah the Swift. And, sure enough, there she was, hurrying towards him showing the 3 card that proved she was paired with him.

The crowd roared as the four pairs of opponents threw down their cards and faced each other.

Neridah looked down at her hands, then up at Lief. "I am rather afraid, I confess," she said in a low voice. "I really do not know how I reached the finals. And you are one of Mother Brightly's favorites, are you not?"

Lief stared awkwardly back at her. He had fought several women the day before, and had learned that it was unwise to think of them as anything other than dangerous opponents. Besides, anyone who had seen Jasmine at work knew better than to underestimate a fighter just because she was female. But Neridah looked so gentle. She was as tall as he was, but slender and graceful as a deer, with a deer's huge, dark eyes.

"The . . . the crowd," he stammered. "We must . . ."

"Of course!" Neridah whispered. "I know I must try my very hardest. And I will not blame you for doing what you must. Whatever happens to me, my poor sisters and my mother will have the 100 gold coins I have already won. Mother Brightly has promised."

"You need not fear . . ." Lief began gently. But at that moment the starting bell rang, and like a snake, Neridah's foot lashed out and caught him on the point of the chin, knocking him flat on his back.

The crowd laughed and booed.

Lief scrambled to his feet, shaking his head stupidly. His ears were ringing. He could not see Neridah at all. With amazing speed she had darted behind him. Savagely she kicked the backs of his knees, and he stumbled forward, gasping in pain. In moments she was darting around him, leaping and kicking at his ankles, his knees, his belly, his back, making him turn around and around like a confused clown, flailing with his arms while always she stayed out of reach.

She was making a fool of him! The crowd had begun jeering, chanting his stupid false name, "Twig," and laughing. A wave of anger cleared Lief's head a little. If Neridah was fast, so was he. He jumped backwards, away from her, so that she was forced to face him. Warily, they circled one another. Then, without warning he sprang forward, catching her around the waist and throwing her to the ground.

She fell and lay gasping, one arm limp and helpless. All Lief had to do was finish her. Stop her from rising to her feet. Kick, or hit . . .

But tears were welling from her eyes as she struggled feebly in the sand. "Please . . ." she whispered.

For one split second, Lief hesitated. And that was enough. The next moment Neridah's "helpless" arm was darting forward and her hand was seizing his ankle. Then the crowd was roaring as she leaped up, jerking his foot off the ground. Lief staggered, crashed to the sand, and knew no more.

✳

Meanwhile, Barda and Doom were wrestling, trying to push each other over. They were very evenly matched. Barda was taller, but Doom's muscles were like iron and his will even stronger. From side to side, back and forth, the two men swayed, but neither made a mistake, and neither gave in.

Wherever you have come from, Doom of the Hills, you have had a life of struggle, thought Barda. You have suffered much. And he remembered the sign that the scar-faced man had made in the dust of a shop counter, the first time he had seen him. The sign of the Resistance. The secret sign of those who were pledged to defy the Shadow Lord.

"What are you doing here, Doom?" he panted. "Why do you waste your time fighting me when you have more important work to do?"

"What work?" hissed Doom, the long scar showing white on his gleaming skin. "My work — now — is to grind you into the dust — Berry of Bushtown!"

His lips twisted into a grim smile as he said the name. Plainly he was sure that it was false.

"Your friend Twig is down and will not get up again," he sneered. "See, behind you? Hear the crowd?"

Barda struggled to keep his concentration, refusing to look around, trying to close his ears to the howls of the people. Yet he could still hear the frenzied chanting: "Neridah! Neridah! Kick! Yes! Again! Finish him!"

Doom's grip tightened and his weight shifted. Barda staggered, but only a little. "Not so easy, Doom!" he muttered. He gritted his teeth and fought on.

✳

Jasmine could see nothing but Orwen's huge shape circling her, hear nothing but his savage grunts as he lunged for her, and the beating of her own heart as she sprang aside. Her mind was working as fast as her feet.

All the competitors she had fought the day before had been larger than she was, but none of them had been Orwen's size and weight. If she allowed herself to be caught in this giant's bear-like grip, he would crush her. She knew she had to be like a bee buzzing around the head of a great beast. She had to irritate him, tire him, so that he made a mistake.

But Orwen was not stupid. He knew what she planned. For a very long time she had kept out of his reach, spinning and jumping, landing sharp, painful little kicks on his ankles and knees. His face was running with sweat, but his steady gaze had not faltered.

Again she leaped away from him. For long minutes she had been trying to turn him to face the sun. And she had nearly done it. One or two more moves . . .

Then, suddenly, Orwen's expression changed. He was looking over Jasmine's shoulder, his eyes filled with horror. Was it a trick? Or . . .

Behind her there was a terrible sound — the sound of someone choking, in agony. And the crowd was roaring: "Glock! Glock! Kill! Kill! Kill!"

Orwen lunged forward. Jasmine darted aside, but almost immediately realized that the man was not looking at her. He had forgotten she was there.

Joanna was down, pinned to the ground. And Glock was kneeling over her, his huge, hairy hands gripping her neck, shaking, tightening, his teeth bared in savage glee as he watched her life ebb away.

Then Orwen was upon him, heaving him aside like a bundle of rags. The watching people shrieked with excitement. Glock's snarl of shock and fury was cut short as he thumped heavily to the ground. Orwen threw himself down beside Joanna, cradling her in his arms.

She was so limp and still that Jasmine thought at first that she was dead. But as Orwen called her name, her eyelids flickered and her hand fumbled towards her bruised throat. Orwen bent his head with a groan of relief, unconscious of everything but her.

And so it was that he did not sense Glock staggering to his feet and coming for him. He did not hear Jasmine's sharp, warning cry. He paid no heed to the crowd rising in a fever of excitement. The next moment, Glock's locked, clenched fists had pounded down onto the back of his neck like two great stones. Orwen fell forward without a cry, and did not move again.

✳

Barda and Doom were still fighting, struggling in a grip that neither would break. They were alone in the arena now. Dimly, Barda was aware that two people had been carried away while Glock, held back by three strong officials, still raved at them with murderous rage.

"Glock is a madman!" Doom growled. His voice was full of loathing.

"And are *we* not madmen?" panted Barda. "Whichever one of us wins will surely have to fight him. Do you want 1000 gold coins enough for that?"

"Do *you*?" hissed Doom, his dark eyes flashing. "For my own purposes I am condemned to this. But you — surely you are not. We have given a good enough show. If one of us falls now, he is free to go on his way. Think!"

Barda thought, and faltered.

It was the smallest hesitation. One tiny gap in

the concentration that had armored him for so long. But it was enough for Doom. A twist, a mighty thrust, and Barda was off balance and staggering.

The other man's fist crashed into his jaw. Barda saw bright pinpoints of light. Then the ground was rushing up to meet him. In seconds he was lying on his face in the sand, dazed, his head spinning, his whole body aching, listening to the crowd howling Doom's name. Through his pain he wondered if Doom had tricked him, or done him a great favor. Had this defeat been because of Doom's wish, or his own?

10 - The Champion

our finalists remained: Neridah, Doom, Glock —
and Jasmine, for she had been pronounced the
winner of her bout, even though Orwen had
been felled by another.

Jasmine had only had a few brief moments to
find out how Lief and Barda were faring. Both were
poorly, but Mother Brightly, anxiously hovering over
them, had told her that, like Joanna and Orwen, they
would soon recover. Their injuries were not too serious, and they would be not much the worse for their
defeat.

Seeing that her friends were in good hands, Jasmine allowed herself to be taken to the center of the
arena to join Glock, Neridah, and Doom.

Foaming mugs of Queen Bee Cider were brought
to them. The dark-haired young serving man was
plainly excited to be serving such great ones. He of-

fered the tray to Doom, who took a mug with a word of thanks.

"Why do you serve him first?" shouted Glock furiously. He snatched another mug from the tray, tipped it up, and drained it dry.

The young man, plainly startled and frightened, began gasping words of apology.

"All is well," said Doom quietly. "Do not upset yourself."

Blushing scarlet, the young man held out the tray to Neridah and Jasmine. Neridah took a mug and drank it in a gulp. Jasmine, however, shook her head.

"Thank you, but I do not like Queen Bee Cider," she said. "I have had water, and that is enough."

As the young man stared, Glock grabbed the rejected mug. "All the more for me!" he crowed, gulping the cider greedily.

He turned to Jasmine, wiping his dripping mouth with the back of his hand. "Pray that you are not facing me next round, little water-drinking Birdie. I will crack your bones like eggshells. I will . . ."

A strange expression crossed his face. And at that exact moment, Neridah, beside him, gave a strange little sigh, bent at the knees, and fell to the ground. Glock gaped at her, then at the empty mug in his hand. His hand went to his throat.

"Poison!" he croaked. He turned, staggering, and pointed with a shaking finger at the young man with the tray. "You — " he croaked.

The young man dropped the tray and took to his heels. By the time Glock, in his turn, had crashed senseless to the ground, he was already lost in the crowd.

People were running towards them, shouting and pointing. Jasmine stared at Doom.

"This is your doing!" she hissed. "That boy — you knew him!"

"What rubbish you talk," he snapped.

Jasmine narrowed her eyes. "You think that if the others are out of the way — if you fight only me in the finals — you will surely win," she said slowly. "But you are wrong, Doom."

He turned away so that she could not see his face. The officials had reached them now. They were shaking Glock and Neridah, gabbling and exclaiming. Only Jasmine heard Doom's reply.

"We will see," he said softly. "We will see."

✳

If fighting Orwen was like fighting a bear, this is like facing a wolf, Jasmine thought, as she and Doom circled each other in the center of the arena. A lean, cunning wolf.

The man was dangerous. Very dangerous. Her every instinct told her that. She feared him as she had never feared a human being before, yet she did not know why. She searched for a reason, then thought she had found it.

He does not care if he lives or dies, she thought,

and despite herself she shivered with dread. She saw a tiny spark leap into Doom's eyes and dodged just in time as he lunged for her.

The crowd, cheated of the semifinal contests and angry because their favorite, Glock, could not fight again, was in an ugly mood. A roar of boos and shouted curses rose up as Doom missed his prey by a breath. They were tired of this circling and dodging. They wanted action. They wanted blood.

Breathing hard, Jasmine whirled to face her enemy again. His mouth twisted into a mocking smile. "Where is your boasting now, little bird?" he jeered softly. "Why, you cannot master your fear enough even to put up a good show for the crowd. Run home and hide your head in your mamma's lap!"

A flame of white-hot anger ran through Jasmine's body, burning away the fear. She looked up at Doom, and with satisfaction saw the smile fade as he sensed the change in her. She saw his mouth tense, and a wary look creep into his eyes.

"You are tired, old man," she hissed. "Tired to your bones."

And as she said it, she knew that it was true. His long struggle with Barda had sapped his strength and dulled his reflexes. Why else had he missed her when he struck?

"Catch me if you can!" she grinned, and half-turned as if to run.

Taken by surprise, Doom took a stumbling step

forward. She whirled around and kicked, whirled and kicked once more. She leaped away from him as he snatched at her, leaving him clutching the empty air. She jumped and attacked again and again.

With savage pleasure she heard his grunts of pain and anger, heard the crowd begin to cheer. Their excitement was mounting and so was hers. The game went on and on. Doom could not touch her.

The arena was a blur. She felt nothing but her own desire to punish and hurt. It was as though her blood was bubbling, as though her anger had turned into energy, surging around her body, making her feet and hands tingle. Laughing, she danced backwards as Doom came at her again, tall and glowering. The crowd howled. The roar was deafening. So loud . . . why was it so loud . . . ?

She stepped back — and her heel hit solid wood.

She glanced behind her in shock and saw a wall, and above it, a mass of red, shouting faces. Only then did she realize how she had been tricked, how foolish her anger had made her. Little by little, Doom had pushed her to the edge of the arena. She had her back to the low wall that surrounded it. And he was closing in on her.

She sprang up, up and back, landing surefooted on the top of the wall as so many times she had landed on tree branches in the Forests of Silence. Behind her the crowd was screaming. But Doom was close, very close, leaning forward, and his hands were reaching for her ankles. Hands like giant spiders. Arms like thick, hungry vines . . .

Pure instinct drove her to jump, to spring up and out towards him. For a split second his bent shoulders were her tree branch. Then she had thrust backward with her feet, launching herself into the air once more, sending him toppling forward. She heard him cry out, heard him fall crashing against the wall as she turned in the air and landed lightly on the sand far behind him.

She landed poised to run. Her only thought had been to escape. But her leap for freedom had done far more than that.

Doom lay crumpled by the wall, unmoving. The crowd was on its feet, shrieking her name. Slowly, in wonderment, Jasmine realized that the fight was over. She had won.

✳

"So — it is all over for another year! And what a thrilling contest our final was at the last!" laughed Mother Brightly, as she hurried Lief, Barda, and Jasmine back to the inn after the presentation ceremony. "A little slow to start, perhaps. But then the fun began!"

She patted Jasmine's shoulder affectionately. "You are a popular Champion, my dear. There is nothing the crowd likes better than agility beating strength."

Jasmine was silent. The gold medallion hung

heavy around her neck. A bag of gold coins was heavy in her arms. And her heart was heavier than both.

She felt sick at the thought of what she had become for a short time in that arena. A beast who took pleasure in hurting and punishing another. A fool who forgot everything in the heady delight of battle. She had been as vicious as the loathsome Glock. As drunk with violence as that reeking, bellowing crowd. If her conceit had been her undoing, as it so nearly had, it would have served her right.

Lief and Barda glanced at one another over her head. They knew her well enough to guess a little of what she was feeling. But Mother Brightly could not imagine that Jasmine was anything but proud.

"To tell you the truth," she chattered on, lowering her voice, "I was very pleased to see that person Doom brought down. A proud and glowering man — with an unpleasant past, I am sure. I am certain that it was he who arranged for the cider to be drugged. He skulked away, you know, as soon as he woke, not even waiting for his 100 gold coins. Surely this shows that he has a guilty conscience."

"Have Glock and Neridah woken?" asked Lief.

Mother Brightly shook her head sadly. "They still sleep like babes," she sighed. "They will not be able to leave here till tomorrow. But Joanna and Orwen have left already. Joanna was limping badly and Orwen's head had a nasty lump, but they would not be persuaded to remain." She sighed again. "It seems that having gotten their hands on the gold they had no further use for Rithmere."

Lief had no desire to stay any longer than he had to either, and plainly Barda agreed.

"Sadly, we must hurry away, too, Mother Brightly," the big man said tactfully, as they moved into the inn. "But we need to buy some supplies before we leave. Can you recommend — ?"

"Why, I have everything you need!" Mother Brightly interrupted. "I sell all manner of travellers' supplies."

And so it proved. As soon as they had fetched Kree and Filli from their room, the companions went with Mother Brightly to a storeroom stacked to the roof with packs, sleeping blankets, water bottles, ropes, fire chips, dried food, and dozens of other useful items.

As Lief, Barda, and Jasmine had suspected, everything was very expensive. But they had plenty of gold to spend and, like other winners before them, they were happy to pay more so as not to have to wander the town. Within half an hour they had everything they needed. Then, at Mother Brightly's insistence, they ate for the last time in the empty dining hall.

Lief did not enjoy the meal. He was plagued by the uncomfortable feeling that all was not as it should be. His skin kept prickling, as though they were being spied upon. Yet who could be watching them? Neridah and Glock were still asleep. Joanna, Orwen, and Doom had left.

He shrugged the feeling off, telling himself that he was being foolish.

11 - Easy as Winking

Mother Brightly was in high spirits all the time they were eating, but afterwards, when she had brought their weapons to them and they were preparing to leave, it became clear that something was on her mind.

In the end, she bit her lip and bent towards them. "It is hard for me to say this," she said in a low voice. "I do not like to spread bad tidings about the Games, or Rithmere. But — you must be told. It has been known for Champions, and even ordinary finalists, to meet with . . . ill fortune, on their way out of the town."

"You mean they are attacked and robbed?" asked Barda bluntly.

Mother Brightly nodded uncomfortably. "The gold coins are a great temptation," she murmured. "Would you be offended if I suggested that you leave

505

the inn by a secret way? There is a back door —
reached by a passage that runs from the cellar. The
cider barrels are brought in that way, but few people
know of it, and the back street is narrow, and always
deserted. You could slip out unseen, easy as winking."

"Thank you, Mother Brightly," said Lief, clasp-
ing her hand warmly. "You are a good friend."

✳

The passage from the cellar was long, low, and dark
and smelled sickeningly of cider. Their boots clattered
on the stones as they shuffled along in single file,
Barda bent almost double. They had divided their remaining gold between them, to make it easier to carry,
but still it weighed heavily on their belts. Already sore
from their battles of the day, they were soon very stiff
and uncomfortable.

"We should, perhaps, have stayed the night at
the inn and set out in the morning," groaned Lief.
"But I could not face the thought of one more hour in
Rithmere."

"Nor I," muttered Jasmine, breaking her long silence. Kree, hunched on her arm, squawked agreement.

"At least we have what we came for," said
Barda, who was in the lead. "We now have enough
gold to fund the rest of our journey — and more besides." He paused, then added awkwardly: "You did
well, Jasmine."

"Indeed," Lief agreed eagerly.

"I did not do well," Jasmine said in a low voice. "I am ashamed. The man Doom jeered about my mother. He made me angry. He *meant* to do it. He wanted me to forget myself — so I would perform for the crowd."

"He tricked himself, then," said Barda. "For in the end he lost and you won. Think of that, and forget the rest." He paused, and pointed. "I see light ahead. I think we are at last reaching the end of this accursed tunnel."

They hurried forward, eager to see the sun and to stand upright.

As Mother Brightly had told them, the passage ended in a low door. Light showed dimly through the crack beneath it. But as Barda drew the bolt, and the door swung open, a flood of sunlight poured into the passage.

With streaming eyes, almost blinded by the welcome glare, they crawled through the doorway one by one. And so it was that, one by one, they were cracked over the head and captured. Easy as winking.

✳

When Lief came to his senses he was covered by some rough, foul-smelling cloth — old sacks, perhaps. His head was pounding. He was gagged, and his wrists and ankles were weighed down by heavy chains.

He became aware that he was being painfully

jolted and bumped. He could hear voices, a jingling sound, and the plod of hooves. He realized that he was on the back of a cart. Whoever had attacked him was carrying him away from Rithmere. But why?

The Belt!

With a thrill of terror he dragged his chained hands to his waist and groaned with relief as his fingers met the familiar shape of the linked medallions under his clothes. His money bag was gone. His sword, too. But the Belt of Deltora was safe. His captors had not found it. Yet.

His groan was answered by the dull clank of chains and a sigh beside him and a muffled cry from a little farther away. So Barda and Jasmine were in the cart with him. He was absurdly comforted, though of course it would have been better if one of them at least was free. Then there might be some hope of rescue. As it was . . .

There was a guffawing laugh from the front of the cart. "The ticks are waking, Carn 8," a harsh voice said. "Will I give them another knock?"

"Better not," said a second voice. "They have to be in good condition on delivery."

"I don't see that this lot's worth the trouble," the first man growled. "The big one might be all right, but the other two are rubbish! Especially the scrawny little female. Champion my eye! She won't last five minutes in the Shadow Arena."

Lief lay rigid, straining his ears to hear more

508

against the sound of rain, fighting down a feeling of dread.

"It's not our business to say what's worth the trouble, Carn 2," answered the other voice. "It's the old girl who answers to the Master, not us. The pod was told that from the beginning. The Brightly woman supplies the goods. All we have to do is deliver them undamaged."

Lief felt the blood rush to his head. Beside him, Barda made a strangled sound.

"The ticks heard us," sniggered the man the other had called Carn 2.

"What does it matter? They're not going to be telling anyone, are they?" sneered his companion. "Or d'you think that black bird's going to spread the word? It's still there, you know. Right behind us."

They laughed, and the cart jolted on.

✳

The journey continued hour after hour. Lief slept and woke and slept again. It grew colder and darker, and then it started to rain again. The sacks that covered him became sodden. He began to shiver.

"We'd better stop and get the ticks covered up," Carn 8 growled at last. "Give them some grub and a drink, as well, or they'll be dying on us. Then we'll be in the muck."

The cart jolted off the road, and finally came to a stop. The next Lief knew he was being hauled out of the cart and dumped roughly onto the ground. Agonizing pain shot through his head and he moaned aloud. Only the cold rain beating on his face kept him conscious.

"Be careful, you fool!" roared Carn 8. "How many times do you have to be told? Any broken bones Brightly didn't put in her report and we're in the Arena ourselves! Do you want to end your days in gladiators' leather, fighting a Vraal? Get him under the canopy, and be quick about it!"

The other grumbled. His face and shoulders loomed out of the darkness as he bent and grabbed Lief under the arms. And it was then that Lief's worst suspicions were confirmed. Their captors were Grey Guards.

✳

The Guards had made a rough shelter for their prisoners by stretching oiled cloth between the lowest branches of a tree. Barda, Jasmine, and Lief huddled together under this canopy, shuddering with cold.

Kree, who had followed them all the way from Rithmere, perched on Jasmine's shoulder. But he could not help them. There was no chance of escape. Their leg irons were fixed to an iron peg driven into the ground.

The gags were taken off and they were given water and some chunks of bread. Then the Guards moved away. Dimly, through the darkness and the rain, Lief saw them crawl together under the cart where it seemed they were planning to sleep.

"I cannot eat weighed down by these chains," Jasmine shouted.

"Hold your tongue or I'll cut it out and throw you into the Shifting Sands, orders or no!" bawled Carn 2. "We passed by the Sands just an hour ago."

"Lief, is the Belt safe?" whispered Barda.

"Yes," Lief whispered back. "Did you hear — ?"

"Yes. We are not far from the Shifting Sands. But this news is of little use to us as we are. Mother Brightly fooled us well."

"I thought *she* was the fool," Jasmine hissed bitterly, breaking off a tiny piece of bread for Filli. "But the secret way out of the inn was a trap."

"The whole of the Games is a trap! With gold coins as bait." Lief clenched his fists. "What better way to lure the best and strongest fighters, and make them show how good they are? And dear old Mother Brightly is there all the time, to make sure that as many finalists as possible walk tamely into captivity when it is all over."

Barda shook his head in disgust. "We heard on the highway that few Games Champions are ever heard of again. Now we know why. They do not run away to spend their money in peace. They are taken to the Shadowlands to die battling wild beasts and each other for the amusement of the crowds."

"And their gold coins, and even the Champion medallion, are taken to be used again!" Jasmine hissed. "It is monstrous."

The rain eased, and they heard snores coming from beneath the cart. The Guards were asleep. With new urgency they began struggling to free themselves, though in their hearts they all knew that it was no use.

They had long given up their efforts and were dozing fitfully when Kree gave a startled squawk and there was the tiny sound of cracking twigs behind them.

"Be still!" breathed a voice. "Do not speak or move until I tell you. I already have your packs and weapons in a safe place. Now I am going to unlock your chains. When you are free, follow me as quietly as you can!"

12 - No Choice

A short time afterwards, astounded by their un-
expected release, the three companions sat
back on their heels in the shelter of a cave and
stared in amazement at their rescuer: Doom.

Impatiently, he waved away their thanks.

"Listen carefully," he said. "We have little time. I
am the leader of a group sworn to resist the Shadow
Lord. We have been suspicious of the Games for some
time — certain that they were not all they seemed. My
purpose there was to see what was happening, from
the inside. Your presence upset my plans. I tried to
scare you off — "

"It was you who locked us in our room!" Lief
broke in. "You who attacked us."

"Yes — and got cut for my pains." Doom grimaced, touching the cloth at his neck. "I was trying to
stop you from competing — to protect you."

513

"Why?" Barda asked bluntly.

"When first I saw you in Tom's shop something about you interested me. I was hurrying on business of my own and could not stay. But ever since, wherever I have been, I have heard whispers about three travellers — a man, a boy, and a wild girl, accompanied by a black bird. Wherever these travellers go, it is said, part of the Shadow Lord's evil is undone."

Lief gripped Barda's arm. If word about them was spreading, how long would it be before the Shadow Lord became aware of them?

But Jasmine, who still could not make up her mind to trust Doom, had something else on her mind. "You allowed us to be captured," she accused. "You crept away after the finals, but you did not leave. You hid in the inn, watched, and did not lift a hand to help us."

Doom shrugged. "I had no choice. I had to find out how the trick was worked. I had intended that animal Glock to be proclaimed Champion, and suffer whatever fate was in store for him. But he took the drugged drink intended for you, girl, and instead of losing to him, as I had planned, I had to find a way of pretending to lose to you."

Jasmine drew herself up. "You played your part well," she said coldly. "In fact, I would have sworn that you *did* lose. Or am I mistaken in thinking you hit your head on the wall, and slid down it almost unconscious?"

Doom's grim face relaxed into a half smile. "You will never know, will you?" he said dryly.

"If it had been Glock who had been captured, would you have rescued him?" asked Lief curiously.

The smile disappeared. "You ask too many questions," growled Doom. "What is certain is that I must save him now, for he and the woman Neridah will be following in your footsteps tomorrow, and I cannot release one without the other. It is unfortunate."

He stared broodingly out into the rain for a moment, then turned to them again. "A group is waiting not far away. Among them is Dain, the boy who helped me at the Games. He will lead you into the mountains where we have a stronghold. You will be safe there."

Barda, Lief, and Jasmine glanced at one another.

"We are grateful to you," said Barda at last. "And I hope you will not take this amiss. But I fear we cannot accept your offer. We must continue our travels. There is — something of importance we must do."

Doom frowned. "Whatever it is, you must abandon it for now," he said. "I could not risk trying to kill the Guards. It was dangerous enough stealing your weapons and supplies from the cart while they slept below."

"They have our gold, I think," sighed Lief.

"Yes, I saw them take it," Doom said. "But their master will care nothing for that. It is you he wants. When they wake and find you gone they will track you wherever you go. They will not rest until you are found."

"All the better, then, that we do not lead them to your stronghold," said Barda calmly. He put on his sword and pack and began crawling from the cave. Doom put a hand on his shoulder to stop him.

"We are many, and at our base we have ways of dealing with Guards," he said. "You had better join us. What could be more important than our cause? What is this mysterious mission that cannot wait?"

Barda, unsmiling, pulled the restraining hand from his shoulder and continued crawling from the cave. Jasmine and Lief followed. Outside, the rain still fell and the sky was black and starless.

Doom appeared beside them, silent as a shadow. "Go your way, then," he said, his voice very cold. "But say nothing to anyone of what I have told you this night, or you will wish you had gone to the Shadow-lands."

Without another word, he disappeared into the dripping bushes, and was gone.

"How dare he threaten us!" hissed Jasmine.

"He is angry." Lief felt very low-spirited. His head ached, he was cold, and he was sorry to have parted with Doom on bad terms. "I think he is a man who rarely trusts. Yet he trusted us. Now he fears that he was foolish to do so, for we would not trust him in return."

Barda nodded slowly. "I wish it could have been otherwise," he said. "He would have been a valuable ally. But we could not risk it. Doom would not be content to let us keep our secret. And there are spies everywhere — even his band may not be safe. Later, if we succeed in our quest — "

Kree squawked impatiently.

"We will not live to succeed in anything if we do not move on," Jasmine said. "It is nearly dawn."

"But which way do we go?" Lief looked around him in frustration. "We have no idea where we are, and we do not even have the stars to guide us."

"You are forgetting Kree," Jasmine smiled. "He followed us. He knows exactly where we are."

They began to walk, Kree fluttering ahead of them. Soon they found a tiny stream which had been swelled by the rain. They plunged into it and splashed along its bed for as long as they could, hoping that the water would disguise their scent.

All of them felt bruised and ill and longed to rest. But the thought of the Grey Guards following them like evil tracking dogs drove them on.

Dawn came, and with it the sun, struggling feebly through the clouds. Soon afterwards they reached a narrow road heavily marked by puddled cart tracks. On the other side of the road was a wooden fence and beyond that a stretch of stony land ending at a row of low grey hills. Kree flew to a fence post and flapped his wings impatiently, hopping to the left.

"If we walk along the fence, we will at least leave no tracks," murmured Jasmine. "Hurry!"

Gathering themselves for the effort, they leaped across the road, climbed the fence, and began moving along it, Jasmine balancing on the top, and Barda and Lief edging uncomfortably along with their feet on the middle rail.

After a short time they reached a crossroads. The fence continued around the corner and on into the distance where it was lost in the grey hills. And right beside the corner post stood a huge, weathered stone. It was as tall as Lief. Words had been carved on it, but so long ago that many of the letters had disappeared.

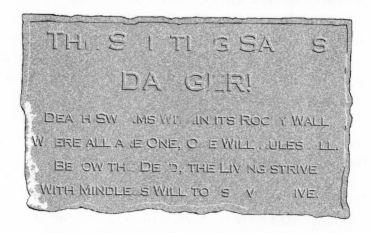

"The Shifting Sands. Danger!" Barda squinted at the stone. "That much I can make out, but what the smaller writing says I cannot say. Too many of the letters have been worn away by wind and weather."

"I think the first word is 'Death,' " said Lief in a low voice. He leaned out from the fence and touched the stone, tracing the letters with the tips of his fingers. Hesitantly, using touch as well as sight, he began to read.

"Death swarms within its rocky wall,
Where all are one, one will rules all . . ."
"Go on, Lief!" Jasmine urged, as he paused.

Lief shook his head, frowning. "The next two lines are more worn than the others. They seem to say something like: 'Be now the dead, the living strive . . . With mindless will to survive.' But that does not really make sense."

"It makes enough sense to tell us that the Sands are not going to be pleasant," said Barda dryly. "But we knew that, I think."

Jasmine's mind was busy with practical matters. "Since the verse talks of a 'rocky wall' I would guess that the Sands are just beyond the hills. But we will have to cross the plain to reach them. The stones may hide our tracks, but there will be no way to disguise our scent."

"It cannot be helped," said Lief. He climbed over the fence and jumped gratefully to the ground on the other side, flexing his cramped fingers. "Besides, we have been very careful. The Guards have surely lost our trail by now."

"I would not count on that," muttered Barda. But he also climbed to the ground and after a moment Jas-

519

mine jumped down to join them. They set off, almost running over the bare ground, glancing often behind them. Despite his hopeful words, Lief looked back as often as his companions did. The idea of Grey Guards silently following, the idea of a deadly blister flying unseen towards him to explode on his back, made his skin crawl.

It became warmer as the sun climbed steadily behind its veil of cloud, and steam began to rise from the wet ground. The grey hills ahead were also quickly shrouded in mist. So it was only when the companions actually reached them that they realized that these were not ordinary hills at all, but thousands of huge boulders heaped together to make a high, natural wall — the "rocky wall" of the verse.

They began to climb and soon lost all sight of the ground below. Everything around them was white. The air grew thick and all sound was dulled. Cautiously, one step at a time, they clambered to the top of the rock pile, then, even more cautiously, began to edge down the other side.

As they neared the ground, a sound met their ears — a low droning, so faint that at first Lief thought he was imagining it. And the next moment, without warning, he was below the cloud.

Slowly he turned away from the rocks to look at what was beyond. The breath caught in his throat. Sweat broke out on his forehead.

They had arrived at the Shifting Sands.

13 - The Shifting Sands

S and. Nothing at all but deep, dry sand. As far as the eye could see, high red dunes rolled away under a low, brooding ceiling of murky yellow cloud. There was no sign of any living thing, but the low droning sound filled the place, as though the very air was alive.

Lief slithered down the last few rocks and his feet sank into the grainy softness beneath. A feeling of dread had settled over him — a feeling as strong and real as any taste or smell.

I have been here before.

This was the place he had seen in the vision of the future the opal had given him on the Plain of the Rats. The terror that had haunted his dreams was about to become reality. When? In an hour? A day? A week?

Through his fear, he heard Jasmine speaking. "It

521

is impossible," she was saying, as she jumped down beside him. "If the gem is hidden here, we will never find it!"

"The Belt will grow warm when the gem is near," Barda reminded her. He, too, was plainly sobered by the size of the task ahead, but refused to admit it. "We will mark the sand into sections and search it, square by square."

"That could take months!" Jasmine exclaimed. "Months — or even years!"

"No." Lief had spoken quietly, but they both turned to him. He struggled to keep his voice steady. "This gem is like the others. It has a terrible Guardian," he said, staring out at the still and secret dunes. "And the Guardian is already aware of us. I feel it."

Or is it the Belt that feels it? he thought, as he moved out into the sand, like someone in a dream. Is it the Belt that feels the danger?

But he dared not put his hands on the Belt of Deltora. He knew that if he touched the opal — if he saw the future again — he would turn and run.

He closed his eyes to shut out the sight of the barren land, the glowering sky. But beneath his lids he still saw red sand. And the hungry, jealous will that was drawing him to itself, as it drew everything, everything in this place to itself, was stronger than ever.

He began climbing the first dune. His feet sank

deeply into the rippled sand, making every step an effort. He struggled on.

"Lief!" he heard Jasmine cry. Her voice penetrated his dream, and he opened his eyes. But he did not stop.

"We have only to move on," he called, without looking back. "The Guardian is very near. We will not have to search for it. It will find us."

✳

In a very short time they were surrounded by high dunes and had lost sight of the rocks. But their trail showed clearly behind them, so they were not afraid of becoming lost.

They had discovered that the dunes were not as empty of life as they had supposed. Red flies crawled from the sand as they passed and flew up to settle on their hands, faces, arms, and necks, biting and stinging. Scarlet lizards with long blue tongues wriggled out of unseen holes and preyed in turn upon the flies.

"But what eats the lizards?" asked Jasmine, and drew her dagger.

Shortly after that they passed a strange object lying on the sand. It was round, leathery, flat, and wrinkled — like an empty bag, or a gigantic, flattened grape that had been split along one side.

"Is it some sort of seed pod?" wondered Barda, looking at it.

"Like no seed pod *I* have ever seen," Jasmine

muttered. Filli chattered nervously into her ear and Kree, riding on her shoulder, made a worried, clucking sound.

Lief's scalp was prickling. He was haunted by the feeling that they were being watched. Yet nothing moved but the flies and the lizards. There was no sound but the low, faint droning, which he had decided must be wind moaning around the dunes, though he could feel no breeze and the sand was still.

They had reached the bottom of one dune, and had just begun to climb another, when Jasmine, who was now in the lead, stiffened and held up her hand.

Barda and Lief stopped. At first they could hear nothing. And then, floating on the still air, there was a voice, growing louder by the moment.

"Carn 2! Never mind the flies. Keep moving!"

Lief looked frantically behind him. Their trail showed clearly in the sand. Their footprints were like arrows, pointing to their position. There was nowhere to hide. No escape.

The droning sound seemed to become a little louder, as though, Lief thought, the wind was excited by their fear. And just at that moment he remembered a trick he used to play back in Del. A trick that had fooled Grey Guards before, and, perhaps, could fool them again.

Gesturing to Barda and Jasmine to follow his

lead, he began to step backwards, carefully fitting his feet into his own footprints. When he had reached the bottom of the dune, he leaped to one side to lie motionless in its faint shadow.

His companions copied his every movement. When they were all huddled together, Lief covered them with his cloak, which blended quickly with the sand.

They waited, still as stones.

The Guards appeared, struggling in their heavy boots. They ran down the side of their dune, and began following the tracks up the next.

Then they stopped, puzzled. For, halfway up the dune, the tracks appeared to stop dead.

"They have been taken!" growled Carn 2. "As I told you they would be, Carn 8. I told you it was needless to follow them into the Shifting Sands. We are putting ourselves in danger for — "

"Be silent!" snapped his companion. "Do you not understand, you fool? We have disgraced the Carn pod. We let a Champion and two finalists escape. Our lives are worth nothing — less than nothing — unless we get them back. They may not have been taken. They could have buried themselves in the sand. Dig! Dig!"

He began to burrow into the sand with both hands. Grumbling, Carn 2 crouched to join him.

Then, suddenly, the dune seemed to erupt beneath them and, with shocking speed, a huge, hideous creature sprang from the collapsing sand and seized them, lifting them off their feet.

The Guards shrieked in terror. Paralyzed with shock, hardly able to believe their eyes, Lief, Barda, and Jasmine lay rigid beneath the concealing cloak. The monster had been perfectly hidden in the dune. Waiting. One more step, and they, instead of their enemies, would have been its prey.

Lief stared in fascinated horror. The creature was eight-legged, with a tiny head that seemed all mirrored eyes. Dozens of leathery bags, like the one they had seen lying on the ground, hung from its body. Sand still poured from its joints and crevices. It regarded its captives without curiosity as they struggled and swung in its terrifying grip. Then it opened its mouth, leaned forward . . . and abruptly, mercifully, the screaming and the struggling stopped.

It had all happened in seconds. Sickened by what they had seen, Lief, Barda, and Jasmine remained huddled under the cloak, not daring to move.

Delicately, using its pincers, the monster picked the clothes from the dead bodies of its prey, like a bird shelling snails. The companions watched as clothes, boots, money bags, Jasmine's medallion, metal canisters of blisters, slings, clubs, and water bottles thudded onto the sand. Then the creature sat back on its spiny haunches and began to eat, taking its time. Lizards and flies crawled out of the sand in the thousands to feast on the scraps that fell from its mouth.

Lief buried his face in his arms. He had no love for Grey Guards. But he could not watch this.

✳

The lowering yellow cloud blotted out the sun so completely that Lief lost all sense of time. For what seemed like hours he, Barda, and Jasmine lay motionless while the creature ate its fill and slowly the bags hanging from its body swelled till they looked like gigantic grapes hanging from a stalk.

"They are stomachs!" breathed Barda in disgust. Lief shuddered. And even Jasmine, familiar with so many weird creatures in the Forests of Silence, wrinkled her nose with distaste.

At last, the flies and lizards scattered and the beast stood upright. One of the swollen stomachs, bigger than all the rest, tore away from its body and rolled to rest in the sand, leaving only a ragged stump behind. Seemingly unconcerned, the creature crawled forward and settled on top of it.

"What is it doing?" breathed Lief, unable to keep silent.

"I think it is piercing the stomach and laying an egg inside," Jasmine whispered back. "That way, the hatchling will have food while it grows."

Barda turned his head away.

But the sand beast had already finished its egg-laying and was moving again. Sluggishly, it ambled through the ruined dune in which it had hidden and climbed the next, soon disappearing over the top. The companions waited a moment to be sure it would not return, then climbed stiffly to their feet.

Without hesitation, but still gripping her dagger, Jasmine hurried over to where lizards and flies still swarmed over the Guards' bones and the blood-stained tatters of their clothes. Beating away the scavengers, she began rapidly sorting through the rags, putting aside in a small pile things that would be of use: the Guards' slings and blisters, their clubs and water bottles, the money bags. After a moment she looked up, startled.

"The money bags burst as they fell," she called in a low voice. "Most of the coins spilled out. But they are not here any longer. They are gone! And so has my medallion."

"That is impossible!" Barda strode towards her and himself began searching. Lief followed more slowly. His attention had been caught by a flat patch of sand just beyond where his friends were crouching. What he saw there made his flesh creep.

"The creature was blocking our view for hours as it fed," Jasmine was insisting. "Something or someone crawled in unseen and took — "

"It cannot be!" Barda was growing impatient as he fruitlessly searched the tumbled sand.

"Look!" Lief's voice sounded choked, even to himself. He cleared his throat, and pointed.

The smooth patch of sand was covered with hundreds of strange, circular marks. Marks that had not been there before.

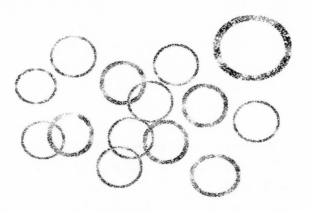

14 - Terror

Jasmine stared. "Never have I seen tracks like these," she said finally. "What creature could have made them?"

"We cannot know," Lief said flatly. "But whatever it is it is something that does not fear the sand beast, and something that likes gold. Perhaps it likes gems, too. Perhaps it is the Guardian."

"But surely the sand beast is the Guardian!" Barda exclaimed.

Jasmine shook her head. "I think it is just one of the creatures of the Sands," she said positively. "We have just seen it lay an egg. What is more, we passed an empty stomach skin on our way here. That hatchling had already emerged to fend for itself. There could be hundreds of sand beasts here. There could be thousands."

Barda cursed under his breath.

The low, droning sound drummed in Lief's ears. He stared at the circles on the sand. They seemed to mock him. He tried to look away, but his eyes kept being drawn back to them. He forced his gaze up to the sky — but there was no relief there. The unchanging roof of cloud seemed to press down on him, hemmed in as he was by faceless dunes. And all the time fear plucked at him like the flies which had returned in force, stinging, stinging . . .

Suddenly he could stand it no longer. With a muffled cry he leaped upon the tracks and kicked at them, destroying them, digging his heels deeply into the soft sand and scattering it everywhere.

"Lief! Stop!" he heard Barda call. But Lief was past listening. He shouted and fell to the ground, beating and tearing at it. Barda and Jasmine ran to him, trying to pull him to his feet. He fought them away.

There was a soft shifting sound and a low rumbling. Then the earth began to move. Lief heard Barda and Jasmine cry out. And just in time he grasped their hands as huge columns of sand began to thrust themselves upward all around them.

Jerked off their feet, the three tumbled together, rolling helplessly, blindly, as the sand roared and quaked beneath them. Lief could hear Jasmine screaming for Kree, and the bird's answering screech. He could hear his own voice, too, groaning in fear.

There is something here.

He knew it. He could see nothing, for his eyes

were tightly closed against the stinging sand, but he could feel a terrible, rage-filled presence all around him.

And he knew what it was. It was the thing that had been drawing him on. The thing that was hungry for what it sensed he could give it.

It wants the Belt . . . It will not rest until it has . . .

Then, suddenly, he felt the power withdraw. And immediately, as quickly as it had begun, the storm ceased and the ground quieted.

He lay still, dizzy and panting, as the last of the flying sand fell around him like rain.

With a rush of wings, Kree landed on Jasmine's arm. He was unharmed, though powdered all over with red dust. He began ruffling and preening his feathers, trying to clean himself. Filli chattered excitedly inside Jasmine's jacket. She murmured to him, calming him.

Lief brushed at his face with trembling hands.

"An earthquake," mumbled Barda. "So — that is why this place is called the Shifting Sands. We should have realized . . ."

"It was not an ordinary earthquake," snapped Jasmine. "It cannot simply be chance that Lief was kicking those marks away when it began. Lief, why did you do that? What is wrong with you? Are you ill?"

Lief could not answer. He was staring blankly around him.

Everything had changed. Dunes had collapsed and formed again in different places, and great valleys had opened where hills had been before. All tracks and signs that had previously marred the sands were gone. The ruined dune, the place where the Guards had died — both had disappeared.

He, Barda, and Jasmine may as well have been dropped from the sky into a part of the Sands they had never seen before. Only the low, droning sound was the same.

"Lief will not speak to me!" he heard Jasmine say to Barda in a frightened voice. She sounded very far away.

The sun was still blanketed by the clouds above. Lief could not tell which way was east and which way west. And he had been spun and tumbled so many times that he had no idea from which direction he had come.

So this is the beginning, he thought.

His glazed eyes fell on a mark in the sand, quite close to where he was lying. His throat seemed to close as he stared at it, and understood its meaning.

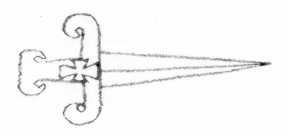

Lief felt Barda take him by the shoulder and shake him. He licked his lips and forced himself to speak. "Do not worry. I am all right," he said huskily.

"You do not seem all right," Barda growled. "You are acting as though you have lost your wits!"

"It is Jasmine who has lost something," murmured Lief. "She has lost her dagger — the dagger with the carved crystal set in the hilt."

"Oh, did you find it?" Jasmine exclaimed. "I am so glad. I dropped it just before the sandstorm ended. It was my father's. I thought it was gone for good!"

"So it is, I fear." Lief pointed to the drawing on the sand.

Jasmine and Barda gaped, speechless.

"The thing whose anger caused the storm accepted the dagger as tribute and left us in peace while it took it away," Lief murmured.

"The circles in the sand! They were not tracks, but pictures of the gold coins, and the medal!" Barda gritted his teeth. "What sort of creature is this? Why does it leave marks to show what it has taken?"

Lief shrugged. "Why do sculptors carve figures of stone, or shop owners list their wares upon their windows, or fools write their names upon trees and walls? To show what they love. To show what they own. To leave a message for all who pass by that way."

Jasmine was looking wary. "You are talking very

strangely, Lief," she said. "I do not like it. You speak as if you know this thing."

Lief shook his head. "It is beyond knowing," he said.

The verse they had seen carved on the stone at the crossroads kept running through his mind.

Death swarms within its rocky wall
Where all are one, one will rules all.
Be now the dead, the living strive
With mindless will to . . . survive.

He knew that he did not have the last lines quite right. But two words he was quite sure about.

Mindless will.

A thing of mindless will ruled the Shifting Sands and all that was precious in that fearsome place it gathered to itself. The terrifying creatures who shared its domain could have the flesh of their victims. The Guardian wanted only the treasure the victims carried.

For the first time since entering the Sands, Lief touched the Belt under his shirt, checking that the fastening was secure. As he did, his fingers brushed the topaz, and suddenly his mind cleared.

It was as though a dusty veil had been ripped from a window, allowing light and air to enter. But somehow he knew that the flash would not last long. There was another power at work here, and it was ancient and terrible.

535

He whirled around to Barda. "We must move on," he said urgently. "Light is fading, and the place we seek is far from here, for the Belt is not yet warm. But I want you to fasten us together so that we cannot be separated. I must be in the middle, tied very tightly."

Grimly, Barda did as he asked, using the rope they had bought from Mother Brightly. It was light, but very strong. Lief tested it, and nodded. "Do not release me, whatever I say," he muttered.

His companions nodded, asking no questions.

They drank a little water. Then they set off, weapons drawn, linked together by their lifeline, as darkness slowly fell.

✳

The night brought no moon, no stars. The cloud hung above them black, black, and it was very cold. They had lit a torch, but the light it gave was small, and they jumped at every shadow. For a long time Barda and Jasmine had wanted to stop, but always Lief had urged them on.

At last, however, they refused to listen to him any longer.

"We cannot go on like this, Lief," Barda said firmly. "We must eat, and rest."

Lief stood shaking his head, swaying on his feet. All he wanted was to lie down, yet somehow he knew that if he slept he would be in danger.

But already Jasmine had untied her end of the

rope, dropped to her knees, and begun fumbling in her pack. In moments she had scraped a shallow hole in the sand and thrown the Guards' clubs into it.

"Never have these been put to better use," she said, laying the torch on top of the smooth, hard wood and adding some of Mother Brightly's fire chips for good measure. "Soon we will have a fine, cheering blaze."

She beckoned impatiently and Lief, unable to resist any longer, flopped down beside her. Barda, too, came to the fire. Seeing that Lief lay still, he groaned with relief, untied the binding cord from his own waist and stretched out.

The fire rose, crackling. The heavy sticks began to glow. The heat grew and spread.

Barda held out his hands. "Ah, wonderful!" he sighed with satisfaction.

And that was the last Lief heard. For the next moment, there was a great roar, the sand heaved, and the world about him seemed to explode.

15 - The Center

Lief was alone, among rippling dunes that had no ending. He knew that somehow the night had passed. Light was filtering through the thick, yellow cloud. The sand beneath his feet was warm.

It was day. His terrible vision had come to pass, as he had always known it would.

He remembered the sand rising beneath him in darkness and tossing him into the air. He remembered the sound of Jasmine's and Barda's voices shouting his name. He remembered the burning coals of the fire spraying through the night, dying as they flew.

But that was all. Now there were only his own tracks trailing off into the distance over smooth, sandy wastes. Now there were only the dragging, useless tails of the rope still tied around his waist. Now there was only the droning sound, louder now, filling his ears, filling his mind.

He was clutching something in his hand. He looked down, and willed his fingers to open.

It was the painted wooden bird that Jasmine had put in her pocket in Rithmere. He must have found it, picked it up, after . . .

Numbly, he slipped the little object into the top pocket of his shirt. His legs were aching. His throat was parched — dry as the sand itself. His eyes were prickling. He could hardly see. He knew he must have walked for many hours, but he had no memory of it.

The Center.

He was being drawn towards the Center. That much he knew. His strength was almost gone. He knew that, too. But he could not stop, for if he stopped he would sleep. And if he slept, death would come. That he knew most of all.

He staggered on, reached the foot of another dune, took a step to begin climbing. Without warning his legs gave way underneath him and he fell. The sand cushioned him, soft as a feather bed. He rolled onto his back, but could move no farther.

Sleep.

His eyes closed . . .

In Del, friends are laughing, splashing in the choked and overflowing gutters, picking up gold coins. He wants to go to them. But his mother and father are calling . . . And now he sees that the gutters are choked not with garbage but with buzzing red bees. The gutters are overflowing with Queen Bee Cider that is pouring from broken barrels lying in the street, running to waste. The bees rise up in an angry cloud. His friends are being stung, and Grey Guards are watching, laughing . . . His friends are dying, calling to him, but he is so tired, so tired. His eyes keep closing as he staggers into the humming red cloud. His arms and legs are heavy, weighed down. Behind him his mother says, "Softly, softly, boy!" and he turns to her. But her face has turned into the face of Queen Bee. Bees cover her back and arms and swarm in her hair. She is frowning, screeching harshly at him, shaking her fist. "Smoke, not fire! Smoke, not fire . . ."

Lief's eyes flew open. The screeching went on. Something was circling high above him, a blurry black shape against a dull yellow sky.

Ak-Baba! Run! Hide!

Then he blinked, and saw that the circling shape was Kree — Kree, soaring lower, calling to him. He tried to sit up and found that he had settled so deeply into the sand that he had to wrench himself free. Sand had already covered the whole lower half of his body, his hands, his arms, his neck . . .

He scrambled, panting and trembling, to his feet. How long had he been asleep? What would have happened if Kree had not woken him? Would he have slipped deeper and deeper into the sand until at last it covered him? Would he have woken even then?

540

The dream was still vivid in his mind. And suddenly he understood what it meant. The words of the verse rushed back to him. "Not 'be now,' but 'below,' " he whispered. "Not 'survive,' but . . ."

"Lief!" Barda and Jasmine had appeared at the top of the next dune. Shouting, they began to slide down towards him. Lief felt tears spring into his eyes at the sight of them, and realized that he had thought they were dead. He began staggering forward to meet them.

Jasmine screamed, piercingly. She was pointing behind him.

He turned, and saw what had emerged from the dune at his back. It was another sand beast, even bigger than the first. Sand still poured from the joints of its legs. It had been stalking him, but as he met its mirrored eyes it froze. In moments, he knew, it would spring.

Backing away, holding its gaze, he felt for his sword, then, with horror, felt himself falling clumsily, entangled in the trailing ropes that had tripped him. The next moment he was struggling in the sand, his sword trapped beneath him. Wildly he scrambled to his knees, hearing Jasmine and Barda shouting, knowing it was too late, feeling as though he was caught in a nightmare. The monster lurched forward . . .

Then it jerked, with a grating cry, as a blister exploded on its body. It staggered, lunged again, then toppled sideways as another blister found its mark. Its spiny legs kicked, and it began to spin, digging great trenches in the sand.

One ankle still caught in the rope, Lief crawled away, sobbing and gasping with relief. Jasmine came panting up to him, hauling him to his feet, freeing him from the rope. Barda was right behind her, a sling still in his hand and another blister at the ready.

Lief began to choke out his thanks, but Barda waved him away. "If I have saved your life, Lief, it is not the first time, nor will it be the last, I fear," he growled. "It is my fate, it seems, to be your nursemaid."

Shocked and deeply hurt, Lief took refuge in sullenness, and turned away.

Barda took him by the shoulder and spun him around. "Do not turn away from me!" he shouted. "What are you playing at? Why did you run away alone? Why did you not try to find us after the quake?"

He was shaking with anger. And slowly Lief realized that it was the anger born of shock, fear, and worry. It was the anger he had sometimes seen in his parents' faces, when he came home long after curfew. When he took risks.

"Barda, I could not — " he began.

"There is no time for this now," snapped Jasmine, her eyes on the monstrous creature thrashing in the dune. "Argue another time. We must get away from here, and quickly. The beast is not dead. It may yet recover and come after us again."

"Do not worry," said Lief quietly. "Where we are going, it will not follow."

*

They walked for many hours, but spoke little. It was as if Lief was listening to something that neither Barda nor Jasmine could hear, and they themselves grew more and more silent the closer they came to the Center.

They saw it long before they reached it — a lone peak rising high from a flattened circle and ringed by rounded dunes. It shimmered against the yellow sky, alien and mysterious in the fading light. A mighty cone with darkness at its tip.

"A volcano," hissed Barda.

Lief shook his head. "You will see," he said.

Filli crept, whimpering, under the shelter of Jasmine's collar. She whispered comfortingly to him, but her green eyes were dark with dread.

The droning noise grew louder as they approached their goal. By the time they had reached its base and slowly begun to labor upwards, the air was vibrating with sound.

And finally they had reached the top, and were looking down into the peak's hollow core. A whirlpool of red sand roared far below, flying in the darkness as though driven by a mighty wind.

But there was no wind. And the sound was like the humming of bees in their countless millions.

The Belt burned around Lief's waist.

"What is this?" Barda was breathing hard, staring down, his big, blunt hands gripping his sword.

Softly Lief repeated the rhyme carved on the stone. And this time, the last lines were complete.

"Death swarms within its rocky wall
Where all are one, one will rules all.
Below the dead, the living strive
With mindless will to serve the Hive."

"The Hive . . ." Jasmine repeated slowly.

"The Sand is the Guardian," said Lief.

Barda shook his head. "But — it cannot be," he breathed. "The sand is not alive! We have walked upon it, seen creatures — "

"The creatures we have seen are crawling on a much larger host," said Lief, his voice very low. "The dunes we have been treading are only a covering, made up of the long dead. The living work below. Serving the Hive. It is they who collect the treasures that fall. It is they who make the marks on the surface. They who cause the storms."

"The gem — "

"The gem, dropped anywhere on the Sands, would at last be drawn to the Center," Lief murmured. "That is why we are here."

He tore his eyes away from the whirlpool within

the core and turned to Jasmine. "We need smoke," he said. "Smoke, not fire."

Without a word she knelt and began pulling things from her pack. Her hands, Lief saw, were trembling.

His own hands were not very steady as he gave his sword to Barda and took the rope in exchange. But as he knotted the rope around his chest, he was half-smiling, and his voice shook only a little.

"I fear you must be my nursemaid again, Barda," he said. "Again I need your help and your strength — and your rope as well. But this time, I beg you, do not let me go."

16 ~ The Cone

Lief crawled over the lip of the pit and stepped into empty space. He dangled, swinging gently to and fro, looking up at Barda's and Jasmine's worried faces and their hands, the knuckles white, gripping the rope.

"Slowly," he mouthed. He saw them nod, and their hands move. Then, gently, he began to sink through the core of the cone.

Lief's cloak was bound tightly around him and its hood was drawn closely around his head and face, covering all but his eyes. I must look like a big grub in a cocoon, he thought. But no grub would be so foolish as to invade a hive. If it did . . .

Shuddering, he turned his mind to other things.

Smoke from the dampened torch, well padded with wet rags, billowed around him. He was not certain it would help, but certainly no other weapon would be useful here. Besides, ever since his dream, Queen Bee's words had kept coming back to him, and surely that was for a reason.

My guards do not like sudden movements, and are easily angered. Why, even I must use smoke to calm them when I take their honey from the Hive . . .

He could remember the words so clearly. Strangely, here, at the droning, swirling hub of the Sands, his mind had cleared and sharpened. Perhaps the Hive was no longer calling him, because it had no need. He was where it had wanted him to be all along.

He looked up. His friends' faces were tiny now. He was hardly able to see them against the glare of the sky. And below, the seething mass that was the Hive was whirling, rising to meet him.

He braced himself, closed his eyes. Then he felt it, like a hot, rough wind, a stinging whirlwind, sucking him in. It spun savagely about him, whipping him, pressing in on him, with a sound like thunder.

It was too strong. Too strong!

He could not see. He could not breathe. Spun in a raging torrent of sound, he did not know which way was up, which down. He knew only one thing:

The Hive cared nothing for him. To the Hive he was not food, or a captive prize, or even a hated enemy to be defeated. To the Hive he was nothing but the carrier of the thing it desired. The Hive would suffocate him. It would rub the clothes from his flesh and the flesh from his bones. Then it would have what it wanted. What it had wanted from the beginning.

The Belt of Deltora.

Panic gripped Lief by the throat. He began to struggle, to scream —

Softly, boy, softly. Gently, gently!

The crabbed old voice was as clear in his mind as if it had spoken right beside his ear. It was like cold water splashed in his face.

The screams died in his throat. He opened his eyes. He forced himself to be still, to stop gasping for air, to breathe evenly.

He opened his eyes a fraction. Through the narrow slits he saw that the smoke pouring from the torch had at last begun mingling with the whirling red.

And the whirlwind was quieting. The Hive was slowing, and thinning. It was retreating to the darkness at the sides of the cone. And the thing that its fury had previously hidden was at last revealed — a glistening pyramid rising through the cone's center.

Slowly, carefully, Lief reached up and tugged the rope once. His downward progress stopped with a slight jolt as, far above, Jasmine and Barda received the signal.

For a moment he simply swung in space, staring, fascinated, through the drifting smoke, at the astounding thing the living Sand had built, tended, and guarded for years without number.

It was a towering pyramid of cells made of gold, glass, gems, and bleached, white bones.

Lief told himself that he had expected this — or something like it. But the reality was beyond anything he could have imagined.

Anything that would not decay, or would decay so slowly that it would have to be replaced only after centuries, had been gathered and used for the building. Skulls and bones of every shape and size were packed side by side with glass bottles and jars, coins, crystals and gems, gold chains, rings and bracelets, and yet more bones. The individual parts, small and large, had been fitted together with such care that the tower glittered like an enormous jewel.

It was an awesome sight. And unbelievably horrible.

It was a pyramid of death. How many human beings had been stripped of life for its sake? And what was stored inside those secret cells? The Hive's young, no doubt. Eggs, then tiny squirming things, packed in the thousands, nursed and cared for, fed on a disgusting brew of decayed red flies, dead lizards, and whatever else slipped beneath the sand. Till they grew into — what? Not insects of any kind he had ever known. Not insects at all, perhaps. Some other form of life he could not even imagine. Some tiny unit that would become part of the ancient thing that had lived on while all around it changed. The Hive.

Shaken with disgust, Lief ached to kick and tear

at the tower, to see it fall and smash to pieces in the darkness below. In that darkness, no doubt, the giant Hive Queen lurked. He almost felt he could see her bloated shape, rippling in the depths, laying eggs, eggs without number.

But he knew that if he attacked the pyramid the Hive would be upon him. The smoke would not hold it back.

And the Belt was throbbing and burning. Somewhere in this gleaming tower lay the gem he was seeking. Was it the diamond? The amethyst? The emerald? He could see clear, purple, and green stones among those that sparkled in the pyramid. But which was the precious One?

He pulled his cloak and shirt aside to reveal the Belt, and looked down at it, peering through wreaths of smoke. He could hardly see the topaz and the ruby. But the opal shone, dancing with sparkling lights so that it seemed alive.

What did that mean? He struggled to see in his mind the words about the powers of the opal in *The Belt of Deltora*.

†   **The opal, symbol of hope, shines with all the colors of the rainbow. It has the power to give glimpses of the future, and to aid those with weak sight. The opal . . .**

What came next? Lief screwed his eyes tightly closed to help him to think, but after a moment he opened them again, shaking his head desperately. He could not remember the end.

He looked up to the top of the pyramid. He knew that the gem was most likely to be there. It had been dropped into the Shifting Sands just before King Endon was overthrown. That was only a little over sixteen years ago, and the pyramid had been growing for many ages.

The first thing he saw was Jasmine's dagger, fitted point downwards into the very tip of the tower. It had been the last thing taken, so was at the top. One day the metal would rust away. But the crystal cross would survive, and other finds would take the place of the metal parts.

Below the dagger, neatly arranged, were many gold coins, and the Champion medal from the Rithmere Games. They were locked in place with a mass of shining white bones.

Lief shuddered. Not a scrap of flesh still clung to the bones, but he knew that they were all that remained of Carn 2 and Carn 8, the Grey Guards. The Hive worked quickly.

He realized that the pyramid seemed clearer than it had before. For a moment he wondered why that was. Then he saw that the torch was smoking less. It was starting to die.

His stomach lurched. For how much longer would the Hive stay droning at the sides of the cone? As the smoke thinned . . .

He looked below the bones and saw some small glass pots, some bracelets, two rocks, and what looked like the jawbone of a horse. And below that —

His heart seemed to miss a beat. There, pinpoints of light piercing its smooth, dark blue surface, was a stone like a starry night sky.

The forgotten words from *The Belt of Deltora* flashed at last into his mind.

. . . The opal has a special relationship with the lapis lazuli, the heavenly stone, a powerful talisman.

The lapis lazuli! There it lay, carefully wedged into place, supporting the roof of an as yet empty cell. The fourth gem of the Belt of Deltora.

He reached for it, then abruptly drew back his hand. If he pulled the stone from its place, the things resting upon it would surely topple and fall. Then the Hive would attack. He would be dead before he could carry his prize to the surface, and the lapis lazuli, and the Belt itself, would be lost.

His only hope was to replace the gem with something else. Something of about the same size. Frantically, he felt in his pockets, though he knew he had nothing — nothing . . .

Then his fingers touched something in the top pocket of his shirt. Something small, hard, and oddly shaped. He pulled it out.

552

It was Jasmine's little wooden bird. And it was just the right size.

The Hive droned with growing suspicion. It was waking, becoming active, as the smoke began to disappear. Holding his breath, Lief reached again for the lapis lazuli. But this time he grasped in his other hand the little wooden bird.

He eased the lapis lazuli from its place. It warmed in his fingers, and moved easily, more easily than he expected, as though it wanted to be free.

The opal is calling it, he thought, feeling the answering warmth at his waist. He felt the lapis lazuli slip into his hand, and quickly pushed the little wooden bird into its place.

Not quickly enough. The top of the tower trembled. The droning from the walls of the cone became louder, more alert. The red cloud swayed inward. Its outside edge just touched the bare skin of Lief's chest, searing, burning. He smothered a scream of anguish.

Quietly, quietly . . .

Sweat dripping into his eyes, trying to screen out the pain, Lief lifted a hand and tugged at the rope. Once, twice . . . Beside him, the pyramid swayed. If it should fall. If anything should fall . . .

The dagger toppled from its place, turning in the air. Lief snatched at it one-handed, just managing to catch it by its tip as he rose beside it, the dying torch tucked under one arm.

With agonizing slowness, he was drawn to the surface. Below him, the droning sound was rumbling, rising, as the Hive closed in, circling the pyramid once more. The Hive did not yet know it had been robbed. It was still sleepy and distracted because smoke still drifted in the air. The smoke was faint now, so faint . . .

But it was still working its magic as Lief crawled into the fresh air above.

And as he stood up and turned joyously to Barda and Jasmine, as he opened his hand to show them the heavenly stone, the clouds that had covered the sky flew apart like torn rags. The stars and the moon beamed down again upon the dark earth like a blessing, and the lapis lazuli sparkled back at them like a tiny mirror.

It slipped into the Belt and glowed there, alive under the moon.

Lief turned to Jasmine. "I had to leave your little bird behind. But I brought you this in exchange," he said softly, and gave her the dagger. Wordlessly she took it, slipped it inside her jacket, and held it close.

Lief swayed and Barda gripped his arm. "The lapis lazuli is a talisman, Barda," Lief whispered. "We will be safe now. But let us leave this place."

※

Lief said little else as the companions walked slowly down the smooth red of the peak. At the bottom he let Jasmine smooth healing balm over the raw patches on his chest. It eased the pain a little. It made the long journey back to the edge of the Sands bearable.

They had the stars to guide them now. They had the lapis lazuli to offer protection against the dangers of the night. But it was not until they had reached the rocks that edged the Sands, and had climbed out onto solid land, that Lief was able to speak of what he had seen.

"Thank the heavens that you and the Belt are safe," murmured Barda when he had finished.

"And now," said Jasmine more cheerfully, "we have the fourth stone. Only three more to go. And surely they will be easy, compared to this."

Lief was silent. It was some moments before his friends realized that he was asleep.

"They *will* be easy, compared to this," Jasmine insisted, turning to Barda.

Barda was looking down at Lief's exhausted, sleeping face. He was thinking how much older the boy looked. He was thinking of all they had been through. What might yet be to come.

Jasmine would not be ignored. She tugged at his sleeve. "Barda! Do you not agree?" she demanded.

Barda was not wearing the Belt. The opal could not give him glimpses of the future. But a shadow crossed his face and his smile was grim as he answered.

"We shall see, Jasmine," he said. "We shall see."